Lindenvale Brothers Book One

THE HOUSE ON LINDENVALE HILL

CASSIDY COLE

Cover Design: Cassidy Cole

Editing & Proofreading: Lunar Rose

Print ISBN: 979-8-9914281-0-1

Ebook ISBN: 979-8-9914281-1-8

ALSO BY CASSIDY COLE

Lindenvale Brothers Series

The House on Lindenvale Hill

Lachlan Park Trilogy

Little Ugly Truths

Standalones

Tame Our Wild

*To the ones who love hard and effortlessly, even when it feels like
they should have nothing left to give.*

AUTHOR NOTE & CONTENT WARNING

Dear Reader,

The House on Lindenvale Hill is the first book in the Lindenvale Brothers Series and can be enjoyed as a standalone.

First off, I want to let you know that there's a dog in this book, and nothing bad happens to sweet Rossco. So you can read peacefully with this in mind!

This book contains mature themes, dark content, and sensitive subject matter that may be triggering for some readers. If you feel inclined, please read the trigger warnings on the next page before picking up this story. Please note that they may contain spoilers!

Your well-being and mental health come first.

XOXO,
Cassidy

TRIGGER WARNINGS

The House on Lindenvale Hill explores dark and potentially triggering themes, including kidnapping, drugging, power imbalance, stalking, group sexual situations, sexual violence, dubious consent, suicide (on-page depiction in a flashback & descriptions), sexual harassment, postpartum depression, and an on-page road accident. Please consider your well-being before choosing whether to continue reading.

ONE | TARYN

Fresh starts suck.

I should know; this is only the billionth time in the last ten years that I've found my feet firmly planted in a place far different from what I got accustomed to. When comfort begins creeping in, it's usually when I can leave everything behind without hesitation. It's easy. It always has been.

The thought of moving is exhilarating.

Making the jump is thrilling.

But as I glare daggers at the piss-yellow two-bedroom home I rented blindly one night after an email from Zillow recommended it, I think my fingers and common sense may have been affected by too many glasses of wine.

I scan the yard sluggishly. There are months of overgrown weeds overtaking the yard and wriggling through the flower beds in front of the deck and at the edges of the driveway. The white paint coating the shutters is beginning to chip, enough that I could dig my fingernails under and pick it off, watching the paint flutter to the ground. The outside of the house itself isn't horrible, but nature's fight to reclaim the structure makes it look like no one has touched it in years. Like one of those abandoned homes you expect a character to come across in an apocalyptic novel. But it's the solid wood door that has unease plummeting into my gut with a force that has my feet feeling like they are sinking into the cement below the soles of my shoes. That one aspect alone should've stopped me from deciding to rent this place.

But no.

I am a twenty-three-year-old woman living alone. If someone waltzes up to the door and knocks, seeing them first automatically gives me an advantage. I have the upper hand because I can either hide around a corner and pretend I'm not home or at least assess their exterior look to make sure they aren't going to murder me the second the door swings open.

Appearances say a lot about a person, but I'm at a disadvantage if I can't see them, especially since there's no peephole.

And that's red flag number two. The first one was ticked off on my little mental sheet when I pulled up and raised the paper listing I printed off. I held it up, glancing back and forth at the image on the paper and the house in front of me as if it were a before-and-after picture. But just my luck, I get the before house. The shit house with a grungy and unkempt yard.

The photos of the shell of the house and yard had to have been doctored up...a lot. Or the images on the listing were from a home that sat here fifteen years ago—maybe twenty.

And the online catalog shows a tire swing. It was silly to look forward to, but it gave the place a lively character. I felt drawn to it because I always wanted a house with a tire swing growing up—any swing, for that matter. But yet again, I'm disappointed because the only thing left on the branch of the willow are two short and different lengths of rope, frayed at the edges, swaying in the soft breeze where one used to be.

It's silent and eerie.

And one hundred percent, undoubtedly, the house on the

street that all the neighbors scurry around and avoid for obvious reasons.

I expect this house to be deserted at the end of a dirt road, not surrounded by pristine family homes on both sides of the street with their white picket fences and off-the-lot SUVs.

Okay, they might not have the white fences and brand-new vehicles, but that's what I visualize compared to the piece-of-junk shack I'm about to live in with my green-and-white 1992 Ford F150 parked in the driveway.

The feeling of dread settles deep in my stomach, churning until it turns sour.

I let my head fall back and release a frustrated sigh, the weight of all my bad decisions resting on my forehead.

I fucked up. Bad.

I grip the leash tighter and scrunch my face, closing my eyes. Maybe when I open them, it won't be there. I crack open a lid; the rickety house is blurred in one eye's line of sight but still as clear as day.

"Goddammit," I mutter.

Might as well get out all my cursing now before my second interview tomorrow. I can't let the principal know that the girl he's looking to hire to be his second-grade teacher has a mouth on her. That wouldn't bode well in my favor since I moved here without securing the job first.

Stupid, I know.

I peek down at Rossco sitting next to me, his sweet face already lightening my foul mood. He always makes it better.

Kneeling beside him, I glide my palm over his black face and across his thick body. Looking at his face, you would think he's just a lab, but underneath all that coarse dark fur, he has the full-out border collie personality. Outside, at least. Other than that, he is honestly the most chill dog in the world and the only constant relationship I've had since I brought him home from the shelter four years ago.

My hand drifts to the large white patch on his stomach, and I dig my nails into it, scratching him.

"Whatcha think?" I ask him, tilting my head. "For you, it's much better than the apartment because you actually have a yard now." It's a brown yard with dried weeds and dirt, but he loves dirt. Laying in the dirt, digging in the dirt, swallowing dirt that coats his ball. He'll love it, so it shouldn't be a problem for him.

His tongue whizzes out, licking a slobbery trail up my arm as his tail drags across the sidewalk back and forth.

"Should we go see the inside?"

A squirrel dashes up the trunk of the lone willow in the yard, and his head jerks in that direction. His gaze locks on to it.

Reaching for his collar, I remove the leash, letting him sprint to the base of the tree. He plops his butt down, staring up as the creature remains perfectly still on a branch. Rossco needs to stretch his legs anyway after the last few days of splitting up the twenty-three-hour drive.

One thing is certain: this weather is nothing compared to the hundred-degree weather back in Tucson. I stand up, absentmindedly running my palms over my arms. It has to be, what, nearly seventy-five degrees? It's a late summer afternoon, and it still feels cold. Yet I'm also not used to this fresh, crisp, and moist Washington air.

Wandering to the mailbox painted the same chipped yellow as the house, I open it and reach inside, pulling out a cream-colored envelope. I wonder how long this house has lingered here, waiting for the next tenant. Ripping it open, I take out the single sheet note and the house key.

Who the hell leaves the house key in the mailbox?

I glance around at the other houses and back at my new home for the time being. There is no way I'll stay here for a year. If I get hired for this position, hopefully I can find a nicer place.

I unfold the letter, smirking at the few handwritten lines.

We hope you enjoy your new home. Thanks for giving it a chance; we are sure its character and charm will be to your liking.
Sincerely,
The Donahue Family

Releasing a snicker, I fold it up, tuck it back into the envelope, and slip it into the back pocket of my jean shorts before walking over to my truck in the driveway—a truck packed with all my belongings under the blue tarp I secured everything underneath with bungee cords. A muscle throbs sharply in my back, reminding me that I slept in the driver's seat last night while Rossco snored peacefully in the passenger seat.

Shit. This house better be fully furnished, as the listing said.

Opening the door, I take out my large suitcase and the reusable grocery bag I have with Rossco's food and water bowl, as well as his various toys.

Before I know it, I'm staring at the front door, contemplating all the decisions I've made that have led me here. On the other hand, my dog looks perfectly content looking up at me, his tongue flopping around, and his mouth set in a way that makes it look like he's smiling. It stirs the confidence in my gut round and round, and I force a smile.

You can do this, Taryn.

It's not as bad as it seems, Taryn.

Just open the damn door and put your mind at ease, Taryn.

I place the key in and jiggle it a little before it gives way. Nudging the door open, the musty smell and the still and silent darkness hit me. When my eyes finally adjust to the scene before me, my shoulders drop, thankful that it's in somewhat good condition compared to the outside.

Ahead, where the living room is, light filters in from the

sides and middle crack in the curtains, creating a line of light on the dusty and scraped wood floors.

Rossco brushes past me, zooming into the small entryway, first running into the living room to sniff the plastic sheets covering the furniture. Once satisfied that he's sniffed every inch, he takes off through the hallway to the right, scoping out the rest of the place.

I leave the door open, take a left into the kitchen, drop the bag in my hand on the four-person round dining table in the corner, and leave my suitcase on the floor, approaching the windows. I throw open the curtains, the layer of dust covering the fabric taking flight and shimmering like dirty glitter in the natural light.

Lifting the sleeve of my flannel to my mouth and nose, I try to keep myself from inhaling it into my lungs. I reach into my pocket and take my phone out, navigating to the notes app. I add another item to the grocery list: *Pick up cleaning products and bleach.*

Who knows how long it's been since this place was properly cleaned.

A few hours later, the sun falls away and I walk about my room, unloading several suitcases. Folding my clothes neatly, I place them on the queen bed raised on one of those metal frames while Rossco is sprawled out on the mattress, chewing on some loose strands of his rope toy. Dua Lipa's "Houdini" drifts through the Bluetooth speaker on the mahogany dresser as my stomach growls over the beat, patiently awaiting my pizza from Crocks—a small pizza joint and bar.

If there's one thing I learned from the small pamphlet of restaurants and phone numbers the owners so kindly left on the kitchen counter—because they couldn't manage to do much else—it's that Cedar Creek Cove is much smaller than I thought it was. Despite that, it has that small-town West Coast vibe that I've been wanting.

It wasn't just the population of fifteen thousand that called to me, but the quaint town nestled on the Columbia River with breathtaking water views. It may seem like an insignificant town to outsiders, but its main street has stopped tourists headed from Portland to the coast because of how well-kept and picturesque it is. It's one street lined with cute shops, businesses, and restaurants on the water of Cedar Creek flooding into the Columbia.

I also learned from their Visit Cedar Creek Instagram page that they also have a Saturday summer market that attracts new visitors from all over the state because of the apples.

I hope to stop by there this week since I don't have much to do until school starts back up in a month.

That is if I get the job.

My second interview is the day after tomorrow, and my skin is buzzing with anticipation. Considering the population, the job can't be *that* competitive. At least, that's what I'm telling myself.

Cedar Creek High has around one thousand students, and its elementary, junior high, and high school buildings are on one campus up on the side of the mountain that overlooks the town. Honestly, I'm crossing my fingers and toes that informing the principal that I was moving here would work well in my favor and give me an edge in securing the position.

I was in Tucson for over a year, and it felt too long. I loved my teaching position there because it was my first professional teaching job, but there came a day when I needed more— desired a different change of pace that I couldn't find in Tucson.

One Saturday a month ago, I was scrolling through jobs when I spotted the second-grade teaching position with a *hiring immediately* tag. It didn't take much thought. I'm impulsive that way. I have years of experience bouncing around because of my parents, who are to thank for that side of my personality.

I applied for the job; they did a background check, and not

even five minutes into the virtual interview, I told Alaric Sinclair, the principal, that I was moving to Cedar Creek. It just spewed out of my mouth flawlessly, and it was settled. I put in my notice with the school back in Tucson and began packing everything in my apartment.

My blood bubbles and pops, excitement and nerves flowing through my veins.

This was probably stupid.

A major move to a place completely different than what I'm used to, with no job.

But damn, it's elating.

And luckily, the house has grown on me in the last several hours.

A flash of light through the window catches the corner of my eye. I dodge all the suitcases thrown on the floor, stepping over them to reach the window. Pulling back the fabric of the curtain more than it was, I peer out into the yard, blanketed by darkness with only a minuscule amount of silver light from the crescent moon above.

I scan the row of houses across the street from mine, cars parked in the driveways, their windows reflecting the solar sidewalk lights. Just as I'm about to turn back around and finish my task, my pulse batters against the inside of my neck at the black SUV-bodied vehicle on the other side of the street that wasn't there earlier.

The make and model of the car are nearly impossible to figure out in the dark, but as a hooded figure shifts in the driver's seat, the hairs on my arms stand on end, sending a bolt of fear that clenches every muscle. I get closer to the window, telling myself it's just a vehicle—probably someone the neighbors know.

Being alone in a new place with a house as unnerving as this makes me hyperaware of everything—aware of each little sound and every draft that tickles my skin.

Examining my yard again, my heart thumps rapidly, lurching into my throat. A second figure leans against the willow tree in the shadows. Their hands are tucked into their pockets, their face hidden by a black hood.

My nose caresses the glass to get closer as the doorbell rings. The soul in my body escapes at the exact moment Rossco throws himself off the bed and chaotically sprints to the front of the house, the wood boards groaning under his weight. His barking vibrates the floorboards under my bare feet, rattling me more than I already am.

I slowly walk through the dark hallway to the front door, my eyes fastened onto the wood as if I'll magically get some X-ray vision and see who the hell is on the other side.

It's the first night, and this solid door is already going to get me murdered. I knew it. Should've trusted my gut feeling the second I pulled up to the house.

Nervously, I grab onto Rossco's collar and hold him back as I sluggishly open the door, my hands tightening around the knob from the terror pulsing through my body.

When the door opens fully, the sight in front of me is even more disturbing.

There's no black vehicle on the other side of the street.

No hooded figure leaning against my tree.

Just a knee-dropping, gorgeous man grinning at me with a pizza box in his hand.

TWO | TARYN

I pump my legs faster, the chill morning air whipping against the moisture clinging to my face and wetting the strands of hair on my scalp. Inhaling deeper breaths, the earthy aroma of moss and fresh rain fills my senses.

God, it feels good to run. To jog off the alarm that gripped me last night. It's still lingering under my skin.

After hours of sleep denying me, I concluded that the long drive from Tucson to Washington and the over-exhaustion were to blame. My brain hallucinated those dark phantoms—the one in the SUV and the one leaning against my tree—and I refuse to think otherwise.

Yes, the house is sketchy as hell, but it's a great neighborhood. A quaint one. Or at least it seems to be, but I guess I can't judge it that quickly, considering I've not been in town for a full twenty-four hours.

After my pizza was delivered by that god of a man, I took it to my room. My gaze kept wandering to the willow tree outside where the figure stood, and I knew I couldn't sleep unless I put my mind at ease.

I threw on a sweatshirt, grabbed my phone and Rossco for

protection, and walked outside with jittery limbs. My pulse raced as the shadows from the branches danced from the breeze as if they were shaking with laughter at my delusion. Thousands of invisible legs tapped against my arms, my skin crawling anxiously. I gradually wandered over to the willow tree, the light from my phone only catching dead grass and weeds on the ground until a little shimmer and pop of color froze me in place. My fingers were cold and white as I grasped Rossco's leash tighter. I dragged my feet across the dirt and inched closer. His curiosity piqued, his nose examining the object eagerly, while I, on the other hand, wanted to run in the opposite direction.

Sitting upright, in the same spot the hooded phantom stood, was an apple. Its skin was practically perfect and void of imperfections, with a coating the color of freshly drawn blood.

Unable to help myself, I picked it up, rotating it in my hands. My eyes flitted around the quiet yard one last time, the sense of being watched settling deep in my bones.

I ran back inside and ate my pizza in bed while *How to Lose a Guy in 10 Days* played on my phone. I needed a romantic comedy to relax my freaked-out state of mind. Occasionally, my focus casually drifted to the apple sitting on the dresser. The movie helped as a distraction, but so did picturing thick muscles clad in a gray Crocks logo T-shirt and a chiseled jawline that could slice through my skin. His wavy brown hair was styled messily, some pieces flopped over and resting against his forehead.

His tan face showed me he had been kissed by the sun a lot this summer. The patio lights reflected in his sage green eyes— irises so light against the darkness that I had difficulty not feeling entranced by them.

They were hypnotic.

So much so that he just smirked at me while I stood there with my mouth parted. He wished me a good night before handing me my pizza and strolling back down the sidewalk. But he didn't have a car, at least not right outside on the street anyway. He just strolled around the corner where the neighbor's trees were against the sidewalk and disappeared. It wasn't until he was gone that I floated back to reality and realized I had never paid him.

If all the men in this town look like that, then I may genuinely be screwed.

My feet batter against the concrete, Rossco's paws pounding the ground beside me as we pick up speed. My running playlist blares in my ears, and I can't help the smile that breaks across my face when the sun strokes my skin.

It rained last night, but it's beautifully gloomy out this morning, with the cloud coverage keeping the late summer temperature at bay. I know birds chirp around me, but I can't hear a word they say. I'm too lost in the beat of the music, and my own head swarming with thoughts.

There came a point last night when I looked out the window at those figures and thought about my parents. How they don't know where I am. They don't know that I've moved not once but twice since they left for Spain. The sad part? I haven't told them about my last few moves because I honestly don't think they care.

It's not that they don't love me or pay attention to my whereabouts; it's just that they adore their lifestyle more. They find contentment in constant travel, moving from one place to the next before they even have the chance to change their address with the post office. Not that they've ever done that, anyway.

The last I heard, they were in Madrid. Or was it Murcia?

I can't remember. It's been over a month since we last had contact, so they could be in a completely different country, for all I know. Ever since I graduated high school, they've been living life as they always wanted to because they put those dreams on hold when they discovered they were pregnant with me. I was a "happy accident." So, instead of being able to travel the world like their original plan since they never wanted kids, we moved from state to state.

One of the questions I was asked in my virtual interview for the second-grade teaching position at Cedar Creek Elementary was: "How good are you at dealing with hard situations and change?"

Pretty damn good at it, Principal Alaric Sinclair.

I didn't answer it like that, but I wanted to.

Instead, I told him how I constantly adjusted and found the positive aspects to focus on despite moving a lot while growing up. At first, I hated it. I was never in one place long enough to make authentic friends or relationships. That's one of the reasons I've never had a long-term boyfriend.

I have a steady relationship with my pink rabbit vibrator, though. So that must count for something.

Anyway, so much change happened that it eventually felt normal. Handling life adjustments became as easy as breathing. Which is why nothing about this move scares me.

Besides the two spine-chilling figures lurking outside the house I blindly rented for myself.

Shit. Maybe it's haunted. I didn't consider that.

Rossco and I round a corner of the street. The neighborhood of houses ends before a dead end where the road meets a thick forest.

The towering red cedars and Douglas firs are so tall on the tree line that they shroud everything under them in a darkness that reminds me of an enchanted forest.

It isn't until I pass the last few houses on the block that two towers of rock ascending into the sky on both sides of a metal gate come into view in the distance. A gate that must be twelve or more feet high.

Slowing my pace, my breath escapes my lungs at a ragged tempo as I examine the intimidating entrance. Scanning the structure, I notice the forest line is behind a smaller fence with golden oak posts, the same color as the sign hanging below the arch. I'm too far away to see the black words scrawled across.

It's as if the property is claiming this part of the land.

The road behind the entrance and trees gradually climbs upward on the small mountain, where a veil of morning fog rests gently on the tops of the trees.

I pull myself and Rossco to a stop, huffing out tattered breaths, and glance down at my Apple Watch.

Three miles from the house.

Wow, I've never run this far willingly. Usually, I only go a mile or two. I guess I did have a lot of anxiety to run off.

Reaching up to the wild strands of brown hair strapped across my sweaty forehead, I tuck them behind my ears and swipe my damp fingers on my high-waisted black running shorts.

I wasn't following directions as I ran—just kept going and going. Turning left and right without thinking, where it felt natural. And I ended up here.

Absentmindedly, I inch closer and closer. It's as if the long metal spikes on top of the gate are like long claws reaching out, piercing my skin, and tugging me toward it.

It's magnificent and obscure.

It nags the curious part of me.

Unable to keep my eyes from wandering the entrance, I take a couple more steps toward it until a small, delicate voice somewhere in the distance stops me. "Amazing, isn't it?"

The statement has my head turning toward the source, a small elderly woman with a hose watering the soft pink and maroon flowers lining her sidewalk. Her glasses rest on the curve of her nose. She smiles at me.

It's seven a.m., and she's already out here early doing yard work. I peek behind her at the impeccable white home with modern black window frames and facades. By the looks of it,

I'm assuming she moved with a husband—maybe—and retired here.

I was so focused on running and captivated by this oddly dark and elegant property entrance that I didn't realize the houses kept increasing in size as I neared.

"By the way you're staring at it, I assume you're not from around here, hun," she presumes.

I flick my eyes over her petite figure in the wine-red shirt that hangs loosely on her frame. Her loose jeans have splotches of dirt from gardening, based on the pile of weeds on the side-walk beside her.

Turning back toward the gate in the distance, I respond, "No. No, I'm not. I just moved here."

"Lindenvale Hill."

I twist my head back to her slowly. *Why does that sound vaguely familiar?* "What?"

She compresses her lips and nods. As she approaches me, the woman places the hose down and removes her gardening gloves one at a time.

I scrunch my brows.

She twirls a finger in circular motions near her temple. "I see the gears turning in that head of yours."

How can this dainty old woman send shivers down my spine? I fight the urge to wrap my arms around myself when a breeze skims my body. My bare legs break out into goosebumps.

"Lindenvale Hill Orchard is the largest apple producer in the country. I'm sure you've seen their labels before." I ponder what she is saying a little harder. "The crow and the apple?"

The crow and the apple...

The familiarity hits me. "Oh!" I react, unable to keep the light bulb moment from registering in my tone. She nods again. "I mean, I've seen their label in grocery stores before, but I don't know anything about them."

She stays silent.

Flashes of their branding filter through my mind, remembering the black background logo with a red apple and the outline of a crow. "Kind of a dark aesthetic for an orchard, don't you think?"

She shrugs, slowly wriggling her hands back into the pink floral gardening gloves.

She doesn't answer me, so I ask another question. "Aren't orchards usually open to the public this time of year? With a company as big as this one, I'd assume—"

"Hasn't been open to the public for some time now. Five years, I believe." My mouth snaps shut since she catches me off guard. Her admission piques my interest. "Not sure who would want to visit anyway. It doesn't stop customers from buying the apples, though. I think they even gained more popularity after the incident."

Incident?

"What incident?"

She peers around at our surroundings and lowers her voice to a whisper. We are the only ones on the sidewalk, and everything else around here is motionless and quiet besides the leaves in the trees rustling from the light breath of the wind.

"Christian, the CEO of Lindenvale Hill Orchard, was arrested and sent to prison for the murder of Jane Lindenvale after she disappeared."

I narrow my eyes at her. "Jane Lindenvale?" I ask.

"The wife." My body freezes, my heart thumping wildly because a news story I remember seeing long ago starts piecing together. "Those poor kids. I can't image what they've gone through the past several years without parental guidance." She follows my line of sight, shaking her head as we lock eyes on the gate. "They are seen around town but mostly keep to themselves now."

"Surly, the orchard is still running..."

Her high-pitched laugh pierces my ears. "Of course it is! This orchard is one of the many reasons Cedar Creek Cove does so well. The Lindenvales are millionaires. Their apples are seen in every market and grocery store from here to the East Coast."

My lips twist to the side in thought. Rossco pulls at the leash and licks up her pant leg, tired of remaining obedient and still in a stranger's presence. I completely forgot he was here. Weirdly enough, seeing this place and interaction has made my brain hazy.

She reaches down, scratching him behind the ears, and he wags his tail hectically in appreciation.

"But they must have workers—packagers...people to run the machinery. Right?"

She straightens. "Sure do, but the packaging headquarters is off the property. As far as I know, there is a machinery barn for the workers somewhere on the 5,120-acre property. Besides them and the workers coming in and out, that gate always remains closed."

Holy shit.

My jaw flops open, my accidental outburst making her jump. "Over 5,000 acres of apple trees?"

"No, no, dear. The house sits on a hill and is directly in the center of one mile of apple trees in each direction. The rest is forest all the way up to their fence line. It's quite a remarkable plot of land, if you ask me. I believe the backside drops down to the banks of the Columbia, but I've never seen it. There is a reason why a lot of people covet the property."

"Well, who owns it now? You know—since the husband is in prison."

Her chest rises and falls in annoyance, hinting that she is getting fed up with all my questions.

"Grandma," a voice calls. "I have breakfast ready."

Simultaneously, both of our heads shift in the direction of

her house. Waiting on her front porch is a man. He must be in his mid-twenties because of his smooth skin, facial hair, and build.

"My grandson," she informs. "We are in town visiting him for the week. I should go."

She begins to walk away from me, but I shout, "Wait!" Her body goes rigid in anticipation. I swallow. "Who owns it now?"

Images of last night flicker through my mind. My neighborhood is only a few miles away, but this town is small. I'd like to know who I'm sharing it with.

Or, more accurately, what monsters I'm sharing it with.

She glances at me over her shoulder, her eyes flashing with a fusion of warning and amusement. "Welcome to Cedar Creek Cove."

THREE | TARYN

My truck rolls to a stop in one of the parking spaces in front of Cedar Creek Elementary's two-story brick building. The freshly manicured lawn meets a blue-and-red climbing structure with slides, swings, monkey bars, and a basketball court, surrounded by red alders and maple trees.

The sidewalk leads to a set of double doors surrounded by massive glass windows.

The corners of my mouth lift upward.

I can see myself here.

Unlike the last school I attended, this one looks well-kept. They care, hopefully meaning they value their kids and teachers, too.

I turn off the ignition, taking notice of the brand-new-looking black Ford a few spaces away from mine with a lift that raises it slightly higher off the ground.

My truck looks like a piece of junk compared to that beauty. I run my palms over the worn and peeling leather steering wheel. But I love this truck. She did get me here successfully, after all.

I grab my purse off the passenger seat, open the door, and jump out. This place is downright deserted, except for the principal and me.

The last interview was hard. My heart was beating rapidly, and the principal was...daunting. He was seated farther back from the camera in his office, reading off a long list of questions, some related to teaching and others not. Several random ones caught me off guard, but that's an interview for you. Thinking on your feet is essential.

I answered them one by one and felt pretty good about it. Excitement swirled in my stomach when the call came through about a second in-person interview. But then I remembered I explicitly told him I was moving to Cedar Creek. That probably boded well in my favor. Everything after that was a breeze. I looked up rentals, secured that shithole, packed my bags, and Rossco and I were on our way.

Using my hands, I smooth the white halter-neck blouse and black pencil skirt that drops just above my knees. Peering at my reflection in the driver's window, I check my makeup one last time, patting the light amount of concealer under my eyes with the pad of my finger to ensure it's not cakey. I usually only wear a little makeup, but I accidentally put on too much this morning because my hands needed a job instead of shaking.

The halter top might have been a questionable decision, but I didn't have much to choose from regarding interview attire. Combined with the top and skirt that immaculately hug my curves, cakey makeup might make me look like a stripper.

I don't need him thinking this young teacher came directly from a pole.

Not that there's anything wrong with that; it's just not a vibe I need to release in this defining moment. If this doesn't work out, I can see if Crocks is hiring bartenders. Then I could get to know that handsome guy who brought me my pizza.

That can be plan B.

Glancing at myself one last time, I remove and reposition a bobby pin that slipped out from my low, messy bun.

I close my eyes.

Please, let this work out.

"Here goes nothing. No pressure or anything," I say to my reflection in a pathetic attempt to boost my confidence.

Dropping the keys into my bag, I stroll up the walkway. My heels are boisterously tapping on the sidewalk, the echo spiking my adrenaline and nerves. When I approach the double doors, I reach out a hand. Suddenly, I'm nearly hit in the face as it flies open without warning.

"Shit," I stammer, leaping backward to avoid the corner contacting the side of my face.

When I look up from the ground, I'm met with a very stern and disapproving scowl, probably at my language.

Off to a great start, Taryn.

I clear my throat and reach out a shaky hand. "Alaric—" I shake my head, "Principal Sinclair, I'm Taryn."

His attention first locks on the tips of my heels, roaming up my body leisurely. An unforeseen mix of heat and chills follow their wake. I didn't even know that was possible. When Alaric's bold, light green eyes clash with mine, I withdraw a breath. He narrows his eyes at me through his glasses, and mine widen of their own accord, no matter how hard I try to stop them.

Oh, my dear Lord, Principal Alaric Sinclair is the definition of a young and nerdy Greek god.

How old is this guy? I'm sure it's slim pickings here for hiring teachers and staff, but this specimen is one I wasn't expecting.

He leans against the frame in his gray slacks and a white button-up that pulls against his tight muscles. The top few buttons are undone, showcasing strands of his chest hair as dark as his stylized, messy brown hair. My eyes flit up to his perfectly cut jawline with a dusting of hair that creates a shadow.

He gives me a once-over, and my clit throbs.

If one person's appearance could make me wet, I think I just found them.

It's probably good that he was seated far back from the camera during the virtual interview because I would've been as distracted as I am now.

But I need this to go well, so I clear my throat again, shoving my outstretched hand closer to him.

He narrows his eyes before dropping his hand, adorned with a silver watch, into mine. My focus snatches onto the little bits of ink on his skin, peeking out from where the cuffs sit on his wrists.

"Miss Meyers, right this way." He motions me inside but takes off ahead, leaving me behind to shut the door.

Kind of a dick move if you ask me, but it gives me a brief moment to peek at the ass on him. God, if this guy is my superior, I am going to be completely screwed.

The door clicks behind me, and I speed-walk through a room that, from the couches and round tables everywhere, appears to be a common area and cafeteria combined. My shoes hit the white tile aggressively as I try to catch up to him, the sound ringing through the space.

He turns left down a hall and then another left into an office—his office, because there is a sign on the outside of the door that says, *Principal Alaric Sinclair*. He moves around his desk, motioning at the chair across from him.

"Please take a seat, Miss Meyers."

"Taryn. You can call me Taryn."

He raises a brow. "This is a professional relationship, Miss Meyers. I'll stick with exactly what I called you."

My eyes flit from side to side, astonished at his harsh tone. Now, my nerves are skyrocketing.

Great.

I put my purse on the second chair and plop down across from him. Looking out the large windows facing the playground, I attempt to muster enough confidence before I look at him again.

He folds his hands on the desk. "Now that you are sitting in my office, I assume you have settled here?"

I swallow and take a deep breath, meeting his gaze. "Yes, sir."

His posture solidifies at that label before he shifts uncomfortably in his seat. Other teachers must not call him that. *Noted.*

A moment of awkward silence sits between us before I continue. "I officially moved here a few days ago and have been working on getting everything in order. Transferring my certificates is easier since Washington and Arizona have a reciprocity agreement. Now I'm getting ready to take the necessary exams and doing the other steps needed to join your team here at Cedar Creek."

Hell yeah. That was a pretty good response if I do say so myself.

He gives a curt nod. "That's great, but this interview is going to be a little different."

His forwardness sends adrenaline flowing through my veins, feeding my already overdriven heart.

"Okay," I draw out.

"I want to get to know a little more about you so we can ensure you will fit in with our staff and our students."

Fitting in with students shouldn't be a priority for teachers since students are at school to learn and grow, not make friends with the teachers. But if it's important to him, then I'll enlighten him.

I nod my approval, and he begins asking questions.

"Do you have any siblings, Miss Meyers?"

That's a strange question to start with, but whatever. "I grew up as an only child, I'm afraid."

"Would you say the stereotype that only children are more reserved and spoiled fits you?"

The fuck.

"Um...no. I have a bachelor's degree in elementary education and love how I can impact young children's minds. Show them that despite their differences, they are worth something —" I swallow because this answer I'm giving hits me hard thinking about my parents. "Even if they don't believe they are. I consider myself to be a giver, Mr. Sinclair. Being an only child made me realize my passion for being around young children since it was a part of life that I missed out on. Because as much as I teach them, I think they teach me more."

He tightens his lips, his heated eyes roaming over my face, studying my reaction while I analyze his. I think he is pleased with that answer. But it's difficult to tell since his face lacks emotion. Maybe he's like a fish and doesn't have facial muscles —he relies on his body language to react. Alaric's strong frame relaxes, so I take that as a positive sign.

"And what about your family life?"

"What family life?" I joke, trying to lighten the mood.

His brows draw together, observing me suspiciously.

We need to pop some of those buttons and loosen that shirt a little more, Alaric. Maybe then you could take a breath.

I tilt my head. "Chill, it was a joke."

"You told me during the virtual interview that your parents travel a lot, and you moved around several times growing up. You must talk to them often."

I surprise myself when the honesty in my heart beats the answer I came up with in my head. "My parents are very immersed in their traveling endeavors, so I don't bother them with meaningless updates all the time. We send texts here and there, but other than that, I am mostly on my own and keep to myself."

He lifts a finger, pushing his glasses farther up to sit on the arch of his nose. "Friends?"

"I just moved here, so none yet and none I keep in contact with—" *Positivity, Taryn.* "But I look forward to creating meaningful relationships with the other teachers and exploring more of Cedar Creek."

"Can you cook?"

I roll my eyes. The muscle in his jaw pops as he shoots me a disapproving look.

Why is that important?

Leaning my back against the chair, I knit my arms together, mimicking his position. "I know my way around a kitchen."

"Do you have any questions for me yet?" he asks.

I lick my lower lip in thought.

Yeah, I have a few questions for you. Like, how old are you, and what kid shoved a crayon up your ass?

Before I have time to answer, he says, "No questions? Moving on." He places his elbows on the desk, folding his fingers together. "What about pot and drug use? Have you used them before? What about arrests?"

Who the hell is this guy?

The water on the stove in my chest boils over and onto the burner. "What kind of question is that?" I snap, pinning him with my stare. "You did a background check, did you not?"

He reclines back in his chair, crossing his arms over his broad chest. "Of course I did," he counters like I should know the answer to that. "Had to make sure you're a good girl..." His eyes drop to my chest as his head cocks to the side. "And right for my students," he finishes. "Now answer the question, Miss Meyers," he says hard-heartedly.

Plan B it is.

I stand up from my seat and step forward, resting my palms

on the surface. I lean over, glare down at his handsomely irritating face in those black-rimmed glasses, and gift him with the fakest smile I can manage. "Do you want me to pull down my panties so you can drug test me, sir?"

His muscles harden under his shirt. Alaric's burning gaze holds mine captive—his eyes appearing like sagebrush in a desert being licked by flames. They send liquid heat rushing between my thighs until it's an intensity that's difficult to ignore.

"If you speak to me like that again, I'll bend you over this desk, rip them off, and shove them in your hot little mouth as punishment for using a tone like that with me."

My limbs tremble.

I wonder what else his mouth could do if it were put to better use.

But I have more self-respect than that. So, I stand up and straighten my posture, giving him a nod. "Thank you for meeting with me about the position, Mr. Sinclair, and hitting me with all those arbitrary questions. But I'm over this conversation and will not beg you for this job." The confidence stirring in my chest expands. "I hope you'll have better luck finding a teacher who will drop on their knees for you because. It's. Not. Me."

I reach for my purse, not sparing him a second look. But it's not until I exit his office that I realize I may not have to. With the size of this town, it's only a matter of time before we see each other again. And if that happens, I only hope our next interaction is a little more pleasant than this one.

FOUR | TARYN

I've been zoned out for the past fifteen minutes, my focus not straying from a limp piece of lettuce. Grabbing my fork next to my plate, I flick my wrist, pushing it around.

Well, it wasn't limp when I ate my house salad, so the fact that it's floppy is proof of how long I've been sitting motionless at this table inside Crocks. Maybe I have some superpower I'm unaware of, and it wilted under the heat of my hellfire stare.

That interview was...unbelievable.

It was one of those moments that felt like a complete and utter blur because my mind was blindsided by how bizarre and nonsensical it was. My mentality still doesn't know how to process it.

After whipping out of the parking lot, I headed home to let Rossco out. I watched him chew on a stick for a while in the yard and rip it into unbelievably tiny shreds as I attempted to gather my wits so I could make a logical decision about what to do next.

Eventually, my stomach growled with hunger, so I left Rossco in the backyard and changed out of my interview attire. I slipped on a pair of jean shorts, a fitted white tank, and a hunter-green flannel while I worked up the courage to jump in the truck and make the ten-minute drive to Crocks.

My stomach required food, but I also had the motive to plead for a job. Luckily, the piece-of-shit house I'm living in has extremely low rent. Like, way below the average for even a town this quaint. Which was why it was so easy to rent it blindly. Even now, with my financial status—thanks to my saving money abilities—I could go a few months without a job if needed.

But I'd rather not be bored out of my mind.

I worked at a diner in high school, so maybe I'll be able to secure a job here with no issues. Unless they need someone to flip pizza dough, which is completely out of the question due to my severely uncoordinated nature.

I lift my head and peer at the dark wood bar with rows of liquor bottles behind it. The bartender wears the same gray Crocks logo T-shirt that the delivery guy had on the first night I got into town.

I wonder where he is. Just a glimpse of his panty-dropping smile would lighten my foul mood.

The scent of baked crust and fried food wafts through the air, mixing with the aroma of hops from the bar. Vintage-style pendant lights hang over some of the tables and the whole length of the dark-finished wood bar in the back. The soft glow from the sconces on the wall creates a relaxing atmosphere. One of the back walls is almost entirely made of windows, giving customers a view of the bay where Cedar Creek flows into the Columbia. The setting sun casts orange trickles of glittery light across the water as night draws closer.

I shift in my seat at a table for two next to some windows that look out into the row of parking spots along the street. Only a few people and families are scattered about the place beside me. So, when a middle-aged man with a dark, graying beard pushes through the double doors to the kitchen, I decide to shoot my shot. His walk and strong presence give him a manager-type aura.

Here goes nothing.

Slinging the strap of my crossbody bag over my shoulder, I push my chair under the table before making my way to the bar. The bar is nearly empty, but one elderly man with a beer in front of him sits a few seats down from where I'm standing.

The man behind the counter grabs a cup from the dish rack and a towel from the bar and dries it off.

I clear my throat. "Excuse me," I interrupt, my voice emerging hoarser than I intend it to.

He turns toward me and smiles. His dimples show despite his facial hair. "What can I get for you?"

I swallow and lick my chapped lips, trying to wet my sandpaper tongue. "A job if you have one."

The man chuckles, his eyes roaming over my appearance. "Sorry, darling. We aren't hiring at the moment."

My heart drops. Shit.

"Oh—are you sure?" I ask as if making him contemplate his response will change his answer. "I could buss tables, wash dishes…" I point to the glass in his hands as he works around the rim, polishing it with the towel.

"I'm sorry. I can't afford to bring someone else on right now."

"You're the owner?"

A corner of his mouth tilts. "Sure am. Have been for the last ten years. And I take it you're not from around here?" He furrows his brow.

My shoulders slump, and I sigh. "How does everyone know that?"

"Well, it's not often that we have young people asking about jobs. And if they do, it's kids who have lived here for a while— they're familiar to everyone. You, on the other hand," he dissects me under his gaze, "have a presence and pretty face that would be hard to miss if you did live in this town."

My eyes widen, and I smack my palms on the countertop as if I can transfer my excitement into the wood and not appear as desperate. "What about a delivery driver? Do you need one of those?"

He glides a hand over his beard. "I mean, it's a good idea, but I'm not sure we get enough calls to consider hiring a delivery driver."

"Oka—"

Wait, what?

A few seconds pass between us before he looks at me strangely. "Are you all right?"

My nails dig into the wood surface of the bar while my face continues to harden in bewilderment. "What do you mean, 'consider hiring a delivery driver'? You have one."

Creases form on his forehead. "No, I don't. I'd know if I had a delivery driver."

"Maybe it was another pizza place, then?" I think out loud to myself, though I'm positive I called Crocks.

He places the glass on the counter, the clank against the wood causing me to jump out of my skin. "We are the only one in town."

I know what I saw.

"I placed an order on the phone with you two nights ago. A delivery guy showed up at my door with my pizza in the *same* exact shirt you're wearing," I exclaim, gesturing to his shirt. "I'm not crazy."

He watches me apprehensively, probably making his own assumptions about my unhinged state.

Maybe I am going insane. Seeing things.

"Sorry, I don't know what to tell you. We've never had a delivery driver." I close my eyes, releasing a frustrated breath. "But if you are looking for a job, you can try The Honey Hut, it's a bakery and coffee bar down the road. She might be hiring and need the help."

Nodding, I soften my tone and drench it with sweetness. I feel bad for possibly putting a damper on this guy's night. "Thank you. I'll reach out to her." I hold out my hand. "Thank you, Mr...."

He places his burly hand in mine, the size consuming mine. "Harrison Crock."

"Nice to meet you, Mr. Crock. I'll be back."

He smirks.

I start to ramble. "I won't be back to bother you about a job —unless you change your mind—but I'll return to eat your pizza. And your salads, because those are really good too." I chuckle.

"Sounds good. I'll see you again..."

"Taryn," I smile, and he drops my hand.

On to plan C.

Sauntering out the front door of Crocks, I'm hit with a wave of fresh air. The floral smell from the barrels decorating the sidewalk and the woodsy scent from the trees make me stop in my tracks. It's calming. Soothing.

I walk between two parked cars and glance both ways before crossing to my truck across the street. I peer up from the pavement, my eyes locking on something sitting on my hood. Something that sure as hell shouldn't be there.

Gaping at the apple, goosebumps spread over my body. Someone is watching me. It's the only reasonable explanation. I study my surroundings. Buildings and businesses line this side of the street, but I don't spot anyone or anything that stands out besides this damn apple. Plus, all the establishments besides Crocks appear closed since it's eight o'clock at night.

It's only day three of living in this stupid town, and I have no idea who is messing with me and why. Maybe because I'm the new girl, and according to Harrison, new people don't move here often.

I'm an easy target.

I'm glad I can entertain their boredom.

Balling my hands into fists at my sides, I dig my fingernails into my palms. Spinning back around, my feet move, marching straight back into Crocks. I am not touching that apple.

If I'm going insane, drinking won't hurt.

Harrison lounges on the other side of the bar, and when he spots me, I flatten my lips in a line and exhale a breath he can hear. "I'm going to need a drink."

He grins. "I thought you might need one. First one's on the house."

FIVE | TARYN

The funny thing about alcohol? It's like one of those teeter-totters my third graders would play on. Piled on one side are all the things you don't want to think about—the things you want to forget. Then, on the opposite sits the garbage can of junk you threw away a long time ago.

When I drink, the things I want to ignore and everything I believed I had let go of from the past come to the forefront of my mind.

Alcohol numbs certain parts of you but makes you painfully aware of others simultaneously.

Like the fact that I honestly don't have a family, and my parents couldn't care less.

Like the reality that I'm entirely alone.

Like the bitter truth that I'm stuck with a year lease in a town that's already driving me to the brink of madness.

But hey, I've got a cute dog at home and a bartender in front of me who keeps handing me free drinks because I think he pities me.

And when you're like me and want to feel absolutely nothing because the only person to blame for your unfortunate luck is yourself, the only solution is to keep drinking until a point where everything shuts off, and the world becomes dark.

For a few hours, anyway, until you wake up with a massive hangover and feel worse than you did before.

I'm not at that point. But my fingertips are numb, a telltale sign that I'm buzzed.

After Harrison Crock got me a drink, I downed it in less than ten minutes. He told me about the club downstairs, and I was intrigued. Apparently, it's also a part of Crocks, but it's the hangout spot when the sun goes down, and the locals or tourists want a club-like atmosphere. I'm glad he pointed me toward the stairs because I need the distraction.

However, no matter how many drinks I consume, I can't shake the feeling of eyes following my every move.

I'm just paranoid. And drunk.

I twist on the barstool, watching the liquid slosh around in my beer glass as I twirl it in circular motions. It is something so simple, yet it's entertaining.

The dark-haired bartender with pattern tattoos crawling up his arms and neck reaches over and snatches my glass from my hands.

I stare at him, dumbfounded. Clucking my tongue, I tuck a strand of hair behind my ear. "That was incredibly rude. I still had several sips left!"

He tosses the glass into the sink and returns to stand in front of me on the other side of the bar. Up until now, I have only seen the gray Crocks T-shirts, but the one he wears is black.

He presses his hands onto the counter and leans over them, getting closer to me. "I was going to get you a fresh drink, but if you prefer that one..." He pauses, letting me think about it.

Reaching for my phone tucked into the back pocket of my jean shorts, I glance at the time. Eleven.

I roll it over, debating whether I should have another or

request an Uber home. Thinking that hard makes me nauseous.

Do they even have Ubers here?

Plus, I left Rossco outside in the fenced backyard, so he should be content for another hour.

"What are you going to give me?" I ask.

He tilts his head back and forth thoughtfully and glides a hand over the back of his neck, giving me a flash of his muscular biceps. Maybe he would kindly take me home once his shift is over. I've never slept with anyone, but he's hot and friendly, and I've had enough drinks already that my body craves something more than my vibrator.

He eyes me up and down. "How about a margarita?"

I hum in approval. "Sounds great!"

He leaves me and wanders into the back kitchen. A minute later, he reappears, tossing a red apple into the air. I trace its movements, observing it rise and fall into his palm. I'm too wasted to let the sight of it affect me. I can't be spooked out by the sight of the fruit my entire life.

He places it on a cutting board and picks up a knife, cutting it down the center. The juices leak out, glistening on the wood from the overhead pendant lights. Similar to upstairs, there are sconces on the walls, which are turned off to allow the flashing strobe lights to flicker on the dance floor in the middle of the space.

It's a little classier down here. Around the floor are leather chairs, round tables, booths, and one pool table in the corner, where bikers are challenging each other to a game. A jukebox and dartboard are on the opposite side of the room.

The knife taps against the cutting board as the bartender slices the apple into thin sheets.

I hop off the stool. "I am going to use the restroom quick. I'll be right back." The rush of alcohol bolts through my body, impacting my head.

I make a beeline for the bathroom—down a short hallway with the kitchen doors at the end—and reach up to massage the skin on the side of my temple as my brain pulses against my skull.

Damn, maybe getting another drink wasn't a great idea.

Staring at the floor through slightly blurry vision, I lower my hand, and my face smacks against something hard. A set of hands grip my forearms to steady me as I sway.

Goddammit.

I lift my spinning head enough to stare at the chest directly in front of me, clad in a black sweatshirt. Heat rushes to my cheeks with embarrassment. The warmth from his rough hands sears through my long-sleeved flannel.

He clears his throat, and I swallow.

"Oh my God, I'm so sorry! Excuse me," I apologize, hurrying away from him to the bathroom to avoid eye contact. I knew it would make me feel worse since I wasn't paying attention to where I was going.

Exiting the stall in the bathroom, I stride to the mirror and stare at myself. What am I doing? I don't drink like this when I've hit a low. I mean, this is much lower and more problematic than the situations I usually find myself in, but I don't resort to alcohol.

My eyes sting with unshed tears. I wish I could call my mom. I wish I had the type of relationship with my parents growing up where I could pour my heart out to them about my issues, even if they were simple, juvenile things that every girl went through. Where they would stroke my hair and tell me everything would be okay. Or maybe my dad would offer to kick a few guys' asses for hurting me.

Sometimes, when I turn my phone on, I long for a text. Or a missed call notification. But always being the first to reach out is exhausting—asking them how their day has been and learning their latest whereabouts even when they don't seem to care about mine.

I know they trust me. Trust that I'll make good decisions. Adulting like adults do. But I wish they wouldn't just assume I'm okay and put in the effort to ensure I am. There's a big difference; sometimes, all we need to know is that someone out there thinks about our well-being. That someone misses us completely because life would be different if we weren't a part of theirs.

I want someone to adore me like that. I want a relationship with people who genuinely can't breathe without me around, and they are a mess if the words between us go unspoken.

Peering at myself in the mirror, I notice the whites of my eyes are bloodshot, the hair near my forehead sprouting out in every direction like unruly, overgrown weeds.

Turning the knob, water pours out of the faucet, and I wet my hands, running them over my face, below my eyes, and up through my hair to slick the bun back to look a little more put together than I feel.

The cool water temperature takes down my body heat a notch and feels refreshing. My tank top has slipped up a little, higher than usual, to expose more of my tan stomach. Thank you, Arizona sun. I'm glad I could soak it up while I had the chance. I still need a ride home, and looking sexy might help. Not that asking strangers for a ride is the best idea, but I need to get home somehow unless I want to sleep in the back seat of my truck, which wouldn't be the first time.

A remix of "All Around the World" by R3HAB grows louder as I go back to the bar and situate myself on the stool. Ten or so sweaty bodies move and grind on the dance floor, my eyes following their movements. Watching them from the stool raises my temperature as if their body heat radiates from them in heavy waves and soaks into my clammy skin.

Most of them appear to be around my age or a little

younger, while everyone on the perimeter chatting and drinking is of various ages. Since there wasn't a bouncer to get in, I'm guessing Crocks is a go-to and unmonitored place for younger folks wanting to let loose and throw a couple of drinks back.

My ruby red margarita awaits me when I rotate my stool to face the bar. My mouth waters, the tumbler with a cinnamon sugar rim and apple slice, validating my decision to have one more drink.

The bartender nods to someone behind me nonchalantly. Sneaking a peek over my shoulder, I see dancing individuals, their bodies illuminated in the dark by the green and pink flashing lights. Everything beyond that is black and blurred.

Someone must have waved at him for another round.

My attention finds the bartender again, and I smile. "This looks so good. Thanks for the drink."

He grins and leans over the bar, holding my eyes. "You don't have to be so polite here. Most tourists just slap a tip down and get on their way."

"I'm afraid going on my merry way isn't an option since I'm here for good." For a while, anyway.

He raises a brow, and I lift the straw to my mouth, taking a long sip of the apple margarita.

Oh my gosh, that's so good.

The tartness from the lime and sweetness from the apple perfectly combine to create an explosion on my taste buds. I suck some more down and drift my finger over the rim. Lifting it to my mouth, I lick off some cinnamon sugar. He grips the edge of the counter in his fists while he tracks my movements.

"And I also need to make some friends since I'm not getting on my way and out of Cedar Creek anytime soon." I give him a single wave. "So, I'm Taryn."

He stares at me, I think. His attention seems to be barely slipping past me to something else. "Xavier."

I pick up the glass and tip it toward him. "Thanks for the drink, Xavier."

He bites back his grin. His lips hold my attention as my brain gets a little fuzzier, like one of those old televisions when it starts to lose connection. Or like radio static clashing with a really good song.

"With a name and face like that, you're bound to get into some trouble around here." Registering his words takes a second longer, and I set my glass down.

Propping my elbow on the counter, I hold my weighted head up. When I give him my attention again, it feels like several minutes have passed. Great, I'm reaching that drunk state where I'm blacking in and out.

"Thanks for the compliment." Or at least, I think it was one. I honestly can't remember what he said.

I straighten back up, hoping the shift in my posture will feed a little energy and control back into my body. Xavier's voice is saying something, but it sounds like an unintelligible noise drifting to my ears underwater. My breathing starts to slow, but my heart beats faster, the flashing lights spurring my dizzy state.

I think I'm going to be sick.

Peeling my sticky thighs off the seat from the sheen of sweat coating my skin, I move to stand, but I wobble. Stumbling, I force myself to regain my balance.

Air. Yeah, I need some fresh air.

I hurry toward the door leading to the hallway of stairs that goes back up to the main level of Crocks. The music blares in my ears. The bar to my left and the dance floor to my right begin tilting the moment I burst through the door to the stairwell. I place my foot on the first step, pausing because I don't even think I have the energy and capability to crawl up all of them right now.

Alarm bells are banging around in my head.

Something is wrong. Think, Taryn. Think.

The drink. My heart plummets into my gut.

The apple margarita.

I slap my hand against the railing of the stairs, trying to suck air in and out of my shriveling lungs. I'm on the verge of having a panic attack because I know what happens next. I have never been slipped a drug. This is what I get for being negligent and stupid. But it doesn't make it any less wrong.

Hot tears stream down my face, my body weakening at a rapid pace to give itself over to whatever Xavier put in my drink. My knees are about to give out when a hand splays across my lower back, keeping me from falling backward.

Maybe someone has found me, and they'll help. That thought drifts away with more of my awareness when another hand wraps around my forearm.

They pull me upward. My head lolls back, my watery eyes locking onto a pair of green ones under the shadow of a hood as my heartbeat slows. I try to study their face but my damn eyes won't focus.

Another arm in a black sleeve worms its way around my stomach. And a fourth hand, a gloved hand, caresses the side of my face tenderly before covering my mouth. I try to inhale air into my lungs, but the leather glove transforms the sound into a muffled moan.

There are too many hands on me.

But I'm too tired to move.

And just as the little sliver of my mind that's still coherent screams at me to fight, I go limp, and darkness drags me under.

SIX | TARYN

I should've known that sometimes, the smallest things turn out to be the most venomous. They sink their teeth in, releasing a deadly poison that either hits your nervous system and bloodstream rapidly or causes a slow and agonizing death.

It's been four days, and Cedar Creek has already punctured my skin with its fangs, killing me quickly.

My eyes flutter, the dark room around me distorting into a hectic ombre of deep grays and blacks.

I groan, using the little strength I can muster to flip myself from my back onto my side. Reaching up to rub my fingers in circular motions on my temple, I struggle to alleviate the throbbing in my skull.

Maybe I'm not dead. *Hmm.*

My hand glides across the surface I'm on, caressing a soft material. The scent of fresh cotton linens with a hint of lavender tickles my nose. What is that other smell? Paint, maybe? The blend of fragrances brings more consciousness through the haze the more I try to breathe in and out calmly.

I fully peel open my heavy eyelids, rapidly jerking my body

to an upright position. My body sinks into the plush bed, the room around me coming into focus.

What the hell happened last night?

More importantly, where am I?

The early morning dawn casts long fingers of shadows across the room from the panel of arched windows in both the front and back of the room. A small amount of light reflects off gold Victorian embellishments and trim around the A-frame ceiling.

One of the navy-blue walls has a dark walnut dresser pushed up against it and a matching vanity with a large mirror. On another side of the room, across from the bed, are a cream-colored accent chair and a floor-to-ceiling bookshelf—but because of the tilt of the A-frame, the shelf doesn't fit against the ceiling seamlessly. On the other side of that is a railing that looks like it leads down to some stairs.

My eyes bounce around, taking in my surroundings.

This has to be a dream.

I toss the comforter off my legs, releasing a breath, relieved I'm still fully clothed in what I wore to Crocks. My head swims, trying to recollect everything that happened last night. The last thing I can remember without any disturbance is when I walked out of Crocks after he told me he wasn't hiring.

Swinging my legs over the queen bed with a navy duvet and pillows to match the room's aesthetic, I rub my eyes, still laden with sleep. God, my body aches. Pushing past the pain, my feet contact the cold wood floor. Standing up, I scan the room again, my eyes landing on the bedside table with a lamp, a small old-fashioned clock, and a glass of water; next to it, a fresh bowl of fruit.

But what's outside the window has my blood freezing, turning to sharp icicles in my veins. I wrap my hands around my upper arms, advancing one slow step at a time.

All I see is sky.

A sky of dawn tormented by dark rolling clouds.

Closing my eyes and inhaling a deep breath, I fail to keep my weak body from shaking.

I approach the arched window, my eyes widening in horror at the nightmare that crawls across the ground and the soft rolling hills below.

Wherever I am, I'm high up. And for miles, the only colors are deep forest green and dreary gray.

My pulse thunders.

As far as I can see, there are only impeccable rows of apple trees until they blur in the distance—the morning fog devouring the rest I can't see.

SEVEN | CAMERON

5 HOURS EARLIER

Crocks has always been a favored hideaway spot of mine. And occasionally, a striking tourist struts through that door, completely unaware they've walked into a den of vipers ready to bite because there's not much else to eat in this damn town.

Or maybe they are reckless and figure that the local hangout spot is an excellent place to find dick and get laid. And finding one isn't usually a problem for them.

Like I said, beautiful women step foot in here all the time, but after settling my eyes on *her*, I may have found my new addiction. And it's about fucking time I had someone new who can hold my interest for more than a few seconds. Someone to help me forget who my heart craves.

I turn my head, staring at my reflection. The only dissimilarity between us is his shorter-cropped hair under his hood. He sits down and places a cigarette in his mouth, letting it hang between his lips. Reaching into the pocket of his jeans, he removes a lighter. My ears perk at the click as he holds the flame steady to the end, the cherry from the cigarette casting an orange glow on his features.

He inhales a deep breath, holding it in before exhaling a curtain of smoke that floats over his face, dispersing into the air above him. "That girl can hold her weight."

I smirk at my twin. "One more drink, and we'll be the ones holding her weight."

Brennan's wicked smile mirrors mine before my eyes lock back on Xavier behind the bar. He's making the "special" drink we bought her while she finishes in the bathroom.

"You gave Xavier the apple and the Rohypnol?" I ask.

"Yep," he says, popping the P. He takes another drag. "Questioned me in the back about why he couldn't just use one of the other apples they have."

Because they aren't as immaculate as the one I picked on my run this morning. Its skin was as flawless as an apple could possibly be—just like the one Brennan left under the tree and the one I left on the hood of her truck earlier.

He drums his fingers against the table impatiently and leans back, stuffing his hands into his sweatshirt pocket. "She accidentally ran into me on the way to the bathroom but was too nervous to look at my face. Embarrassment is a cute color on her."

I saw. She was too focused on looking at the floor, planting one foot in front of the other so she wouldn't trip. I'm not going to lie, a spike of jealousy jolted down my spine since he got to touch her first. I could've run my fingertips over hers when I handed her that pizza box the first night she was in town, but I zoned in on my control and forced myself not to.

It was fucking difficult not to touch her.

Especially since we had been watching her walk about her house for an hour before she looked out the window and saw me in the driver's seat and Brennan leaning against the willow tree in her yard. We were covered head to toe in black pants, hoods, and leather gloves.

Her curiosity was so fixated on Brennan against the tree

that I pulled the car away without her noticing. I quickly took off my sweatshirt, grabbed the pizza she ordered from the back seat, and snuck up to her front porch to ring the doorbell.

When she opened the door, I stood before her in a gray Crocks shirt I borrowed from Xavier. Her eyes penetrated mine, those beautiful brown irises flashing with terror from Bren and me scaring her. I swear I could feel the vibration of her heart beating through the porch, each shudder shooting straight to my cock.

"But...he wants something in return since this could get him fired if anyone finds out," Brennan tacks on.

Xavier gets away with too much shit to get fired. Harrison would never throw him out on his ass. He's his best bartender and has been for the last three years since he moved here.

"What did he want?"

A corner of his mouth lifts. "Me." He relaxes an arm over the back of the booth, releasing a sigh mixed with a breathy chuckle. "He said I should bring her along."

I narrow my eyes at Xavier on the other side of the counter, observing as he pours the red mixture into the glass. My eyes roll. "You would've let him fuck you anyway."

"True. But bringing her along? Damn, that would be hot."

Bren and I shared with him once, and now Xavier expects to join in on the fun every time?

Fuck that. Not happening. Not with her.

I grind my teeth. "She hasn't consented to anything." *Yet, but she will.*

Reaching for the ashtray, he grinds his cigarette into the glass, stubbing it out. "And when she does, I'll let her know the option is there if she wants it."

Brennan and Xavier have an open relationship and are always on the prowl for a third. They crave pussy too much to give it up, but they both like dick too.

Bren and I may share, but I have a feeling it will be a challenge this time. The jealousy is already festering, rotting me more than him.

She appears from the hallway, my adrenaline spiking as she returns to her seat. Sliding back onto her stool, the knot on her head looks a little different, as if she fixed it up in the bathroom.

When Taryn notices the drink in front of her, Xavier gives me a single nod, letting me know we are good to go. She must catch his gesture because she peers over her shoulder, examining everyone around the dance floor. Her eyes roam back and forth to look for who Xavier nodded to, but it's too dark. She doesn't see us, even though my focus and Bren's is locked on her.

With our hoods up and black attire, we blend into the background on the other side of the room from Taryn and the bar. There is something almost predatory about how we observe each movement she makes. But our sweet, innocent, soon-to-be roommate is oblivious to us. My blood crackles with energy, fueling my impatience.

With all the individuals on the dance floor, I only catch glimpses of her between sweaty bodies grinding. The neon strobe lights flash in the darkness, but the bar is well-lit enough to illuminate her side profile.

She turns back around. Lifting her drink, she takes a sip, tipping the glass toward Xavier in thanks as they exchange more words. It looks like she loves the margarita by the way she keeps diving in for more.

Taryn doesn't know that sweet and pretty things can be disguised to hide their deadly nature. After this, I may need to teach her a lesson about leaving her drink alone with strangers around.

Tsk, tsk, tsk, Taryn.

She stirs the mixture with her straw, causing my heart to pound savagely in my chest with anticipation. The muscles in her back and shoulders start to relax a little more.

Anytime now.

The light from Brennan's phone screen illuminates his face as he pulls up his messages. "I'm letting Colt know we'll be home in less than an hour so we can get her through the house without all the questions."

Bringing Taryn home will be like walking through the door with a new pet everyone has been awaiting. But in our case, we've been waiting for years.

Preparing.

Planning.

I narrow my eyes on my brother. "Which is why we waited until tonight, dumbass. Everyone should be in bed so we can slip her in quickly and quietly." The main reason we needed the Rohypnol.

I've always been entirely against the idea of drugging someone, but there's a first time for everything. She would've undoubtedly put up a fight if we had gone with one of the other methods we contemplated. I probably would've found a little too much pleasure in that, anyway.

The minutes excruciatingly drag on. A flash of movement by the bar has my eyes darting from Bren to Taryn. She pushes herself off the stool, her gaze steady on the doorway leading to the stairwell. She hurriedly walks toward it as the drug starts to pull her under, causing her body to sway from side to side. She pushes through the door and disappears, but not for long.

My pulse batters, and I clap a hand on Bren's shoulder. "It's finally go time, brother."

He snatches his black gloves from the table, and I remove mine from my sweatshirt pocket. We slip them on as we hustle across the room, dodging sweaty people scattered about.

I give Xavier a nod in appreciation before we exit the bar.

When we push through the doors that lead up to the main level, it's only us and our girl alone in the stairwell. She is one step up, hunched over. One firm hand grips the railing in a death grip with white knuckles, and the other is pressed against her forehead.

With one glance, Bren and I share a conversation with unspoken words. He gives me the signal, and we advance toward her.

Her frame can no longer support her weight. She sinks leisurely toward the floor like an anchor, losing a battle with the ocean's depths—plunging into the deepest trench until nothing but darkness shrouds her.

A groan slips past her soft pink lips when Brennan splays his hand across her lower back to keep her from collapsing and wraps his fingers around her upper arm.

Tugging her upward, he pulls the side of her body flush against his frame, but Taryn's head falls backward. Her flushed and heated cheeks are wet with tears. Those beautiful eyes struggle to find mine, but they pierce into my soul with the intensity of a goddamn pneumatic drill that can obliterate concrete into thousands of tiny pieces. God, they are breathtaking.

Nice to see you again, beautiful.

But I don't think the recognition crosses her.

I press my chest against her back, snaking one of my arms around her waist to keep her steady. She moves, her ass brushing against the front of my jeans. Fuck, if she's already making my cock swell like this, it won't be long before the nearly microscopic sliver of self-control I have left vanishes.

Lifting my gloved hand to her head, the leather glides over her smooth and tear-stricken skin as her eyes flutter closed. Bren holds her tightly while I sweep her small, warm body into my arms.

Her sugared citrus perfume envelops me all the way to my

car. It's time to get her home so she can infect my head and our house with that scent. And just like me and my brothers, *they* will soon be obsessed with her, too.

EIGHT | CAMERON

Dirt crunches below the tires, kicking up a plume of dust behind us as I pick up speed through the orchard. The car curves around the bend where the cliff drops off—the rushing Columbia River lashing against the rocks below.

I can almost hear Dad's deep, anal-ridden voice sternly ordering me to slow down. But the adrenaline surging to every nerve ending has my foot heavy on the gas pedal.

We emerge from the sharp turn, my black Aston Martin DBX passing between two sides of apple trees lining the road. It's only half a mile farther until we reach the house.

I spare a quick glimpse over my shoulder. Taryn lies on her back across the back seat with a blanket sprawled across her legs. Her hands are folded over her chest, the same way a corpse in a casket looks before you bury it. But unlike a corpse, her chest is rising and falling softly. The comparison almost makes me laugh.

She might not be conscious, but we aren't dicks. We want her to be comfortable even if she isn't awake. Dad taught us to be gentlemen, after all—although some manners have escaped us over the last five years.

"Do you think she will like the room?" Brennan asks, pulling my attention back to the dirt road as we hit the solar lights spread out on both sides, guiding us the rest of the way.

The house emerges on the hill; the porch sconces a speck in the darkness. As we draw nearer, all the other lights in the house are off except the kitchen on the bottom floor and the tower. *Her* tower soars over the rest of the four-story stone Victorian home directly on our hill in the center of a circular yard until it meets the line of apple trees on each side.

Our unique slice of heaven that she will, hopefully—eventually—come to love like we do.

I answer his question about the attic, my voice turning gravelly at the thought of her not liking it. "I hope so. Between all the hours of working, refurnishing that room, and family time, we all did our research. We know what she likes."

He nods, looking ahead.

It takes us a few minutes to appear from the orchard, but we hit the base, inclining up the small hill. We reach the circular driveway in front of the house and pull to a stop.

Bren and I open and close our doors simultaneously. I round the car to his side, where he already has the back seat door open. She lays peacefully, breathing evenly through her parted lips. A strand of hair is glued to her soft mouth—lips that are taunting the hell out of me. I envision all the ways I could claim them; her on her knees with them wrapped around my cock, her lips on mine while at the same time I finger her tight cunt so I can swallow and devour her pants from the euphoria, her gentle tongue that I imagine tastes as sweet as that apple margarita she drank earlier.

I could cave in to my urges. I could force myself to be temperate with her so that when she woke, she would be entirely oblivious that I had brought her unconscious body pleasure. But the thought that she could willingly give herself over to me is stirring whatever patience I have left.

Before my brother has the chance to say anything, I lower my body through the door and drop down, wrestling to get an arm under her back. I reach my other hand under her legs, scooping her up into my arms. Shifting my body to get a better hold of her dead weight, I lift her from the car and take a step back.

He grips the doorframe and arches a dark brow. "You realize she's here for all of us and not just you, right?" He chuckles, slamming the door, the sound echoing through the night and harmonizing with the chirping of crickets. "You can't get all territorial over a girl who's here to serve more than one purpose. You said you wouldn't get attached."

"Shut up, asshole," I mutter, approaching the sidewalk. "I want her to stay."

"We all want her to stay. More importantly, we should do whatever we can to ensure she *wants* to stay." He shakes his head. "Because we are fucking screwed if she leaves and tells someone what happened."

I exhale a frustrated breath. I know. We already have one of us behind bars. It wouldn't look good if three Lindenvale sons landed in prison with felonies for abducting a young teacher.

Did it stop us? Absolutely not.

Maybe prisons do family blocks.

Dad told us to protect this family at all costs, and that's precisely what we are doing. Colt may have his own twisted reasoning behind his actions, but ultimately, my brothers and I have the same objective.

It's just eccentric and a little idiotic.

One of her arms sways back and forth as I take the steps up to the porch, and Brennan grabs it, placing it on her stomach. We reach the front door, and he walks into the foyer first. I follow, and he shuts the door behind me.

Since the lights are all mostly off, I assume Colt is in his cabin, located on the backside of the house, at the edge of the yard.

He played his part. Now we are doing ours.

Brennan draws nearer to us, swiping his fingers across her clammy cheek. He tucks the dark strand of hair behind her ear that was attached to her lips. "But that doesn't mean we both can't have some fun with her while she's here."

I mischievously grin. "Can you imagine how beautiful she would look with one coc—"

"Bren...Cam." The delicate voice drifts through the dark foyer from the stairs on the left wall that go up to the second, third, and fourth floors.

I jolt in surprise, nearly dropping Taryn. "Fuck!" I attempt to resituate my arms to get a better grip on her.

"Language, Cam," Brennan scolds from beside me.

We both glance up at the staircase as our baby sister stares at us with sleepy eyes and pouty little lips.

So much for everyone being asleep.

She grips her light pink nightgown in her fist, looking between us. "Is that the girl? Why is she asleep?"

Bren and I gape at each other, struggling to find an answer. How do you explain to your sibling, who can't tie their own shoes and is just learning to spell, that we kidnapped her new nanny?

Her light brown hair, so similar to our mother's, falls in natural waves over her shoulders. She peers at us with those vibrant blue eyes.

"You should be in bed, Elena," Bren whispers, keeping his voice low so we don't wake Tristan and Jessica, our other siblings.

My cursing probably already did that.

"Did Colt not say good night?" he asks.

She rubs her tired eyes and nods.

"You just couldn't sleep?" I ask.

Her head bobs again, and my heart stutters.

I glance at Taryn, unresponsive in my arms. The heat from our bodies pressed together creates a layer of sweat that encases my skin.

Damn, I need a shower. Mostly so I can release some tension in my dick before I'm tempted to lay a finger on her.

Or in her.

I look back at Bren. "Can you take Taryn upstairs?" I gesture to Elena with my head. "I'll get her to bed."

He narrows his eyes. "I'm surprised you trust me to take her to bed."

"If I find you in it with her," I threaten, "that's when we'll have an issue."

Our eyes hold steady while he approaches me and holds his arms out. I transfer her weight to Brennan, and he walks up the stairs, passing Elena. He smiles at her, but her wide eyes stay locked on an unconscious Taryn like she's the most interesting thing she's ever seen.

He says the words we say to her and Tristan every single night without fail. "I love you, Elena."

Someday, I'll have to explain to her why we did what we did to Taryn—why we abducted her. We will have to justify it. But at this age, she'll never understand why we went through these immense lengths for her. She may be five, but she's smart like Jess and as vigilant as our mother used to be.

I'll have to defend why we bent our morals. That we did it for her and Tristan since Jessica is leaving and won't be around to help.

But a part of me knows that we brought her here for us, too —Bren, Colt, and I. But since my twenty-seven-year-old brother is hard-headed, Colt won't admit it. He wants her, too, in more ways than one. But he's also too tenacious to acknowledge he's tired of those whores he has on speed dial coming in and out of his cabin nearly every night.

"Love you too, Bren," Elena responds quietly when they disappear into the darkness.

I can tell she's exhausted by how her attention slowly finds me again. I walk up the first few steps to her and bend down. She jumps into me, and I cradle her in my arms, her tiny limbs wrapping around my abdomen and neck.

It's sad to think that one day, it will be the last time I'll hold her like this, and I won't even recognize it as the last time.

I start walking her back up the stairs and into the hallway toward her room when her nervous voice stutters, "Is—is she going to be like a mom?"

My heart skulks into my throat, and I swallow.

Tristan barely remembers Jane, our mother. He only has minuscule glimmers of who she once was and what she looked like. As he gets older, those memories slip further and further away, like she did. Eventually, Mom will be nothing but a recollection of small moments that are hard to reach and hard to place. His mind was so undeveloped and innocent when everything happened.

On the other hand, Elena never had the chance to know her. Our mother disappeared when she was a couple weeks old, leaving my father to care for all of us on his own until his arrest later that year.

But at twenty-four, fatherhood suits me well. At least, I like to think so. Bren, Colt, and I were shoved into that role overnight, taking care of this family and keeping the company afloat.

I place my palm to cradle the back of her skull and walk into her bedroom, which is only lit by the blossom night-light in the corner and the moonlight outside her window. She likes to sleep with the curtains open at night, thinking it helps keep the monsters and nightmares away.

"Not if you don't want her to be like a mom," I respond, leaning over the bed with her in my arms. "She'll probably be more like a best friend."

She lets go, plopping onto the mattress, and wriggles her tiny body under the purple covers. "Sam at school is already my best friend."

Lowering myself to the edge, I sit there and scan the expression on her face, noticing the faint indent in her right cheek from her pillow. She must have fallen asleep for a few hours and woken up.

I shrug. "Nothing wrong with having a few best friends."

Her lips twist to the side thoughtfully while she picks at some threads on her comforter.

"You wanted me to say yes, didn't you?" Her eyes flit up to mine, her irises looking like blue crystal balls in the darkness. "You wanted me to say she'll be like a mommy."

Her nose wiggles. "Sam said her mommy and daddy took her to get a new backpack and new crayons. She has a mommy and a daddy, and I don't have one."

I bit my tongue, trying to ignore the sting in my eyes at her sad words. Fuck the world for making my baby sister go through this. She doesn't deserve any of it.

My voice comes out hoarse. "You still have a daddy."

She looks back at her fingers, fiddling with the thread. "Colt said Daddy isn't coming home."

Goddammit, Colt.

I understand we don't want to get Elena's and Tristan's hopes up that he's coming home anytime soon, but cut the kids some slack. They're too young to know how brutal and unforgiving this world can be.

Out of all of us, Colt took Dad's arrest the hardest. Jane may have vanished five years ago, but my father did not kill her, despite what my mom's family thinks. He couldn't have.

Colt feels differently. He's holding on to something that has turned him inside out from the brother he once was. At first, I registered it as depression from her disappearance. Then, our father's murder trial eight months later, where he was found guilty, added to whatever misery was coursing through him. But all these years, it hasn't been depression. It's been anger.

Anger toward what? I'm not sure.

"I'm sure Miss Taryn would be happy to take you back-to-school shopping."

Her features light up as much as possible for two in the morning. "Promise?" She holds out her pinkie finger, which has a light coating of pink nail polish that Jessica gave her.

My pinkie swallows hers. "I promise." She nods drowsily and pulls the covers up to her neck. She's tired. I lean over her blanketed body, pressing my lips to her forehead. "Sweet dreams, Elena. I love you."

I stand up, examining her light blue pastel walls with purple and pink stripes that my brothers and I painted last week. She wanted a change since she saw we were painting Taryn's room. Like always, we were drowning in work from the orchard, but we carved out some time since she persistently begged. She said it needed to be all her favorite colors. I smile to myself. I don't think she'll ever have a favorite.

Sneaking out, I quietly shut the door behind me and stroll down the hall, passing Tristan's and Jess's rooms. I jog up the stairs past Brennan's bedroom and stalk toward the door at the end of the hallway with stairs beyond that lead up to the tower. It used to be the attic until it was refinished for Taryn.

My room is the master bedroom on the first floor because I have windows that look out onto the driveway. And, of course, Colt has his cabin, which Mom and Dad had specially built for him before everything went to shit.

I reach for the door, surprised to find it unlocked. I don't expect her to wake up anytime soon, but I figured Bren would lock it behind him as a precaution. We don't want to risk her running away when she has the chance, though Bren and I would find immense pleasure in the chase. She can try, but she'll have a hell of a time escaping us. We have her right where we want her to be, and we've done everything possible to ensure it stays that way.

I reach the top of the stairs and see Brennan with her phone. Taryn is tucked under the covers, her dark, mid-length hair draped over the pillow as he types away on the screen beside her. He must have taken her hair tie out. That thought is validated when I catch the black band on his wrist as he engrosses himself in his task.

I walk over to the side of the bed, peering down at her, my fingertips tingling.

But I can't touch her.

Not yet.

"There." Bren stands up and places her phone in his pocket. "If she finds her phone in the house, we can track her from it. And I changed the passcode, so she won't be able to unlock it if she does."

Brennan leans over, reaches for the black box on the nightstand, and holds it out for me. Knowing what's underneath the lid sends a hurricane of unease rolling through my chest, causing acid to burn the inside of my throat.

This is so fucking wrong in so many ways, but we can't afford to screw up and take risks.

Not with her.

Opening the lid, I take out the alcohol wipe and the white syringe. Come tomorrow morning, she's going to be confused as hell and extremely pissed off. But I'm eagerly anticipating the look she'll get when she realizes it's Brennan and me.

Her phantoms.

I reach for her hand, stroking the skin on her knuckles with my thumb.

Welcome home.

NINE | TARYN

I peel open my eyes, the nightmare before me a solid, living, and breathing thing. Dread digs its sharp claws under my skin, pulling and gnashing to constrict every muscle in my body sprawled on the mattress.

When I woke earlier, getting out of bed and trying to put together the pieces from last night while I stared out the window evaporated the little energy I had. The only plausible solution was to drift back to sleep and shake off the frightening, realistic dream.

I did drink, after all.

I sucked down more alcohol than usual, and I knew it might have been my mind conjuring up and keeping me trapped in a realistic hallucination until I would wake.

But that's not the case. Not even close.

I stare at the A-frame above me, inclining up and up. It whirls the dizziness in my head, and I have the urge to empty my stomach all over this expensive and soft comforter.

The natural, gloomy light from the windows on both sides of the room glistens off the dark wood paneling on the ceiling. I inhale deeply to help combat some of the nausea, but instead, it makes my senses aware of the faint stench of fresh paint hanging in the air.

This room was recently painted.

And if everything looks like it did when I woke a few hours ago, I hate that I'll love this room. Blue and gold are two of my favorites, especially together. Which directs a spike of discomfort skirting across my skin because it can't be coincidental. Can it?

I release a growl, sitting up to figure out how the hell I'm going to get out of this mess and figure out where I am. The second my eyes settle on the room caging me in, my hand flies to my chest in horror. The poor heart in my sternum thrashes against my ribs.

A man—a young man—is leaning his weight against the walnut vanity in front of the bed with a black sweatshirt and his hands tucked into his pockets. His hair is short, his eyes piercing as they hold me captive figuratively and literally. My body is painfully aware of his unrelenting focus.

I rub my eye sockets with my fingers and open them again. The familiarity of the man in front of me slowly appears through the haze in my brain the longer I scan his cut jawline and muscular frame.

"Sleep well?"

But the words didn't come from his mouth.

No, they come from somewhere else in the room.

Turning my head, I lock my eyes with another person seated in the accent chair in the corner. He's nearly an exact replica of the first one, but this guy's hair is slightly longer and mussed. The type of hair that anyone's fingers would itch to pull through. The light shining through the arched windows near him reflects off the cords in his muscular arms and vibrant sage green eyes...

Noooo.

I grip the covers in my fists in a death grip, trying to hide my body even though I'm still in the same clothes as last night. The combination of their eyes on me is enough to scorch me to the bone and turn me to ash.

Their gazes are intense.

My mouth falls open while the one seated in the corner hooks his lips into a smile. I can't remember how to speak, let alone breathe.

He's the one who delivered my pizza. The ghost delivery god who apparently didn't exist when I talked to Harrison Crock.

I manage to snarl, flicking my eyes between them as I free my anger. "You fucking drugged me, you motherfucker—"

"*Ah, ah, ah,*" The one leaning against the vanity tsks. "The first thing we'll have to do is silence that foul mouth of yours." My breath is ripped from my lungs. "You'll only be allowed to speak like that when we allow you to."

My eyes turn into slits. "Excuse me?"

"Rule number one." The one in the chair cuts in, and I whip my head toward him. "Ensure *they* are happy at all times."

"Rule number two," the other continues, snagging my attention again. "Convince them everything is normal. Their minds are fragile."

"And rule number three." The one with longer hair in the accent chair snags my focus. These two are giving me whiplash with their back-and-forth. "Trying to escape and acting out will not be tolerated, and you will be punished."

I shoot daggers at both of them, wishing my glare alone could slice through their perfectly toned bodies and bleed them out on the floor so I could run. But then I remember their rules.

Fuck their rules.

Counting, I hold up my pointer finger. "So, you stalk me." They study my hand as I extend a second. "Drug me." I throw up a third. "And abduct me, and you expect me not to freak the fuck out?"

"Language, Taryn," the short-haired one scolds, and the hairs on my arm stand on end, hearing my name. "Unless you want to be punished now." He shrugs. "Which Cameron and I are not against. We could also call Colt up here, but he might be extra pissed off that you took him away from work."

The one lounging in the chair—Cameron—places his elbows on his knees and leans forward. "Brennan and I are quite looking forward to it, so if you want to continue," he motions toward me, "by all means."

I intertwine my arms over my chest and don't let my concentration stray from him. "Both of you should go to hell."

I don't want to take my eyes off either of them since I have no idea why I'm here or what they are capable of. But keeping an eye on them simultaneously is impossible since they are on opposite sides of the room.

I am at a disadvantage. A tremble racks through my body at the thought.

The fire in Cameron's eyes raises my temperature as we hold each other's attention. A muscle in his jaw pops. "Do you use that mouth with your students?"

I shift uncomfortably. How does he know I teach?

His tongue swipes over his bottom lip smoothly, and I latch on to the motion. He has a nice mouth, I'll give him that.

He has a nice *everything*. And, of course, that perfection had to be duplicated because God couldn't just make one of him. And then I remember he said another name.

Colt.

Shit. Are there three of them?

I grip the bedsheets. The layer of moisture collecting on my hands from the nerves is too much to ignore. "I haven't even been in town for a week. How do you know I'm a teacher?"

The twins share a look, something flashing behind their eyes that I can't read. The corners of their lips lift.

I interrupt their private and wordless conversation. "People will come looking for me— They'll wonder where I am."

Brennan rolls his eyes. "You didn't think we'd bring you here without doing our research, did you?" He swipes a hand over his cropped hair and drags his palm down the back of his neck.

"We couldn't bring just *anyone* here, Taryn," Cameron states.

My chest rises and falls, and I pick at the hem on the duvet to busy my fingers, tingling with fear.

Brennan continues, "Whoever we chose needed to have unique circumstances. Someone who could disappear without raising many questions because there's nobody to notice they're gone."

Both of their voices echo in my head. Their words are on a constant loop that's inescapable in my current exhausted and post-drugged state.

Out of the corner of my vision, Cameron rises to his feet, moving toward me as slowly as a predator on the verge of sinking its claws into its prey to render it helpless.

"We've waited a long time to find someone whose circumstances and qualifications blend as perfectly as yours," he mentions softly. Almost lovingly, but I know better.

Something about Cameron's inflection has my heartbeat bursting like the crackle of thunder. Tears form behind my eyes at the impact. He stands at the edge of the bed next to me, and I glance up at him, allowing the first tear to fall.

Because they know. They somehow know I just picked up everything and moved to a town where nobody knows me.

They recognize I'm alone.

Helpless.

And I'm starting to understand that their knowledge of my

situation and who I am is greater than they're leading on. But the question is, *how?*

"You need to eat and drink something," Brennan says, motioning toward the bowl of fruit and glass of water on my dresser that's been there since I woke up the first time to this nightmare. "It will help with the nausea."

I glare at him. "How do I know you aren't trying to poison me? You did roofie me—"

Cameron silences me by stretching for the bowl. His fingertips reach into the blend of strawberries, sliced apples, green grapes, and kiwi. He pulls out a sliced strawberry and slips it between his lips, crunching through the flesh and into the fruit. The juices glisten on his mouth as his tongue darts out, swiping the sweetness away.

I swallow, wetting my dry mouth. "I'll run. I'm quite good at it."

"Please try. Cam and I have always found pleasure in..." Brennan's gaze trails over my body. "...hunting."

Cameron lifts his hand to his mouth, running his thumb over his bottom lip in thought. "I'll make you a deal." My breathing stops. "If you decide to try and run and happen to make it over the fence that surrounds the entire property, we won't chase you. We'll let you go."

Brennan raises a brow at his brother.

"But," Cameron continues, making my heart plummet into my gut, "if we catch you before you reach the property line, we get to punish you using whatever method we want."

Brennan smirks, liking the idea.

Cameron leans over me. His hot breath skims the shell of my ear, sending shivers down my spine. "Even if you did run," he whispers, "this property is eight miles of orchard and forest. Every way you turn looks exactly like the direction you just came, and Bren, Colt, and I have memorized every inch of this property. We'll see you before you see us."

I remain silent and motionless at the thought of the punishment they would choose. I try to stop it, but I can't keep the heat from rushing between my legs. I attempt to shove the thought away, ignoring my sick mind, but the more my mangled brain contemplates their threat, the more curious I get.

Brennan stares at me inquisitively. "Do you consent?"

Oh, God. But it's a chance to escape without them coming after me. I should be grateful, yet the dread churns in my gut like a swarm of angry hornets.

Challenge accepted.

I inhale a breath, giving an unsteady nod to agree.

"We need a verbal confirmation, Taryn," Brennan commands.

"Yes—" I choke out. "I'll take the deal."

Cameron backs away from me and smiles maliciously at Brennan. His head tilts. "I hope you understand what you're agreeing to." I don't. I have no idea what I'm agreeing to, but if it's a chance to escape, why wouldn't I? "We'll check on you in a little while."

I snatch the pillow behind my back and chuck it across the room, hitting Brennan's thigh. He arcs a brow at my attempt. "What if I need the bathroom?"

Brennan shrugs. "There's a half-bath at the base of the stairs to the left. The main door is the one that will be locked."

My blood boils. "You can't just lock me in here all day!"

They start to head down the stairway, going down far enough so that I can't see them but can hear their voices. "You need to calm down! We don't want you to frighten them," one of them shouts, but I haven't been around them long enough to tell whose voice it is.

Them?

And then my brain ruptures when it remembers something. "My dog!" I screech. Wet, hot tears pour down my face now at the thought of Rossco alone. "Just please bring me my dog," I whimper. But the sound of the door cuts me off, and I release a sob.

Rossco has been home all night by himself in the backyard. He must be hungry. Concerned.

Completely and utterly alone.

But I guess that's one thing we have in common.

Because even with the twins and whoever *them* is in the house, I've never felt as isolated as I do now.

TEN | COLTEN

"I'm not going to get her fucking dog."

Cam folds his arms over his chest, glaring at me while Bren lights up a cigarette—an addiction he picked up a few weeks after my father was arrested to help combat his anxiety.

I have enough shit to worry about right now as is. Someone has to keep this property maintained and the company running. Between the books, logistics, physical labor, and keeping this family high above water, I can't fuck around like my twin brothers. And I say *high above water* because we know too damn well that even touching the water gives it the authority to drag us back under. My siblings and I spent too long fighting to get out of the current fed by all the family issues caused by my father; it won't fucking happen again.

I played my part.

I got her here.

It's done.

She's been too much of a distraction already.

I toss the wrench aside and tug the oil pan closer. The metal grating across the concrete floor produces a screech that raises the hairs on the nape of my neck.

Wiping my grimy black hands on the red towel on my lap, I lean against the massive back tire of our green tractor. Propping one arm on my knee, I release a frustrated breath tainted with annoyance.

"It will only take you an—"

I crush the cloth in my fist, aiming for Cameron's dick. It soars rapidly but contacts his stomach. His grunt of surprise fills the air, along with more tension than there already was between us. The towel lands on one of his boots.

"What the hell, man?" Cameron barks.

Bren conceals a snicker beside him.

I push myself to my feet, marching toward him. "I am swamped around here, and you two need to start pulling your weight again!" I point a finger at his chest. "Why don't you two go fetch her dog? I have more important things to do around here, and peak season is approaching."

Cam throws an arm out. "Because Bren and I have to go get the damn truck she left at Crocks!"

They should've thought about that and the dog when they made their plan. But no, they wanted to play with their food. On the other hand, I have no problem demolishing it right there and reveling in the fight they give me before hopelessness dawns on them. It's poetic.

"It will be easier to get back to normal once she's settled," Brennan mentions. "She's just being—difficult right now."

I hold back the smirk that's attempting to pull at my lips. Thinking about her feisty personality and foul mouth has the blood rushing straight to my cock.

"I hope so," I agree sternly. Their matching green eyes magnetize toward each other's. "You need to forget about how she makes your dicks feel for one goddamn minute and remember that the reason why she's here in the first place is that I need your help around here, and Jess is leaving for school. I'm not paying you to be pussy-whipped."

Lindenvale Hill Orchard doesn't run independently, and I'm getting exhausted. I always thought one day I'd receive the family inheritance and all that comes with it, but it's different when you can prepare for it versus it getting dumped on your shoulders overnight.

I had barely any responsibility, was mourning, and woke one day with everything on my shoulders. It's a lot of fucking weight to carry, and it's been slowly dragging me to the depths.

"You're one to talk," Cameron snips, breaking the silence. "Do you think we miss those women coming in and out of your cabin every night?"

They're a warm cunt. A release. Nothing more. Because all relationships are hopeless, and someone is bound to end up with a knife in their fucking heart.

They are the ones who willingly come back because they enjoy my particular taste in pleasure. And keeping them on a repetitive loop will keep me from indulging in the one thing I'm afraid I'll want.

Raising my arm to my head, I wipe off the bead of sweat dripping down my brow. I glance down at the ink snaking across my arm, admiring how it glistens from the moisture under the shop lights.

Running my tongue on the inside of my bottom lip, I peer out the two large doors pulled back to give a view of the edge of the orchard across the field. Keeping my eyes trained on the trees, I follow the movements of their branches and fruit swaying from the steady afternoon breeze. The circulating air carries the scent of approaching rain, the smell bringing a little clarity when I inhale deeply.

We thought about every detail but somehow forgot to figure out what we were going to do with that damn dog. Though I know Tristan and Elena won't complain, they've been begging me for one ever since we watched *Homeward Bound* a month ago.

So much for wanting to avoid attachments.

Reality is brutal. People and things come and go, leaving nothing but a hollow space in your mind where they used to be —which is why abducting Taryn was the best option. A way to protect my delicate family and young siblings from any further heartache after losing the two people who were always supposed to be there.

Until they weren't.

After everything I've studied about Taryn Meyers, this method keeps her from escaping once she's committed. Because once she meets Elena and Tristan, she's bound to get attached. Her nature—the teaching part of her soul—is compassionate and warm.

Maybe it's a form of manipulation, but sometimes, we resort to eccentric methods to protect the ones we love.

But I know her history. She floats from one place to the next, barely staying long enough to create meaningful connections. Taryn can't stay still for long, and if we didn't take the measures we did, she would bolt.

I won't fucking let that happen.

She was walking through life like a ghost anyway.

But she's our little ghost now.

After my mom's disappearance and seeing my dad thrown behind bars for being the monster he is, this family is fragile. And I am barely holding us together. We need someone who can help. Someone who is steady. Jessica leaves for college soon and we didn't have time to waste trying to convince Taryn to work for us. We did things the traditional way at first, going through résumés of candidates who may have been a decent fit. But we weren't looking for *decent*. We weren't looking for someone who would be temporary.

We needed someone more permanent.

Taryn fits the role perfectly, even if she's being forced into it.

The twins gaze a hole into the side of my head, and I face them. "Fine, I'll go get the damn dog."

Cameron straightens, folding his arms over his chest with a satisfied look crossing his features.

"But..." I warn. "She's not, under any circumstances, allowed to have it in the house until it becomes better acquainted with the kids. I'll keep it around my cabin until then."

"Wow, you hear that, Cam?" Brennan smirks. "Colten's using Elena and Tristan as an excuse because he's afraid of the dog." He chuckles. Some of the smoke from the cigarette gets sucked down wrong, and he hunches over, having a coughing fit as Cam slaps his back.

Asshole.

MY TRUCK ROLLS to a stop in the driveway of the old yellow house, my pulse hammering as I give it the first good glance since I bought it from the Donahues three months ago.

Our grandparents—the Donahues—no longer wanted to have an attachment to the Lindenvale name because of my father, and finally put it up for sale after packing up and not looking back. After Jane's disappearance, my mother's parents left everything behind to start over. Left their home to rot and wither away just like their hearts after losing their only daughter.

The speculations about Lindenvale Hill are dark. Some people think she ran, leaving her husband and children behind, since her body and car have never been found. Others believe something more sinister lurks behind the fence and through the miles and miles of forest and orchard. They think the only way to learn the truth is to listen to the trees when the wind blows through them, as if their rustling branches and leaves are whispers.

It's a bunch of bullshit.

And because of all the whispered theories and secrets, the property I once loved is now plagued.

This home, my grandparents' house, has been unoccupied for four years. The paint is slowly chipping away, and the yard has been left to be reclaimed by nature. The deck and wood floors are aged and whine under any amount of weight or pressure.

I wonder what her first thought was when she looked at this place.

When I posted the rental on Zillow, I used old photos— pictures that made the place appear like a quaint and peaceful home. I carefully crafted an email that was a convincing advertisement. The hook of the rental was the unbelievably good deal on rent.

I needed her to want it.

It's a shithole. It is. But she wasn't going to be living here long anyway. It was just one step of the plan and served its purpose.

Now, I don't want to look at it anymore. All I see when I stare out the passenger window is an impeccable yard, the grass thick and green below the tire swing my brothers and I used to mess around on. I can imagine the ghost of childhood Jess sprinting out the front door and down the steps of the deck, wanting to join us like she always did because hanging with her brothers was the only place she ever wanted to be.

When I open the door and finally step outside the truck, cheerful voices blend with the breath of the wind blowing through the willow leaves. My parents' and grandparents' laughs drift from the backyard, coating the back of my throat with unwelcome emotion.

The visions play behind my eyes, the air heavy and suffocating with the feeling that warmed my body back then—when my parents were happy. When our family was whole and content.

But it wasn't until after Tristan was born that things started to change. The slight shifts in my parents' relationship seemed loud and obvious, but I was the only one of their children to notice. And what my twenty-two-year-old self witnessed the night before she disappeared will forever haunt me.

As I walk down the sidewalk, everything fades, blurring into oblivion because the laughter is dead.

The memories are dead.

This house is dead.

There may not be a body, but I know she is, too.

Because she promised she'd come back.

And she never has.

I hustle with my head down, fumbling with my key in the lock, and enter the house, heading straight for the back door.

I focus my mind. Get in. Grab the things she'll want. And get out and back to work.

Lifting my head, I see the beautiful black lab lying on the other side of the glass door on the deteriorating deck with its head on its paw.

It must hear me because as I near the door, its ears perk up, followed by its head, revealing the white patch of fur on its stomach. But just when I think it will bark and get territorial, it stands up, its tail wagging back and forth, comforting my unease.

Nice and easy now.

Slowly peeling back the sliding glass door, I keep my eye on it while the animal keeps its eye trained on me.

I expect its eyes to darken with suspicion, but they're calm. We exchange a look that relaxes the muscles in my back as it comes closer and sits in front of me. I tilt my head, glancing underneath it—or *him*, shall I say.

Reaching for his head slowly, I begin scratching his head with my black-stained fingers from working on the tractor.

"Hey, boy," I greet gently.

He licks my arm, his tongue leaving hot trails that chill my arm a second later. The little slaps and nibbles almost make me smile.

Taryn lives alone, for Christ's sake. She should have a dog that protects her from monsters like us.

After digging through the pantry to locate the dog food, I feed him a bowl that he scarfs down while I stroll into her room curiously. I push open the door, the old hinges creaking.

She slept in here. It may have only been a few nights, but it was long enough for her scent to soak into the sheets. The sweat that glistens on her skin, the hint of perfume she wears, the rose shampoo she uses—because it's labeled in the shower —all blend together, creating her distinctive, lingering scent, hitting my bloodstream like a drug.

The first time I got a whiff of the sugared vanilla and citrus radiating from her, I wanted more.

And admitting that was my first mistake.

It only becomes an addiction if I give over dominance.

But before I know it, I'm standing in front of the mahogany dresser, running my fingertips over the wood before they drift of their own accord to the brass handle of the top drawer.

Pulling it toward me, my breathing ragged, an array of colored lingerie is folded neatly in piles. I reach in, running my calloused and dirty hands over the perfectly clean garments, trying to picture what set she is wearing right now.

Picking up a red pair, I rub the see-through lace on the pads of my fingers and draw it closer to my face. But I stop, gritting my teeth.

My eyes fall closed. Tilting my head side to side, the taut muscles stretching and pulling, I crack my neck to clear my head, which has been slowly deteriorating since I saw her email pop up in my inbox.

Clenching the material in my hand, I toss it back into the drawer and slam it shut, rattling the floorboards under my boots.

Obsessions have the power to destroy you, and Little Ghost will not become one of mine.

ELEVEN | TARYN

Time passes slowly when you're trapped.

Too. Damn. Slowly.

My pulse thumps in my ears, a steady cadence now that I've been left alone since the twins, Cameron and Brennan, waltzed out like this was the most normal thing in the world. Kidnapping. As if abducting a random girl is an act they have committed several times before.

I've never been as fully aware of my surroundings until now. Every minuscule sound or movement somewhere beyond the door freezes my blood solid.

Over the last several hours—which excruciatingly feels like days—I've been training my ears to catch every noise that drifts through the house. I've heard doors shut, the floorboards creak, a pitter-patter of footsteps running somewhere, the trickle of rain tapping the rooftop, a conversation between crows, and murmurs of voices that sound like the phone noise in the Charlie Brown movies whenever he picks up a call.

I've gaped blankly out the window for far longer than I assume is healthy. With the various levels of shingles spread out and cone-shaped roofing, my gut rolls, knowing that I'm at least three or four stories up.

For a while, I analyzed my situation. I peered at the outside world, noting things that may eventually help my escape. Thunderous clouds glide over the expanse of the orchard, unleashing steady amounts of afternoon rain.

Or is it evening?

Honestly, I'm not sure because the damn clock on the bedside table has motionless minute and second hands stuck at two o'clock.

The apple trees rolling over the hills in the distance disappear into the haze, and if there is one thing that's utterly indisputable after contemplating where I'm trapped, only one place comes to mind. Because when that old woman described what was beyond the gates, I could see it vividly. Almost as if I had been there before.

Lindenvale Hill.

The uneven roof below my window spans out far enough that I don't have a clear view of what's directly beneath. The educated part of my brain wants to guess that it's a driveway of some sort, though I only see a paved road leading down the hill with freshly mowed grass on both sides until it turns to gravel, vanishing into the dark orchard.

So far, the only movement I've caught outside is the swaying of oak branches in the yard, crows soaring through the air, some on the roof darting their heads in different directions, and a black SUV leaving the driveway.

The same SUV I saw parked outside my house the first night I moved into town. My phantoms aren't identityless anymore because now I know who they are. I'm resisting the urge to grab the fork they left with the fruit bowl and stab their eyes out when they walk back up those stairs.

To my entertainment, this room, or tower, has another window facing the back of the house and the hill that quickly crawls down a faint decline to a smaller cottage-type cabin. I can see it perfectly from my window. It has exterior stone walls, wood beams, and framing with the same golden oak color as the fence at the front gate.

To the side of it is a decent-sized garden with plants in raised beds and vines weaving through arches. The flowers in that garden are the only burst of color outside compared to the rest of the front and back yards. I stood at the window for almost an hour to catch any movement coming in or out, but the curtains were drawn. If they were open, though, I'd be able to see inside without any issues.

Directly behind the cabin, it flattens to the orchard since it's 360 degrees. How do I know that? You may wonder since I can't see the other sides of this massive castle in my tower.

Because the identical bastards put a framed bird's-eye view map of the entire property above my bed, in the corner is the Lindenvale Hill Orchard logo—half a red apple combined with a black crow. They put it on the wall to remind me that attempting to run is a reckless idea. There's one mile of fruit trees in every direction until it reaches the forest line. One part of the property drops off the cliffside into the chilled waters of the Columbia.

The smart part of my brain tells me to stay put—form a solid plan. But their threats mean nothing to me. I don't want to stick around long enough to discover who *they* are.

And under no circumstance do I want to find out what I'm forced to do to keep *them* happy.

Fuck their happiness.

The sky is darkening now, and a little trail of solar lights flick on and illuminate the road on each side of the driveway.

Awesome. It's night now.

Grasping onto whatever little sanity I have left, I slump down the stairs. The locked door is straight ahead, and to the right is another door leading to the half-bath. I walk into it, feeling like Harry Potter confined under the stairs. It's simple—just a toilet, a sink, and a mirror—but it's better than a bucket or having to hold it.

Somehow, I lost my hair tie. I'm not sure if it's somewhere in the bed or if I lost it when they drugged me. So much of my memory is a blank void. Every time I reach into the profound section of my cognizance, it's just blackness.

My mid-length hair hangs loosely around my shoulders in a disheveled mess, strands hanging over my eyes like I'm the ghost in the attic that haunts this house. And if they kill me, I swear to God I will be the demon that haunts these halls and screws with their untouchable lives.

I'm pathetic.

I've barely been here a day and am about to lose my damn mind.

On my way out of the bathroom, my focus locks on the doorknob, and I grasp it again for the fifth time today, wiggling it again and again, thinking maybe if I jerk hard enough, it will magically unlock. It doesn't.

"Ugh," I growl under my breath, hitting the wooden door with my fist.

As if on cue, footsteps fall right outside the door at the bottom of the staircase, and my pulse jumps at the same time as my feet. With each step, I scramble up the stairs with my heart lurking further into my esophagus. Flinging myself around the banister and over to the bedside table, I seize the fork next to my untouched bowl of drying fruit. It's a pitiful weapon choice, but at least it's something.

The door opens and closes a second later, the stairs creaking under the individual's weight. Except it's not as loud and boisterous as when the twins left me this morning. It's softer. Delicate.

I back my body against the window as a head of straight, long brown hair seizes my attention. A face comes into view that halts my breathing. The girl's gaze finds mine, and her rosy lips pull up into a genuine smile. When she's at the top of the stairs, I take in her emerald-green tank top and ripped skinny jeans.

She's younger than me, judging by her flawless skin and kind green eyes.

My hand lowers with the fork, but I'm still on guard.

She scans my body in my shorts and flannel, and for some reason, her focus on me makes me feel vulnerable and bare.

"Hi, Taryn." Her soft greeting only increases the rapid pace of my overworking heart.

I stand before her, unmoving. "Um...hi," I stutter.

Her gaze drops to the fork in my hand, and she smirks. "Nice weapon, though I'm sure it wouldn't have done much good."

My fist grips the metal tighter.

I don't have many options in here, bitch.

She folds her hands in front of her, and I look her over again, my muscles tightening a little more.

"Oh my God," I breathe, "did they abduct you too?"

Her burst of laughter heats everything under my skin. "Definitely not! I'm afraid you're the first victim my brothers have brought here—and you'll be the only one."

My shoulders fall. "Brothers?"

"Cameron, Brennan, and Colten. Can't say I was fully on board with this plan, but when they see something they like and something they want, well..." Her confession makes me swallow. "It's hard to convince them otherwise."

The silence hangs between us, the air so heavy that I'm fighting to get any oxygen into my shriveled lungs.

"I'm Jessica," she smiles. "But you can call me Jess."

You have some pretty messed-up-in-the-head brothers, Jess.

"So, are you their little messenger or something?" I wave a finger over her figure. "The one they sent to convince me that everything will be okay if I listen to their rules and don't run."

"Yes and no," she answers.

"I'm sorry, *Jessica*." Her name spews out of my mouth like it tastes horrific on my tongue. "It's going to take a lot more than sending their sister to calm me down after being drugged and kidnapped from a bar."

She grins.

She grins at me as if she finds me amusing and watching me spiral is the most entertaining thing. Like I'm a little caged animal she and her brothers get to observe through the glass, waiting for the moment I'm docile enough to play with.

"Now I know why they haven't been able to stop talking about you since they chose you. You're fiery."

I narrow my eyes. *I'll show them fiery.*

"Chose me? What does that even mean?" I ask firmly.

She shrugs. "My brothers aren't impulsive. They think through their moves. Study...watch. Then, strike when all the pieces finally click, and there's little room for error. Especially Colten. They're smart and have been very patient until you came along a month ago."

"In a few days, someone is going to notice I'm mis—"

Wait. Did she say a month?

I haven't even been in Cedar Creek Cove for a week.

I stare blankly at her, the gears rotating in my head. "You said *month*, Jess. I just moved here."

She widens her eyes, rocking slowly on her heels. She knows she said too much. She changes the subject, "You didn't eat the bowl of fruit I made you."

"Not hungry."

"Would you eat if I brought you something better?"

I shake my head, but my stomach protests my response, releasing a growl. Jeez. I haven't eaten anything since lunch yesterday. Yet I also don't want to consume anything they offer me. I mull it over for a second, my eyes darting around the room while she waits, so I don't have to look her in the eye.

She starts to hum a tune.

"Maybe," I say.

She gives a contented smile and turns, heading back down the stairs. "I'll be right back."

When she gets down the stairs, a bit of hope festers that she'll be so immersed in her mission to feed me that she forgets to lock the door. Of course I'm wrong. It closes, followed by a click that makes my stomach drop. I set the fork on the dresser and drop myself on the edge of the bed.

Waiting.

Waiting.

And flipping waiting because there's nothing else to do.

When I start to think she's forgotten about me, the door opens again. She walks up the stairs with a plate in each hand and two bottles of water tucked under her arms.

The smell of baked crust and melted cheese wafts through the room, and I hastily sit up in response.

She hands me a plate, placing the two water bottles on the comforter before she crawls up on the other end of my bed. She sits across from me, crisscrossed with her plate in her lap as if we're best friends about to share secrets, and blah, blah, blah.

She's not my friend.

I'm here against my will.

She picks up the slice of pizza on her plate and folds it in half, smiling at me before putting it in her mouth. Her chewing makes my mouth water.

Fine. *You win, Jess.*

I eat my pizza—only to fuel myself and have the energy I'll need to escape. We hang out in the stillness, with only the rain drumming against the roof.

"So, are you the *them*?" I question suspiciously, swallowing.

Her head tilts back and forth. "Not exactly. But you are here because of me."

I still, my eyes turning into little slits. "Why, because of you?"

"I start my freshman year at the University of Washington soon. I won't be here to take care of them anymore while the boys work during the week and take care of the family business."

Business. *Lindenvale Hill Orchard.*

She gestures to me using the hand that isn't holding the slice of pizza. "Hence, why you're here."

Not for long.

A thought blooms in my head. The door at the base of the stairs has a gold knob with only a small hole that goes through it. So, I'm assuming that the other side is the flip lock.

I place my pizza plate on the bedside table and tuck a strand of hair behind my ear, seeing it's completely dark outside when I look over my shoulder out the window.

"Thanks for the chat and the food...Jess," I try to keep the bitterness from my voice, "but I'm exhausted and want to be left alone for a while."

A melancholy look crosses her features, and she nods.

She's a nice girl. I'll give her that. But I'm not going to make friends with the sister of two—three if you count whoever Colten is—sociopaths who belong behind bars. And from what I've heard, she already has one family member in prison.

"Okay," she sighs. "I'll leave you alone for the night." She crawls off the bed with her plate, gets to her feet, and grabs one of the water bottles off the bed, leaving the other as she walks to the top of the stairs and pauses, looking back at me. "Maybe I'll see you tomorrow."

Not a chance in hell.

I give her a fake grin, and she leaves me alone, the lock once again clicking into place.

Waiting a few seconds, her footsteps retreat down the hall until there's only the sound of my breathing. Leaping off the bed frantically, I move to the center of the room, peering around for what I'm looking for.

Everyone should be asleep in a few hours, the perfect time to make my escape.

"Think, Taryn," I mutter, my eyes darting over the picture frames on the wall with oil paintings of landscapes. I scan the bookcase and the corner of the room with the accent chair.

I grab one of my breasts in each hand, pressing my fingers into my bra, but my heart plummets.

Come on! There must be something.

But then, my gaze lands on the bedside lamp with three thin pieces of wire on the top of the shade that connect in the middle. It shines like the heavens opened, and I might not be completely screwed after all.

"Aha!"

Reaching for the lamp, I unscrew the bulb, remove the shade, and sit on the edge of the bed, ripping the white fabric. I twist, turn, and bend the wiring, my breathing turning erratic when a bark turns every muscle in my body rigid.

It happens again, making the backs of my eyes sting.

I'd know that bark anywhere.

I drop the lampshade to the mattress, the pads of my feet pounding across the floor to the window at the back of the room that faces the backyard.

Nighttime is fully blanketing the house now. The sky is still enclosed in a thick layer of clouds, only letting a small sliver of silver moon peek through here and there.

My eyes frantically scan the hill that drops down to the part of the yard that flattens out to the cabin. The curtains are still drawn, so I can't see inside the large windows. The grass and the sidewalk leading to the front door are illuminated by lights on the exterior part of the house and posts in the garden.

But then I see it. A figure in jeans and a gray sweatshirt with their hood up strolls down the sidewalk to the house, carrying a linked chain in one hand and a rope in the other.

But it's not just any rope—a rope toy.

And sprinting up to them happily, wagging his tail, is a dog.

My. Fucking. Dog.

I clench my fists at my sides, digging my nails into my skin, the sting muted as the hooded stranger throws the toy for Rossco across the yard as they lean over and screw something into the wet grass.

Their hands work hooking up the chain, the whole time keeping their back to me. A whistle sounds in the air, and Rossco runs back to them, the toy flopping in his mouth. They grab his collar and secure him to the chain in the yard, scratching behind his ears before shoving their hands into their pockets.

I grit my teeth, smacking one palm against the glass, giving them a look that could kill.

If only it would.

The figure straightens, and I withhold my breath. They glance over their shoulder, their face barely visible in the shadow the hood is casting.

My arms and legs break out in goosebumps. Even though I can't see their face, I feel their eyes on me.

And when the shadow casted across their features moves, it's enough to brighten the sinister tilt of their lips. Everything I felt before this is nothing compared to the fear their gaze injects into my veins.

TWELVE | TARYN

My fingers ache, but I zone in on the intense feeling of determination bubbling under my skin.

Determination to get out of this house undetected.

Determination to get Rossco and sprint through those trees as fast as my legs can carry me.

Determination to reach the property line.

I pause, picking at the lock. *A deal is a deal.*

They told me to give them consent to use whatever means they find necessary if they find me. Fear crawls over my skin, feeling like the legs of a thousand spiders tapping against me. But the twinge of excitement that accelerates my breathing is what worries me.

If it weren't for two hot twins threatening me and keeping me hostage, I'd probably vomit thinking of all the things they could do to me. But the disciplinary methods that flash through my head when I picture them...Yeah, I shouldn't want to explore that. Not even a little.

But the way their mouths moved mesmerized me. The way the cords in their arms popped, and muscles tightened, encouraged a faint throb in my core that still lingers. Even just a simple glance from those pairs of sage green eyes made me feel like they were the snakes slithering through the moss to capture their prey. And I happen to be the target.

I was so entranced by Cameron and Brennan earlier that my head inadvertently nodded before I could thoroughly think straight. Because I wondered what it would be like to be captured by them.

Handled by them.

If the words that emerge from their mouths are so hypnotizing, imagine what their bodies could do to mine.

I shake my head at myself. *Focus, Taryn.*

My hands move frantically, working the thin piece of long metal through the tiny hole in the doorknob at the base of the stairs.

My pulse jumps unexpectedly. Leaving the wire in place, I flatten my palms on the door and press my ear against the cool surface. Hearing them coming could save me from a very unpleasant interaction if they're up.

Nobody came to check on me after Jessica left. After she disappeared down those steps, I felt a strong wave of guilt settle over me when I contemplated how rude I had been to her. She tried to be nice, but that doesn't change the facts.

Since then, I've been tearing apart the lampshade, which is lying in pieces on the floor next to the bed. I paced the room and listened intently, trying to hear and sense any vibrations or noises that drifted through the house. For the last hour, it's been dead. Fortunately, the rain has ceased, allowing other sounds to come through clearly, making me fully alert.

A light layer of sticky moisture rests on my skin as my hands return to the doorknob, getting back to work. The scrapes on my fingers from snapping wire into something good enough to pick the lock sting with every move I make.

Come on! This has to work.

Changing the angle, I purse my lips and jiggle it a little more when, finally, a click has my adrenaline bursting.

Closing my eyes, I huff out a breath in relief. Yes.

Bending over, I make sure my shoes are tied, thankful they left them near my bed. Then, slowly, I twist the doorknob and step out silently into the dark hallway.

I have no idea where my phone is, and I have no flashlight, but luckily, little outlet lights are spread out along the base of the hallway, guiding me. Three more closed doors are on this floor, but my eyes are zeroing in on the staircase at the other end of the hallway.

Step by step, one foot is deliberately placed in front of the other. My breath is held in my lungs as if it will make all my other movements lighter.

Please don't creak. Please don't creak.

Just as I make it to the top of the stairs, the wood floorboards whine under my weight, and I freeze, waiting to hear footsteps or something, but I don't.

Taking the stairs, I make my way down one flight. Turning around the corner to the second, my feet pad quietly but quickly down the next set of stairs and another. Shit, this house is massive. I don't pay any attention to the interior, small elements that I pass, or Victorian décor because once I escape, I'm gone.

My next priority is leaving Cedar Creek. After storming out of that job interview, there's nothing to keep me here.

Nobody will force me to stay here.

When I reach the bottom of the staircase, the foyer with a looming ceiling opens to a living room to the left and an intimidating kitchen to my right. I see the front door, and my nerves and anticipation of getting out of this house carry me toward it.

Reaching for the handle, I stop. Next to the door, against the wall, is a wooden coat rack and storage bench with jackets and sweatshirts. But what has my feet glued down a little longer than I have time for are the small pairs of shoes. More specifically, the pink glitter ones reflecting glimmers of light from the patio drifting through the windows.

I shake my head to clear my mind.

Rossco is in the backyard, but I'd rather run around the house through the soft grass than attempt to find the back door and risk being seen or heard.

Flipping the lock, I pull open the door quietly and step out into the cool night air. It brushes against my clammy skin, covering my body from head to toe in chills. I may be running all night, but being lost in the orchard or surrounding woods with Rossco sounds better than being trapped in that room.

Run far and fast and pray to God that they don't know this property as well as they said.

Inching the door closed, I take off down the patio, to the sidewalk, and around the house through the grass. The dew from the earlier rain hangs off the blades, the water already soaking through the fabric of my Nikes.

Rounding another corner, I see him down the short decline, my boy curled up in the wet grass, sleeping next to a water bowl. Reducing my pace, his soft ears perk, and he whips his head up, making eye contact with me.

I can't help the small smile that lifts my lips. "Hi, boy," I murmur.

Standing on his feet, his tail thrashes back and forth with excitement. Delicate whimpering noises reach my ears. It's the sound he makes when he hasn't seen me for a few days, and it accelerates my pulse. Sprinting toward him, my arms fly around his frame. My fingers scratch the skin behind his ears to get him to calm down, but his body jerks in my hold.

"Shhhhhh— Shhhh, Rossco," I whisper, slamming my eyes shut, praying nobody hears him.

Running my hands across his thick coat, it only takes a

moment before his whines stop. The cottage beside us is entirely dark. I hope the monster who's in there isn't awake. That thought alone has me desperately reaching for Rossco's collar and removing the chain. Once it's removed, he glances up at me.

"Let's go," I whisper, ensuring he's starting to follow me before I break into a full-out sprint across the yard.

His body bolts in front of mine, and we run. And run until the expanse of the yard transforms into an expanse of apple trees lined in perfect rows on each side of us. The crescent moon is the only light penetrating through the branches, their arms with dangling red fruit feeling like long fingers reaching out to keep me captive.

I loved the movie *Snow White* growing up. I was innocent enough to dwell on the beautiful parts where a girl finds refuge with the dwarves.

They weren't her family, but they became family.

This feels identical to the forest in the movie.

Shadowy.

Haunting.

The silhouettes around me in every direction are alive, making my skin crawl and burn under the gaze of whatever is watching me.

There may be millions of apples in these trees and crunching beneath my feet, but just like Snow White's story, none grant wishes. Because the apple in my drink—alongside the poison the twins gave me—had me waking up to a nightmare and not a fucking prince.

My feet pound into the damp earth, and after five minutes of running, I can't take any more and hunch over, heaving. I'm a good runner, but all around me is the same.

The haunting trees.

The heavy air brings tears to my eyes and burns my lungs.

This orchard is already driving me to the brink of madness,

and it will only take a few more steps to shatter any sanity I have left.

I don't know where we are going or how to get out, but I understand that if we keep running straight for a mile, we'll eventually reach the edge of the forest.

Maybe letting the forest floor swallow and kill me would be easier.

But life isn't that kind.

I place my hands on my hips, trying and failing to suck deep breaths into my lungs. Rossco is fifty or so yards ahead of me, and his presence gives me the confidence I need to keep going.

Taking a step, something grabs onto my flannel, jerking my back into a hard wall of muscle. A piercing scream escapes my lips and echoes through the orchard—the rest drowned out by a large, calloused hand that covers my mouth, silencing me. I struggle to breathe, the faint scent of oil and dirt from his palm overpowering the musky air.

Just as my brain thinks it's one of the twins, a gravelly hum emanates from the throat behind me. And it's not one of theirs. They brush their mouth against the shell of my ear, tsking me. That sound overpowers the thrashing of my heart, increasing the panic.

Although I may have only heard it a few times, I recognize the tone and wish I didn't.

His laugh warms the nape of my neck. "Where do you think you're going, Little Ghost?"

THIRTEEN | TARYN

His rough hand is plastered on my mouth, and the one snaked around my waist soaks in the tremble that racks through every bone in my body.

The lips against my ear tilt upward, tickling the skin there. My eyes flutter closed, preparing to brace myself. His hands vanish from my body, making me colder than I already was. I turn toward him unhurriedly, fearing what I might see.

My eyes instantly magnetize to his, my lungs shriveling into raisins that deny me oxygen.

His irises are black under the silver moon, leaking through the trees and contrasting with the shadows. They are deep and bottomless, and I know instantly that he will be the thing that drags me under. Because I recognize what his eyes look like under fluorescent office lights and framed by charcoal-rimmed glasses. A glacier green that takes my breath away, but the magic evaporates when his mouth opens, breaking the spell. Eyes that I'll never escape from even after I'm buried six feet underground.

My mouth parts, and I stare at him as a sadistic grin holds me completely still.

"A—Alaric," I breathe. I retreat a step, my back hitting something hard. My hands drop, magnetizing to the apple tree behind me.

His head cocks to the side, his mouth faltering as if in disappointment. "Try again."

I swallow, my focus dropping to the dark ink on his wrists under the sleeves of the gray sweatshirt he wore earlier when I glared at him out the window. His hair is messier than the last time I saw him but lightly styled, and his glasses and nice attire are gone.

He's mouthwatering standing before me, messy and rugged like this.

And that's a problem.

When I remain silent, he steps into me, placing one hand above my head on the tree. He tucks a strand of loose hair—wild and frizzy from sweat—behind my ear. "I'm a little offended my brothers didn't talk about me more. Or warn you, should I say."

He places the pad of his thumb directly on my flushed forehead, rooting me to the ground. He drags it down the middle of my face, over the curve and bridge of my nose, and my top lip until his force becomes more demanding, pulling my lower lip downward. I don't even realize I'm holding my breath until the inferno in my chest makes me release a sob. He smirks.

My eyes widen, and I choke on the lump in my throat. "Colten."

He is at least a foot and a half taller than me and peers down into my damn frightened soul. The heat from our bodies creates something suffocating that envelops us.

He pulls his lower lip between his teeth. "I love how my name sounds on your tongue when you're running for your life."

Liquid heat rushes between my legs, dampening my underwear. What the hell is going on? My body is confused. *You should not be reacting like this.*

"I—" He cocks a brow at me. "I don't understand..." I force the words. "You interviewed me for that teaching position. You're a principal, and you're fucking kidnapping young girls!"

"If it makes you feel better," his eyes roam from my shoes up my toned legs, landing on the swell of my breasts peeking out of the white tank top below my open flannel. "Nothing about you is *young*."

I open my mouth, but the words don't emerge.

"Also, I'm not a principal," he says flatly as if I'm senseless for even thinking he was.

"But you interviewed me—virtually and in the office. You asked me professional questions!" *Well, the first time.* The gears in my head spin and spin.

"I, unfortunately, remember our time together in the office very well. It took every ounce of restraint not to throw you over that desk and shove something other than your panties down your throat to shut you up."

"I would've rather killed myself with the letter opener and bled out on that desk."

A muscle in his jaw pops. "Red is my favorite color, Little Ghost. That wouldn't have stopped me."

Gooseflesh breaks out over my arms, and I inadvertently knit my arms together. "You're incorrigible."

His eyes haven't left mine once. "Only for you, Little Ghost."
I feel flattered.

He sighs, rubbing a hand over his jaw. "My brothers and I went to school there. I have copies of keys. Access—"

"But the second-grade teaching position..." Tears form in the corners of my eyes, and my nose tingles. "It's not a real position. Is it?"

His evil grin has me pursing my lips to hold in another sob. I was fucking catfished by a job listing.

"Why?" I whisper, my breath still labored from running.

He steps into my body again, and I swallow, wishing the sharp claws of the shadows would reach through my body and end me so I don't have to live in this nightmare.

The hard ridges in his chest brush against my breasts. "Because we needed someone gentle. Caring. Someone with no ties who can vanish and not raise suspicion. And what better way to find that perfect person and learn everything about them than through interviews and background checks, Little Ghost."

The first tear falls, and his eyes track the movement. It drips off my chin, the soft earth soaking it up.

"Why do you keep calling me that?" I mumble.

"You know why."

My eyes squeeze shut.

Colten's voice chills me to the bone. "There's nobody to look for you, is there? Nobody who will notice you're gone."

He's wrong. I may go weeks between checking in with my parents, but at some point, they will realize something is wrong when I don't contact them.

Right?

Someone will notice. I refuse to believe that my parents are so out of touch with their own daughter—their only child— that they won't wonder why she hasn't called or texted.

Colten whistles, the sound vanishing into the night, disturbing my thoughts. What is he do—

A moment later, Rossco emerges, his black coat blending seamlessly with the darkness. He runs up to Colten, panting, happy, and entirely oblivious that this man is more of a predator than he is.

If teeth could kill, I'd bet on Colten. They would probably still look flawlessly white afterward.

Reaching into his sweatshirt pocket, he pulls out a leash

that makes my pulse hammer. Colten bends down, hooking it to Rossco's collar.

"Run."

My voice trembles. "Wh—what?"

Standing to his feet, he grins. "You have about one minute until they're here. I suggest you start running."

Huh?

I reach for the leash, and simultaneously, he retreats a step. I grit my teeth. "If you're letting me go, I want my dog."

His low, menacing laugh rings in my ears, his green eyes piercing mine. "Yes, I'm letting you run, but you're not going anywhere. My brothers find pleasure in the chase, and it wouldn't be much of a hunt if I held you here, would it?"

I peer at him through watery eyes. "You're taking Rossco and leaving me here with them?"

His eyes bore into me. "I can't be here to witness what they will do to you."

A tremor seizes my muscles, making my lip quiver. "Why? What are they going to do?" I whisper.

I flinch as his hand, the one not holding the leash, darts out and wraps around my throat, the pads of his fingers pulsing into the skin below my ear. His sleeve hikes up further on his right forearm, revealing the ink embedded in his skin. He tilts my head upward before I can get a good look at the tattoo, which looks like decaying leaves.

His voice is low, hot, and sticky, dripping down my spine. "Unlike my brothers, I don't share. If and when you find your-self being punished by me, I will be the only one you submit to. I'm not as forgiving as they are."

His hand withdraws from my throat, and his lips draw closer to my ear. My eyes flutter, his hot breath causing my legs to shake.

"I feel your erratic pulse, Taryn." My name coming from his mouth weakens my knees. They're barely holding me up. "You and I both know, as badly as you want to escape, your curiosity is desperately telling you to find out what we'll do to you when you pull a stunt like this."

His body leaves mine, leaving my brain and limbs a quivering pile of mush. Colten turns around, walking back toward the direction I came from, with Rossco trotting beside him.

His voice echoes through the orchard. "You're wasting time, Little Ghost."

I blink long and hard, inhaling a deep breath into my burning lungs before turning and running. Again.

But I barely make it one hundred yards when something whooshes through the air beside my head. Coming to a halt, I stare at the object that fell from one of the trees in front of me and crashed onto the ground.

Oh. My. God.

I'm unable to remove my eyes from the apple lying with an arrow straight through the flesh.

They were serious when they said hunting.

FOURTEEN | TARYN

Horror flows through my body as easily as a drug. I smack my hand to my mouth, choking on air I'm so desperately trying to breathe as I stare down at the hunting arrow.

Someone grips my shirt and yanks me around, releasing a sob from my body. Cameron's and Brennan's heads are tilted, with barely a hint of a smirk playing on their lips. They find my fear of them amusing, and I'm not too fond of it.

"I'm glad we didn't have to wait longer for this," Brennan says to Cameron as he slowly moves behind me, his body heat staying constant with his proximity.

"We knew you'd be clever, but we also thought you'd be more observant," Cameron teases.

I gape at him, wishing the flames behind my eyes could light him on fire. What does he mean by 'more observant'?

"Four floors and you somehow managed to oversee the cameras in every hallway and the one above the front door," Cameron mutters disapprovingly.

There are cameras?

I hold his eyes firmly. Shit, is there one in my room?

Brennan reappears from behind me and stands at my side, his chest brushing my shoulder. "You owe us a new lampshade."

A profound laugh has me whipping my head back toward Cameron. "Fortunately for us, your first punishment will be far better than we thought." I swallow his warning. "Hey, Bren," he calls to his twin, his eyes not leaving mine. "I'll bet you her tight hole that she'll be clenching her thighs together before we are both done with her."

His foul mouth drops a whale onto my chest, the weight so heavy I can barely get half a lungful of air.

Brennan swipes a thumb over his bottom lip, giving me a shit-eating grin that causes my blood to simmer. "And I'll bet you her tight cunt that she'll be begging for us to touch her before we're done with her."

The conversation that flickers in their eyes as they stare at one another tells me they've made a deal.

Too bad. I won't satisfy either one of the bastards even though my clit is throbbing at the thought.

I clench my jaw hard enough to shatter my teeth, and they circle me like ravenous sharks, Brennan coming to the front of me and Cameron pressing into my back. Cameron's cold fingers drift along the nape of my neck before they lightly pulse into my throat and demand my head to incline upward, so I have no choice but to glare at his brother looming over me. I'm not short by any means—5'6"—but they're both over six feet tall, and honestly, they're so intimidating I'm trying my best not to cower.

Cameron's belt buckle is digging into my ass. It hardens, releasing a strangled gasp from my throat.

Oh, shit. That's not his belt buckle.

I don't like to consider myself a virgin. Technically, I am, since I've never had sex in the traditional sense, but I guess it depends on how someone defines it. I moved around so much

—and did online classes for my bachelor's in education—that one night, at age nineteen, I decided I wanted to claim all the power.

It was just me, a glass of wine, and a toy I bought online in my bed alone, and it was perfect. Freeing. And I've never once regretted having that moment to myself. Plus, I always thought it would evaporate some of the pressure of penetration when that time came.

I have never touched a man in this way, let alone been touched by one. But it looks like we are skipping that phase and going straight to the threesome.

Colten's voice plays in my head:

"You and I both know, as badly as you want to escape, your curiosity is desperately telling you to find out what we'll do to you."

God, I hate that in the bottomless depths of my messed-up soul, I want to find out. Find out if my body will betray me, and I'll either be so wet and horny that I'll beg to be touched, or I'll clench my thighs together because I need something more there.

There is an imposter in my brain. A little splinter implanted itself, telling me I want more. It's a parasite, growing more impatient and taunting me with each passing second—whispering and telling me to push them harder and find out.

What does that say about me if I indulge in this situation and let my curiosity win?

They drugged me. Abducted me. Maybe if I fight back hard enough, they'll get annoyed and let me go. Or I'll find myself six feet in the ground, and they'll use my body to give nutrients to the trees.

"Criminal activity must be a family trait you inherited from your father." I laugh shakily. "I guess the apple—sorry apples, don't fall very far from the tree."

Brennan's eyes darken while Cameron's hold on my neck

turns demanding. He uses his force to shove me downward, my knees diving into the soft, wet earth.

I peer down to avoid unpleasant eye contact, but Brennan leans down. Gripping my jaw with his fingers, he forces my head up. "What better way to punish you for that mouth than to stuff it full of cock."

Cameron's fingers lightly skid across the nape of my neck. They tangle in my hair and pull violently enough that my head stings. "A deal is a deal, Taryn." His breath skids into my ear.

My eyes flutter closed at his reminder, my heart thumping so hard I'm afraid it's going to burst through my chest and plop onto Brennan's boots.

With Brennan's hand still on my chin, his thumb glides across my lower lip, and he pushes it between my lips. His skin resting against my tongue tastes like salt with a hint of soap.

"Nod, if you remember that you consented and understand what happens next," Cameron says from behind me.

Oh, shit.

I should stop this. I should really, really stop this. Yet, my bitch of a body betrays me, and I nod, giving in to the temptation. I nearly clench my thighs together but remember their bet.

The hand pulling at my hair vanishes, and I yelp with Brennan's thumb still in my mouth when Cameron slaps my inner thighs with the palm of his hand. "Spread your legs apart," he commands.

The shock from his demand keeps me motionless. The insides of my legs begin to tingle, and when I don't move, he smacks both again, driving me to whimper around Brennan's finger. Brennan's eyes don't stray from mine once, but my focus falters to his grin. A grin that widens as a tear cascades down my cheek.

Cameron's husky voice, drenched with eroticism, peppers my skin with goosebumps. "I sure as hell want to see the moment you get so needy that you press these gorgeous thighs together."

Slamming my glassy eyes shut, I inhale a breath through my nose. I shift my weight on my knees, picking one up and then the other, spreading my legs wider for him.

His fingers snake through my hair again behind me, holding me still as Brennan withdraws his thumb from my mouth. The clanking of a belt has my eyes frantically flying open, and I don't have any time to prepare before his thick cock is jutting out, the wet tip only an inch from my mouth.

Instinctively, I lick my lips. My heart is an earthquake shaking in my chest. There is no way I'll be able to fit all of him in my mouth.

"Stick out your tongue, Taryn," Cameron orders.

I timidly follow his orders. Brennan picks up his dick, pumping himself a few times before slapping it down on my tongue.

The bead of precome hits my taste buds just before he guides himself into my mouth, the girth forcing my lips to stretch apart. The bulging vein on the underside of his cock glides against my tongue. Breathing in and out of my nose, he keeps going further unhurriedly. The tip hits the back of my throat, making me gag. Wet, hot tears cascade down my feverish flesh.

Cameron keeps my head steady by holding on to my hair while Brennan thrusts, pushing deeper. A few tears glide over my lips, the salty flavor combining with the saliva pooling in my mouth. Gurgling sounds, heavy breaths, and Brennan's groans fill the orchard around us with the company of nearby crickets.

His hips move wildly, slamming the back of my throat so hard that I moan around his cock. Because of his size, he can barely thrust himself entirely in my mouth.

I hate that the thought going through my head is that I

hope I am deep-throating correctly. The way he grips his long-sleeved shirt and tugs it farther up his abdomen to expose his tattoos—highlighting the V-line that directs straight to his erection—makes me think he's enjoying himself. A small burst of pride hits me, but I shove it away.

I may be enjoying this situation more than I want to, but it doesn't change what these assholes have done to me.

He tilts his head back. "Fuck."

"How do her lips feel wrapped around your cock, brother?" I can hear the shift in Cameron's tone, giving away the malicious grin plastered on his face.

"Like heaven." Brennan looks back down at me, driving in and out of my mouth. His finger glides along a corner of my lips. "I knew this dirty mouth of yours had better uses."

A strand of hair whips out, sticking onto my face from Brennan's rapid movements. Cameron removes it from my sweaty face, tucking it behind my ear. The combination of having a cock down my throat for the first time and another pair of hands touching me has my skin sizzling with electricity.

I need more.

But I don't want to ask for more because this whole situation is so fucked up, and I wish I weren't enjoying it. I also don't want either of them to win their little bet.

I'm going to win this one.

A growl rumbles from Brennan's chest. "Look at those tears dripping on my cock." I blink more away, opening my puffy and watery eyes to hold his. Brennan's thrusting becomes more chaotic, and I begin choking.

Combined with the makeup from the other night still lingering on my face and hair that hasn't been brushed in a day, I'm sure I'm a mess. But it doesn't matter because he grunts and pulls out, white streams of release hitting my chest and dripping between the valley of my breasts.

I lean back and rest on my knees, still spread open since I

don't want to risk closing them. I force the cool air into my lungs and hunch over, trying to regain any of the energy that was mouth-fucked out of my body. Not even thirty seconds have passed before the twins' footsteps shuffle and their shadows move in the corners of my blurry vision.

When I glance back up, they have swapped positions. Cameron stands before me in those hot, soft sweatpants and a white T-shirt that perfectly stretches across his strong frame. My eyes loiter on the veins swelling in his biceps.

He reaches for the hem of his shirt. Removing the entire thing in one smooth, swift movement, he discards it on the ground next to us. Unlike Brennan, his body is wiped of ink—a beautiful blank canvas of hard muscle. Little spots of freckles sprinkle across areas of his skin. My eyes trace over them, connecting the faint dots until my focus drops to the drawstrings hanging in front of the bulging ridge of his cock confined in his sweatpants.

I swallow, my lips stretched and throat sore. The corner of his mouth lifts, finding amusement that after sucking dick once, I'm already staring at him like I'm ravenous and craving more.

I cringe as the pads of rough fingers from years of hard work graze my neck and tangle into my hair. Brennan pulls, not hard enough to have pain shooting through my skull but enough to sting. He tugs upward gently, and I take the hint to rise straighter on my knees again.

"You didn't think you were done, did you?" Cameron laughs.

The tears start falling again. I'm wet and horny, and my chest is sticky from Brennan's release. My mouth aches, and all I want to do is curl into bed, even if it's back up in that tower where I can get some sleep. I need to sleep so I can fight the mind-numbing fatigue and wake up and think more lucidly.

"This is supposed to be a punishment, Taryn," Brennan reminds me.

Cameron presses his finger below my chin, tipping it upward. His heated eyes capture mine.

"God, I'm in hell," I mutter.

"Your skin is glistening like you are. Are you dripping for your handsome devils?" Cameron smirks, reaching for the band of his sweatpants.

My attention focuses on the ripple of his muscles as he moves. The tips of my fingers sizzle, pleading with me to reach for him, but I don't.

He drops his sweats, revealing his gorgeous, thick thighs and a cock standing to attention. A shiver bolts through my body, seizing every muscle.

I stare up at Cameron with animosity in my eyes.

Cameron wraps his fingers around his width, his eyes darting over my face. "You're so pretty when you glare at me on your knees. This look alone could make me come."

My eyes roll, but he steps forward, and I open my mouth, letting him guide himself in. My eyes widen at his size. Up until this moment, I thought they were the same size, but my lips stretching further tell me I'm wildly wrong.

His hips slam forward, and when he hits the back of my throat, I gag around him, releasing a growl from him.

A flutter of panic courses through my veins as Brennan begins to move my head back and forth while Cameron thrusts between my lips. Tears pour out of my eyes as they both quicken their paces, Brennan using my head and mouth to swallow Cameron's cock as Cameron thrusts into my face ruthlessly.

They are both unrelenting.

Loud moans break through all the sloppy sounds, and it takes a second before I realize I'm the one making those noises.

"Goddamn, your hot mouth is perfect, taking every inch of me," Cameron grunts, and I whimper around his glorious cock.

"Tell my brother how badly you want to be touched," Brennan entices in my ear like one of those little devils on my shoulder. "Or beg me to reach between your legs with my fingers while he fucks your desperate little throat."

His erotic words sink into my ears and straight down through my body, making my pussy throb so uncontrollably that my knees move together of their own accord. I smack my palms onto Cameron's thighs for stability as mine draw together.

"*Shitttt*," he hisses, my grip on his thick muscles pushing him over the edge.

Brennan stops moving my head when Cameron jerks, his cock pulsing in my mouth as a hot stream coats the back of my throat.

"Look at you with Brennan's cum all over your tits and mine on your tongue." Cameron bends over, his face so close to mine that his hot breath fans across my heated cheeks. "Swallow every drop, Taryn."

Damn, I wish those words didn't turn me on. Surprisingly, I listen to him, swallowing.

He pulls out of my mouth, leaving it empty. Cameron smirks as his gaze locks on my thighs. Gripping his pants, he pulls them up and tucks his length back inside. "Oh, look at that, brother. Your taunting backfired. I win."

Ugh.

I was bound to lose. They practically set me up for failure. My thighs were burning, spread apart like that, but the ache between them was stronger.

Standing, my exhausted body attempts to hold itself up on wobbly legs, my bones liquid with the rest of me. If only the ground could soak me up with the rain from earlier this evening. Dirt and blades of grass are plastered to my knees, indented from kneeling for so long.

I wipe my mouth with my sleeve and close my eyes, the tiredness taking over quickly. Or at least that's what I'm blaming it on because I'm not sure I can look the two of them in the eye right now. The way the air and their gazes are still crackling against my clammy skin is a big enough hint that they know I liked it.

I grumble when two strong arms wrap around me and sweep me off my feet. I hook my arms around Cameron's neck and lean into his chest, too tired to care that I should be shoving him away and trying to run again. His scent of wood, leather, and a hint of cinnamon envelops me, the sleep dragging me under as they wrench me farther into their underworld.

They're taking me back.

"You guys are going to carry me all the way back?" I question drowsily.

"We have two pairs of perfectly functional arms." He clears his throat, attempting to remove the sexy rasp in his tone. "This is nothing, sweetheart."

I sigh. "You're awfully full of yourself, aren't you?"

Cameron lowers his voice to a whisper. "I won a bet. Next time you run or break one of the three rules, you'll be the one who's full of me."

FIFTEEN | TARYN

It's been three days.

Three long days of being trapped in the tower because of the Lindenvale brothers, with nothing to do but read books off the shelf and contemplate all the life decisions that led me here.

They have visited off and on, bringing me food and keeping me company, though I don't want it. Their presence mainly consists of them sitting in the room while I ignore them—or escorting me to the shower on the fourth floor in Brennan's room.

They are always waiting there when I get out, and it's infuriating. I have privacy, but don't have it at the same time. I'm just thankful that the night they brought me back into my room, all my clothes were folded neatly in the dresser drawers. I don't even want to know how they got them, but I strongly suspect Colten broke into my house when he went to get Rossco.

Jess hasn't visited since the first time, and I almost wish it were her keeping me company instead of the twins. Flashbacks of the night I sucked them off in the orchard invade my mind every time they sit in my room and watch me. My blood scorches the inside of my veins whenever it crosses my mind, leaving a blistering guilt that terrorizes me when I'm alone.

I despise that they hold that power over me now. They know it, too.

I've only seen Colten a few times out my window. He's either going in and out of his house or caring for Rossco. And they both disappear during the day, which pisses me off because the need to embrace Rossco is overwhelming. To at least have some trace of a constant before everything went to shit. They won't allow him in the house or my room. When I asked why, they just said, "Because Colten said so," and left it at that.

That solidifies the thought that Colten is the one who holds all the power around here. It wafts off him in tangible waves. For some reason, my body is in tune to know whenever he's near. The hairs on my arms stand on end, and chills flurry across my arms. And then, when I approach the window, he's there. Never long enough for me to finish the monologue of curse words I mutter under my breath.

The last few nights, around one in the morning, the slam of a car door has stirred me. I would wake up, rush to the window facing the backyard, and see a woman strut down the sidewalk in ridiculously tall heels that could wedge between those cracks in the concrete. She would knock on the door and wait, rocking on her heels before he opened the door.

He always pulls them inside hurriedly, but only after making direct eye contact with me. His sly smile grates my every fucking nerve because he knows I am there plastered against the glass like one of those barnacles clinging to a ship's hull. I'm plagued by curiosity and boredom.

Embarrassingly enough, I would linger patiently, waiting and squinting as if I could see what was going on through the curtains. Sometimes, I would catch movement behind the slit, bodies disturbing the light coming from one of the rooms on the side of the cottage.

The woman wouldn't leave until an hour later, looking more dilapidated than when she arrived. Her dark figure rushing out was lit by only the solar lights lining the sidewalk, her shadow floating across the silver blades of grass from the moon.

Both nights, it was a different woman. The first had long black hair, tight jeans, and a black lace cami. The other strutted across the pavement in those damn five-inch heels wearing a trench coat. And by my intuition, I'm assuming there was nothing or very little underneath.

My skin crawled while my brain conjured up the worst because Colten gives me that vibe.

The whine of metal hinges alerts me, and I sit up in the bed, placing the thriller I'm reading in my crisscrossed lap, wondering which twin it will be or if it's Jessica finally deciding to visit me.

Cameron appears, walking up the steps in jeans scuffed with mud and a black T-shirt. He strolls to the foot of my bed, my heart unexpectedly thrumming when he smiles.

"Good morning," he says casually.

I glower at him. Hard. "I. Want. Out. Of. This. Room."

His neck slopes, his eyes narrowing on me. Standing up straighter, he flips his head back, gesturing toward the door. "Let's go then."

I taper a brow. "Are you serious?"

Because I'm not kidding around. I need to step out of this room, or else I will go stir-crazy. Then I'll take apart the new lampshade they replaced and stab myself repeatedly with a piece of metal instead of using it to escape again.

"Yes, but I need you to listen to what I'm going to tell you first."

The strumming in my heart ceases, the artery leisurely

slinking into my throat. I attempt to swallow it down. "Okay." My voice shakes nervously.

He paces back and forth on the wood floor, the look crossing his face a heady blend of discomfort and urgency.

"We told you we brought you here for them," he starts.

Yes. I remember that quite well because I still have no idea who "they" are. Whenever I let my mind wander to theories about why I'm specifically here for *them*, I want to throw up.

My eyes don't stray from his.

He shakes his head, out of breath already. "We wouldn't have done anything like this if it weren't absolutely necessary." *Yeah, I'm sure.* "They are really fucking important to us. And we were entirely serious when we said they have fragile minds. They need more than we can give them right now, and with Jess leaving—" He sighs, pulling his fingers through his hair. "We need someone who can be a constant for them." He walks up to the side of the bed, his look stern as he points toward the door. "They need someone constant, Taryn. There is nothing we wouldn't do for them, and though these are the circumstances, we're still compensating you for your time."

Wait...what?

My brows draw together, my eyes expanding with confusion. What the hell does he mean by 'compensating me for my time'? I open my mouth to ask, but my jaw slams just as quickly when he continues.

"We are paying you triple what a teacher's salary would be. Honestly, they'll be a lot fucking easier than the things you probably deal with all the time. They have been through a lot. They've dealt with *us* while we run around doing all the other shit we have to do for this property, and they—"

I throw my hands up. "Who are *they*, Cameron?" I shout.

Lifting his hand, he drags it down his face, groaning. He narrows his eyes at me. "And no cursing. Sometimes Bren, Colt, and I let it slip, but you have to try...not to do that."

He's breathing like he just ran a mile, his chest rising and falling in a way that makes me think he'll pass out from lack of oxygen.

"I need you to promise me you'll stay calm when we get down there," he says. "Or at least hold all your thoughts in until we leave the room. Then, we'll talk to you about it."

"That doesn't help my anxiety whatsoever!" My frantic heartbeat pulses to my fingertips, gripping the book on my lap. "You're freaking me out more than you already have."

"Promise me," he whispers, a hint of pain seeping through the words.

My stomach is doing somersaults, flipping and swooping, making me nauseous. But I nod sluggishly.

My voice is steady despite all the questions creating a ruckus in my head. "Okay."

He exhales loudly, his body visibly relaxing more than it was, and starts to walk to the other end of the room and down the stairs. I get up, my hyperactive bare footsteps on the polished wood floors telling him I'm following.

The door was already open; he didn't even bother to shut it when he came up. He takes the last step, vanishing into the hallway. I speed up my pace, my eyes on his figure advancing down the hallway since I've already seen this fourth floor.

There are gray walls, the lower half with wainscoting to add texture, and white Victorian crown moldings, with one of those damn cameras I missed high in the corner. Ornate gold décor, sconces, and patterned runners line the hallway leading to the staircase. I pause a few times, admiring the few paintings of Douglas firs and the Pacific coastline encased in gold frames with a nearly illegible signature in the corner.

"How long has this house been here?" I ask, hastening my steps to catch up.

Cameron shrugs. Each hallway looks the same, with four doors on each floor. This house swallows me whole. It's huge.

I place my palm on the railing, letting the smooth, finished surface glide under my hand as we descend to the bottom floor. Sadly, the worry consuming my being doesn't rub off onto the varnish.

"My great-grandfather started the first plot of apple trees on Lindenvale Hill in 1910. His sons carried on the orchard, creating new plots to expand the business over time. The house started as a one-story home on the hill, but my grandfather made renovations. And then when widespread distribution started, and we became one of the country's leading apple producers, my dad gutted everything and built everything you see now."

"And the cottage out back?" I ask.

A chuckle slips through Cameron's tone. "My parents built that for Colten since he'll never leave. Eventually, Colt will officially inherit Lindenvale Orchard," his voice deepens, "and everything that comes with it. The cabin, as we call it, was built for him so he could still live on the property but not have to live with my parents. Well, when they were here anyway."

We reach the last set of stairs, which open into the grand foyer with the wood coat rack and storage bench against the wall. An extensive set of windows faces the patio with a gray furniture set and hanging pots of ferns and flowers. The few steps lead to a sidewalk with lush greenery, which leads to a circular driveway I can't see from my window that faces the front lawn.

He steps down onto the main floor, taking a left as the foyer expands into a massive living room. My head falls back to scan the ceilings with plasterwork and gold accents. The windows allow bright natural light to filter in, reflecting off the walls painted a muted forest green instead of gray.

At the back of the room, a vast fireplace large enough to crawl in has engravings on the mantel and a television. A decorative rug sits on the dark, polished hardwood floor, with brown furniture set around a large wooden coffee table front and center.

This house is striking and intimidating. But what's even more daunting isn't Colten, Brennan, or Jess lounging on the couches. Not even close. It's the boy with his head down, playing with a Nintendo Switch on a chair in the corner, and the beautiful little girl sitting on Colten's lap with her head on his chest and her eyes trained on me.

SIXTEEN | COLTEN

It's been over a minute, and nobody has said a goddamn word—just heavy breaths, eyes darting back and forth, and the voice of a crow outside somewhere on the patio roof.

Taryn stands rigid at the foyer's threshold, where it turns into the living room. She's dressed in tight black yoga pants that mold to her curves and a tan Nirvana tank top, her eyes wide. I don't think she's blinked. If I focus hard enough, I can feel her rapid heartbeat vibrating the floor, the soles of my shoes soaking up the brisk drumming.

I enjoy it far too much.

She huffs out a frustrated breath. "What the fu—"

I shoot her a judgmental glare, her lips slamming together quickly. Her large chestnut eyes roll with her irritation.

"Taryn, this is Tristan and Elena," Cameron introduces, gesturing to Tristan, immersed in his game in the corner on the chair, and Elena, who is on my lap, shyly gripping my T-shirt in her fists.

They don't get introduced to many people. Sure, they attend school and have activities, but we primarily keep to ourselves up on the hill. This is the first time anyone else has been living in this house.

It may take an adjustment period. For all of us.

Taryn knits her arms together, her bare foot tapping on the floor lit with a ray of sunlight from the windows. She's spewing with anger, unable to contain it as her eyes dart back and forth between them.

It might be a long adjustment period.

"Cameron, can I talk to you outside?" she grits through her teeth.

Fuck no.

"You can talk here," I say flatly, pulling a growl from her throat. I almost smile.

"Okay. Fine. So, you kid—"

I cock my head, pinning her with a stare. "Watch it," I seethe.

Elena stirs on my chest at my angered tone, strands of her soft, naturally curly hair tickling my neck. Her eyes haven't left Taryn's once. Tristan, on the other hand, couldn't care less.

Taryn purses her full pink lips, lips I watched wrap around Cameron's and Brennan's cocks a few nights ago like a good little whore taking her punishment.

I swear I could smell her arousal wafting through the trees, the scent turning me around and rooting me in the shadows with Rossco while I watched them.

Watched her.

And I shouldn't have.

I'm not a voyeur. I don't find any amount of pleasure in observing. I would rather be the one touching. Fucking. Owning their body because I crave that control, and that's what gets me off.

The other night was an abnormality.

The way she took their dicks to the back of her throat on her knees with her thighs spread apart had me growing painfully hard. She may have resisted at first, but she clenched her thighs at the end, telling me she wanted to be filled. It made me want her.

Which is problematic because she's off limits.

So, after the twins came all over her tits and poured down her throat, I walked back to the cabin and immediately called Britt, ordering her to get her ass to my place.

I found that pink rabbit in my little ghost's underwear drawer at the rental that afternoon before she escaped. It's currently burning a hole in my bedside table.

When I brought it back to my place, I wondered how she touched herself with it. What she thought about. Finding that toy was like a bomb straight to the wall I built, convincing myself I'd never touch her because she's here for Elena and Tristan.

Not for me.

Not for Cam and Bren.

She's here for them.

I called Brennan and Cameron and told them I saw her bolt with Rossco. I followed her while they found us using the tracker they implanted under her skin the night they brought her home. After they were finished with her, I knew they were returning her to the tower. Visions flickered behind my eyes of Taryn touching herself in the dark after my brothers used her like that, maybe desiring her pink toy to get her to the precipice.

If it weren't for Britt coming over that night, I wouldn't have trusted myself not to barge in and validate that Taryn was wet and craving more, even if she was reluctant to admit it.

If I keep myself satiated and dive into a hot piece of ass every night, it will lessen the craving to touch her.

I prefer sex long and hard, but that night with Britt took much longer than usual. It wasn't until the image of my little ghost writhing under me appeared instead.

That's all it took for me.

God, I am so fucked.

"We are here to answer your questions," Brennan tells Taryn, dragging me out of my thoughts. Jessica sits next to him, her legs crossed and foot bouncing. I know she hates this and hates to leave, but she needs to. "But think about your questions first before they leave your mouth," he forewarns.

Taryn scowls at him and swipes her hair behind her shoulder. "Why am I here?" she probes, her gaze darting to each of us.

Cameron walks into the living room, lowering himself to the arm of the couch Elena and I are on. "We needed someone more permanent when Jess leaves for college in a month. After all this family has been through, we can't have another person leave us."

Her eyes flash to mine, shimmering with a blend of pity and concern.

She causes the pulse in my neck to pound harder.

Sure, we could've asked her to be our live-in nanny—or even hired one. We had plenty of chances to be up-front and honest with her about our situation once Jess leaves for college. But my brothers and I don't trust easily. And the truth is, nannies and babysitters are temporary. We weren't looking for someone who would bail when we needed them the most. When you've experienced loss, even the people who barely touch your life can leave a gaping hole when they're gone. A void you never knew could cut so deeply.

Taryn is different. She's an independent and kind spirit who seems to have no ties to anything or anyone, from what I learned from our few interviews for the teaching position, making her an easy target compared to other women we considered. The likelihood of anyone even realizing she's missing, or that we took her, is slim.

By abducting her and keeping her here, we are protecting ourselves.

Shielding our vulnerable family from someone we could've easily hired just for them to leave us as quickly.

We didn't have time to convince Taryn and give her the chance to say no. It's not ideal, but I'd do anything to protect my siblings, even if it means bending morals and taking an unconventional approach to ensure she doesn't leave us.

Taryn considers Cameron's words. It's only been a few days, and I can already tell she has a soft spot for him. It awakens a pang of jealousy that shouldn't be there in the first place.

"Oh. Uh— So I'm like a nanny then?" She thinks harder. "An enslaved nanny."

"An enslaved nanny getting paid way more than any second-grade teacher ever would," I clarify.

Elena sits up, pushing a strand of hair out of her eyes. She turns her head to peer up at me. "What does enslaved mean?"

I assume Tristan looks up for the first time, wondering the same thing. But he doesn't say a word. He never has much to say; he listens. A lot.

"See, young ears pick up everything, Taryn," Brennan retells her, crossing his arms and slouching into the back of the couch. "Remember the rules."

I tighten my arms around Elena's small frame. "It means she's not going anywhere."

Elena nods and pushes herself off me to stand. She wearily approaches Taryn in her purple fluffy slippers and pajamas that she usually doesn't get out of until around eleven. Which, looking at the watch on my wrist, is thirty minutes from now. A reminder that I have shit I need to get back to.

But this family matter needed my full attention.

Elena gazes up at her, the first hint of a genuine smile flickering across Taryn's face, but then her lips twist to the side, and it falters. It's like one of those indecisive neon signs when it can't decide if it wants to be on or off and just flickers.

Taryn shifts her focus to Tristan, and his head immediately drops back to his game, avoiding her. "How old are they?"

"Tristan is seven, and Elena is five," Jess speaks up for the first time since Taryn came downstairs.

"Am I—" She swallows. "Teaching them? Homeschooling?"

Jessica shakes her head. "In a few weeks, you'll take them to school. I'll go with you, of course, up until I leave. You'll take them to after-school activities and sports on weekends and hang out with them when Cam, Bren, and Colt are out in the orchard or doing business things—pretty much anything a nanny would do."

She huffs out a laugh. "You'll trust me to leave? What if I tell someone what the Lindenvale children are actually up to on the hill besides avoiding everyone?"

"You can try to leave, but we'll always be able to find you," Cameron informs her.

Her eyes transform into little slits as she glares at him.

"Also, if you run or decide to tell someone, I can access all your bank accounts," I enlighten. Her head whips toward me so hard I'm surprised she doesn't get whiplash. I nod. "Pretty good savings account for a teacher that moves constantly and eats out all the time."

She shifts her weight, uncomfortable in her skin under my stare. I know she eats out regularly from studying her bank statements. You can learn a lot about someone by their spending habits. Now, I have a sneaking suspicion she lied about her cooking abilities in her interview. If so, she should get disciplined for that. Blood rushes to my cock at the thought. I move to distract myself, placing an arm across the back of the couch.

She releases a shallow breath. "How did you..."

While I was at the house the other day, I went through

some of the boxes still unpacked in her living room. Digging through it all wasn't difficult since she only moved with belongings that could fit in her truck bed. I found a storage container containing account documents, passwords, old taxes, and other vital documents.

You should be more careful with personal belongings, Taryn. You never know who's lurking, waiting to steal that information.

"Doesn't matter," I quip. "All that matters is that everything you've worked for can be gone instantly. So, it's either you have nothing in your bank account with Citibank, or you play house and make more than you'll ever see in your profession."

She blinks blankly at me a few times, the only sign of apparent anger in how her fists ball at her sides. Taryn's knuckles are so white I expect the bones in her fingers to burst through the skin.

"Want to come see my room?" Elena's small voice impeccably slices through the tension in the room.

Her tiny hands hold that power.

Taryn glances down at her, but Cameron gets up as she opens her mouth, cutting her off.

"I think Miss Taryn has had enough for today, Elena. You can show her tomorrow," Cam says softly.

I catch Taryn dramatically rolling her eyes and mouthing *Miss Taryn* to herself.

I bite my bottom lip to withhold my smile at her frustration, but it still shows.

"No! I want to. Can I? Please..." she drawls. Taryn's begging has my eyes drifting to the ceiling in a pathetic attempt to ignore the word's hold on me. And God. The way she says it? Yeah, I could have her repeating that one breathy plea all day long. "I need to be out of that room for a little while, or I will go insane."

Brennan eyes her suspiciously.

If Little Ghost wants to run again, she won't get far. At this point—after the other night—I bet the twins are itching to drag their rough hands all over her soft tan skin with a dusting of freckles.

Jess stands to her feet. "I can go up with them." She turns her head toward Tristan. "Do you want to come up with us, Tristan?"

His focus doesn't stray from the device. The only answer he gives is a brief shake of his head as his light, dirty blond hair flops onto his forehead. Tristan is a quiet but kind kid. Sometimes I wish he would give me more, but he knows I'm not his father.

With Elena and Tristan, I've dipped the tip of my finger into what fatherhood is like.

Elena was a newborn when Mom disappeared. But sometimes, it's hard to shake the feeling that I've failed with Tristan. When Christian, my father, was arrested, Tristan was barely two. He doesn't remember anything; if he does, he keeps quiet, keeping the memories of that horrific night in his head.

The mistakes I've made with them—my family—over the years are immeasurable, but I have matured enough to comprehend them. I have matured to understand that those moments are a blip in time, and I hold the power to decide what kind of man I am after my faults. Am I the man who lets his errors devour him or the one who stares straight ahead, using those mistakes as a guideline for things I never want to revisit?

Five years ago, I looked forward to becoming a father—seeing a new generation of little Lindenvales love this property as much as I do. It's amusing how fast directions can change.

Cameron, Brennan, and I were thrown into the father role because my narcissistic father let himself go and let his obsession control him. We were three young men—the twins, nineteen, and me, twenty-two—who were irresponsible one day with only the worries of working and sleeping around with whatever piece of ass we could find. Then, instantly, it was diapers, learning how to bottle-feed, and balancing accounts. We got the weight of a multimillion-dollar company dropped on our shoulders, all the while trying not to fuck up our family further.

Tristan doesn't talk very much. He goes to school and comes home either to dive into schoolwork or play video games. I was against getting him a Switch at first, but this kid has been through so much that I hate saying no to him if it's the one thing he finds joy in.

Taryn crosses her arms. "I also want to see my dog."

Elena jumps up and down. "I want to see the dog too!" Her lips pout. "Colt hasn't let me see it yet."

Tristan's head whips up at the mention of Rossco.

At first, I was worried about having that dog around Elena and Tristan, but he follows me when I work outside, tending to the plots and trees. Or he curls up by my desk at the shop and keeps me company. I had a staff meeting with all our workers yesterday, and he lounged by me the entire time. The whirr of the chainsaw doesn't seem to bother him, either.

I've grown to like him.

"Fine," I stand up, running a hand over my white shirt with our logo in the corner. "I have work to get back to." I keep my gaze locked on Taryn, but my tone is directed at my brothers. "Jess can keep an eye on her today. You two have shit to get done. Meet me at the shop in half an hour."

The twins nod and rise to their feet.

Walking past Taryn on my way to the door, I withhold my smile as her breath hitches in response to the slightest brush of my shoulder. I enjoy knowing I can paralyze her in place. Imagine the influence I'd have if her entire body were at my mercy. Taryn's sugared citrus scent wraps around me like a cloak, and already, I know that smell is going to be the distraction I don't need today.

Stepping into the fresh air, I regret telling her she could see

Rossco. He's easy company. It's not hard to understand why she loves that damn dog so much. His presence makes work more bearable when he's around.

And as much as I despise admitting it, over the last several days, I've looked forward to the end of the day. And I refuse to believe it's because of the pretty face that stares out the window every night in the tower, seeking me out.

SEVENTEEN | TARYN

"He's fast," Elena yells, her chuckling bright and happy like the warm late summer breeze gliding against my skin.

She throws the ball again for the millionth time, utterly unfazed by the slobber coating her hand. The ball rolls across the front yard, stopping just before the gradual decline of the hill. She sprints, her pink sneakers leaving footprints in the damp grass. She runs to catch up to Rossco, both of them content and breathing hard.

Tristan sits nearby, picking at blades of grass, and adding them on top of the pile he's created. He doesn't like being told he needs to spend some time outside without the Switch. That order came from Cameron before he went to the shop, not me.

Despite being forced to be their nanny, I don't feel it's my place to order them around yet. I'm still completely uncomfortable with all this, but Elena eases some of the angst. Is it acceptable to be jealous of a five-year-old with a stunning smile and natural curls?

I know the Lindenvales are millionaires, but the thought that I'm making triple a teacher's salary to sit here on my ass and watch two young kids churns my stomach into knots. Already, it's easier than the thirty children I had in my classroom last year. But Elena and Tristan's three brothers seem to make up for the twenty-eight kids I don't have.

God. I shouldn't be okay with this.

I shouldn't be here complying with their rules when they've put me through hell. The sad part? Colten was right; there's probably nobody looking for me, and it's not like I have anywhere to go or a job to get back to. The tower is ten times nicer than that house I'm renting, and I've come to appreciate it now that I'm allowed to be out of it.

"If I would've known a dog would tire her out like this, I would have begged my brothers to get one a year ago." Jess laughs on one of the outside patio chairs beside me under the porch.

I adjust my black baseball cap and brush back some sweaty strands of hair sticking to my forehead. We are in the shade, and it is still scorching out here. I place it back on and lounge back, glancing up at the cloudless sky. It's a beautiful day, a blue blanket covering the orchard that spans a mile in front of us.

Thankfully, the fresh air in my lungs calms my head and brings some clarity. Now that I can focus on my surroundings better, I can see the distinct plots of trees. A cloud of dust disperses into the air in the distance, probably from machinery or a vehicle on the gravel road.

It's peaceful out here, surrounded by hanging plants under the porch. I was tempted to bring the book I've been reading outside, but I thought it might be rude to ignore Jess.

Thousands of questions are swarming in my head, and she's more likely to answer them than the twins.

I faintly smile. "Yeah, Rossco has a way of tiring me out too. Outside, at least. Inside, he couldn't be lazier."

Elena crashes her knees into the wet earth and flops onto

her back, breathing heavily. The sun kisses her milky white skin. Rossco drops the ball onto her stomach, and she giggles.

I observe the sun beating down on her little exposed arms and hastily sit up. "We should get some sunscreen on them."

Jessica meets my eyes. "Already did. I put it on them while you were upstairs."

I slump back against the cushion and nod. "Can I ask you something— Actually, can I ask you a few things if I'm going to be trapped here?"

Jess presses her lips in a thin line and nods.

"I don't know anything about your family, just what I've been told." By one old woman living directly outside the gate, but still. I don't know anything.

She sighs and twists a strand of straight brown hair around her finger. "I assume you want to know about my mom and dad." She doesn't phrase it as a question, but her tone, laced with sadness, tightens my chest. She keeps her eyes on Elena and Tristan, wiping her hands on her jeans.

"My mom was always a bright person," she begins. "The one whose presence would light up a room even if she weren't smiling. She had that effect, and it wasn't hard to understand why my dad fell in love with her." She swallows. "I remember watching them in the kitchen. The way he'd hug her behind her back and place his chin on her neck to watch her cook. The way he would kiss her was my favorite part. Most kids hate seeing their parents like that, but for me...it set my standards for what I want with someone someday."

I scan her face as she picks at the pink polish on her nails, the same color chipping on Elena's.

"Anyway," she continues, "it seemed like everything changed one random week. My dad was devoted to the company, and my mom had her hands full with me, three teenage boys, and Tristan—who was only one at the time. They fought more than usual, out in the open around us and not in their bedroom like they normally did. It just —changed."

Her eyes settle on me. I may have questions, but I see them dancing in her eyes, too.

"When Mom got pregnant with Elena, she was a shell of herself. My dad lashed out more, spent lots of time in the office in the shop, and Mom always seemed to have dead eyes when she looked at him. Two weeks after Elena was born, she was gone. The few months after that were even stranger."

"What do you mean?"

She shakes her head. "Our grandparents were always close to us, but after Mom left and never came back, she didn't contact them or us at all—just vanished."

Her eyes flutter closed, and she draws in a deep breath. "A month later, after no contact, my grandparents raised their suspicions to law enforcement that my father was involved with her disappearance somehow. That week, cops and investigators were all over our property like ants, and my dad was around his lawyer more than us. They took some samples of a few large stains and smaller ones in my parents' room as evidence to test. My dad claimed it to be red wine they spilled one night, but after the report came in a few weeks later—" She clears her throat, and I clench my hands in my lap. "It was her blood. They arrested my dad early that next morning, and none of us has seen him since."

My mouth opens, but her story evaporates anything on my tongue. It's one of those stories where your head is consumed by thick fog and swishes around like liquid because there is too much to process. I can't even begin to understand what it would've been like for all of them to experience that.

"You don't have to say anything or apologize," she mutters, picking at a hangnail on her thumb. "He's been at Washington State Penitentiary for over four years. He writes us letters, but Cam, Bren, and I are the only ones who write back." She faintly smiles. "Elena draws him pictures even though she has no memory of him. And, of course, Tristan doesn't have a lot to say, but he tries."

My heart plummets into my stomach like the chaos of an avalanche destroying everything in its path. The cold snow drifts over my skin, leaving chills in its wake.

A short exhale breaks past her lips. "Sorry, I know that's a lot for you to process."

Not as much as it has been for them to process. No wonder the Lindenvale children keep to themselves up on this hill.

"Do you think he did it— Your dad? I mean, there's been no body." I don't know why I say it. I'm sure she's considered that brutal fact enough to drive her to the brink of madness.

She pulls her bottom lip between her teeth. "No. But there was a lot of blood...There was also enough circumstantial and behavioral evidence to charge him. Honestly, I don't know what I believe."

When I went inside to go to the bathroom, I wandered around the house to get acquainted with my prison for the next...however long they plan on keeping me. Jess looks like her mom. I've seen the family pictures framed in a few hallways, on mantels, and in the kitchen. Their smiling faces, frozen in time, are a stark contrast to the broken family I've found myself trapped with. Her mom had shoulder-length light brown hair, but their arched brows and button noses are the same. Jane Lindenvale was beautiful. I can see some of her features in all of them, and I'm sure that haunts them sometimes.

I shift in my chair to face her, placing one foot on the cushion and wrapping my arms around my knee. "What about Cameron, Brennan, and Colten? What do they think? Do they think he did it?"

The breeze floats through her hair, blowing some across her lips. She picks it away with her finger. "Brennan writes to Dad, but he bottles up his emotions pretty well. I think he only writes because he feels guilty if he doesn't. Cameron loves hard and trusts hard—with everyone. He doesn't believe Dad could do something like that." I give her a weak smile because even though I barely know them, her descriptions seem spot-on. "Colten, on the other hand, doesn't like mentioning or talking about my father at all. He remembers everything too well. Sometimes, I wonder if he knows more than us."

"Why do you say that?" I listen intently.

"Because the night before she disappeared, my parents were having the biggest fight they've ever had. Something shattered, and Colten gathered us all in Brennan's room and told us not to come out until he came and got us. I remember hearing the front door slam once and a second time a few minutes later."

"Did he ever come to get you?"

The perplexed look that passes over her glassy eyes forms a lump in my throat.

She languidly shakes her head. "We stayed in that room the rest of the night until morning. But when morning came, Colten was gone, and so was Mom. He didn't come back until three days later. Even then, he didn't seem the same and hasn't been since."

My eyes expand. *Three days later.* After something like that happened? Unease scrapes under my skin. I hug my knee tighter, trying to suppress all the other questions that continue developing.

What happened during those three days he was gone?

Where was he?

We both turn our heads, laughing as Elena runs around in circles with the ball, trying to dodge Rossco as he leaps for it. His body crashes into her petite frame, sending her flying and sprawling out across the lawn.

Jess and I gasp, rising to our feet, but Elena jumps up and

giggles so loud that it sends the crows flying off the patio roof. Maybe it's her contagious happiness, or he's tired of being bored, but Tristan finally joins her. He wanders to the rope lying in the grass, piquing Rossco's interest in the toy. He picks it up, and Rossco darts for it.

My body warms, feeling Jess's eyes on me. "We never talk about it," she sighs. "Well, sometimes we do, but Colten shuts the conversation down pretty fast. I know you hate this situation, but I'm glad they brought you here when they did—before I leave for school." My chest rises and falls a little heavier. "It feels good to talk to someone about it. Each year, I think my brain gets a little fuzzier about it all."

I'm relieved she shared, giving me more insight into their complicated family history and why they've made the decisions they have. But I'm not a therapist. I don't have wise words to share or advice. How the hell does someone get past something like that? I may not talk to my parents, but I know they are there if I need them.

The Lindenvale children have nobody; they only have each other. And when my eyes settle on hers, the reality of my situation sinks further into my gut, hardening the truth into something solid.

They once only had each other. Now they have me.

EIGHTEEN | TARYN

The sweltering steam hangs heavy, coating my already-dripping skin. I draw the hot air into my lungs, letting the warmth cascade down my throat and soothe my exhausted mind.

The last few days have dragged on. I'm one second away from crashing onto Brennan's fluffy memory foam bath mat and drifting to sleep right here since it's nearly one a.m.

One moment, I woke up trapped in the tower, and the next, I was running around with Jess, learning to care for the two children I'm nannying for. Forced to nanny. But even when I say *forced*, my tongue is shit at convincing my brain that's reality. After learning about what happened five years ago, I feel for Elena and Tristan.

My heart aches for all of them.

It doesn't make it right to abduct someone, not even a little bit. But they are close, and I've never had to ponder the extreme lengths I'd go to for my family because I don't have what they have. It's not something I can relate to.

In a way, it's surviving—watching out for themselves when the two people who were supposed to be there for them aren't.

Each day I've been here feels less and less like I'm trapped against my will. I have money flooding into my bank account, a beautiful room, a massive house, a stocked fridge, and a pantry I don't have to pay for. My dog may not be allowed inside the house, but he's here and has already settled into the enormous yard. If I drag him somewhere else or back to that piece of junk I rented after this, I'm sure I'll get those big, brown, pouty eyes from him that make me reevaluate my choices.

It's a nannying gig that someone would be idiotic to turn down if they came across it on a typical job-searching site. But sometimes, the feeling of being confined floods my veins. I've always had the free will to go anywhere. I've never been restrained. And although they aren't locking me in the room anymore, this property is starting to close in on me.

Jess wasn't wrong when she said the guys have a full schedule running the company and tending to the orchard. I've barely seen them besides at dinner, breakfast, and occasionally when they return to the house for lunch.

Jess and I keep the kids busy enough, and after spending more time with her, I genuinely enjoy her company. She's sweet and has a personality I would've loved in a sister if my parents had ever decided to have another child. When we are sitting at the table coloring with Elena while Tristan joins us on his tablet or Switch, it almost feels like we are sisters in a way. Our hair color is similar enough.

"Shit," I mutter, my eyes darting desperately around Brennan's matte black bathroom for my clothes.

My skin was itching to shower so badly that it didn't even cross my mind to grab a pair to change into. The massive walk-in shower with tan tiles and gold accents is relaxing. It's one of the reasons I don't mind taking an hour-long shower. I sit on the floor with my arms wrapped around my knees while the water cascades over my head, drifts down my neck, and the ridge of my back like a boulder under a waterfall.

Wrapping the towel tight around my breasts, I tuck it in, gritting my teeth. I have to enter Brennan's room practically naked.

Please be out of the room.

Gripping the door handle, I repeat the silent prayer in my head, eagerly hoping that he needed to leave the room for a glass of water or to smoke since he's restricted from doing it in the house.

I exit the bathroom and am hit with a wave of dry, chill air that peppers my damp skin with gooseflesh.

At least, I think it's the air. Or it could be that I'm wrong. So. Unbelievably. Wrong.

Brennan lounges into his fluffy pillows propped against his headboard. His bed is impeccable, and so is his muscular frame in only a pair of dark gray joggers hanging low on his hips and a book in his hand. His pattern tattoos dance across his skin, down his chest, and onto his stomach. He flips a page, the tendons in his arm rippling below his skin.

Like the bathroom, this room is nearly completely black, with a tan area rug under his king-size bed and a charcoal duvet. Each time I breathe his scent of leather, orange spice, and a hint of smoke, it drips down my throat, covering me from head to toe in tingles.

The light from the lamp flickers across his tan skin. His lack of a farmer's tan makes me think he works outside without his shirt on. God, what he must look like—

"Are you going to come get in bed with me?" His raspy voice startles me, but his focus stays hooked on the book in his hand.

"Um— What?" I stutter.

He flips the page carelessly. "You've been staring at me for over a minute, and you're standing in a towel. So, if you're not going to drop it for me and crawl onto my lap, then I suggest you move on before I make a move."

My stomach leaps.

Not knowing what else to do to fill the sexual tension, I point upward, knowing my room is above his. Sometimes, I hear his headboard tapping against the wall, and muted sounds come from this room around two or three in the morning.

"I...forgot my clothes in my room." I fold my arms over my breasts, nervous that his gaze has magic abilities and may somehow whip the towel off my body. "Don't you get enough action in here already? You seem to do quite well at luring your victims here."

Something the Lindenvale boys have in common.

Other people may not come in and out of this property besides workers, but they have no issues tempting women into their beds. No wonder both Cameron and Brennan have their own floors. Sadly, the floor and walls of the attic are thin. Unfortunately, even though Jess told me all the other rooms are soundproof, I can still hear...certain activities that take place in his.

He lowers the book to his lap and cocks his head, evaluating me. "Victim," he corrects.

My eyes roll. "Well, whoever she is, you two are loud." I may not catch voices, but I sure as hell can hear the furniture he's trying to pound into the wall along with whoever is in there with him.

"He."

My eyes lift to the ceiling in thought. *Hmmm.*

"Whoever *he* is," he repeats. "You know him," he mentions casually.

I barely know anyone in Cedar Creek besides them, Alaric, who frustratingly turned out to be Colten, the old woman I met on my walk, Crock, and...

My eyes flit to his, and he grins maliciously. "Xavier?" I exhale. "You and him? But you...Uh—"

"Fucked your throat and came all over those gorgeous tits?" His compliment drips down my spine like honey.

I clear my throat. "Yeah."

"Xavier and I are bisexual." He places the book on the nightstand, kicking his legs over the bed to stand while I mull it over.

Xavier is the one who drugged me, but now it's clicking together. What a perfect little scheme they had at the bar.

Assholes.

Brennan approaches me, his smoky and spiced scent hitting me like a wall. The impact hits my knees, releasing a flurry of tingles.

"Tell me, Taryn." He circles me, pressing his bare chest into my back, his rough fingertips gliding delicately across my collarbone. The heat from his chest collides with my shoulders. A pang of shock surges through my body when his breath hits the curve of my neck. His lips hover over my flushed skin. "Have you ever been with two men before?" His words pour through my ears like venom, petrifying me in place.

Acting thoughtlessly, my neck slopes further, my body craving his lips on my skin. His question hangs like a thick haze, and I shake my head. I still haven't even been with one man, but the thought of two simultaneously sounds...

Thrilling and terrifying.

Since that night in the orchard, I have had all this sexual tension and curiosity pulling at each ligament in my body. Brennan and Cameron are the ones who caused it, and now whenever I see them, my bitch of a brain tells me I want more. That it's okay to feel this way despite being abducted and held against my will.

It's messed up, but I've never been so turned on.

"We would go slow with you." His lips barely stroke my neck, and my eyes flutter closed. *Oh, shit.* "Ease your body into it. Ease you into fitting both of us." I swallow. His fingers travel across my shoulder to the top of my spine. They dip below the towel, his touch spreading like wildfire as if he could disintegrate the towel still wrapped tightly around me. "We don't mind sharing," he whispers.

"You and Xavier?" I murmur, processing his comment.

"Xavier and I. Cameron and I...occasionally." My legs wobble, and he grips my shoulders to steady me. His dark chuckle is a beautifully haunting sound. "Xavier and I have been looking for someone to be our third for a long time."

"Why don't you just force me into it like last time? You seem to take what you want anyway."

His fingers thread through my hair, the wet strands brushing against my back. "That was your punishment. We won't take it further than that unless you ask us to."

Unless I ask them to.

It's not going to happen, though I've fantasized about it more than I like to admit.

He removes his hand from gripping my hair and walks back to the bed, plopping on his mattress. He picks up his book and opens it to the page he was on, refusing to meet my eyes. "Go to bed, Taryn."

I stand there speechless and, embarrassingly enough, aroused. Turning around, I walk out of his room and open the door to my tower, my feet feeling heavier with each step I ascend.

Clearing the last step, I notice something different out of the corner of my eye. I glance out the window facing the back-yard, admiring how the full moon casts light on the grass, the blades like silver swords. It's almost entirely dark outside, besides the moon, the stars, and the solar lights along the path. Rossco isn't in the yard like he usually is, so I'm assuming he's inside with Colten somewhere. But that's not the only unusual thing.

The curtains in Colten's cabin are always closed. But tonight, there's one area with the curtains open—the room on the side of the house closest to the garden.

With the tower high and the house lower in the yard, I can only see part of the carpet and what looks like an accent chair with a side table and a glass of some amber liquor.

I grasp my towel, pulling it tighter and tucking it in to secure it around myself. Strands of wet hair drip onto my collarbone, the water skating down my stomach. I approach the window closer, nearly tumbling back when Colten steps into view behind the window.

God, these Lindenvale brothers are going to be the cause of my death.

He stands in front of the chair with his back turned to the window in nothing but a pair of jeans. The black tattoos embedded in his skin are on full display, running over one arm, across his shoulder, and down part of his back. I practically press my forehead to the glass, wanting to see the artwork, but it's blurred from this far away. If I focus enough, some of the shapes on his back look like feathers.

He lifts an arm, pulling his fingers through his tussled hair. My mouth unexpectedly waters when the muscles in his back ripple and flex. Whatever thought I'm forming evaporates from my mind as quickly as the water droplets on my overheated skin.

He's irritatingly hot.

He may terrify the shit out of me, but at this moment, I'm itching to touch him—to find out if the palpable intimidation he exudes could soak into my fingertips and seep into my bones.

But it looks like someone else gets that privilege. A brunette with long, curled hair stalks toward him. She nods at something he says while wetting her lips and dropping onto her knees. Her large, bare breasts bob, sending a shock wave of ice scraping against every nerve ending.

I want to look away, but my eyes are glued to what's happening before me.

He shifts his position, giving me a side profile of both of them. Colten fiddles with his belt, whipping it out of the loops effortlessly as if he had done that motion a million times before. And I'm guessing he has since he slips the leather back into the buckle and fastens it around her neck. The woman eagerly reaches for his jeans, where the band of his boxers peeks out. She tugs them down to his ankles, letting his erection spring free.

My hand flies to slap over my mouth.

Oh my God.

She's completely bare; he's glorious and...naked. I can see *everything.*

The size of his cock hits me like a baseball bat to the backs of my legs. I'm about to be on my knees for this man purely from the sight of his dick. He won't even know he has two women on their knees for him.

He holds that much power, and my stomach churns at the thought that he has this effect on me after everything. It might as well be as big as a baseball bat because, holy shit, he looks massive even from here.

He bends over, saying something into her ear, and she nods submissively. Grabbing the leather belt around her neck, he wraps it in his fist. Her tongue darts out, and he pulls on the belt, tugging her head toward him, and effortlessly slides his cock between her lips. His other hand, the one not clutching onto the leather, grips the nape of her neck, thrusting in and out of her mouth deliberately. I observe them as liquid heat rushes between my legs.

I shouldn't be watching this.

I should be crawling into bed.

But the window is open.

Ugh. It's his own damn fault.

The strong muscles in his shoulders stiffen, his head falling backward in pleasure. Seeing him all ragged like this makes my clit throb and my chest rise and fall more hectically with each breath I'm struggling to take.

I wonder what he's thinking about.

He claims her mouth like a man who's been celibate for years, which is flustering since women come in and out of his house every night. I nip my lip a little too hard when he buries himself to the hilt. She struggles, her arms gripping onto his thighs, but he still holds her there until he's ready to let her go. Her body convulses, choking on his cock. He releases her head, and she jerks back. Saliva drips down her chin and onto her breasts as she sucks in the air he deprived her of.

That's how I looked that night with Cameron and Brennan in the orchard. Their hands in my hair, gripping my neck, shoving themselves down my throat. Fire swarms in my lower belly, imagining it.

The woman bats her lashes at Colten, flinching as he reaches down, pinching her nipples.

I try to swallow, but my dehydrated throat is making my tongue feel like sandpaper. The water from my strands of hair trapped under the towel around me drips down my rib cage, the cool droplets doing nothing to chill my burning temperature.

I'm unable to understand why she enjoys being treated like that. But I can't get the night with the twins out of my head, so maybe there's a twisted part of me that finds pleasure in feeling helpless, too.

His hold on the belt becomes more forceful when he hauls her to her feet. Colten faces me now as he backs her into the window. She's nearly touching the glass, but then he shocks me when he grips her hips and flips her around to face me.

My panic meter is teetering on extreme.

Back away from the window, Taryn.

He turns her face, pressing his solid frame against hers, so her cheek and breasts are plastered to the window like she's one of those gooey holiday stickers I used to put on the window in my classroom. He arches her ass up in the air, sliding his hand between her thighs as a shock wave of tingles sparks between mine. As if he senses my presence, his head tilts upward, his gaze capturing me hostage.

Shit. Shit. Shit!

Colten's stare incapacitates every part of my body, but even acknowledging my presence doesn't stop him. His fingers drift between her thighs, back and forth. The tremble that racks through my body is catastrophic, and somehow, I think he senses it by the cunning smirk transforming his mouth.

Colten knew I was here the whole time. He purposefully left the curtains open, knowing I'd be watching from the attic like a ghost.

He removes his hand, using the same one to grip his cock as he tears a package with his teeth, slipping on a condom. Pushing his hips forward, he thrusts inside her, smacking his palm flat on the window for stability. I swear the vibration of the glass shudders through the yard, through the bones of the house, and straight to my clit.

He throws his head back again while shoving hers more aggressively into the glass as he drives into her ruthlessly.

Two can play this game.

A spark of courage shocks me, my trembling fingers dipping to where the towel is tucked, securing it around me. Plucking at the white cloth, I let it cascade down my body like water, turning it into a puddle at my feet. I see the reflection of my naked body in the mirror, my rosy nipples hard from the air conditioning traveling across my skin.

I shaved *everything* in the shower tonight because I never know when the next punishment will be in store. He can't see the lower half of my body, but it's still exciting and nerve-racking to let myself confidently have this moment.

It takes only a second for his eyes to find me again, exposed behind the window. His entire body goes rigid, solidifying whatever glimmer of boldness is bubbling in my veins.

I'm the one smirking now, and it feels good—freeing.

I could play a little more. Push it further. See how he likes to be toyed with.

Gliding my fingertips over my collarbone, I reminisce about how Brennan touched me. They slide down my chest, and I fondle my breasts, letting a whimper escape my throat that sounds thunderous in the silent void of my room.

My eyes focus on his sternum; the subtle hint of his chest rising and falling from this far away is mesmerizing. He's breathing harder than he was before. I'm making him breathless, and that authority goes straight to my stubborn head. It's time to push him a little further. He deserves every bit of torture for what he's put me through.

Holding up my middle and ring fingers, they hover in front of my lips.

Colten slowly shakes his head in warning.

I nod, saying yes.

He crashes his palm against the window so hard that I'm surprised he doesn't shatter the glass. He's giving me a glare that could kill me, but he can't touch me.

I'm untouchable. At least right now.

I chuckle, feeling lighter than I have in days.

Slipping my fingers in my mouth, I swirl my tongue to wet them. His thrusting movements slow as he watches me. I remove them, place them on my stomach, and leisurely slide them down my clammy and heated skin, not letting my eyes stray from his.

He shakes his head, telling me *no* again, but I don't listen.

My fingers slip between my soaked seam, and my mouth falls open, releasing a moan that causes Colten's body to constrict and jerk instantly. He strikes the glass angrily with his fist a few times before he pulls out, gripping the condom hastily and tossing it carelessly to the side before he climaxes all over the woman's back.

To be honest, I completely forgot she was there. I only saw him and me in this battle.

Withdrawing my fingers, I raise the wet middle one at him, and it glistens in the lamplight. The last thing I gift him is a fuck-you smile before spinning on my heels. I know without a doubt in my mind he's going to be pissed beyond what I thought possible.

I don't care, nor do I spare him a second glance.

I crawl into bed naked, waiting for the guilt to eat me alive. But it doesn't. I'm soaking in it right now, and it feels fantastic.

There's so much tension stirring and pulling at my body right now that I need to find another way to release it.

I need to go on a run tomorrow morning.

NINETEEN | COLTEN

It's only eight-thirty, and two hours of sweat cling to my neck. The sun pelts my back with its weak morning rays, tensing my body more than it has been as I walk up the yard leading from my cabin to the back door of the main house.

There's dirt lodged into the cracks of my hands, the smell of burnt wood gripping my clothes. I got up earlier than usual, deciding to take out my frustration on the piles of dead branches I've stacked up in the various plots of apple trees over the last few weeks.

Glancing up at Taryn's window towering above me, the blue sky dotted with clouds reflects off the glass.

My fists clench at my sides. Last night was...I don't even know what words to use.

I'm fucking pissed at her.

Fucking hot for her.

And completely and utterly fucked because I can't touch her. And if I do, once won't be enough.

I left the curtains in my office open on purpose last night, knowing my little ghost would be watching me as she has every night from the moment she arrived.

She's so curious, and she hates herself for it. I knew Taryn was watching me, though I initially didn't acknowledge her. Her gaze dragged across my skin like her eyes were the flame to a match, burning me alive and turning me animalistic.

Britt faded away, and the only thing consuming my thoughts was Taryn in her room—her body needy and pussy dripping from me taunting her.

I expected her to be a good little ghost and observe as I claimed Britt's throat. But then I smashed Britt against the window, and my resolve faltered. There Taryn was, standing in the window, exactly like I knew she would be. We stared at each other for a few minutes while she stood in nothing but that damn towel. Of course, the moment I closed my eyes for a second, I opened them to see her standing completely naked.

It caught me off guard, but she was playing me just like I was playing her. Her hands floated over her perky breasts, and when she held her middle and ring fingers up to her mouth, I knew what was about to happen.

Her mischievous smile and disobedience were bringing me closer and closer to coming, my thrusting into Britt quickening.

When I shook my head to tell her no, to not touch herself, I expected she'd push back.

A part of me wanted her to.

What I didn't anticipate happening was to come the exact second she inserted her fingers into her cunt.

That has never happened before. I take my time with sex—drag it out and edge them on until they are begging me to let them come. But Taryn was so distracting and making me fucking savage. And that moan that escaped Taryn's lips when her jaw dropped, and she thrust her fingers inside her—

Goddamn.

I couldn't hear the noise, but I felt it as if the current transferred through the bones of the house, across the yard, and through the floor straight to my throbbing cock.

Britt thought it was her doing—that I couldn't hold myself back.

It wasn't her. It was the ghost in the attic taunting me, her little parting gift, her glistening middle finger.

I'm losing control around her, so I tried overworking myself first thing this morning. But every time she crossed my mind, the hurricane in my chest raged, and my dick hardened when her naked body crossed my vision.

I open the back door, welcomed by a blast of cool air against my burning skin. Walking through the hallway to the foyer, I listen for voices, but it's quiet.

Too quiet.

I saunter past the staircase and take a right into the kitchen. Immediately, I see Tristan and Elena sitting at the dining table in front of a set of arched windows with a view of the expansive circular driveway. Elena hums happily as she dips her spoon into her cereal bowl while Tristan eats his and plays the Switch at the same time. They are accompanied by a few of Elena's stuffed animals placed in the other chairs.

She does that when Cam, Bren, and I can't have breakfast with them. Not a morning goes by where seeing our seats filled doesn't bother me. But two other people are missing from the table.

I wander to the coffeepot, take a mug out of the cabinet above, and pour a glass, observing as my two younger siblings immerse themselves in their sugary breakfast.

By themselves.

They shouldn't be alone.

I approach Elena and press my lips to her hair like I do every morning if I can return to the house. "Where's Miss Taryn?"

Her response is immediate. "Running," Elena says innocently with a mouthful of cereal.

My muscles tauten.

I tilt my head, clenching my jaw. "Miss Taryn is running?"

Elena scoops up a spoonful of fruit loops and bobs her head. "She wanted to go on a run. She said to eat my cereal while she's gone, and then we'll play with my stuffed animals when she gets back."

Adrenaline shoots through my bloodstream, reaching a dangerous level. "Where is Jess?"

She shoves a spoonful in her mouth. "Sleeping," she answers around the silverware.

My focus finds Tristan, who is flicking around a couple of Honey Nut Cheerios floating on the surface of his milk.

"Did she take Rossco, Tristan?" I ask.

He nods.

"When did she leave?" I push harder.

He shrugs. It's always simple reactions and answers from him. "A little while ago."

I doubt the twins know since they left around six this morning for a meeting at the packaging headquarters located off the property.

Whipping out my phone, I navigate to our tracking app for her microchip. The little blue dot slowly moves across the screen, down the long driveway. She's near the big bend in the road near the cliff—the mile mark for the orchard before it drops to the Columbia below—where it continues through the forest to the front gate.

Fuck.

Looks like Little Ghost is finally going to receive her punishment from me for disobeying the rules. My hands itch in anticipation, but my cognizance reminds me why I shouldn't touch her. It takes one taste—only one touch for an obsession to grow and eat away at you.

My features harden, and Elena scans my facial expression. "Is she in trouble?" she asks softly.

"You know how sometimes I say I'll spank you if you aren't

listening or if you talk back?" She nods nervously. "Well, Miss Taryn isn't listening."

Her little blue eyes expand so large I'm afraid they'll pop out and float in her cereal bowl.

I remove my truck keys from my pocket and point at Tristan. "You two stay here. I'll be back."

They both nod as I place my mug on the table and march out of the kitchen and through the hallway to the back door. Before I know it, I'm heading straight for my driveway, focusing on the black Ford I bought last year.

I climb in, not bothering with the seat belt as I throw it into reverse. When I get it turned around, I slam on the gas, taking the road around the hill and the side of the house where it intersects with the main driveway.

Dust billows behind me, the speedometer reaching thirty miles an hour, pushing the pulse in my neck even harder. My truck breaks through the threshold of the orchard, apple trees lining each side. My eyes are locked on the blue dot on the phone screen in my hand.

"When I find you, Little Ghost," I growl, shaking my head as I get closer.

Then I see her. She's in little black running shorts and a green fitted tank top that hugs her figure. Her ponytail whips back and forth, almost matching the pace of her feet pounding into the gravel with each step. Rossco runs ahead of her, and for a second, I think she's too distracted to hear my truck barreling down the road, but then she looks over her shoulder and increases speed.

She's in a full-out sprint now.

I slam on the gas and tug the wheel to the right, whipping the truck past Taryn. One tire rolls off the side onto the grass, so I can safely get around her, but I also want to scare the shit out of her. Once I'm past her and Rossco, I jerk back onto the road and slam on the brakes when I'm a safe enough distance in front, throwing it into park. I can see where the plot of trees abruptly stops in front of the truck—the bend in the road a little farther on the cliffside.

I glance in the rearview mirror, clutching the wheel with my fists, and she stops. She places her hands on her hips, attempting to catch her breath. I throw the driver's side door open and stalk toward her with pure irritation.

She walks backward in a pathetic attempt to avoid me. "Colten," my name emerges breathlessly. "What are you doing?" She swallows, placing a hand on her chest. "How did you find me?"

I slant my head. "Running, Little Ghost?"

Her eyes dart between mine, her body tensing when I stand directly in front of her.

A bead of sweat cascades down her temple. "Yes," she answers, and I arch a brow. Taryn shakes her head. "I mean, yes, but no. I am running, but I'm not *running*," she huffs.

I point to her and then Rossco, who's plopped down in the shade under one of the apple trees, panting away. "You just wanted to go on a run?" I question disbelievingly. "Had a little energy you needed to run off?"

She crosses one arm over the other. "As a matter of fact, yes. And you're to blame." She gestures to me.

"Why am I to blame?" I counter.

She rolls her eyes and licks her bottom lip. "You know why. You aren't a saint, Colten. You intentionally left those drapes wide open!"

"And you stood there watching as I spread *her* wide open, Little Ghost."

Taryn's jaw pops. "I saw you wrap your belt around her neck. I was watching to make sure you didn't choke the poor girl to death! After all, you have a very questionable track record with women." Her fingernail taps against one of my pecs, my heart thrashing at her touch. "For all I know, you keep your curtains closed so I can't see all the corpses from your visitors every night scattered around the floor."

I smirk. *Nice try, but I know you stand there observing to catch when they leave.* My mysterious activities have piqued her interest.

My arms fold across my chest, her gaze falling from my eyes to my biceps, where the decaying leaves transform into crow feathers on my forearm. Her fingertips drum into her thigh as if she's trying not to touch me.

"So, you're telling me you don't stand at that window and watch them leave after I'm finished with them every night?"

She takes a step toward me. "Doesn't mean you don't have some stuffed in your closet to use later," she banters.

The sunlight glistens off the sheen of moisture coating her skin, my eyes locking on a drop gliding down the valley of her breasts in that tight tank top. I bet they taste as good as they look.

"I prefer my women very much alive and begging to be fucked," I reply honestly.

Her lips part just as the breeze blows a strand of her brown hair across them. I'm unsure if the breeze or my words cause her to shudder, but I hope it's the latter.

I take another step toward her, forcing her breasts to clash against my chest. I lower my tone, brushing my fingers across her jawline. *Did you like watching?* "Did seeing me fuck her make you wet?" Her erratic breathing hitches, making my cock twitch. "Did you crawl under those covers and finish what you started with your fingers?"

She slaps my hand away with hers. "Yep," she pops the P. A corner of her mouth lifts mischievously. "And the entire time, I thought about your twin brothers," she says dryly.

That one response from her fucking mouth is like a missile straight to the wall I built. Red-hot fury flows through my veins, detonating any ounce of self-control I have. The memory of her smart mouth in my office and what I said I'd do if she talked to me like that again has me swiftly throwing her five-foot-something frame over my shoulder.

She keeps belting my name and squirming in my hold, but my rough hand smacking her ass shuts her up.

She weighs the same as a sack of apples. But I'd bet my soul to the devil that Little Ghost probably tastes sweeter.

TWENTY | TARYN

I went on a run.

A run.

I wasn't running away.

I wasn't escaping.

I was blowing off steam.

But somehow, I still find myself draped over Colten's shoulder like I'm the sweat rag he's using after a workout at the gym. His muscles flex under my frame, and my eyes roll. *What it must be like to be that gym towel skating over his body.*

Rossco is in the distance, rolling contently in the grass shaded by trees on the side of the road. His black body continues shrinking in size as Colten marches me to his truck to take me back to the house.

I squirm, resulting in his palm smacking my ass again. The sting tightens every muscle in his firm hold. A whimper escapes my lips.

We reach the truck, and he flings the door open and effortlessly tosses me into the passenger seat. The center console digs into my back, and my legs hang off the seat out the door.

"Ready for your punishment, Little Ghost?"

"Colten, I was just on a run! I swear," I squeal, my heart bashing against my ribs so violently I'm afraid they are going to explode.

He tsks. "Maybe so. But you've broken some of the other rules, too." I tilt my head, not understanding. What did I do? "You left Elena and Tristan alone."

"Jess is there!"

"She's still asleep, Taryn," Colten responds.

My eyes pierce his. "Semantics. You can't tell me she gets up with them every morning when they wake up. You're just digging for reasons to punish me!" My clit throbs at the thought.

He smirks, making him appear like a dark god. "Do you remember what I said that day in the office when you used that tone with me?"

Yes. I don't have to think about it because I've thought about it more than I want to.

"Do you want me to pull down my panties so you can drug test me, sir?"

"If you speak to me like that again, I'll bend you over this desk, rip them off, and shove them in your hot little mouth as punishment for using a tone like that with me."

Oh, God.

I shouldn't want him to touch me, but my limbs are vibrating with the need to feel his hands on me. He reaches for the band of my shorts and tugs them down, his eyes falling to the red lacey thong I'm wearing. His jaw flexes, and I know he sees the spot on my underwear that shows him the reaction I have to his presence.

He places his palms on the seat and leans over me, holding my eyes captive. "I keep my promises."

Drifting his hands up my thighs, my legs fall open spontaneously to give him better access. When Colten's thumb contacts my clit, the slightest touch sends sparks bolting through my body. He moves in circular motions, the wet material on my sensitive bundle of nerves forcing me to lean against the center console. I grip the seat, my lashes fluttering at how talented his fingers are.

"Look how soaked you are."

I inhale a sharp breath.

My panties rub and tighten against my skin painfully, and I don't realize what's happening until the sound of material tearing reaches my ears. Chills break out across my skin, and I sit up, my eyes magnetized to his heated ones. He holds up his hand, my torn underwear hanging from his index finger.

"Open wide," he orders.

I swallow, letting my legs fall open wider.

His head tilts, unamused. "Open your mouth."

Oh, shit.

I shake my head at the same time he nods. Inhaling a deep breath, I open my mouth, and he shoves the red material in with his fingers so my own arousal is sitting on my tongue.

Colten grips my thighs and tugs me to the very edge, granting himself easy access because of the lift he has on his truck. He adjusts the seat, sliding it forward. He rests one of my feet on the dash and slides the other between the wall and the headrest, spreading me completely open.

I try to speak to tell him I've never done anything like this before, but it comes out as gibberish through the underwear he stuffed in my mouth.

He laughs at my attempt and places his palm on my chest, pressing my body back down. The other hand slithers below my tank top, pushing the material up my abdomen. He cups a breast, my heart thumping when he moves to the other, pinching a nipple, and my back arches at the pleasure I get from the pain.

His eyes lock onto my dripping core. "God, this cunt is

perfect, wet, and ready for me to take whatever I want; however, I want."

He keeps one hand switching between my breasts while the other lowers to my pussy. He swipes a finger through my center, spreading my arousal around as he presses his thumb to my clit. Colten's movements are precise—so mind-bending that my nails are digging into the passenger seat hard enough that I wonder if they'll pierce through the leather.

I lift my head to watch him, and the moment he meets my eye, his head tips down, his hot breath fanning over my pussy. He grins against me before gliding his tongue up and down my seam, controlling his movements like an oral mastermind. He holds my gaze, and I moan when the tip of his tongue flicks my clit, stirring the warmth in my belly. By the way his eyes scan my face, I can tell he enjoys watching me watch him. Warmth floods through my body, melting me into the seat.

He straightens and slaps my pussy, making me screech through the panties in my mouth. "Do you think you'll like coming on my fingers more than yours?"

His words pour over my blistering skin like lava, searing me to the bone. My already muddled breathing from running is turning into pants with every erotic and filthy sentence emerging from his mouth.

Holding up his middle and ring finger like I did last night, he spits on my core and shoves them into my wet pussy with his palm facing upward. He immediately finds the spot that has my body shaking beneath him and my eyes rolling back into my head. I moan, hearing the wet sounds that his fingers and my pussy are making.

His head falls back down, his tongue magically over-working that other spot that has specks of white dotting my vision. All three sensations of his fingers thrusting in and out, and my panties rubbing against my tongue while his flicks up and down, licking and sucking, have my vision blurring and tears gathering in the corners of my eyes from how good it feels to be touched.

Colten glances back up at me. While one of his hands works inside of me, the other reaches for the panties in my mouth, pulling them out. He tosses them to the back seat.

"Did my brothers make you feel this good?" he asks seriously, the pace of his talented fingers starting to make the corners of my vision blacken.

"No," I breathe, nearing the crest of my orgasm. "Oh, shit. Colten—"

He pulls his fingers out and stares at my core. "Your cunt is so pretty when it's flushed and begging for more than just my fingers."

The longer he stands there, the more it fades, and fades, until my heart plummets, wanting more. But I know he won't give it to me.

His whistle slices through the air, making me jump. "Let's go, Rossco," he yells, walking around the front of the truck to the driver's seat.

I sit up, my body sore and aching from the position he had me in, and I pull my shorts up. He opens the back door, letting Rossco climb in before he situates himself in the seat next to me.

I reach for my seat belt angrily and secure the buckle. "You're an asshole."

The only response I get from him for the entire ride back to the house is his vexing smirk. I'm thankful the silence ends when he pulls around the roundabout, and we both hop out, heading into the house. But I'm marching straight to the bathroom on the bottom floor near the kitchen.

I need to get out of here.

Not because of Cameron and Brennan.

Not because of Jess.

Not because of those two sweet little faces in that kitchen with me this morning.

It's because of *him*. Colten fucking Lindenvale.

"Miss Taryn!" I don't even bother to stop and speak to Elena as she runs toward me from the living room.

Parading straight past her, I walk toward the back entryway but take a left into the bathroom and slam the door. The sound and vibration shake the whole bottom floor.

If Jess isn't awake, she probably is now.

I turn and press my back against the door, sliding down it with my knees propped up, and release the tears I haven't managed to cry since I got here.

I sob into my arms, feeling completely helpless and trapped, but between my sobs, I hear a sweet little voice on the other side of the door in the foyer—loud enough that I can understand them.

"You made her mad," Elena says, I'm guessing to Colten.

Colten says nothing.

"She's going to leave," Elena shouts. "I like her, but you had to spank her and make her sad!"

I chuckle through the tears, not believing my ears. He told her he was going to spank me?

He remains silent.

"She's going to leave because of you and never come back, just like Mommy and Daddy," she screams, the tears evident in her voice, the tone shattering my heart into millions of tiny pieces.

Her little footsteps pound on the stairs. She's headed for her room.

"I'm sorry, Elena," Colten apologizes loudly. "I'll fix it—I'll talk to her."

But Elena doesn't respond; there's just another slam of a door—this one soft and innocent.

I close my eyes, resting my head against the door. My heart

softens, wanting to wrap her in my arms and tell her I'm not going anywhere. It's almost been a week of being trapped on the hill, and this kid is already getting to me.

Making me attached. And that's a problem.

Because as badly as I need to get off this property after this morning, I think the tiny human upstairs needs me more.

TWENTY-ONE | COLTEN

I fucked up.

I should've ignored my dick for one goddamn second and called the twins when I found out she ran—was running...whatever—and had them take care of Taryn since they already touched her once.

"Did seeing me fuck her make you wet? Did you crawl under those covers and finish what you started with your fingers?"

"Yep. And the entire time, I thought about your twin brothers."

She raided my head with her manipulation and sharp tongue. She knew exactly what to say to shatter every ounce of my resolve. As if she knew the woman I saw writhing beneath me and taking my cock wasn't Britt, but her instead.

Red flooded my vision when she said she was envisioning my brothers. Each word was a needle puncturing through my skin, the ink leaking through muscle, riding the current of my veins until the image of my brothers with her tattooed itself on my brain.

Dusk covers the hill with a clear navy and purple sky, the color reflecting off the wall of windows at the front of the house. I flip the steaks, watching as the smoke from the grill on the patio spirals up into the air. I'm so on edge and tense that the sizzling meat grates against my skin.

Elena hasn't talked to me all day, and Taryn has been avoiding me and staying in her room. Jess scowls at me suspiciously every time I see her, suspecting something went wrong between Taryn and me. I've been fuming with myself, not wanting to discuss it with Jess after a five-year-old yelled at me.

Eventually, I drove all my anger into work, driving the ATV around to fertilize and burn piles. After that, I mowed the plots and moved irrigation, and as if that wasn't enough to reduce the self-loathing, I went to my office to answer emails and check accounts, hopping on the occasional phone call. My evening ended with me releasing any energy and tension I had left in our gym in the shop.

When I got back to the house, it was nearly eight, and the sun was setting. I didn't bother to shower. I just wanted to avoid the scrutinizing looks from my brothers, so I grabbed the steaks out of the fridge and found myself at the grill.

Grilling calms me. So here I am, chugging water, watching the sky darken with each passing minute as the meat hisses.

The screen door slams, and Cameron appears beside me with a beer. He lifts it to his lips, a drop of water from the condensation dripping down the glass and onto his hand. My mouth waters at the thought of feeling the hoppy carbonation on my tongue.

Five years sober, and I've never struggled as hard as I am now. I clench my fingers around the tongs, resisting the urge to snatch his beer from him and take a swig. But taking one drink to numb my issues could force me down a path I'd rather not explore.

His eyes bore into the side of my head as I flip a steak. I snap my eyes to his. "Why the fuck are you staring at me like that?"

"You want to tell me why all our girls are moody as hell?

Bren and I haven't gotten a word out of them. Tristan hasn't spoken either, but that's normal for him."

Our girls.

The muscles in my back constrict. A wave of guilt washes over me, and at the same time, the breeze shifts the smoke in my direction.

He takes another drink and leans against the pillar. "We contemplated periods being the cause, but Elena is *way* too young for that."

I stay silent, my eyes fastened on the meat.

"There's a letter from Dad for you on the counter."

As if my body wasn't strained enough, my frame solidifies. "Place it in the drawer with the others," I say, void of emotion.

He knew what my answer would be. He didn't even need to ask.

Cam releases a sigh. "It's been almost five years, Colt, and he'll be there for eleven more."

I grab the plate next to the grill and stack the steaks. "We've had this conversation. He doesn't deserve a word from me, you, or Bren, and Jess—" I raise my voice. "And he sure as hell doesn't deserve drawings from those two young children in there," I point to the house, "who don't even know they're writing to a man who let his fucking addiction take their mother away from them."

His knuckles turn white around the bottle. "We still don't know if he's the reason she's gon—"

I slam the grill shut harder than I mean to, but my blood is boiling as hot as the flesh of these steaks in my hand. "Cameron," I warn, not wanting to talk about this.

They don't know it, but I was there. The amount of blood in my parents' bedroom burned into my eyes right before Mom ran out the front door to her car and drove away, with my father trailing in his.

He came back early the next morning.

She didn't.

And I left for days because I couldn't face him after what I saw.

There's no guessing or theorizing what happened—no giving that callous man any benefit of the doubt.

I didn't speak a word to him the three months leading to his arrest—not that he gave me much of a chance since he was drowning in a bottle of scotch every night.

The responsibility of this family and company might have been dumped on my shoulders, but watching the bright blue and red flashing lights of vehicles speeding up our driveway while I held a sleeping baby Elena in my arms was a pinnacle moment. Well, that and watching the bastard with his hands cuffed getting shoved into the back seat of a cop car.

I vowed then, staring down at Elena's innocent face as the cop cars disappeared into the fog consuming the orchard, that I would protect this family at all costs.

I was twenty-two. I knew it would be hard, but I understood I could be better than him. For their sake, I would be better than he was.

This is the reason I can't touch Taryn again. She is off limits as much as that beer bottle in Cameron's hand.

Obsessions have the power to destroy you.

Addictions have the dominance to control you.

And the twins may be able to play with her, but I'm the one who can't afford to fuck up.

She's the one thing this family needs. I will not obliterate that just because I can't keep my hands to myself despite how right she feels. How good it felt when her soft skin melted into my palms. How confusing it was when even the slightest touch made me want to shove her away but tug her into my chest at the same time.

I hand the plate of steaks to Cameron. "Please take these to the table. I'll go get Elena and tell Taryn dinner is ready."

He nods and takes a swig of beer before returning to the house. I follow, but instead of heading for the dining room where I hear Jess and Bren chatting, I take the stairs and enter the dark hallway on the second floor.

Elena's door is cracked, the light from the lantern stars the twins and I hung shining through the opening. I press my hand to the door, pushing it open enough to see Elena curled into— I freeze.

Elena sniffles, holding in a sob that shakes her chest. "Colt sc-scared you."

Taryn sits crisscross on the floor with Elena on her lap. Elena leans into her embrace, clutching her T-shirt in her tiny fists.

"He did scare me, but he just wanted me to come back to you," Taryn soothes, stroking her soft, tousled brown hair.

I swallow, all my focus devoted to them.

I'm ashamed. Frightening Taryn into staying here is calculating. Everything we have done is screwed up, yet my brothers and I refuse to let her leave. I feared my father, but I don't want Elena to be frightened of me.

"But if he scares you m-more," she cries, "you'll leave, and won't come back. Mommy and Daddy have n-never come back."

I place my hand on the doorframe, hanging my head. This conversation is making me nauseous. Another reason why we can't let Taryn—

"I'm not going anywhere, baby," Taryn coos, rocking her to stop the tears.

Elena peers up at her, her blue eyes puffy and red in the yellow glow of the lanterns hanging from the ceiling.

"Promise?" Elena sniffs, holding up her pinkie finger.

Taryn smiles, holding out hers as their fingers intertwine. "I promise...at least until you don't need me anymore."

Until you don't need me anymore.

Those words echo in my eardrums. Because there will come a day when we don't need her anymore, and she will walk away.

My heart plunges into my stomach, the vessel churning with the acid. The reality is we can't keep her forever. Eventually, Elena and Tristan will be old enough to take care of themselves, and she'll have no use here.

She's here now, and she's not leaving. She promised she wasn't.

Elena twirls a brown lock of Taryn's hair around her finger. "I think I'll always need you," she says so softly that I barely hear it over the hammering in my chest.

Elena is attached. Cameron and Brennan are getting attached. So, I shove my emotions further into the bottomless depths of my soul, telling myself I won't get attached too. I need to tread lightly with her. Around her.

I push open the door farther and peek my head in, clearing my throat. "Dinner is ready."

Their heads whip toward me simultaneously from being startled. Taryn's eyes search mine, and she nods.

"Why don't you go wash up, and I'll meet you downstairs?" she says, lightly tapping Elena's back with her palm.

Elena gets up and walks toward me, her glassy eyes looking me over.

My apologetic tone is strained. "I'm sorry, Elena."

She wraps her arms around my legs, pressing her flushed face into my dirty jeans. "It's okay."

She escapes the room, leaving Taryn and me.

Taryn walks toward me; each step she takes is loud and thunderous, though she's creeping toward me at the pace of the pet turtle my brothers and I had when I was ten.

My arm is still propped on the door, the heat between us sizzling and crackling the closer she gets. A bolt of lightning flashes when she peers into my eyes with those big brown ones.

"You do terrify me," she chokes out, her gaze not straying from mine. "But my weakness is feeling responsible for caring for kids like that." Her eyes glisten with unshed tears. "It's one of the reasons I became a teacher. But you already knew that because you asked me about my weakness in that first interview. And you're using it, using *me* to your full advantage, because you knew the moment I met them that I would care too much to walk away. And I think that's why you chose me."

The only thing I can manage to do is nod. She's right. She was the perfect choice. Yet her words don't make me feel remorse for my actions.

If I die a greedy man who made choices for his benefit, then my soul deserves to rot in hell. But if I die a selfless brother because I put my family first, then I can burn in hell knowing I gave my soul so I could protect theirs.

That's why I continue to let them write letters—why my siblings are oblivious to what happened that night after we all heard the glass shatter. Their hearts don't deserve to be plagued like mine.

I've kept the truth from them so they would never carry the pain of knowing their father stood before the woman he was supposed to love, clutching a bloody shard of glass in one hand and gripping the neck of a bottle in the other.

So, I am a selfish man.

Taryn is here because I'm a selfish brother.

My siblings heard the fights. They witnessed the screaming and the decay of their marriage. But the weight of the truth about how our parents' marriage ended is mine to bear alone.

They deserve to grow up in a world where love is worthy and isn't destined to fail.

Taryn points out the door, her lecture muted in my ears. The hollow feeling in my chest intensifies. I always feel nothing for anyone unless it's the five people downstairs I'd give my life for.

She glares at me. "But I'm staying for Elena and Tristan. Only. For. Them."

I exhale a long breath, repeating her words. "Only for them."

With this pace, Elena and Tristan are bound to fall for her. Now that I'm stepping back, so will my brothers. And everyone will fall hard since nobody else has shown them this type of dedication besides me. Taryn's staying because she's gentle and compassionate. She is putting their needs above hers, though we abducted her and have held her against her will.

Someday, my siblings will grow to understand what that type of affection, that type of love, feels like from someone who isn't blood.

And just because I don't believe in it doesn't mean they shouldn't.

TWENTY-TWO | TARYN

I glide the knife through my steak, failing miserably to ignore the sets of eyes slicing into my skin, similar to how my blade slashes through the meat. The sound of metal cutting through flesh is louder than the deafening silence around the mahogany dinner table. The chandelier overhead, dangling with dainty crystals, illuminates every tense muscle and feature on everyone's face.

Occasionally, a muscle twitches, an audible exhale is released, and a mouth opens as if someone wants to speak and then thinks better of it.

It's remarkable how a glittering chandelier can hold the same effect as a light in an interrogation room. And I can't help but feel like I'm the subject, feeling isolated and scrutinized.

But there are no confessions.

At least not yet anyway.

Cameron's inquisitive gaze imprisons me, making me think he doesn't know the particular activities that occurred between Colten and me earlier.

On one side of me, Tristan flicks around a green bean, watching it roll across his plate. On the other, Jess won't meet anyone's eyes. Brennan and Elena are across from me. She keeps trying to steal the knife to cut her own pieces, but he keeps batting her dainty hand away.

Cameron's eyes narrow in suspicion, the subtle movement causing me to squirm while Colten's jaw hardens further than I deem possible. I could probably slice my meat on his face and not puncture his frustratingly perfect chin.

Cameron snatches his beer from the coaster and takes a drink, slumping against the back of the chair. I shift uncomfortably under his unmoving glare.

"Can someone tell me what's going on?" Cameron says, speaking the first word since we've sat down.

The clanking of cutlery on glass plates halts, leaving only the sound of heavy breaths from everyone at the table. I didn't think the silence could intensify, but I was wrong.

Colten's eyes find mine, and I falter, shifting my attention to my half-eaten plate.

Elena peers around and stabs a small piece of meat, plopping it in her mouth. "Colt spanked Miss Taryn today."

A gasp slips out of my throat, my eyes widening in mortification at the same time Brennan chokes. Some of his beer escapes his mouth, spraying the table. He sets the glass down while his eyes dart between Colten and me.

"Elena," Jessica snips. "Where did you hear that?"

Her eyebrows pull together. "Colt said she wasn't listening, so he went and spanked her and brought her back home."

Somehow, I manage a nervous glance at Cameron, noticing the slits in his eyes as they bounce probingly between Colten and me. "You ran again."

"Running. I went running!" I knit my arms over my chest. "Like, for exercise," I clarify because nobody seems to understand.

"How far did you go?" Brennan asks, clearing his throat.

Colten picks up his napkin, wiping the corner of his mouth. "She almost made it to the cliffs," he informs with a flat tone.

Cameron cocks his head.

"You guys are ridiculous," I mutter. "If I'm going to stay here, I need to get some fresh air by myself once in a damn while."

"Language, Taryn," Cameron warns. "You don't want to be spanked again, do you?"

I think he's joking...I think.

Either way, his threat emanating from the depths of his throat has goosebumps peppering my skin.

"Well, since we got that out of the way," Jessica sighs sarcastically with a roll of her eyes. "I need to go pick up some things for school before I leave in four days. I'm going to head into Cascade Springs tomorrow."

Brennan lifts his glass to his lips, pausing when he mulls over her comment. "Wait, I thought Cameron and I were taking you in a little over a week?"

She shrugs. "If you guys can take me, I'd like to go earlier to settle into my dorm room and get to know my roommate better before classes start."

Colten places his napkin from his lap onto the table. "I can give you the card to go out tomorrow and buy whatever you need."

"Can I go with her?" All six pairs of eyes at the table snap to me. "I want to go with her," I repeat when none of them utter a word. "I need some new underwear," I manage to speak through gritted teeth.

Colten huffs out a laugh, low and husky. It's a laugh that has no business being so sexy at a moment such as this one. "Not a chance. Not after what you did today."

"I went on a run to get exercise, *Colten*. If I were trying to escape, I would've put up a fight when you threw me in the truck." *But instead, I let you suck on my clit and edge me on because you're an ass who was punishing me for no reason.* I hate to admit that I liked it. "And I didn't put up a fight, did I?"

He raises a brow. "No. You were—submissive."

Submissive.

For one word, it holds enough power to have the cords in my body twisting into knots and sucking all the oxygen out of the room. I'm not the only one who notices the word choice. The corner of Brennan's mouth tugs upward into this blood-heating smirk. Cameron, on the other hand, is glaring at Colten as if he's the one who cursed at the table—that look has marked me several times before. As for me, visions of Colten with that woman, obeying him on her knees, flash behind my eyes.

I give him a fake smile and look at Cameron and Brennan. Cameron has his arms folded across his broad chest, the tendons in his muscles straining.

"Plus, if I were trying to run tomorrow too, I wouldn't leave Rossco here, would I?" I convincingly throw that out there.

Cameron releases a breath laced with frustration. "Fine. You guys can take Elena and Tristan too, because they both need school supplies."

<hr>

A LITTLE HAND whips out to snatch the container of rainbow sprinkles on the kitchen counter. Elena's arm bumps into the jar of cherries, causing the glass to wobble and slide across the marble.

My nanny reflexes kick in, my hand barely grasping it before it can tumble and create a red sticky mess all over the floor. We don't need a dessert crime scene on our hands.

A whooshing sound has my head turning rapidly, but I'm not quick enough. Tristan has an Everest-sized mound of whipped cream in his bowl. There's chocolate ice cream somewhere underneath, but all I see is white fluffy foam loaded with more sugar than he needs.

"Can I have three cherries?" he asks.

I can't help but smile. It's one of the first things he's said to me that isn't a few measly syllables. I nod, hoping this tiny interaction, as small as it may be, will help him feel more comfortable around me. So far, all my attempts to get him to interact with me have failed.

"Go for it." I slide the cherry jar across the countertop to him. He swipes a hand across his forehead, moving strands of long hair out of his bright blue-green eyes.

"I'm done!" Elena's bright voice seizes my attention.

My eyes widen.

Oh, Jesus.

My concentration should've been focused on her more than Tristan. Not only does she have the two scoops of ice cream I placed in her pink plastic bowl, but her mass of whipped cream coated in a layer of chocolate sauce, sprinkles, and five cherries on top is nearly toppling over. It's the ice cream Tower of Pisa.

Her brothers won't be happy with me giving them all this sugar before bed. *Lord, please bring on the sugar crash early.*

"Okay!" I clap my hands the exact second she reaches for the sprinkles again like she doesn't already have enough. "Cameron and Brennan have the movie set up. So, let's take our ice cream into the living room. Yeah?"

Elena nods and hops off the stool, reaching up for her bowl. She runs out of the room in her Snow White nightgown with Tristan following closely behind her.

When I confessed that *Snow White* was my favorite movie when I was her age, she immediately threw on her nightgown and begged the boys to watch it tonight. Of course, they couldn't say no to her small, pouty lips and puppy eyes. Cameron and Brennan are watching it with us while Jess is upstairs creating a packing list for college, and Colten is back in his cabin doing God knows what.

Or who.

Sliding my spoon into my ice cream, I switch off the lights in the kitchen and head to the living room, plopping on the large couch Cameron is on since Brennan is in the recliner, nearly asleep already. Both Tristan and Elena are sprawled out on the floor on top of the bed of pillows and blankets they made earlier.

A chill sweeps across my bare legs, so I reach for the blanket draped across the back of the couch and tug it over my legs. I scoop up some ice cream, savoring the sweet flavor of peanut butter and chocolate dancing on my taste buds as the movie starts.

Partway through the beginning, Cameron rises from the couch and shuts off the main lights, the only brightness coming from the television screen and the porch light drifting through the wall of windows.

A leg brushes against mine, and I turn my head leisurely to see Cameron shifting beside me. His proximity distracts me from the scene where Snow White is frantically running from the Huntsman. The warmth radiating from his skin boosts my body temperature enough that I consider removing the blanket draped across me.

He's close.

So close that his thigh touching mine makes my heart flutter, and my stomach flip. He stretches his arm, draping it across the back of the couch behind me. I disregard him and the intimate moment as Snow White sees the shadows shifting into scarier things.

"Is that how scared you were, running from us that night? As if Bren and I were two huntsmen chasing after you?" Cameron murmurs.

His breath skates across my neck, soaking into my prickling

skin. God, I should just ignore him. Pretend his words don't hold the power to melt me faster than the frozen dessert in my bowl.

I eat another spoonful, and my tongue darts out, slowly licking the cream off the silverware. His heated eyes latch onto my mouth, my slow movements making him shift uncomfortably beside me. Deciding to ignore him again, my eyes find the screen, but my psyche doesn't stray from thinking about him beside me. I'm painfully aware of him and his effect on me.

Everyone remains silent as the movie slowly transitions to the scene where the Evil Queen hands Snow White the poisoned apple. The red color of the fruit holds my attention, memories of the night they drugged me flooding back.

The fatigue.

The nausea.

They spiked my margarita, but I still can't remember anything that followed. I reach into the bottomless depths, my brows pulling together in thought as I dig my fingers through the box of blurred memories that I can't piece together.

Cameron's calloused fingers drift over my neck and tangle in my hair. Each brush of his skin against mine causes me to shiver.

His rough voice lowers to a whisper. "You ate our poisoned apple, and here you are."

Turning my head, I look at Tristan and Elena knocked out on their mountain of pillows and blankets. It's probably from all the sugar I let them have.

I lean back, allowing his arm, draped over the back of the couch, to press into my shoulder blades. "Sleeping death would've been easier," I murmur.

Cameron's dark chuckle graces my ears. His hand glides under the blanket, the pads of his fingertips contacting the skin on my inner thigh, lighting sparklers on my skin.

His warm lips skim the shell of my ear. "But the nightmare is so much sweeter. Wouldn't you agree?"

He drags his hand up and down. Each time he ventures upward, he approaches the hem of my shorts and pauses his teasing movements. The muscles in my jaw clench right before his fingers dip under the thin fabric, forcing me to hold my breath as his warm digits brush against my panties. I unintentionally release a whimper.

Rapidly moving my hands under the blanket, I grab his wrist forcefully to tell him to stop.

This should not be happening.

Not here.

Not with two young kids asleep on the floor below us. But his strong hand moves anyway, and my thighs open a little further.

God, I am so turned on right now, it's embarrassing. I grind into his hand inadvertently, and heat crawls up my neck, flushing my cheeks.

"You can't help yourself, can you?" I feel him smiling beside me, and he takes it as an invitation to dip below the silk underwear; his middle finger glides over my wet seam. His groan rumbles in his chest, the vibration causing me to shudder beside him.

"We aren't thirteen years old, Cameron. You should not be touching me like this here," I quietly say through my teeth.

He leans in closer. "Who the fuck touched you like this when you were thirteen?"

I shake my head, looking at him over my shoulder, noticing Brennan isn't in the recliner. He probably went to bed. "Nobody. That's not what I meant," I sigh. "But you're acting like a hormonal teenager who can't sit through a movie with a girl beside him."

He arches an unamused brow, and I bite back my smile. The flashes of light from the television dance across his features in an array of colors. We sit silently for a second before his jaw pops, followed by a strand of mussed hair that falls onto his forehead. Clearly not caring about our surroundings and proximity to his younger siblings—who are still passed out on the floor—he snakes his arm around my waist and effortlessly tugs me onto his lap.

I choke on my tongue and the air in my lungs at his rapid movements. The solid ridge of his cock presses against my center as he uses the muscles in his arms to push my body down harder, his massive bulge shooting liquid fire between my legs.

His rough hand snatches the nape of my neck possessively. "Then don't grind on my hand because I'll take that as an invitation to glide my fingers into your needy cunt."

My mouth parts, the swirling hurricane of lust growing out of control. The need for him to take me here and now is so strong. I just need *something*. Any kind of euphoria he can give me, especially after Colten fucked me with his fingers and tongue today.

But I've been out of my birth control pills. Obviously, I didn't think I would need them when I moved here since getting abducted by three hot brothers was the furthest possible thing from my mind.

Damn these Lindenvale boys and their hypnotizing physiques. They're screwing with my head, and a part of me wants to give each of them a piece just to see what they do. See if they can probe and dissect the diseased parts of my brain because anyone in their right mind wouldn't be contemplating how each one of them could bring me pleasure.

I scramble off Cameron, tripping over the blanket as I rise to my feet with the same clumsiness of a basset hound tripping over their ears. Ignoring his heated eyes branding my skin, I grab all the ice cream bowls off the coffee table and rush into the kitchen.

It's blistering hot in this house.

I toss the bowls in the sink and grab the container of sprinkles, taking it back to the giant walk-in pantry with the same marble countertops and shelves as the kitchen. I don't need the stool, so rising on my toes, I reach and place the sprinkles back, hoping that busying myself will dampen the need for Cameron to touch me more.

Who am I kidding? There isn't a distraction in the world that could keep me from lusting over him.

The quiet click of a door sends chills through my skin, and I lower to the flats of my feet in panic.

I whip around, my heart hammering uncontrollably.

Cameron has his arms knit over his chest, with the pantry door shut behind him, and a wicked smile lifts his lips. "A win is a win, Princess. I'm ready to claim my reward."

TWENTY-THREE | TARYN

I step backward, my back pressing painfully into the marble countertop as he advances toward me. Each progressive step thunders through the floor and zips through my limbs, making me shake more.

I swallow the dryness in my throat.

He reaches for the hem of his blue shirt, removing it flawlessly to reveal the hard lines of his muscles, each one taut and lickable. Just like I felt the vein under his cock on my tongue, I wonder what it would feel like to drift it over the cords in his neck and down his abdomen.

He tilts his head, increasing the panic coursing through me and flooding straight to my core.

My unsteady voice spills out. "Do you have a condom?" I manage to speak through ragged breaths.

He shakes his head slowly with the kind of speed that I assume psychopaths use. The kind of speed that is terrifyingly thrilling. He steps into my body, allowing my breasts to mold against his chest. The layer of my clothing between us does nothing to dampen the heat emitting from him.

This feels like a dream. That he's not actually here, preying on me in this pantry, despite how badly I want him. How sad is it that I would jump on any of them right now? And just thinking of Brennan and Colten joining in on this makes my insides coil with a neediness I've never experienced.

My teeth clamp onto my bottom lip, my eyes scanning his. "I'm not on birth control."

The breath is expelled from my lungs as his lips curve. "Well, it's a good thing my side of the bet was claiming your ass then."

Somehow, those words ignite a stick of dynamite embedded in my bones. At first, it starts as a tremble in my legs as the sparkling fuse burns. But the second his hands find my waist and wriggle under my shirt, my fragile limbs can barely take the blow, my legs wobbling at his foul mouth and how scared I am about doing anal before anything else. But the need to continue is more governing than my fear.

Lifting it over my head, he tosses my shirt on the floor near the pantry door. He removes my shorts next, and I step out of them, standing before him in my black silk bra and panty set. Cameron's hands clench at his sides.

Oh my God, he's collecting all his control not to devour me immediately. His eyes give him away. The way they roam and lock on to various parts of my body. He's savoring how I'm completely at his mercy.

A delicate animal cornered by a beast with nowhere to run.

The rough pads of his fingers glide up the ridges of my spine, picking away at the clasp on my bra until I feel the material loosen. He gently removes it from my breasts, his eyes not once leaving my cold and hard nipples. I take a step backward, noticing the way his cock strains even more against his sweats as my trembling fingers gracefully slip under the band of my panties.

"Fuck, Taryn," he breathes as I throw them to join the heap of clothes collecting on the floor.

I flip my hair behind my back timidly, letting his hands float up my stomach to cup my breasts. I don't have big tits, but they fit perfectly in his hands.

In Colten's hands.

Cameron removes his sweats, freeing his stiff cock from confinement.

"On your knees for your huntsman, Princess. You're going to swallow my cock first before your ass does."

Oh, dear Lord.

My thighs clench, doing what he says, and I kneel on the finished wood floor. He pumps himself a few times, the bead of cum glistening on his tip, making my mouth open on instinct. Thrusting his hips forward, I swirl my tongue around the tip. A guttural growl vibrates his muscular frame, and I grip his balls in my hand, making him groan before I fit my mouth entirely around him.

He threads his fingers in my hair, moving my head at the same rhythm as my mouth.

"You love sucking that cock?" he breathes. I struggle to move my head up and down to answer him since using words is impossible. "Princesses are supposed to be innocent, Taryn. But here you are on your knees, taking my cock to the back of your throat like a good little whore."

He slaps the side of my face a few times, his dick still working in and out, gliding against my tongue. The sting has heat pooling in my lower belly and rushing to my core.

He pushes his hips forward further, his tip hitting the back of my throat. He holds me there, tears pooling in my eyes as I gag around him and battle for breath. His grip on my hair tightens, and he pulls my mouth off him, my saliva coating his cock.

I suck air into my lungs as he walks to the door and removes the multi-step stool next to the wall, dragging it across the floor.

The scraping of the heels against the wood increases the frantic thumping in my chest. I'm unsure if it's because I'm worried about what will happen or because I'm ashamed of what I'm about to say.

I open my mouth to say something. Anything. Yet, my jaw hangs open like it's another invitation for him to claim my mouth again while I try to muster the right way to tell him. Cameron glances up from the stool to me, the heat that was just on his face a second ago shifting to concern.

He scans my expression. "Taryn, what's wrong?"

"I need to be honest with you." I wring my hands, my pulse pounding.

His brows pull together.

"Do you want to sit down for this?" I motion to the stool.

His eyes remain attached to mine. "No. But you might— Your face is white."

When I don't move, frozen in place by my thoughts bouncing around in my skull, he sits down on the stool.

"Come here," he orders, reaching for me with his sweet tone.

I walk toward him, feeling completely vulnerable under his scrutinizing stare. He grabs my hand and then my waist with his other, pulling me on top of his thighs to face him. I'm straddling his thick legs, his thighs rubbing against mine. Cameron's not pulling me on his cock, touching me, or doing anything of the sort. He brushes a strand of hair out of my face and holds me.

"What do you want to tell me?" he whispers so softly my heart snaps.

"I— Uh..." I inhale an unstable breath and try again. "I have never had sex before."

He goes completely still under me. His eyes widen. "Like...ever?"

"I mean, I've kissed a few guys, but never anything past that."

His hands wander to my ass and flex. "Oh my God, Taryn!"

I slap a hand over his mouth, his breath ragged and moist against my palm. "Shhhh. They are sleeping out there." I remove my hand.

"Brennan and I forced you to your knees, and we weren't gentle about it," he whisper-yells. "We were so close to fucking you right then and there. And I was just about to take your ass in a food pantry, and you're a virgin and have never been fucked."

I shake my head.

He eyes me suspiciously. "If you've never slept with a man, then you're still a virgin—" The following words die on his tongue.

"I mean, I'm not exactly inexperienced."

He swallows, arching a dark brow. "What?"

I never expected to admit this to anyone. But I figured I would have sex the normal way first before trying anal, but here we are. "I didn't want to be inexperienced when the time came. So one night, it was just me, a toy, and a bottle of wine." A toy I am well acquainted with now.

His perplexed look worries me. "Are you fucking with me right now?"

I tilt my head. "Do I look like I'm joking?"

His eyes bounce between mine. "Fuck. I'm honestly trying so hard not to find that as hot as I do."

A faint smile pulls at my lips. I glance down at his cock, and he's not kidding. It's thicker and harder than it was before.

He sighs, placing his sweaty forehead on my chest. "As much as I want to fuck you right now and be the first one to bury a cock in your cunt, you said you aren't on birth control, and the condoms are in Brennan's room."

I nod. "It's okay. I was going to ask if I could use your phone to call my prescription into the pharmacy when I go to town with Jessica tomorrow."

He lifts a hand, his fingers gliding down my red, blotchy

cheeks from the embarrassment. "Thank you for telling me. Despite everything we've already done, I never want to scare you or make you uncomfortable here."

Maybe it's the morality laced in his tone. Or the way his eyes searching mine break through that layer of humiliation from telling him something I've never told anyone. But the way his grip tightens on my body and the quirk to his lips stir a comfort that I've never felt—the comfort of having a friend.

He could've chosen to freak out. To push me away, finding what I did utterly eccentric and repulsive.

There's no hint of judgment.

No trace of disgust.

He's looking at me like he understands and wants to protect me. Which is why I'm feeling bold enough to ask him this, not someone else.

I place my arms around his neck, pulling our faces closer. His hot breath fans across my face.

"You guys have been driving me insane and wild the last few days." His chuckle vibrates my body but then stops abruptly when I whisper in his ear, "Please, make me come."

He quietens, his fingertips pulsing into my flesh while he processes my request.

"I don't care if it's your fingers or your tongue." His firm body shudders underneath mine, his already engorged cock growing harder. "Please just make me come," I beg.

He wraps his arms around me, breathing into the crook of my neck. He stands up and flips us, placing me down on the stool where he was just sitting.

"God, it's so fucking hot when you beg," he groans. Chills break out across my arms under the sheen of moisture from how humid and scorching this room is from our body heat. "And because you asked nicely, I'm going to give you my fingers and my tongue."

I moan, his deep voice dripping onto my flushed skin and

melting through my flesh like lava consuming everything in its path. "Lean back against the door and spread your legs for me."

I do as he says, pressing my back against the pantry door, and place one foot on a shelf to my left as he holds up my right, granting himself better access. His head dips down, leaving a trail of wet kisses on my inner thighs. His hot breath skids across my skin, floating across my pussy like the sweetest breeze. His tongue drags up and down my sensitive center before circling my clit, releasing a chain reaction of one firework after the other from my head to the tips of my toes.

My fingers knit into his hair while his masterful tongue moves and sucks, and I moan at how good it feels when he dips it into my cunt.

My eyes flutter closed of their own accord the second he inserts two fingers, but I slump against the door when he immediately withdraws them.

No. Why is he stopping?

"Open your eyes." His commanding tone sends a shock wave of flurries through me. "I want you to see how needy you are to be filled."

I peel my eyes open, instantly focusing on the fingers he's holding up, glistening with my arousal. "Are you ready to watch me make you come, Princess?"

"Yes," I whimper.

Lifting them to my face, I open my mouth, letting him thrust them inside and move against my tongue, my arousal coating my taste buds.

He shoves them to the back of my throat, and I choke around them. Pulling out, he shoves them back into my already-soaked pussy and finds that spot, pulling his fingers toward him in an up-and-down motion. He is slow with his movements at first, speeding up randomly, then taking his time, but it all builds the swirling in my belly.

His fingers speed up, and his heated eyes hold mine. "I'm

going to give your sweet pussy exactly what it's craving until you're clenching around my fingers in appreciation."

My ass hurts on this uncomfortable stool and in this position against the wall, but the pain adds to the pleasure.

"Fuck, you're so tight, Taryn." His head dips down. "Imagine if this was my cock stretching this pretty cunt," he breathes against me before his tongue finds my clit again while his fingers magically work inside me.

Oh, fuck.

His erotic tone starts to drag me to the edge, and at the same time, his fingers move faster. His tongue drifts against that extremely sensitive spot that has me quivering, his fingers pounding me harder and harder.

I pull at his hair. "Oh shit, Cameron! Please don't stop," I plead. I don't care how desperate I sound. I'll take anything he'll give me.

His tongue swipes again, and every string that's been coiled for the last few days because of these men unravels all over his fingers. My pussy constricts around him, my body jerking from the peak of the orgasm that nearly drags me under into black nothingness. He continues moving his fingers, letting me ride the wave of euphoria until my body softens and my legs fall.

He presses a gentle kiss to the inside of my thigh and stands up, reaching for my hands to help me to my feet. My legs wobble, but he steadies me.

"Your turn," I laugh, but he shakes his head.

"Tonight was your night."

My eyes flit between his, and they're a different color green. Green like the forest surrounding this property that keeps me tucked away on this hill with them.

At least right now, I don't mind it.

That could be the orgasm talking.

"Thank you, Cameron." He smiles at my appreciation. "I mean it."

After putting all our clothes back on, he gets the kids up to bed, and I walk back up to my room. Sleep is nearly dragging me under when I reach the top of the stairs. Padding barefoot across the floor like a sated zombie, something bright pink on my bedside table catches my eye. As I near, there's a small piece of paper folded on some lacey material.

I pick up the paper, unfolding it to read the four words:

Replacing what I destroyed.
- C

My fingers wrap around the vibrant pink panties, the material injecting something that feels a lot like warmth into the section of my heart where I shoved Colten in the back of a freezer, not to be touched. Yet I can't help but notice that the ice has thawed a little.

The tips of my ears warm at the gesture, yet my mind begins to wander.

There's no thaw.

Yes, there is, and you like it.

I exhale, ignoring my inner battle, and walk over to my dresser, opening an unused drawer on the bottom.

I'm not rude enough to throw them away, but I also can't help but contemplate if his little gift has a deeper meaning.

Nope.

There's definitely not.

He will need to find a different method to win me over.

I shove them in the far back, along with any sliver of warmth the gesture gave me at first, and glare at the drawer with as much annoyance as I can muster.

I wonder which one of his hookups left those.

TWENTY-FOUR | TARYN

My sandals clap against the concrete, the cool morning breeze sweeping against my legs and stirring my gray T-shirt dress that falls loosely over my frame. I reposition my crossbody, thankful they returned my wallet and a few other personal things, though I still have no phone.

I'm not sure I'll ever get that back—their trust doesn't stretch that far.

From the little they've allowed me to know about their past, I can't blame them. They've stretched that rubber band before, and it snapped, leaving them with welts that cut deeper than knives in their backs ever could. And I just so happen to be their solution.

Or so they think.

A temporary solution that's plastered over their wounds until they inevitably bleed through because I'm no replacement for a missing mother and a criminal father.

I peer around Main Street, observing as groups set up tents and speed walk to and from their cars, carrying crates and boxes to their designated Saturday market spots lining the sidewalks on both sides of the street. The early-morning sun beats down, the warmth soaking into my bones and easing the tension seizing my muscles after being trapped on Lindenvale Hill.

At least they lengthened my leash a little.

I tear my gaze away from the busy street and lower myself to peer at Jess through the passenger door. "Where are we going? I thought we were heading to Cascade Springs?"

Jess slides her sunglasses onto her head and turns off the ignition, pointing at a building a few down from where we parked. "We are, but we're stopping at The Honey Hut. We need coffee for the drive."

She steps out and shuts the driver's side door, the noise echoing off the row of shops in front of us. She opens the back door to let Tristan out of the back seat while I open Elena's.

She sits in her car seat with her headphones on, her fingers tapping her tablet screen aggressively in an intense game of *Fruit Ninja* that kept her silent the entire ride besides the few angry puffs of air that slipped past her pouty lips.

"Let's go, Little Miss. You'll have an hour's drive to try and beat your high score." I chuckle, reaching over her to unclasp the seat belt.

Elena huffs in defeat, pulling her headphones off and ruffling the two French braids I gave her this morning.

She tosses the tablet into the middle seat and crosses her arms. "It's Bren's high score. He stole my tablet, and I haven't been able to beat him." Placing one hand in mine, she jumps out of the vehicle, her eyes locking on the buildings in front of us. "*Oooh*, are we going to The Honey Hut?"

Flying fruit forgotten, Elena's sparkly sneakers drum on the pavement in pure excitement that her little body can't contain. She doesn't let go of my hand; she tugs me along, and we join her brother and Jess on the sidewalk.

Her infectious energy makes me smile.

And damn does it feel good to be out of that house and off the property.

"Miss Taryn," Elena's excitement holds my attention, "you'll get to meet Addie!"

My focus shifts from the little girl gripping my hand to Jess. "Who's Addie?"

"Adelaide is one of the reasons I wanted to stop here before we head out." She shrugs. "I figured you might need a friend when I leave in a few days. She's Cameron's best friend, and we've been friends since he introduced us."

My brow furrows. "She works at The Honey Hut?"

We stroll down the walkway, Elena pouncing on the sidewalk, attempting to jump over the lines separating the concrete. I gasp in surprise as her petite body jerks mine forward, her momentum causing me to lose my balance and knock into Tristan next to me. I apologize, but he takes a step away from me and picks up his speed, keeping his head down.

Jess shakes her head. "She owns it."

My eyes widen. "She owns it?"

I remember Harrison Crock telling me to check The Honey Hut for a job. One of the few things I remember that night before the twins roofied me.

I'm pretty sure I'm making more money now, being a nanny held captive by three brothers, than I ever would've made with a job like that. Still, I probably would've gone in and asked for a job anyway if things had turned out differently—had I woken up that following day still needing a job rather than instantly having one I never wanted.

"She used to spend every summer here with her grandmother, Sylvia. Her grandmother started The Honey Hut in the late '90s...I think. But she died two summers ago. Adelaide was left with everything and moved here from Seattle to continue running the business."

We stop in front of a shop, its charcoal exterior contrasting with the cream and light-colored storefronts around it. A vintage bakery sign and black-and-white striped awning hang over the sidewalk, concealing us in the shade.

The two large windows facing the street feature a giant decal of a honey wand dripping onto a croissant. There are tall pots of various flowers and some two-person wooden tables, one of which is occupied by an elderly man sipping a cup of coffee and reading the newspaper.

"Wow." My eyes scan the bakery storefront again. "This place looks remarkable for being around since the '90s."

Elena jumps up and down, nearly pulling my shoulder out of the socket.

"Her grandmother had all these big ideas for what she wanted it to look like, but never got the chance to remodel. After Adelaide took over, she put a lot of money into renovations and opened it back up a few months later."

"What's the inspiration behind the name?" I ask curiously.

She smiles, gazing at the decal. "Before her grandfather died, he always used to call her grandma Honey."

My cheeks warm. It's one of those simple things that makes you more attached to a place and its past.

When we walk inside, my eyes roam. The interior aesthetic completely matches the exterior. There's an accent wall coated in dark paint on the opposite side of the order counter. Wood tables fill the space, and vining houseplants hang in the rafters. Natural light drifts in through the front and rear windows. The back of the bakery leads out to a deck with a view of the bay where Cedar Creek flows into the Columbia.

A few people are chatting and working on computers, sipping their drinks, or indulging in their baked goods.

Dainty hanging lights weave through the rafters and hang over glass cases of croissants, cookies, cakes, muffins, and several other pastries, making my mouth water. The one natural brick wall behind the counter pulls everything together. The ambiance of this bakery is impressive for a town of this size. The fact that she had enough money to afford renovations like this is impressive.

My gaze immediately lands on the gorgeous honey-blonde girl who pushes through a set of kitchen doors and reaches into the glass case of various pastries. Her hair is in a messy bun, pieces framing her round face. She has a slim nose and gorgeous, rosy cheeks, probably from running around.

She places a muffin on a plate and calls out a name. She immediately smiles when her attention lands on us walking to the register. She thanks the man who comes up to pick up his order, wiping her hands on her black apron, which covers a short, floral summer dress.

"I was wondering when I would see my favorite customers again," she beams.

Jessica rolls her eyes and stifles a laugh. "You say that to everyone."

"But I actually mean it when I say it to you." She winks at Elena.

Elena drops my hand and peers over the countertop at her. "Adelaide, this is my new nanny, Miss Taryn!"

Her vibrant blue eyes find mine.

This is Cameron's best friend? Because, holy hell, I have no idea how he's not dating her. I would date her if I were into women. Images of his face between my legs last night encourage the pang of jealousy stirring in my sternum.

I swallow, attempting to disregard the unwelcome feeling, and manage a smile to dissipate the tension. "Nice to meet you, Adelaide."

A corner of her lips tugs upward at my greeting, and I can only wonder what thoughts are rummaging through her head at this moment.

I eye her suspiciously. "What?"

"I'm going to go see what Tristan wants," Jess says, leaving me with Elena to find Tristan, who found a table at the back of the bakery near the patio doors.

Adelaide shakes her head. "You are awfully calm for someone who just moved to town and was—" She peers around, her eyes flicking from one corner of the room to the other. She lowers her voice to a level that has my heart thumping louder than her whisper. "Abducted."

I don't miss the hint of amusement slipping through her tone.

She straightens, her voice full of humor. "Cameron is horrible at keeping secrets from me. I'm surprised to see you because I thought it would be months before they let you off the hill. Those boys don't trust easily."

Yeah, I've figured that out.

"I told them I needed to get out, or I was going to go insane."

She lifts a brow. "But you're not running?" There is no hint of judgment laced with the humor in her tone. She's genuinely curious.

She has this aura about her, one that clutches onto the tension swarming in my chest and draws it out in a form of honesty I've never had with strangers before her.

My lips roll, the breath in my lungs expelling leisurely. "Is it horrible to say that I'm making more now than I was with my teaching job?"

She gives me a suppressed grin. Running her hands along the smooth countertop, she says, "Not at all. We do what we do to survive, even if it's unconventional in the eyes of society." She tucks a lock of blonde hair behind her ear. "And there's nothing wrong with making decisions that make us content even if the circumstances want to convince us otherwise."

There's an underlying meaning behind her words—a flash

in her eyes showing me she believes every word. As if she knows the kind of torment your gut battles when you're doing something that's not normal or accepted.

It's only been a few weeks on Lindenvale Hill, and my brain ceased trying to persuade me that this is completely wrong a few days ago when I saw how Cameron and Brennan tucked the kids in one night. They never fail to say "I love you" to each other. Colten too. He may live in the cabin, but he says it before he leaves for the night. The forehead kisses he gives Elena are like missiles straight to my core.

But the reality is always there in the background. Lurking. Festering. Constantly reminding me of the situation when the feeling of confinement settles in.

"And if it makes you feel any better, the Lindenvale brothers are a lot of talk. So, if they threaten you, just take it with a grain of salt. They find...pleasure in threatening something pretty."

"Oh." I think I get what she is hinting at. "Have you and Cameron ever...you know?"

Two lines form between her brows for a second, and then she laughs. "Oh, no! Definitely not. Friends. Just friends. And have been for a very long time."

"All right," Jess says, wandering back toward us. "Tristan wants a double chocolate muffin and a hot chocolate, and Elena wants—"

"Me too!" Elena answers for herself. "And a cookie," she shouts excitedly.

"Make that four chocolate chip cookies," Jess says. "We need a snack for the drive home later, too."

I glance up at the menu, and Adelaide chuckles, her fingers tapping on the tablet in front of us like a timer ticking down until it's my time to order.

Jess orders a vanilla latte while I glance at the pastry case, and since I can't make up my mind, I look back at Adelaide. "I'll have whatever your favorite pastry is and whatever coffee you recommend."

"Okay, so one butter pecan sticky bun and a honey cinnamon cortado for Taryn," she mumbles happily, jotting the order down.

Yeah, I'm happy with my decision to let her choose.

We thank her once we've ordered everything, and she runs around behind the counter, steaming milk, crafting drinks, and grabbing our pastries out of the case. She hands everything to us, and we join Tristan over in the back at a table by the windows.

I settle into the chair, tearing off a part of the bun with my fork. My teeth sink into the warm, gooey butter pecan bread, and my taste buds burst, my mouth watering even more than it was at the smell.

Holy shit, this is honestly the best thing I have ever put in my mouth. And the coffee is better than any place I went to in Tucson before moving here.

Probably a good thing for my wallet that I'm hidden away on the hill, or I'd be here every day supporting Adelaide and trading the amount in my bank account for calories. Not that she'd probably mind.

Tristan lifts his cup, sipping at the hot chocolate. He sets it back on the table, his fingers returning to the buttons on his Switch while Jess talks to Elena about the school supplies she needs.

"You know, I used to have a blue Game Boy. It was my favorite thing in the world," I tell him, trying to get a reaction out of him. I point to his Nintendo Switch. "The Game Boy was like the dinosaur version of that."

He glances up at me, his eyes squinted, scanning my face with so much attitude for a seven-year-old. He raises a brow.

Damn, he gets that brow pop from his brothers. His eyes

analyze me the same way too, with such intensity that I almost want to shrink away from his penetrating gaze.

"Well," I continue, "it was my favorite thing in the world until I left it on an airplane when my parents and I were moving. I was heartbroken. I would always play *Scooby-Doo*. That game was awesome."

"*Scooby-Doo*? That doesn't sound fun." His eyes drop back to his screen as he returns to his game.

It may have been small, but I mentally raise my fist in the air. I finally managed to get him to say more than two words to me.

"Oh, but it was," I respond, attempting to push this conversation further. "You had to run around with Fred, solve mysteries, and try not to get caught by the bad guy. You also had to collect Scooby Snacks that would give you powers to solve the quests."

He regards me, his chest shaking with laughter.

Yes! I got a reaction, and it was laughter.

It's such a beautiful sound I haven't heard him make since I met him.

His lips twist to the side, and he places the green device on the table. "We could get you a *Scooby-Doo* game, and you can play on mine. It might not be the same, though."

My toes to the tips of my ears warm at his kindness. "I would like that. And then I can teach you how to play. Your score would probably beat my ass anyway because you're really good," I compliment, pointing to his device.

His eyes widen as he lowers his voice, a little laughter slipping through. God, I love that sound; it reminds me of Cameron and Brennan's laughter. "You aren't allowed to say that word, Miss Taryn."

I respond with a smirk, and we lean closer together as if we are sharing secrets nobody else knows. It makes me feel closer to him already. I was worried I wouldn't get him to talk to me before Jessica left and that everything would be a struggle after that.

I hold out my pinkie, and he glances at it. "Promise you won't tell your brothers?"

He smiles and hooks his around mine. "I promise."

TWENTY-FIVE | COLTEN

Yanking my fingers through my hair in irritation, I drop my weighted head, swarming with too many thoughts, into my hands.

I need a goddamn haircut.

Squinting downward, I notice strands floating around the surface of my keyboard when my breath falls across the keys. Strands I've pulled out while sitting here, getting no work done. At this rate, removing each strand one by one may save me from asking Jess to carve time out of her last night at home to give me a haircut.

I could pull off being bald.

Men with bald heads have a certain sex appeal when they have tattoos. Right?

Not that it matters. The women I've fucked recently—or used to since I haven't invited a woman here since Taryn observed me with Britt that night weeks ago—focus on my happy trail leading to my *other* head.

Usually, Jess is the only one Cam, Bren, and I trust near our heads with sheers, but the twins take her to the University of Washington tomorrow.

We could teach Taryn—suffer through a couple of bad cuts until she improves, but I don't trust her near my head with anything sharp or pointy. She'd probably accidentally "slip" and implant the scissors into my neck, puncturing a vital artery.

A pang of dejection blooms in my stomach. I swallow, but the growing lump only fertilizes the hollow sensation.

It's always only been us.

The six of us.

Over the last five years, we've produced a balance—an equilibrium that has allowed us to survive the destruction my father's alcoholism caused and the gaping hole our mother left.

I've never wanted to admit it, but I have trust issues.

It is probably not surprising, considering...well, everything.

People's lies and promises are more destructive to the nervous system than the sweetest poison. The difference? We expect the inevitable damage poison causes. We're taught to read the warning labels.

On the other hand, people disguise their words impeccably. They inject their lies into each syllable that lifts off their tongue, making it impossible to see what's below the surface because their inflection seems sincere and honest.

MY MOTHER'S bellowing voice echoes through the halls, her words unintelligible because of the walls and floors separating us.

My siblings' frightened eyes scan my face as I stand in the doorway of Brennan's room on the top floor. Jess has her arms wrapped around her knees, rocking back and forth on the floor. Scared tears stream down her flushed face, and my heart aches with the urge to hold her. To wrap my arms around her protectively.

Our parents have fought before. But this...

Alarm bells are bouncing around in my head.

Brennan is sitting in a chair with his arms wrapped around Tristan, my two-year-old brother's head nestled into his chest, his blue eyes wide. Cameron paces the room, with newborn Elena sleeping peacefully in his shaking arms.

We all heard it.

Shattering glass scraped against our eardrums while we were in the living room just down the hall from their room, the sound raising the hairs on my arms in fear of what was going down between them.

I attempt to gain control of my trembling hands as I shut the door, leaving my siblings inside. My heart lurches into my throat, acid swishing in my stomach with each step I take down the four flights of stairs, their screaming tones increasing in volume the closer I get to the bottom floor.

My mother's scream is cut off by the boom of my dad's voice, the drunken, slurred shouts making me jolt in my skin.

Fuck. Why does this fight sound so much worse than every other one they've had?

I turn the corner, a sliver of soft light shining underneath their closed door at the end of the dark corridor.

Creeping closer, my mother's hysterical voice springs a burning sensation behind my eyes.

I don't want to go any further. Yet the thought of my terrified siblings huddling in the room upstairs injects a minor amount of determination into my bloodstream.

I drag my feet across the wood floors as if it's thick tar, something trying to keep me from seeing whatever lies beyond their bedroom door.

"You're so fucking weak, Jane!" My father's slurred words, combined with her horrifying shriek, shake the floorboards under my bare feet outside their door.

My blood hardens to ice in my veins. Sharp shards that threaten to gut me from the inside out.

Gripping the door handle with quivering hands, I push it open.

My eyes quickly scan the room, and my chest ruptures in two, my eyes widening in horror at the scene before me.

Their vanity mirror is smashed into a thousand pieces, shards dusting the countertop and sharp blades smattering the carpet.

My dad stands with his back to me, and my mom is hidden partly behind him. His head is dropped, his gaze locked on the...

My soul leaves my body, my battering heart thudding to a complete stop.

Blood pools below my father's work boots, the large shard of glass in his hand dripping crimson onto the tan carpet. The knuckles of his other hand are white, gripping the neck of a scotch bottle.

"Colten," my mother gasps my name, freezing me in place. Her face is entirely white, her body shuddering. A sheen of sweat coats her skin, glistening in the lamplight from their matching bedside tables. Tears fall from her reddened eyes, the drips feeling like they cascade down her cheeks in slow motion.

My father's body turns toward me slowly as if another entity possesses him. My mom clutches her hands to her stomach, her purple shirt beneath them staining a deeper plum.

The two people who used to show me what love should look like peer at me with dead eyes.

My father's lifeless irises clash with mine.

The bloody glass tumbles from his fingertips.

Time freezes.

Every movement and every breath between the three of us is in slow motion.

Even the shard of glass falling through the air floats like the heavy snowflakes we get in the winter that plummet toward the earth. It lands flat on the carpet, reflecting my father's crimson hand that pierces my vision.

He was holding the blade of glass.

It's her blood.

I should move. I should do something besides stand here. Run to her, take on my father with my own hands, but the terror grips every muscle in its claws.

My father's shoulders are rigid, and my mom bolts as he lifts the bottle to his lips to get his fix. She sprints past me into the dark hallway, drops of blood trailing her path. I follow her into the foyer, and she reaches for her car keys on the hook. Opening the door, she steps outside into the night air, my wobbly legs carrying me to her as fast as I can manage.

"Mom." I fight through the emotion clogging my throat. She halts on the porch steps. "I'll drive you to the hospital. Please let me take you!"

She turns around to face my pleading voice. Taking a few steps back up to the porch, she approaches me and grips the flesh of my shoulders.

"I need you to promise me you'll stay here with them, Colt. Tell me you'll never leave them!"

I stare into her blue eyes, my lip quivering. "I promise, Mom."

She presses her lips against my hair. "I'll be back—" She shakes her head and taps the skin over my heart, the drumming of her fingertips splintering whatever is left of it. "I'll be right here, always."

I nod absentmindedly, watching as she leaves me on the porch and climbs into her silver GMC Terrain. Driving around the circular driveway, she speeds off, her red rear lights disappearing into the haze of fog overshadowing the orchard.

I'm nearly knocked over a few minutes later when my dad's swaying, intoxicated frame smashes into mine. He tears down the sidewalk, heaves himself into his truck, and takes off after her.

My heart throbs, my lungs somehow sucking in air through the small opening in my collapsed windpipe as my dad's rear lights, too, dissolve into the haze.

I'm left alone, my mother's blood on my shoulders soaking through the material and chilling me to the bone as I peer at the orchard that swallowed them whole.

I DISTRACTEDLY RUB MY CHEST, everything inside my sternum stretching so painfully I think it might tear through my skin and expose the bottomless void. It's holding on to those promises that can cause irreparable damage.

She said she'd be back. She promised.

How can a memory feel so vivid but fuzzy simultaneously?

I didn't leave the porch until my dad returned early that next morning. I sat on the outdoor patio couch, perking up as his headlights shone through the dawn, his truck rolling up the hill.

I waited for her car to follow, but it never appeared.

And when he showed up alone and didn't utter a word to me as he rinsed his bloody hands in the kitchen sink, the crimson water flowing down the drain, I knew she wasn't coming back. Yet, I still held out hope.

Foolishly fucking held on tight to that little flicker of optimism that was buried deep in my soul.

When he offered no answers, no damn explanation, rage and agony consumed me completely.

I left.

I couldn't exist in the same house after what he had done. Without a second thought, I drove to a place on the cliffs we stumbled across when my brothers and I were boys. A place that felt safe. Somewhere where I could yell and curse my father openly, however loudly I wanted to.

I may have bellowed curses to the wind, but I liked to imagine the bastard heard them.

Three days later, I remembered the promise I had made to her. Despite fearing my father, I went back for one reason only.

Them.

And I've never left since.

You think it wouldn't take me this long to respond to an

email when I answer tens a day—requests from privately owned markets, supplier inquiries, human resources, and environmental updates—but when I'm alone, my head is a chaotic little fuck.

I reread the email from our marketing director for the fifth time, and the words start sinking in.

Phillip is begging me to reconsider starting the harvest festival again, which my family used to put on every October in the field near the shop. Well, every October until my dad's arrest. I wanted to cancel it that year, but everyone pleaded with me not to.

I wasn't in the right headspace to host an event that used to be so joyous for my family, but I let it slide. Fair rides were set up, and our usual vendors and bands lined up to sell local products and play on the stage we'd had built the week before. The harvest festival went smoothly—that is, until a group of teenagers dressed up for the costume contest and a girl who went to Cedar Creek High with Cameron and Brennan showed up as the ghost of Jane Lindenvale in a white gown with blood coating the abdominal area and a shard of glass protruding from her stomach.

We couldn't continue the tradition after that.

Fuck. I can't deal with this email right now.

He knows what my answer is year after fucking year, and yet he continues to ask me.

After shutting off my computer and office lights, I head to my truck and make the minute drive home, trying to brighten my mood like I do every day before I step into the house.

It's Jess's last night home, and I don't want my sour mood to rub off on everyone. It does that too often, which is why I stayed at the office a little longer and skipped dinner. When I get home, I'll toss what they left me in the microwave.

When I step over the threshold, the last thing I expect is to see everyone, and I mean everyone, hanging out in the living room. The twins, Jess, and Elena, are in an epic battle of Monopoly, their loud, happy voices softening my temperament.

Scanning the room, I locate Tristan. His body is huddled up against...

Jesus Christ.

Taryn has her legs crossed on the couch in black yoga pants that cling to her curves, her blush pink tank top exposing the delicate swell of her breasts. She has his Switch in her hands, her fingers scurrying across the buttons as her features brighten at whatever's on her screen.

Tristan's body jolts in surprise. "Yes! You got the Scooby Snack without getting caught," he smiles.

Oh, goddamn.

I haven't seen Tristan smile like that in forever. And *she* made him grin like that. He never lets anyone touch his Switch. Cameron tried to play it once, and then Tristan didn't say anything to us for a week. Ignored us completely.

"I knew you'd like it," Taryn singsongs. "I told you this game was awesome!"

His head rests on her shoulder, his dark blond hair flopping onto his forehead. "I don't think I'll be as good as you, though," he responds, pointing to something on the screen.

"It's good that you have a few weeks till school starts. I'll teach you all the tricks before you go back—"

Her soft brown eyes magnetize to mine, her mouth snapping shut when she notices my presence. My body hums in response to her attention on me, but my focus on Taryn tenses her muscles. I love that her body reacts to me in such drastic ways.

Cameron sees her staring at me and stands. "Oh great, you're here. Jess doesn't want to wait anymore to hear about her congrats-you're-headed-off-to-college gift."

A corner of my mouth tilts, but my eyes are still glued to Taryn's. I rip them away, clearing my throat. It's still been fucking awkward since we established she's only here for Elena and Tristan. Which she is. I'm not arguing that, but we are about to be alone with just the kids for a few days when the twins take Jess to school. I'm unsure of how to talk to her.

I nod. "All right, I'll be right back."

Heading to the kitchen, I set my keys on the counter and open a drawer to pull out the white envelope. When I return to the living room, I hand it to Jess. Her eyes beam and flit around the room, taking us in while our attention is on her.

She slides her nail under the flap, tearing it open to remove the folded piece of paper bursting with color from nearly every color crayon existing in this house.

Elena worked hard on it. She tackled this project like she usually does with all her creations—her eyes locked on the paper, her crayons scribbling across while her tongue rested on the inside of her cheek.

She has so much focus and hates being distracted when she's creating things.

Maybe she will grow up to be a painter like Cameron one day. But hopefully, she will share her talent with the world and not just display it on the walls of our home. He has seemed relatively close to Taryn these past few days.

I wonder if he has shown her his studio yet.

An unexpected flush of jealousy runs down the ridges of my spine.

Jess opens it up, smiling at the picture of a stick figure, Jessica, in a triangular dress, standing next to a red car resembling an oval with four circular tires.

Elena's five. To her, this is a masterpiece.

I think so, too.

"Do you like it?" Elena squeals, jumping to her feet from sitting on the floor by the coffee table where their Monopoly game is sprawled out.

"I love it! Thank you," Jess says, wrapping her arms around

her petite frame and peppering her face with dainty kisses. Jess glances between Cam, Bren, and I, cocking a brow. "So, what's my gift?" She chuckles.

Cameron stuffs his hands into his pockets next to me. "When you, Bren, and I get to Seattle tomorrow, we're going car shopping."

Jessica flies off the couch in a flash, tossing her arms around Cameron and me, pulling us closer. I place a hand on her back, savoring the moment. Come tomorrow, there will be a Jessica-sized hole in our lives.

At least until Thanksgiving, anyway.

She runs over to Bren, pressing a sloppy, wet kiss on his cheek that rings through the room. "Thank you!"

"Ugh," he lifts his sleeve to his face, wiping it off. "Could've used less tongue."

Joyful laughter fills the room, but the one that has my skin buzzing and echoing in my ears is Taryn's. She's observing us as if she's watching a movie, her eyes flashing with a warmth that flows through my body to my hands.

I lower myself to the floor next to Elena. She takes my proximity as an invitation to sit on my lap.

"You guys have room for another player?" I ask.

Brennan grabs his car game piece and throws it at Cam, hitting him in the arm. "Cameron's the banker and *somehow* seems to have more money every time I glance at his side." He crosses his arms. "I think we should restart anyway."

Cameron reaches out a hand, sweeping the board clean with a middle finger out, right in Brennan's line of sight.

Elena leans back against me, fanning her money. "Colt, will you be on my team?"

I lower my head, pressing my lips to her hair. "Sure thing, baby girl."

She lobs her money, the colored paper floating to the board. "They beat my ass."

My body goes still.

More accurately, everything in the damn room goes still.

The only sound penetrating the void is Taryn's little gasp of air. She shifts on the couch, her gaze falling to the Switch in her hands, avoiding my gaze.

Interesting.

"Elena, you are not allowed to say that word," Brennan scolds.

She moves uncomfortably in my lap, her little pink lips pouting. "I heard it yesterday when we were at The Honey Hut," she whines.

I arch a brow. "Who said that?"

She cowers in my hold, her little finger pointing at the one person who instantly gave themselves away the second that word left Elena's mouth.

Little Ghost.

Pressing my lips in a line, I hold Taryn's wide eyes and flummoxed expression.

Goddammit, I am trying so hard not to smile.

Work was frustrating today. I expected to come home, eat dinner, and retire to my cabin early like usual. But something feels different. Tristan said more than five words, the vibrancy in his face like a punch to the gut because it's been so long since I've seen it.

Little Ghost may be teaching my little sister profanity, but for the first time in a long time, this house has felt lighter.

The laughter and smiles are livelier.

And I can't help but think she may be the reason for it.

TWENTY-SIX | TARYN

I shift in the bed, the sheets tangling between my legs. Flipping again to my side, releasing a frustrated groan, I accept that sleep may evade me tonight.

My throat is dry, and my body apparently can't find comfort on a mattress that feels like sleeping on a marshmallow after it's been lightly toasted by a flame.

I miss sleeping with Rossco. I miss finding comfort in the way his body curled up at the end of the bed, warming my feet. The way I wake up in the night to soothe him when he's whimpering, and his body lightly shakes while he's dreaming.

I've gotten so used to his presence that now I don't sleep as well as I used to with him around. I'm sure he feels the same since he sleeps outside now. Luckily, Colten got him a doghouse and a bed with plenty of room to curl up inside for the night.

Today was...awkward, hence why the tension still lingers and pulls at every cord and muscle in my body, denying me of rest.

The twins left with Jess this morning, leaving me to watch the kids by myself for the first time.

It was easy.

Painless.

Who knew spending time with a seven and five-year-old would be easier than sharing the same air with their brooding brother who showed up for dinner and didn't bother to utter a word to me all evening?

I received a few glares.

And several scrutinizing gazes that I couldn't dissect.

Teaching his five-year-old sister the word *ass* probably has something to do with that.

Honestly, I'm surprised her little mouth doesn't spill all sorts of other nonsense since Colten, Cameron, and Brennan are no saints.

The moonlight casts long shadows across the floor and up the walls, the light waking me more than I wish it would.

I lose my internal battle and glance at the clock.

It's nearly one in the morning.

Ugh.

Flipping the covers off my body, I toss a white tank top over my purple bralette and pull on a pair of black sleep shorts. Since I sleep in a bra and underwear and don't feel comfortable walking around in such little clothing, I decide it's best to cover myself. I know who lurks in the other rooms in this house. Jess and the twins may be gone, but it would just be awkward if the kids found me since it's only them and me in the house.

I pad down the stairs on feathered feet and quietly open my door, walking through the eerily silent house. The only sounds are my faint steps, my heartbeat, and my shallow breaths. Managing to quietly make it down all the flights of stairs, I step into the foyer.

My skin prickles, the hairs on my arms standing on end, responding to a presence that makes all the sensitive nerve endings in my body tingle.

I peer into the kitchen to my right, only lit by the light on over the stovetop on the kitchen island. Scanning my surroundings, my eyes drift to the dark living room, faintly glowing from the moonlight filtering through the windows, casting shadows across the room.

But it's the shadow sitting on the couch in a far corner of the room that has my heart creeping into my throat.

The silver light dances across Colten's features in an ethereal way. His concentration on me is secure and unrelenting, freezing me in place at the base of the stairs.

Neither of us has moved, and I'm completely aware that I can't see his eyes from this far away, but they feel black and bottomless. The obscure kind that pulls me in, wanting to venture and see how close I can get until I fall into them, and he swallows me whole.

A glass of amber liquid is on the end table. He picks it up, the surface of the alcohol shimmering from the moonlight.

Colten's gaze holds mine.

I slowly part from the staircase and wander into the living room, keeping him a safe distance away.

"Um...I—" I inhale a deep breath. My nipples pebble under my shirt in response to his company, making me feel entirely more exposed than I am. "I just needed a glass of water," I whisper, loud enough that he can hear me, while pointing to the kitchen.

There's no response from him. His chest rises and falls, and the silence stretches between us.

Chills break out across my bare arms and legs. My tone shakes. "What are you doing in here?"

"Elena had a nightmare." His sleepy, deep voice tenses every one of my muscles. "She came to get me."

Shit.

She walked outside by herself at this time of night? The twins and Jessica may be in Seattle, but I'm here.

I fold my arms over my chest, attempting to hide my firm

nipples from his view. Colten's eyes land on the movement, his fingers tightening around the glass tumbler on his knee.

I shift unnervingly. "Why wouldn't she come get me?"

He swirls the amber drink in his glass leisurely. He lifts it to his mouth, but instead of taking a sip, he inhales the sweet aroma. He closes his eyes briefly before setting the glass back on his knee.

"She comes to find me when they scare her more than others. I guess she thinks I'm better at handling nightmares."

"Are you?" There's a nervous edge in my tone.

I absentmindedly step toward him, and he cocks his head, observing my movements.

His eyes roam my body. "I've dealt with my own."

My breaths become shallower, causing my hands to shake. "Delt with your own or dealing with your own?" I ask.

Slits appear in his eyes. "Why would you ask me that?"

I shrug, heart thumping. "There's a big difference."

God, I should ignore him—get the glass of water I came down for and return to my room. Yet something about him keeps my feet firmly planted on the chilly wood floor. He makes me want to push the boundaries.

"You're giving me the vibe that you might be trying to deal with them right now," I continue when he doesn't answer.

Colten lifts a hand to his mouth, swiping a few fingers over his bottom lip before dragging the same ones through his hair. His black shirt hugs his chest and biceps, the cords in his muscles and neck catching the light as he moves fluidly.

I'm not sure why I do it, but I stalk toward him, our gazes sparking and lighting something I should be running from.

Getting close enough that the fabric of his sweatpants brushes against my knees, I lean over, grabbing the liquor in his hand.

Maybe I have a death wish. Or maybe I'm curious what taunting Colten will lead to. His eyes don't leave mine, but as our fingers brush against each other's, molten lava floods through my veins simultaneously as a threat flashes across his eyes.

"Taryn." His husky voice, laced with warning, sends a rush of desire to my aching core.

God, the voice that comes out of that mouth.

A mouth whose words have nearly brought me to orgasm almost as quickly as his tongue pressed to my clit. A throbbing between my legs increases the staccato rhythm of my pulse.

He releases his hold on the glass, inspecting me savagely as I lift it to my lips and draw a mouthful. Swallowing it down, the smoky, sweet flavor bounces off my tongue and burns my throat. I know alcohol doesn't work this instantly, but my flesh tingles just the same.

His fingers curl into a fist on his lap. "What are you doing, Little Ghost?"

I smirk, taking another sip. I lean across his muscular frame, setting it back on the table, my head so close to his that I can feel his hot breath skimming the slope of my neck.

Wetting my lips, I whisper, "Facing my own nightmare."

Before I can even register what's happening, his hand whips out, his fingers wrapping around my throat with such a subtle force I release a strangled noise. He stands the exact moment he rotates us, throwing me on the couch effortlessly. He shoves my back into the sofa with his fingers still firmly around my throat and his body pressing between my open legs.

Oh, shit.

His swift actions and the way he forced me into this position transfers a surplus of tension between my parted legs—the fear inside me sparking and shifting into something much more needy.

His fingers softly dig into my erratic pulse. I'm completely trapped and helpless under Colten's hard physique. Thrusting his hips between my thighs, the massive and hard bulge of his cock grates against my sensitive flesh.

Lightning crackles under my skin.

His lips skim the shell of my ear. "I highly suggest you go to bed, Taryn."

I should. *God, I should.*

Making no effort to move, I give myself over and accept my fate. He's making it nearly impossible to scurry away from him and back to my room. So, I stare at him challengingly, dissecting the look in his eyes, my chest rising and falling beneath him.

His eyes flutter closed, his features contorting in a way that shows me the internal battle he's fighting. When his eyes fly open, my body jolts at the complete shift. His hooded eyes inject venom into my bloodstream, immobilizing me in place.

"Fuck it," he breathes.

His lips crash down onto mine, my body igniting into flames underneath him at the unexpected feeling of his mouth on mine. His cock swells against my core, enticing him to grind on top of me and wrench a moan from my mouth and into his.

Colten's other hand, not capturing my throat, grips my hip bone, tugging my frame flush against his. His touch sears through my flesh and liquifies everything. Hot damn, I'm going to turn into a puddle on the couch for this man.

I wouldn't be surprised if I'm soaked through my underwear and shorts, drenching him through his sweatpants with the skillful way he's dry humping me. His thick erection rubbing against my clit has everything twisting and coiling, begging to be released.

He bites my bottom lip hard, the sting quickly diminishing when his tongue swipes against it. He thrusts it between my lips, demanding further access and deepening the kiss. Our tongues tangle, his sugary, minty flavor sizzling on my taste buds.

Did he even drink the scotch? He doesn't taste like it at all.

Every part of my being floats in space as his dominant tongue, which brought me pleasure a few days ago in his truck, duels with mine.

His minty taste and the spiced scotch lingering in my mouth create a cocktail of flavors that increase my feverish flesh.

Fuck, I've never been kissed like this.

I've never been handled in such a mind-blowing way that tears prickle in the corners of my eyes from the combination of millions of unknown emotions I've never experienced.

Fear.

Lust.

Desire.

Hate.

Pleasure.

He brought the entire storm to play with my lightning.

A groan vibrates his chest, pulsating through my sternum. My sensitive nipples are strained against the lace bralette, begging to be freed and caressed by his teeth or twisted by his fingertips.

Surprisingly, he pulls his mouth from mine, leaving my lips swollen and wet. His hand releases my throat, and his other hand lifts from my hip as he rises from the couch.

Our heavy breathing is the thunder.

The enormous rumble after the lightning strike.

Loud and terrifying.

Colten's hands drag down his face in apparent ire.

And then he's gone.

Colten rapidly paces out of the living room and through the hallway on the other side of the stairs. The back door slams, the tremor shaking the house's bones, rattling me even more than I was.

What the actual hell?

He has some nerve, not bothering to utter a word or spare me a glance after he nearly ground our bodies to a climax and dominated my lips.

My tongue.

My damn mind.

I push myself off the couch, reaching for his glass of scotch, and down the whole thing in a few gulps. It scalds my throat, but my skin ruptures into flares from how angry I am, numbing the pain. The alcohol swirls and swirls, festering in my stomach with rage.

Letting the liquor give me some audacity, I set the glass down and take the four flights of stairs back up to my room. Hurling open the bottom drawer, I remove the hot pink lace underwear he left on my dresser.

Fuck him.

It takes less than a minute for me to erupt through the back door and march down the grassy decline to his sidewalk. Rossco emerges from his doghouse, wagging his tail.

And Colten's rules can kiss my ass. I'm taking Rossco back up to bed with me tonight.

No porch light is on, but the moon is full and bright. All of his curtains are pulled closed, but my ire is directed at his door as if I have a problem with it and not him.

I batter my fist against it and wait a second. My patience wears thin when there's no answer. But my anger doesn't let up. I keep knocking and knocking, knowing at some point he'll have to come to the door and deal with me if he wants to get any sleep.

TWENTY-SEVEN | COLTEN

I still taste her on my tongue.

Her breaths.

Taryn's sweet, soft lips.

The honeyed, spiced flavor from my scotch that she sipped so easily.

I'm still savoring the faint moans she let me swallow when I rolled my hips and groin against her needy center through her clothes. The sounds Taryn made replay on a loop, each passing of the track furthering my craving.

For the last five years, I've worried that alcohol would become my addiction of choice. That I'd be driven to succumb to alcoholism like my father because solving your issues by forcing down bitter liquid is easier than facing issues head-on.

The business.

This family.

This property.

Even the withering relationship he had with my mother pushed his weak cognizance to locate his solution at the bottom of a bottle to numb the stress of it all.

The same pressure I combat daily because of him.

This is why I never give myself to the poison, giving it the power to flow through my veins and devour me from the inside out. It destroyed him rapidly, transforming him into a shell of a man rotting in a cell because his obsession reigned over him.

Lounging with a glass every night reminds me that I'm in control. Inhaling the aroma and being determined never to let it influence my mind shows me that I hold the power.

That's my fix.

My drug of choice pushes me forward to be the best man I can be for my family.

It's a reminder.

I always thought if something would destroy me, it would be the temptation and sensation of liquor. But I couldn't have been more wrong.

It's the taste of *her*—the feeling of her soft skin molding under my hands like putty. Alcohol impacts the brain, but I should've known that Taryn Meyers would be wildly more dangerous.

Like a lily of the valley that my siblings and I would come across playing in the woods—toxic if ingested, but with a sap that can seep through your skin and cause as much damage.

And I've done both.

I let my hands drift over her soft skin. I tasted her mouth. Her perfect cunt.

Because I let my control slip away.

She's infecting my head, and it's taking all my fucking willpower not to barge into her room and pretend that she's the remedy to cure my insanity.

As I walk across my driveway, inhaling the fresh air to compose my racing heart and clear my muddled head, her scent clings to me. Follows me.

I have never kissed a woman I fuck.

It's too intimate.

Has the ability to shift the casual relationship into something I will never allow myself to have.

But the moment I flipped her over onto that couch, she was the numbing agent. I forgot all I stand for as my body melted into hers, and she gave herself over to me.

Her brown eyes saw more than the man who has cowered behind the barricade he built five years ago when he witnessed his father attempt to murder his mother.

Love doesn't fucking look like that.

Love isn't a piece of glass cutting through flesh.

Devotion isn't letting someone's blood drip and soak into the carpet in a family home.

If love can break as easily as their marriage, I swore to myself I'd never want it.

For five years, no woman has slept in my bed. I've always used a condom, and my lips were either sucking on their nipples or attached to their clit. If she said words that were too intimate during sex, I would shove something in her mouth or shut her up by using my cock—resorting to bondage when they get too handsy. Their touch and nails grating against me resembled ants swarming over every inch of exposed skin.

It's been easy. Keeping up with the repetitive cycle and not breaking it once.

Until Little Ghost came along, and I gave her the power to fuck with my head.

Kissing her shouldn't have happened.

And now she has made my principles short-circuit, and it's only a matter of time until...

A hammering sound echoes through the night, mingling with the soft hum of crickets and the occasional hoot of an owl somewhere tucked away in the dark orchard.

The banging continues, hardening my muscles.

What the hell is that?

The sound holds me in place, but suddenly, everything is

eerily silent. My heart strikes violently against my ribs, and when the sound drifts through the night again, my feet move of their own accord across the gravel driveway.

Rocks crunch under my shoes, my skin prickling with irritation every time the *thump, thump, thump* hits my eardrums.

When I round the driveway, and my sidewalk comes into view, my heated blood solidifies into sharp icicles that scrape against my veins.

Taryn stands on my porch, the silver light from the moon highlighting her toned legs in those tiny shorts and the apples of her ass. I keep my steps quiet, holding my breath as I amble down the sidewalk toward her.

Turn around, Colten. Turn the fuck around.

"You better open this goddamn door, Colten," she whisper-yells.

I don't know why she's keeping her voice so low when her banging is loud enough to be heard by the nearest neighbor a few miles away.

Her eyes are locked on the door, so I slip onto the covered porch behind her. Leaning against the beam, I tuck my hands into my pockets.

I clear my throat, announcing my arrival, making her straighten into a statue. "The way you knock on doors is very unpleasant. I think you need to work on your approachability."

She outwardly cringes at my voice. Spinning around, Taryn clutches her hand to her chest. Between her fingers, I notice hot pink material. I eye it deviously, knowing exactly what it is.

"I've been knocking for several minutes! I thought you were in there."

I shrug. "Needed a walk."

She clenches her jaw, avoiding my gaze. My eyes fall to her hard nipples poking through her white tank top in the chilly night air.

I can't catch a fucking break with this woman.

My head tilts. "I thought I told you to go to bed."

Her chestnut eyes roll. "That was before you kissed me. Asshole," she mutters through clenched teeth. "You have some nerve walking away from me."

"You've run away from me several times, Little Ghost. Do you really want to play that game?" She swallows, staying silent. Raising a brow, I stalk forward. "I'm guessing you didn't like the gift."

She pauses, unclenching her fist to reveal the pink panties I gave her. God, she would look so beautiful in those with my cum leaking out of her and into the lace material.

Not helping the situation, Colt.

I want to know why she's here. She's standing before me like a fawn ready to be devoured, breathing heavily with her cheeks and chest flushed a similar hue to the underwear.

All my doing.

It's making me want to do it more.

See how vibrantly flushed I could make her skin.

Taryn throws the wad of lace at my chest, the material falling to my feet. My eyes don't stray from hers as my lips quirk upward, sending her into a tailspin that amuses me more.

She scrunches her nose, making me want to drift the pad of my finger over the dusting of freckles there. "You are revolting and twisted if you think I will wear those. I'm not interested in anything your sluts left behind, Colten!"

My chest vibrates with laughter as I lower myself to pick up the material. "If I remember correctly, your pussy was dripping on my tongue and gripping my fingers a few days ago."

I step into her, the front of my body colliding with her chest. Her ragged intake of breath makes me smile. Taryn's eyes dart away from mine, not wanting to acknowledge my proximity.

Using the underwear hanging off my index finger, I press it below her chin to angle her eyes to meet mine. "If they are my sluts, then what does that make you, Little Ghost?" I murmur.

She exhales shallowly, her irises bouncing between mine like little ping-pong balls.

I release my grip on her chin and walk to my door, leaving her standing there. Opening the door and pushing it open, I enter my house, standing in the dark foyer with the living room and open kitchen to my right and my closed office barn doors to the left. My favorite room as of recently because I know Taryn has a view of it from her tower.

She'd be much safer up there than standing helplessly on my porch.

The farther away I get from her, the more my skin prickles with unease, and my sternum tightens. She sluggishly turns toward me, her rosy lips still swollen from my mouth earlier. Her eyes analyze me through the doorway, her body visibly shaking.

If she decides to break the threshold, there's no turning back.

Because once she's in here, I won't be able to control myself, and divulging my fascination with her is bound to annihilate us both.

Do it, Taryn. I fucking dare you.

I cock my head, challenging her, and place my hand on the door, flinging it closed. Right before it clicks shut, Taryn explodes into my house, breaking the barrier.

My skin crackles with energy—the once heavy oxygen is light and breathable.

Fuck yes.

No turning back now, Little Ghost. You're in my home now, completely at my mercy.

Taryn slams the door shut, the vibration firing a surge of blood that rushes through my veins and straight to my cock.

She shoves her hands into my chest, her small frame no match for mine. "God, after everything you've done, I hate that you make me want you!"

"And what do you think you do to me, Little Ghost?" I wrap my hand around her throat, backing her up until her shoulders hit the front door. Her pulse flutters against my fingers, her chest rising and falling against my forearm. "Because ever since you mouthed off to me in that office, you have been driving me fucking insane. Why do you think I haven't had a woman here since you watched me with Britt?" My grip tightens.

She swallows against my palm, shaking her head.

I lower my mouth to her ear. "Because I can't come unless I visualize you. Unless I imagine that it's your legs spread wide open. Unless I visualize you stuffed full of my cock, your cunt taking every inch because you need all of it as much as I need all of you." She shudders at my words, and I hover my mouth over her lips, feathering my breath across them. "That's what you do to me, Taryn. I've always had fucking control, but since you've been here, you've had it the entire time without even knowing."

She licks her lips, provoking me. Agitating whatever's left of my sanity. "Then take it back, Colten."

Clenching my jaw, my fingers dig into her flesh as her hand reaches up, gripping my tatted forearm that's holding her head hostage.

I crush my erection against her warm stomach, the electrical current between us zipping. "You don't know what you're asking for."

"I do," she breathes. "I lied. I didn't picture your brothers that night when I slipped my fingers inside me."

She's killing me here. I'm barely holding on, the rubber band ready to snap and leave me with permanent scars. The sheen of sweat on my skin chills.

"I imagined you...imagined what it would've felt like—been like—to be her."

My eyes fall shut, allowing the vigilant part of my mind to dig its claws into the unfathomable part of my soul to gather any remaining common sense to prevent me from carrying her to my room.

Her hand drifts up my arm and wrist, her fingers pressing into mine to choke herself more forcefully.

It only takes three words from her mouth to snap the rubber band and break me entirely.

"Take. It. Back."

TWENTY-EIGHT | COLTEN

My mouth magnetizes to hers, the impact as if two waves in a tsunami have finally collided, unleashing the wrath of the merciless sea.

The pads of my fingers press into the delicate cords in her neck, the patter below Taryn's skin tapping viciously against my palm. Our breaths are ragged. Our hands wander, demanding to grip any part of each other we can hold on to. And as the seconds pass, her racing heart syncs with mine.

I lower my body, snaking my arms around her bare thighs. Lifting her frame, her legs weave around my waist, her feet locking, her core flush against my hardening cock. My tongue pierces through her soft lips to deepen the kiss, her tongue eagerly twirling with mine. Her teeth nip my bottom lip, the sting transmitting a shock wave of heat that pulses through my veins and straight to my groin.

Fuck.

Up until I kissed her earlier, I was disinclined to fully comprehend how badly I wanted her. She's been living on Lindenvale Hill for weeks, but Taryn Meyers has been on my radar for months—the little green dot blinking on my screen I craved to lure closer.

From the second her application and résumé hit my inbox for the fake teaching position I crafted—a replica to match a job listing I found for a second-grade position in Oregon—I couldn't think of anything else. My fascination with her festered and gnawed at my patience until she fell into the palm of my hands when she walked into that faux interview.

Turning us, I break the kiss as I shuffle us down the hallway ahead, heading to my bedroom at the back of the house. Keeping my eyes trained on my bedroom door, her mouth glides and explores my neck, the cold tip of her nose trailing up the slope to my ear.

With eagerness, I saunter to the bed, flipping us around so I sit on the edge, and she's straddling me.

Her shallow breathing catches as her focus locks on the view behind me. The entire back wall of my room is windows, the ethereal expanse of the orchard blanketed in night spanning across the edge of the yard. Eyes wandering, she scans my room—the gray walls and wood fixtures—allowing the natural greens outside to be the focal point. Wood beams traverse the ceiling with sconces, and the honey-toned bedposts match the dresser and bedside table.

I'm scrutinizing her features as she takes it all in, memorizing the enthralled look glinting in her eyes while her irises bounce around. She traps her bottom lip between her teeth.

God, I could watch these curious looks flicker across her face for hours and never succumb to boredom. What I really want to do is use my finger to trace those beautiful, inquisitive lines between her brows.

It's like she wasn't expecting a view this phenomenal.

She shifts distractedly, her hot center dragging against my erection bulging below her. The subtle movement has me fanning out my fingers over the apples of her ass and burrowing my fingers to gain some purchase. I leap up, spin us around, and throw her on the bed to trap her underneath me.

A gasp slips past her glossy lips.

I dip my head into the crook of her neck, biting at the tender skin while my hand slips under her tank top. My fingers wander up the smooth expanse of her stomach, digging under the lacy material she's wearing to access her breasts. They've been pleading for my mouth since she found herself in my presence.

"Tell me, Little Ghost," I whisper against her navel as I push up her tank top, and my mouth latches to her stomach. She digs her fingers into the duvet, wriggling beneath me. "What were you thinking about all those times you pushed your pink vibrator into your pussy," I say across her skin.

Her body goes rigid under me as what I asked starts registering. She attempts to get up, but I snatch onto her throat, lightly thrusting her back onto my comforter.

If she didn't like it, she'd be fighting me. Yet her inclination to submit and sink back into the mattress has exhilaration short-circuiting my brain.

"Colten, how did you know—"

The pads of my fingers pinch one perky nipple, forcing something between a groan and a whimper from her.

"Answer the question, Little Ghost," I demand. My firm arms hover my body above hers, and I grab the hem of her tank top to lift it over her head. "If you don't answer me while I'm undressing you, my cock isn't going to be the only thing stretching you. I'll invite your pink rabbit to play too."

A strangled moan escapes her as she shudders.

Hmmm. She doesn't seem opposed to the idea.

That's on the agenda for another day, but she doesn't need to know that quite yet.

Her voice is strangled as I tug her shorts down her legs. "I—I thought..." Even when she's stuttering, it's an addicting sound. "I thought about someone taking what they wanted from me, hitting that spot over and over again that nearly makes me black out from pleasure."

"Yeah?" I arch a brow, admiring how the purple lace set clinging to her frame highlights her skin tone. It'll be a masterpiece when it's on my bedroom floor in shreds. "Who was fucking you?"

My hands wriggle under the panties resting against her hip bones. Grasping the lace, I stretch the material and chafe her soft skin and pussy. My forearms flex as I rip it apart with my hands.

She releases a scream, the skin quickly reddening where the cloth had agitated her skin. It's like I'm marking my canvas—the first stroke of many. Once I'm done with her, she'll be a work of art, all sated and glowing from the high.

"You can't keep ripping my clothes, Colten!"

But I can.

I plaster a hand over her mouth to silence her, her hot breath between my fingers making my dick twitch.

"You gave me full control, Little Ghost." Her glassy eyes unwaveringly fixate on mine. "In that house, you may be theirs, but in this house, you belong to me. Your tight cunt, your ass, this fucking mouth," I growl, slipping my middle and ring fingers between her lips. "I even own the breath in your lungs." My tongue darts out, wetting my bottom lip. "Answer. The. Question."

I withdraw my fingers to let her respond, though I would find immense amusement watching her reply through them.

She shakes her head. "They didn't have a face," she utters nervously.

Interesting.

I don't push further. There's no time to waste diving into the faceless phantom in her fantasies.

From now on, my face is going to be the one that haunts her pretty mind and owns her orgasms. Pondering if my brothers have touched her in any way or form simmers my blood. When it happens again, I'll ensure her body recollects everything I've done to her—like conditioning a dog to salivate at the mere ring of a bell.

She may come for them, but I will possess a piece of that, too.

"Get on your knees for me," I command.

She scrambles off the bed, and I release her from the confinements of her lace bra, tossing it on the floor.

Holy fuck, she is breathtaking.

Taryn's hair drapes over her shoulders like a dark waterfall, her strands ending just above her nipples. Her tits aren't huge by any means, just large enough to fit perfectly in the palms of my hands. I want to think they were designed only for me, but it's thoughts like those that will increase the weight tied around my legs and drag me deeper into an abyss I'll never be able to escape.

She peers up at me, her long lashes casting a shadow that fans against her flushed cheekbones. My taut muscles throb, craving the caress of her fingertips. They're hungry for the feel of her nails scraping against my skin.

I've never wanted to destroy something so badly but simultaneously guard it with my life.

Yep. I'm losing my goddamn mind. I usually despise it when women touch me, and here I am, aching for this woman.

Reaching for the hem of my T-shirt, I tug it over my head, disposing of it in the pile I'm creating of our mingling clothes. I remove my sweatpants next, feeling her gaze anxiously study every inch of me. I stand in front of her, completely exposed, releasing a weighted breath. Taryn kneels in front of me, flawless and motionless, looking like perfection in the subtle glow from the lights as they paint her skin.

My gut twists, feeling her eyes locked on the visible part of my vulnerability. The part of me where there's ink embedded below the surface on the left side of my body.

My tattoos.

Shit. I really should've thought this through—kept my shirt on because I already know she's perceptive as hell.

Her focus isn't eagerly fastened on my rod-straight cock like all the other women I've been with. Instead, she analyzes the black design like a complex book she's struggling to understand. The look that crosses her features starts with fascination and slowly morphs into curiosity. I can see the questions she's forming dancing in her eyes.

Each second she spends dissecting the artwork, she claws deeper into my soul, seeing the pieces that nobody bothered to notice or acknowledge before her.

Unable to keep herself from touching me, she extends an arm, her soft fingers traveling over the tattoo, tracing the branches and healthy leaves of an apple tree drifting over my pecs. The ink covers my left shoulder and back, the leaves decaying and turning into the feathers of crows floating down my arm the farther they get from the single apple inked over my heart.

"I got it for my mom on the first anniversary of her disappearance."

She looks up at me with empathetic eyes.

Shit.

I said that out loud instead of in my head.

My fists clench at my sides, the admission sequestering every muscle in my body. Taryn notices my hesitation, and just as I think she will examine further and ask me something about my mother that I don't want to answer, she senses my reservations about wanting to disclose more information.

Her mouth opens, except she doesn't speak. Her warm hand darts out to capture my balls. She dips her head, allowing her lips to wrap around the tip of my cock. There's no holding back the groan that rumbles in my throat and gravitates toward her. Her tongue swirls in rotating motions, licking up the bead of cum that's gathered on my tip.

Her knowing precisely what I need, instead of talking, sends my heart tailspinning with unusual sensations.

Taryn's eyes expand, suddenly realizing the thickness won't easily fit in her mouth. I thread my fingers through her hair, letting her get adjusted to my size for a minute as her tongue presses against the vein on the underside of my shaft.

"I want to watch you take my cock to the back of your throat," I growl as heat sears every nerve and vein in my body. "I want to see how pretty you look when you swallow every inch and choke around me when it's too much."

"God, this cock," she praises, licking her lips before taking me deeper. Saliva pools in her mouth and drips down her chin onto her tits.

I reach down, using both of my hands to twist her nipples with the rough pads of my fingers. She moans, the vibration penetrating through my cock, igniting a drive to claim her in every fucking way possible.

Gripping onto her skull, I thrust my hips and bury myself to the hilt, taking away her ability to adjust. Her wet gurgling sounds and my groans fill the air when the tip of my dick rams against the back of her throat. Her eyes widen, hands flying to my solid thighs to keep herself steady as she gags around me.

My head drops back, her hot mouth turning me feral. When I glance back down, tears are falling over her bottom lashes.

"I want you to insert two fingers and confirm my suspicions that you're dripping for me."

She nods, full of my cock, and reaches between her thighs.

She already gives herself away by the tremor that torments her entire body before she even enters a finger.

My lips quirk. "That's what I thought. Is your cunt ready to be stuffed full of me, Little Ghost?" Withdrawing my shaft, I admire the way she prepared it for herself, making it glisten with her saliva.

Goosebumps feather across every inch of her skin. "I need to feel all of you, Colten."

Look at her begging for me.

Ready for me.

"On the edge," I nod toward the bed behind her. "And spread your thighs open for me."

Opening the drawer of my bedside table, I pull out a small gold package. She does as I say, spreading her legs, and I stroll up to her, dragging the corner of the condom confined in its package along her inner thigh and across her pussy.

Her eyes flutter closed, and she quivers just before snatching my wrist. "You'll be my first," she breathes, catching me completely off guard.

Those words thrash against my heart.

I know exactly what she does with that pink vibrator. She may not have been with a man sexually, but she's not inexperienced with penetration. The idea of her being untouched by anyone thrills me, which means my brothers may have messed around with Taryn, but I'm the first to claim her.

I am so screwed.

"Birth control?" I ask.

She nods slowly, and I decide right then that I want to feel all of her the same way she craves to feel all of me.

Lowering my body to cover hers, my cock presses against her wet center, molding perfectly.

I'll make it fit seamlessly, too.

I tuck a strand of hair behind her ear, infatuated with the

way her chest rises and falls. Each time her lungs inflate, her breasts sweep against my pecs.

Her expectant, glazed eyes dart between mine.

The pad of my thumb grazes over a reddened cheek. "Your toy might've ruined you, but I'll be the one to wreck you. I'm going to stretch your cunt to fit the size of my cock. And. Only. My. Cock."

TWENTY-NINE | TARYN

As he positions the tip of his cock at my soaked entrance, the groan that emits from his throat is downright savage.

I bury my fingers into the soft mattress. The grunt he made is like an electrical current shooting through his dick and straight to my clit. The aftershock spurs the heat swirling in my lower belly, and he hasn't even inserted his cock yet.

He makes me want to let go completely. Even if he drags me down into the dark depths of his soul, I could acquaint myself with the real Colten—the one who uses dominance as a barrier to protect the vulnerable parts of his heart.

Although if he's right and I've held control the entire time I've been here, does that mean just the mere thought of me chips away at the wall he always keeps guarded?

If I run with the power and wield it in a way that allows me to peer through a hole in the barricade, maybe I'll get to familiarize myself with the man who has clearly never told anyone else before me that the ink embedded under his skin is for his mom.

I saw the flash in his eyes. The disbelief.

It was evident that he didn't mean to confess that fact out loud. I wanted to push further—uncover the hidden meaning behind the apple over his heart. The healthy branches with leaves crawl across his chest and shoulder until they reach his lower arm and abdomen, the falling, decaying leaves turning into the feathers of crows.

It's breathtakingly beautiful and haunting.

There's so much importance in the tattoo. I felt it in the way my fingertips graced his skin, as if the ink would soak into my fingertips and enlighten me. My curiosity is still killing me, but if he somehow felt comfortable enough to let that secret slip, then maybe it's only a matter of time before he trusts me enough to let me in.

He grips my thighs and straightens his posture. With one rapid tug, he hauls my ass to the edge of the bed, using his palms to drift over the sensitive skin on my inner thighs. He softly pushes them into the comforter, opening me up to him.

Lowering himself onto his knees, he situates himself comfortably on the floor. I lift my head, observing as his head moves between my legs, peppering sensual kisses along my skin. He moves deliberately, shifting from one leg to the other, ensuring each gets the attention they deserve.

Colten's skillful tongue trails upward until it contacts my clit. I wince, grinding into his mouth.

His palm contacts my inner thigh with a slap, followed by the nip of my clit. A squeak I've never heard before emanates from my mouth.

"Look at you dripping for me, Little Ghost," he praises against my folds. "I want to see how much you can take before you make a mess on my sheets."

His tongue flits across my sensitive center in slow, teasing strokes. He inserts his middle finger, moving it in a come-hither motion that has my chest tightening and my spine coiling in pleasure.

Without any warning, his finger withdraws, and he pushes my arousal down to my ass, pressing into my other hole. I stretch around him, my body trying to adjust to the intrusion.

Holy hell.

I'm so wet for this man that the pain is brief, momentarily before his finger starts moving more fluidly.

His other hand joins, sliding two fingers into my cunt. The wet sound filling the room forces me to intake a lungful of air. Maybe it's a kink of his if I pass out from the ecstasy.

I shouldn't want that.

On second thought, maybe it would be a kink of mine.

His lips lift into a wicked smile against my clit as if he can read my thoughts. Colten's tongue only provokes the already present stimulation as two fingers glide against my walls and another stretches my ass. My eyes roll to the back of my head, the pressure building and whirling like Colten is the hurricane crashing against my beach and shifting my sand.

"Oh, shit! Colten, I'm going to—"

"You're not allowed to come unless it's on my cock, Little Ghost." Removing his fingers, he wraps them around the base of his cock, pumping himself with my arousal.

His cock is huge. It stretched my lips, but now that he is positioning himself at my entrance again, I'm worrying my bottom lip—chewing like I'm starving when I'm hungry for something entirely different.

His eyes flash ravenously, his thumb rubbing over my clit a few times before he lines himself up and pushes his hips forward.

Oh. My. Gosh.

No dildo or vibrator could've prepared me for this.

Prepared me for him.

The bed is the ideal height, giving him the perfect angle to thrust inside. His eyes stay locked on mine the entire time, his fierce gaze enticing the tension between my legs to snap. My brows pull together, my body adjusting to his size.

His focus not once straying, he continues to bury himself in my pussy and says, "You feel my cock stretching you?" I shiver at his erogenous words as he reaches the hilt and pauses. "*Goddamn*, the way your body responds to me is fucking addicting, Taryn."

My name on his lips is the most beautiful sound.

He hovers over my feverish flesh, worming his hand under the nape of my neck. Weaving his fingers through my hair, he forcefully tugs my head up, the sting egging on my swelling, aching clit.

I can't help it; my gaze snags onto his cock seated fully inside me.

He slants his head at my curiosity. "You want to see how much your pussy loves me?"

"Yes," I exhale, nodding in his grasp.

His hand moves to cradle my skull as he lifts my head up tenderly. Slowly, his hips withdraw, his cock sliding out and glistening.

His pace picks up, our grunts and groans filling the otherwise silent room. He pounds into me over and over again, summoning the darkness that will soon tip me over the edge.

His husky voice pierces through the fog, consuming my head. "You see how swollen you are? Your pussy is weeping for me. It's making a mess of my cock."

I nod, my head weighted and disoriented with desire. Luckily, his hold on my head keeps me upright, or I would collapse backward.

"That's because I'm the first man to claim you. After I'm done with you, your tight cunt is always going to take my cock perfectly. Isn't it?" My answer is how I constrict around him as he repeatedly hits that spot. Dots twinkle in my vision. "*Fuck. Yeah, it is.*"

I am so close.

"Are you about to come?"

Dizzy with pleasure, my eyes drift to the back of my head. "*Mhmm*," is the only response I can manage.

"You aren't allowed to come yet," he growls.

"Stop talking to me like that, or I will," I fire back.

"You and that fucking smart mouth."

He rises and removes his hand from my head, only to snake his arms under my back. He lifts my frame into his arms, keeping his cock fully inside me. My legs wrap around his waist and my arms around his neck as I cling to him for stability.

His hot skin melts into mine. Cupping my ass in both palms, he turns, walking straight out of the bedroom and down the dark hallway. His strong arms lift me up and down, still sliding in and out of me as my lips attach to the cord in his neck.

A faint beep seizes my attention, and I glance up and around at the pristine kitchen with vaulted ceilings and marble counters. The only light reflecting off the furnished wood floors and countertops is the oven light he just turned on.

He lifts me off his cock, lowering me to my feet, the cold wood floor under my toes making me tense. The delicate yellow glow bounces off his taut muscles.

I want to trace every mapping of veins with my tongue. Create an atlas of every cord under his skin.

I glance around the room, but his hands grip the sides of my face, bringing my lips to his in a hot, feverish kiss. His tongue enters my mouth to play with mine, and I hum.

My steps retreat as Colten backs me up to the cold countertop, the edge digging into the ridge of my back. His lips pull away, and he leans over, grabbing something. Peering over my shoulder, I see him reach for an apple in the fruit bowl.

What the hell?

"Wh—" I swallow the weight of nerves lingering in my throat. "What's that for?"

A corner of his mouth tilts. "Don't ask questions. Why don't you be a good girl and open those pretty lips for me?"

He wants to have a snack. Now?

My laugh stutters, my worries turning into flippant words that fall off my tongue in a ramble. "Wow. I thought you had more stamina than that," I tease, running my fingernails across his pecs. "Need a snack already?" His jaw pops in irritation, and I smile.

Grasping onto my hips, he spins me around, placing his hand between my shoulder blades. Shoving my chest downward onto the marble, he uses his other arm to adjust my hips so my ass juts out. His hot body and erection press into my ass from behind while the cold countertop clings to the front of my clammy, heated skin and hardens my nipples to a painful level.

"The apple isn't for me, Little Ghost." If a few words could stop my heart from confusion alone, it would be those. By his tone, I know he's wearing a malicious smirk. "It's to shut your smart mouth while I fuck you senseless."

What?

Reaching for the apple again, his chest leans over my body, pressing me further into the countertop, my hip bones grating against the edge.

"Open wide, Taryn," his husky voice taunts.

I shake my head.

He's going to shove that thing in my mouth.

He slaps my ass, and my jaw instantly falls open from the discomfort. Seizing the moment, he shoves the fruit inside. My teeth sink into the flesh, releasing the sweet juices that sit on the surface of my tongue and trickle down my throat.

Gripping onto his massive length, he drags the tip through my seam. "I have to train your jaw to stay open for long periods of time, so you can swallow my cock."

In one brutal thrust, he impales me. My teeth clamp down on the apple, and the ache in my bones is already present.

"Just like that," he moans, using one hand to lock my body in place against the kitchen counter as the other strikes my skin again. I shriek, quivering beneath him.

"You must like the pain, baby, because you're pulsing around my cock."

God, what is wrong with me? I am so turned on and fulfilled by this that I would be utterly content with dying right now, and I haven't even orgasmed yet.

Wait. Can an orgasm kill you?

If so, I'm betting this one will.

I can see it on my headstone now: *Here lies Taryn Meyers. Resting in peace after she let Colten Lindenvale obliterate her vagina and deliver a heart-stopping climax.*

His flexing hips retreat and then smack against my ass, his dick hitting that tender spot that shoots adrenaline and euphoria to my clit and quickening heart.

Spit and juices from the apple drip down my chin and onto the countertop, tears pouring down my face as my hot cheek moves across the hard surface with his powerful thrusts.

His head lolls backward. I love that I make him this unhinged. But I guess he kind of already was, so maybe it's not me.

The thought is nice, though.

Colten's eyes clash with my watery ones. He smirks, pounding into me to drive himself deeper.

"You take every inch so perfectly. You love being full of me, don't you? The only thing that will taste sweeter than the juice from that apple is my cum on your tongue."

That's all it takes. I moan, the noise muffled by the sweet fruit lodged between my teeth. My eyes flutter closed, my walls clamping around him as I plunge over the edge, soaring through a dark sea of stars.

He rips the apple out of my mouth, and it rolls across the counter.

My orgasm is so intense that his voice sounds like it's underwater with me in my sea of pure bliss. "Fuck, yes. Come on my cock, Little Ghost."

The movements of his hips become more ragged as I begin to shake.

"Colten—" I stammer lightheadedly.

Maybe it's the way I say his name, but his cock pulses against my walls, and he hastily pulls out, shooting white streams that fall in ribbons across my back. He places both palms on the counter, leaning his weight over his arms. His chest rises and falls against me uncontrollably.

Something is flickering in his eyes, but I don't have enough time to analyze the look as he swipes something across my back. My hooded eyes peer into his as he thrusts his fingers coated in his arousal between my lips. His salty flavor mixes with the juice from the apple.

And he's right; he tastes a whole lot sweeter. Lethally sweet.

He doesn't say a word.

Neither do I.

Our weighted breaths are thunderous. And with each passing second, the squall settles and dissipates. But come tomorrow, I have a feeling this is just the beginning of the storm that will devour us both.

THIRTY | TARYN

"O*ooh*, what's this one?" Elena points at the Pinterest pin I pulled up on the desktop computer in the office downstairs. "That looks fun!"

I tilt my head and grin, analyzing the craft photo. "You think so?"

Her palms clap together in enthusiastic interest. "Yeah."

I drag the bar down, scrolling through more pictures. Brightly painted rocks flash across the screen, their smooth surfaces decorated with patterns, others with complex images and inspirational sayings.

Finding an entertaining activity to amuse the kids today was a top priority since it's the second day Jessica is gone, and Bren and Cam still haven't returned from Seattle. Luckily, they should be back tomorrow.

I'm looking forward to it.

Their presence may settle the tension between my ribs.

This silent game transpiring between Colten and me is already making me go haywire.

Well, I guess I can't judge our interactions as silent, considering I've only seen him once since last night. He darted into the kitchen to grab some mail off the counter and bolted straight out back to work before I even blinked.

After getting more...accustomed to each other in more ways than one last night, he cleaned me up in the kitchen and encouraged me to drink a bunch of water. He gulped down several glasses before we returned to his room to collect our clothes. Honestly, I think it was a nervous quirk to keep his brain from detonating. I gathered that much from how one hand was grasped on the counter, the other was clutching the water glass, and his daunting stare was trained on the apple marked by my teeth.

Only a few words emerged from his mouth here and there, asking if I was all right and if he hurt me. For a guy who craves control, he gets awfully quiet and sensitive afterward.

The silence stretched between us, and after a few minutes, I took it as my cue to leave. He didn't have to say anything for me to know that he was uncomfortable with me staying—his tense shoulders and rigid posture were loud enough. He was a gentleman, though, and escorted me back to the house.

Or maybe he didn't trust me to not bolt after what transpired between us.

Frustratingly, it was probably both.

As he walked me up the yard and to the back door, I couldn't help but wonder if he regretted it. The last thing he said to me was good night, and then he pressed his lips to my forehead before I walked in and left him amongst the darkness. I returned to my room and collapsed on my bed, utterly exhausted from the way he commanded my body, stirring reactions I'll never comprehend.

But this morning, I woke up with my lips stretched, jaw sore, and pussy aching from his ruthlessness—spurring the visions of him last night, which have been playing on a repetitive loop in my head.

His hands. His smooth voice. The way he delivered my

orgasm with that damn apple shoved in my mouth like I was a pig on a silver platter ready to be consumed.

When I got up to use the bathroom, I found the bright pink pair of underwear I had stormed over with and a black strappy thong on my nightstand. On top was another note:

Bought these for you.
Only for you.
- C

I shift in the office chair, the wings of butterflies vehemently scraping against my stomach lining at the simple thought of him sneaking into my room sometime in the middle of the night and delivering the note.

Unless he came early this morning before he went to work?

He sometimes gets up to go to work at five a.m., but I was out cold. The floorboards groaning and squeaking stairs couldn't even wake me from my satiated slumber.

If I've learned to sleep through the voices of crows perched on the gutter outside my window in the early morning hours, I can sleep through anything.

My right eye twitches.

Hmm.

I wonder if he watched me sleep.

He practically dislocated my jaw last night with his fruit gag, so I'm sure my mouth was slack while I slept. My room may be in the attic, but at least it's newly renovated, so I don't have to worry about inhaling moths and insect carcass spores.

I would happily let him shove another apple in my mouth. That was the hottest thing I've ever experien—

"Why would we paint rocks? That seems kind of boring." Thankfully, Tristan distracts me before the spark awakening on my skin can turn into a raging wildfire.

"That's what you said about my *Scooby-Doo* game, and you haven't been able to put it down," I smile playfully.

He lifts a finger to his lips, tapping it against his mouth in thought. "You're right. What will we do with them, though?"

I pull up another picture. This one is an image of a rock sitting on a park bench with a painting of the earth that says, *Hug your mother.*

My lips lift. Clever.

"Well, little man, we would paint the rocks and leave them for people to find. It's kind of like a fun game that makes them happy when they see it."

"That's kind of cool, I guess." He shrugs.

"We can paint anything?" Elena drawls.

I nod. "Anything you want," I agree.

"Can we leave them around for our brothers to find?" Tristan asks with curiosity painting his features now. He leans over the arm of my chair to scan the image again.

"Can we take some to The Honey Hut?" Elena jumps.

I smile. "I think that's a great idea."

With her fist pumping in the air, Elena exclaims, "It's like an Easter egg hunt, but with rocks!"

I drum my fingers against the desk. We need paint and flat rocks.

Which means we need to go into town, and I need access to a vehicle.

My eyes bounce between the two of them. "How good are your begging skills?"

ELENA'S HAND is clutching mine tightly as we stroll down the dirt road. She tugs a little harder, and I nearly trip over my feet. It's more like she's dragging me. When she gets excited about something, it goes straight to her feet. Or her mouth, because she won't stop rambling about painting ideas for her rocks.

Tristan, Elena, and I round a corner in the dirt road, a massive shop coming into view at the dead end. Rossco darts ahead of us toward Colten's black Ford in the parking lot as if he can sense his proximity. I swear my dog is more attached to him, and it shouldn't piss me off as much as it does. He lowers his nose to the ground, sniffing around his tires until he gets to the driver's side door. The sight of his truck spurs the vision of him eating me out in the passenger seat. The image of him unhinged. His words. His rough, calloused hands.

I release a breath, and with it, the memory, willing myself back to the present.

The building is striking against the dark greens of the trees. It's the essence of a shop blended with the structure of a barn. The metal exterior is a pale green with giant wood sliding doors and rectangular windows with amber wood framing. It's tucked in the orchard next to a grass field, a ten-minute walk from the house.

It's beautiful.

"This is where his office is?" I ask.

Letting go of my hand, Elena runs toward the giant open barn doors. Rossco becomes disinterested in the truck, finding more amusement in the little girl running toward the building. A whirring sound of some kind of machinery emanates from the inside as they scamper toward it.

Tristan nods, pointing to a large set of windows on what I assume is the second floor. "Colten's office is up there. I like helping him fix things in the shop when he lets me."

"This place looks way too nice to be a shop," I mumble under my breath.

"Cam and Bren said there used to be a party here. There were lots of people and rides, caramel apples, and even a costume contest."

My eyes scan the building as Elena darts between the doors. "Elena, be careful," I yell. I direct my attention back to Tristan as we near the doors. "Like a harvest party?"

"Yeah. Mom and Dad used to have one every year." His mouth pulls downward, the frown making me want to reach for him. "Colten didn't want to do them anymore."

"Well, that's a bummer. It sounds like a blast."

He shrugs. With eyes cast downward, he nudges a rock with the toe of his boot, kicking it into the shop. "He doesn't like us talking about it. But I wish we still had them."

I place my palm on his head, ruffling his hair. "Maybe someday, buddy."

Walking through the doors, my eyes wander the shop. High beams and facades traverse the ceiling. The main lights across the beams are on instead of the two rustic black chandlers hanging over the floor. A staircase leads to a second-floor balcony with three doors.

There's machinery everywhere—tractors, four-wheelers, a side-by-side, and...

"Oh my God, my truck," I squeal.

My feet hastily carry me to the middle of the shop, where my truck is behind a tractor or vehicle of some sort with funky metal arms and a conveyor belt with bins. Tristan follows behind me. I plant my hands on the hood, my heart rapidly beating at the feel of the worn paint beneath my palms.

I was wondering what they were going to do with this. I figured it would get towed or something sitting on Main Street for so long, but it's here.

"This is your car?" Tristan wrinkles his nose. "Why is it here?"

"Because your brothers..." I think over my words carefully, "are storing it for me since I don't need it right now." I peer around, my chest tightening. "Where did Elena go?"

"Up to see, Colten," a deep voice startles me.

Judging by his tattoos and graying beard, a man in his mid-to-late fifties steps out from behind the odd piece of machinery blocking my truck inside the shop. He has a brewery T-shirt on, and his beer belly is stretching the material.

"Oh, um...thanks." I eye him apprehensively.

I had no idea he was there. About gave me a damn heart attack.

"Hi, Johnny," Tristan greets flatly with a single wave. "I'm going to go find Colten."

No. No, please don't leave me.

The man, Johnny, steps out farther from behind the corner of the vehicle with a torque wrench. His large, grimy hands, caked in oil and dirt, grip the handle. There's a tire beside him, so I'm guessing he's changing them, judging from the sound I heard before we came in.

I awkwardly sway on my feet, rubbing my clammy palms on the hood of my car. "I'm Taryn...the nanny."

The corners of his gray eyes crinkle as he smiles kindly, his gaze steady on me. His resolute attention has me reaching up to adjust my black baseball hat nervously.

Great. Being stuck up on the hill is already making me an introvert.

"Don't mind me," he waves a hand, "I've worked at Lindenvale Hill Orchard for the past twelve years. Just wanted to say hello since I may see you around more."

"It's nice to meet—"

"Taryn." Colten's cavernous warning voice booms through the shop, raising the hairs on my neck.

I glance up in the direction it originated from. Colten is standing on the balcony, holding Elena in his arms as she rests on his hip. Rossco walks out of the room behind him, wagging his tail, and plops right down like he belongs there.

Hot damn.

If sexy looks could kill me, this one would. He's in a white

T-shirt and jeans caked with dirt, his hat backward. I swallow, noticing his strained, tatted muscles. I may be a floor below him, but I can see how the light catches on the dips and ripples in his flawless skin.

My ovaries do a little dance. He would be one hell of an attractive dad.

He practically is one.

"Taryn, can I see you in my office, please?" Colten's husky command straightens my spine.

Yes, sir.

I give his employee a curt nod. "Nice to meet you, Johnny."

Propelling myself across the bottom floor of the shop, I take the steps two at a time. Walking through the threshold and into the office, I pause, taking it in. Elena and Tristan are drawing on a whiteboard on the wall with markers, not paying any mind to us.

There is a round meeting table in the center of the office, and Colten's desk is pushed up against some large windows with a view of, you guessed it, the orchard behind him. There are shelves of random books and frames, some with gold awards.

"I'm surprised to see you here," Colten says, leaning on the desk with his arms crossed. Delicious arms that were bouncing me up and down on his—

I walk farther into the room to sit on one of the two chairs in front of the desk, pursing my lips to divert myself. I plop down, his jean-clad knees a hair away from brushing mine.

Why does it feel hotter in here now?

"Yeah. I have a favor to ask you," I answer, wringing my hands together.

He raises a brow, eyes focusing on Elena and Tristan in the corner briefly before settling back on me.

Colten doesn't say anything, so I nervously grip the edge of the cushion on both sides of my legs. "I need to borrow your truck."

"Why do you want my truck?" he questions unequivocally.

"I want to take the kids to town to buy some paint."

He scowls, making me swallow. This feels like a very unnecessary interrogation.

"They have paint."

"Acrylic paint," I clarify. "I found watercolor in the office, but that won't work for our project."

Colten's eyes narrow on mine as if he's trying to dissect my brain and find a lie. It's unsettling.

"Absolutely not. I'm not letting you leave with them."

My eyes roll, and he glowers at my reaction.

"They are innocent children, Colten." I lower my voice to a whisper, "I'm not going to escape with your truck and kidnap your siblings."

I don't know why I say it. Maybe it's my brain doubting what happened last night and how I felt.

He places his hands on either side of him on the edge of the desk, leaning closer. Our faces are so close that we are inhaling each other's air.

"Even if you did, we'd find you and haul your perky ass back here."

Should I challenge him? Probably not.

But the notion of seeing him unhinged again thrills me, and I want to see how in control I really am.

My eyes slice to the kids again. I thought they would help me convince him, but it looks like they are too distracted drawing pictures on the whiteboard and giggling at something they created.

I smirk at Colten. "I think you're full of shit. You'd never find me if I didn't want to be found."

His face inches closer, his hot breath fanning across my face. "Want to test that theory, Little Ghost?"

I hover my lips over his mouth, flitting my eyes between his. With all this natural light in the office coming from the wall of windows behind him, they remind me of spring. The vibrant green that emerges after the pouring rain. Refreshing. Energizing.

"Kind of," I breathe honestly.

His white knuckles grip the edge of the desk. He pulls away, rubbing the nape of his neck with his palm. Turning, he grabs something off the desk. The clanking of metal fills the air as he tosses his truck keys to me.

I catch them, grinning.

"I'll be off around six tonight, and it's almost noon," he glances at the clock on the wall, folding his arms across his broad chest.

"Okay..."

"Take Elena and Tristan somewhere for dinner tonight. If I can't find you by eight," he mulls over his following words, "I'll give you your phone and your truck."

My eyebrows shoot up in excitement momentarily before furrowing in wariness. "Why do I feel like there is a *but* coming?"

"Because there is. If I can find exactly where you are before then, I get to punish you any way I want for challenging me." He smirks devilishly.

My breathing hitches.

Well, this is going to be fun.

There's no way in hell he'll find me; I will make sure of it.

I drag my bottom lip between my teeth. "Game on."

THIRTY-ONE | TARYN

Elena's tongue darts out, licking her lips hungrily as a massive pile of chocolate chip pancakes is placed before her. She swoops her finger through the whipped cream, unable to wait as the woman sets down Tristan's crepes. She sucks her pointer finger clean with a contented *pop* that makes me smile.

She's so easily entertained sometimes.

I'm hoping she'll hit that sugar high and crash so she can sleep peacefully on the hour drive home while I gloat.

There is no way in hell Colten will find us here.

Before we left the shop, he tried to give me his work cell so I could contact him if needed and have access to navigation. I refused. I'm smarter than he gives me credit for. He could've easily tracked that phone, and I wasn't about to hand over an advantage. Luckily, I remembered the route to Cascade Springs.

Our waitress returns with my French toast combo, and I glance at her IHOP name tag as she places it in front of me.

"Thanks, Melanie," I say gratefully.

Yep. I chose IHOP for dinner because I highly doubt it would ever cross Colten's mind to check a place like this. Plus, I am a sucker for breakfast for dinner. The way the kids quietly indulge in their meals makes me think that's something we all have in common.

Or it's because I let them choose meals on the menu that are complete sugar bombs.

Either way, points to me for being the cool nanny.

Seeing them happy has warmth spreading across my cheeks. Jess may be gone now, but I'm hoping I can be enough of a fun distraction that her being gone will hurt them less.

I glance around at the other tables, some with families and others with elderly singles. I still have no idea why he created this competition in the first place. Cascade Springs is one of the bigger cities around Cedar Creek, and I could've taken Elena and Tristan anywhere. It hardly seems fair, but I want my phone and truck back.

The pathetic part is that I don't even care to run. I just want to see if my parents have bothered to reach out. I would be perfectly content with one meager text asking how I am since they won't ask about the new teaching position. Honestly, they don't even know about it.

Or that I've moved.

I shouldn't be surprised since it's been three months since we last communicated, but the silence hurts.

Elena makes a humming noise of satisfaction as she reaches across the table for the syrup bottle. The drips cascade down the glass, creating a sticky ring on the tabletop.

She pulls it toward her, and I chuckle, popping a piece of fluffy egg into my mouth. "I don't think you need any more of that."

Tristan's gaze snaps toward me. "I want more, too!"

Of course you do.

Raising a brow, I glance between the two sweet faces giving me their best begging eyes across the booth from me.

Where were these looks when I needed them earlier?

Locating my knife next to the plate, I slice through my French toast like butter. "Colten isn't going to be very happy with me if I bring you two home all sugared up and hyper."

He'll already be pissed off that I'm going to kick his ass in this little game.

Which reminds me—

I peek up from my plate. "Hey, what time is it?" I ask Tristan.

Picking up his Switch beside him on the booth cushion, he clicks it on, his gaze darting across the screen. "7:50 p.m.," he tells me.

My chest erupts with a little bit of adrenaline.

Ten minutes until eight.

Tristan arches a brow. "Why do you keep asking me the time?"

I place a slice of toast in my mouth, crunching through the buttery bread. "No reason."

Someone at the booth behind me moves, shaking the wall my back is resting against. A large figure appears in the corner of my vision. When I tilt my head up, my eyes clash with those vibrant green eyes that instantly consume mine. With one look, it's as if I just took a nosedive off a cliff into glacier-cold waters that sequester my entire body and turn it into ice.

My stomach somersaults. In excitement or fear, I'm not sure.

Fuckity, fuck, fuck, fuck.

One side of Colten's mouth crooks maliciously. "Your lack of belief in my ability to find someone is amusing."

My lips part, my throat so dry that I couldn't speak even if I wanted to. He sucked all the damn moisture out with just his daunting presence.

"Colten! Look at what Miss Taryn let me get for dinner," Elena shrieks cheerfully. "The nice woman working gave me extra whipped cream!"

The sides of his eyes wrinkle while a raspy laugh shakes his chest.

The moisture is back in my mouth now.

He slips his hands into his pockets. "I can see that."

I've decided that his genuine laugh is my favorite sound. It nearly distracts me from imagining all the possible things he could do to me later. I lost. My punishment for challenging him is on the horizon, and I'd be lying if I said I don't get a trill of exhilaration behind my hip bones just pondering his threat.

He places an arm over the back of the booth, leaning into it. His spiced leather and woodsy scent overpower the sickly-sweet smell of pancakes and French toast wafting from the table.

Oh God. His cologne, natural scent, or whatever it is, makes me squirm in my seat.

I can't keep the whine from mingling with my tone. "How the hell did you know we were here?"

Lowering his body to the booth, he uses his strong frame to shove me closer to the wall so he can sit with us. The equivalent would be him sliding an empty cardboard box across the floor.

He settles in, getting comfortable. Colten's arm brushes against mine, shooting off all sorts of chaotic sparklers that dance across my skin.

A touch so simple, yet mind-bending simultaneously.

"Isn't it entertaining to not know the answer to that? How about we make this even more interesting?"

I knit my arms together, the tops of my breasts breaking out in gooseflesh when his attention lands on them.

My response is flat. "And how would you do that?"

His eyes find mine. "This is the first place I checked."

I press my tongue against the inside of my cheek. He must not miss the irritated look contorting my face because he grins.

He's lying. He must be.

Why the hell would his first guess be an IHOP?

Breakfast for dinner. I thought I was being clever because who in their right mind thinks of that first?

Unless—

My eyes widen. "The kid's tablets! Are you tracking those?"

He shakes his head, and my heart plummets into my stomach.

He knew precisely where we were. In fact, he knew *exactly* where I was when I went out on my run that one morning. The same way that Cameron and Brennan knew my location in the orchard when I tried to escape...

My chest hollows, allowing recognition to flood the space. "Oh my—" The wicked grin on his lips boils the blood in my veins to a temperature that's damn near about to burn me alive. I'm sure there's steam billowing out of my ears.

"Did you microchip me?" I seethe.

He lifts his water—*my water*—to his lips and takes a sip. Then he crunches an ice cube between his teeth, ignoring me.

Answer the damn question, Colten.

I concentrate on the movement of his tongue, wetting his lips. His mouth quirks.

"That's perverted and completely unfair!" I blurt louder than necessary, attracting the attention of a few patrons at nearby tables.

"A win is a win, Little Ghost."

"You cheated!"

"And you didn't ask for specifics on what tracking strategies I would use. That's your fault, not mine."

Ugh.

My mouth tugs downward, and I sulk as I press two fingers to the juncture of my inner elbow. Pressing firmly, I dig my fingers into my flesh, trying to locate anything that feels abnormal or foreign.

Where are you, you little bastard?

Colten side-eyes me. "What are you doing?"

"I'm trying to find my microchip."

"Why would you think it's there?"

I don't know, *Colten*, probably because that's where they put them in *The Hunger Games* when they were tracking all the tributes. Another movie scene plays behind my eyes, and my hand flies to my neck.

His head lowers to mine. "I'll give you a hint: it's not in your upper body."

My eyes narrow for a moment, then quickly expand unusually large. They enlarge to the size that encourages a twinge of pain behind my lids and urges a headache to form.

My head drops to my lap. Uh...is that even possible?

I mean, I guess IUDs are implanted, so it's not...impossible. But that means they would've had to do that the night I was drugged, and usually, they are below the skin somewhere.

Hello, vagina, do you have an intruder in there?

He follows my gaze.

The sigh that leaves him is infuriating. "It's not there either."

I glare daggers at him as if they could slice through his perfectly cut jawline and beautiful eyes. If his eyes bled from my fictional blades, I could only envision them looking like those pinstripe red-and-green candy canes at Christmas that my parents would let me hang on the tree—one of the only holidays where I didn't feel as lonely as I usually did.

His hot lips scrape against the shell of my ear. "And save those cock-hardening eyes for later. I want you to look at me like that when I claim your ass tonight," he whispers, the statement pouring down my spine like hot honey.

Sticky. Sweet. And sinful.

I pick up my fork, stabbing a soggy piece of drenched French toast. "You have no limits."

"Not when it comes to you, Little Ghost."

THIRTY-TWO | COLTEN

I pull my truck around the circular driveway to the front of the house and park behind our SUV, turning off the ignition. Taryn and Tristan hop out of the vehicle in front of me, and she rounds the other side to Elena's door.

I watch them for a moment.

Recently, I always seem to be watching.

Their interactions. Their expressions when they're around each other. It's mesmerizing and fuels the unfamiliar flame billowing in my chest.

She opens the rear door—the top half of her body disappearing into the cab. The illumination from my headlights kisses the muscles in her toned legs. Her feet shuffle on the pavement, her body appearing to be struggling.

What is she doing?

I don't even know why I bother asking the question because she's doing something that will probably drive a hedge hammer straight into the barrier I've maintained all these years.

And I'm fucking right.

She lifts Elena out of her car seat. My little sister's arms weave around Taryn's neck tightly, her legs secured around Taryn's waist.

Tristan maneuvers around her, grabs some plastic bags out of the back seat, and shuts the door for her. Their mouths move, their blurred voices barely reaching my ears. The conversation easily flows between them as if they've known each other longer than a couple of months. Tristan laughs, a vibrant and lively sound muted by glass, but it buries itself into my bones as if I were standing before him, witnessing it for myself.

Goddamn, I wish I could develop superhuman hearing at times like this.

Absentmindedly, I lift my fingers to my breastbone, massaging away the unwelcome ache. Jesus Christ, I wish these spasms constricting my chest would go away. It's only been present at certain times during the day, whenever she happens to be around. Or I think about her.

I should be relieved it's not the signs of a heart attack. I already went down that rabbit hole searching for symptoms on the internet.

Unfortunately, *chest pain when a woman is around* isn't a sign of one.

Whatever feelings I have toward her have been implanted somewhere out of reach—an isolated sanctuary deep within the recesses of my mind where they don't want to be tainted by all the valid reasons why she can't ever be mine.

I've tried to disregard them. Ignore the part of me that wants to feed the urges and consider what we could be if I somehow pulled my head out of my ass.

But if I don't acknowledge the *what-ifs*, I won't have to admit that I like her being here.

That I like the way she is with *them*.

That I love the way she is with me.

Taryn pauses, repositioning Elena's frame so her weight sits comfortably on her hip.

Opening my door, I exit the car and hustle over to her, shoving my keys in my pocket before holding my arms out.

"Let me carry her," I insist.

Her eyes twinkle in the glow from the headlights as she contemplates my offer since they have yet to shut off. She grips Elena tighter, nuzzling their heads together, and a lump lodges in my throat.

"I've got her." She walks quicker, passing me as we stroll down the sidewalk.

"Let me at least get the door for you."

"Is your driving time your reflection time? Because you are being awfully gentlemanly right now." I can't help but clear my throat to suppress the laugh slithering up my throat. "I figured you'd be arrogant when you got out of the car and order me to get the kids to bed so you can tie me to yours or something like that."

Blood rushes to my groin, my cock swelling at the thought of her all tangled up and restrained—ready for me to take what I want; however I want.

I want that.

All of that.

It was her idea, not mine.

To my delight, Tristan is ahead of us and has already entered the house. By Elena's pouty lips and open mouth, I know she is asleep. I quicken my pace to catch up to Taryn as she reaches the porch steps.

"Is that what our marriage would be like, Little Ghost?" slips out before I can fucking think about it.

Can't take that back, dumbass.

Her shoulders solidify, her movements slowing. Taryn's side-eye glare pierces straight through my sternum, forcing my heart into a staccato rhythm that presses against my lungs.

Her plush lips flatten into a line, but the pink flush in her cheeks is unmistakable.

I grasp the handle and open the front door, waiting for her to put me out of my misery and respond to my remark.

She swallows. "Uh...I mean—"

"It's about time! We thought you guys would be home when we got back," Cameron sighs, lounging on the couch with an arm draped over the cushion and a beer in his hand.

Oh, sweet fuck.

Of course, as I'm imagining securing her to my bed and having my way with her again tonight, these two idiots come home a day early.

I won. I found her. I deserve to have her soft lips wrapped around my cock before I bury myself inside her again.

Taryn shifts Elena's weight in her arms and smiles at my brothers. "Did Tristan head up to bed?"

Cameron nods. "He said to tell you he left the rocks on the kitchen counter. Do we want to know why you needed to *buy* rocks?" He furrows his brow. "There are plenty around the garden beds outside."

"I guess you'll just have to wait and see," Taryn teases, a feeble smile playing on her lips. She moves toward the stairs, her gaze bouncing between my brothers and me. "I'm going to get her to bed."

She disappears, leaving me to drag my hands over my face in irritation. "You two weren't supposed to be home until tomorrow night."

Brennan heaves a sigh from the recliner. "Yeah, well, little sister instantly hit it off with her new roommate and didn't want us around."

"She practically forgot we were even there," Cameron adds, bringing his beer to his lips.

"We offered to help her finish setting up her dorm room, but she told us it was fine if we wanted to leave early. A load of shit if you ask me. They giggled and whispered about attending a party tonight when Cam and I walked into the room with the last few boxes."

Cameron's head inclines as he changes the subject a little too fervently. "How's everything been going here? You two seem —more acquainted."

My muscles constrict in response to his statement.

You have no idea, brother.

Their eyes bore into my head from two separate sides of the room. The shifting tension whirling in the air tells me they know exactly what happened between us while they were gone.

And I'm eager to *acquaint* myself with her more, but it looks like my little bros are cockblocking me tonight.

"Everything's been good," I reply. "She wanted to take them to Cascade Springs today to buy some new art supplies for that rock project they're working on."

Brennan's brows shoot up. "And you let her go?"

I bury my hands in my pockets and shrug.

Cameron places his empty beer glass on the coffee table, then rests his elbows on his knees. "Yeah, what's that about? What do they need rocks for?"

"Shit, if I know. But Elena and Tristan are happy, so who am I to interfere with that?"

My brothers' heads tilt as they peer at something behind me.

My deep tone rattles my chest. "What?"

They pin me in place with a glare as the back door shuts and the wood floor beneath my boots vibrates, further anchoring me in place.

Cameron rises off the couch, snatches his glass off the coffee table, and struts past me. "I need another beer."

My skin itches with eagerness to talk to Taryn and finish our conversation. I assume she has headed outside to see Rossco.

I hike a thumb over my shoulder. "I—" Brennan gapes at me as I fumble for words. "Need a shower."

His scrutinizing scowl makes me uneasy. "Okay...Can you come back after? Cam and I want to discuss sales strategy with you before our marketing meeting tomorrow. And we need to talk about soil testing and decide what variety we want to replace section eight with."

We are already well in over our heads with suppliers. Everyone already knows our name and the brand, so I'm not entirely sure why we need to keep pushing. Is it not already enough that our produce appears in nearly every goddamn market across the country?

Marketing may be vital for every business, but when they see our brand, they don't think *they have great apples*. No. My dad fucked that up. Now, they see us and think about the trial. They think about the months authorities spent searching for my mother. They think about the vile man who returned to his kids with blood on his hands but came back without a wife.

Buying produce at the store is routine and straightforward. It's clockwork. And we have no problems whatsoever getting our product out. However, I understand their perspective. Marketing is demanding. I just wish we didn't have to do it.

"We already agreed on the new variety for section eight. Cripps Pink," I tell him, clearing my throat.

Cameron speaks up, brushing past my shoulder to reclaim his spot on the couch. "About that..."

Great. Here we go.

I enjoy working with my brothers, but sometimes, when decisions need to be made, it takes us a hell of a lot longer than necessary. Three different opinions. Three obstinate temperaments.

It's fucking painful sometimes, but at the end of the day, they're still here. And though I may not always act like it, I'm grateful. For them. For all the shit we've gone through together over the years.

By age fifteen, I knew I never wanted to leave Lindenvale Hill. My grades slipped in school because I was too busy playing sports, partying, or slipping my dick into some girl I grew up with up with since Cedar Creek is a speck on the map. I didn't need college, so succeeding in academics didn't matter. I passed, but because my priority was football, and I was too smart to completely suck. That was an advantage.

After graduation, I immediately dove straight into the company with my dad. He gave me an office and his trust and lobbed me into the deep end, challenging me to lead meetings and handle important client accounts. He expected me to tread against rough waters when difficult situations threatened to pull us under.

That was one of the last years when everything was normal. When I respected my father beyond anyone and told myself one day I would be as successful and meticulous as he was.

One night, I stayed late at the office to handle a client who was complaining about pricing fluctuations. It was one of several calls I made that day. By the time the conversation ended, we had lost the account because they had reassessed the client agreement and were unhappy with our increase in prices. It was the third one I'd lost that day. I slumped into his office, preparing for him to lash out. Tell me I'm a disappointment and incapable of running the company I would eventually inherit.

But he didn't. He walked over to his wet bar, grabbed two tumblers, and returned to his desk with scotch. My first glass of straight alcohol was with him.

"You can either let this experience hurt you or fuel your drive. The next move is yours. But a man only fails when he gives up entirely."

That's what he told me. It was a moment in my life when I

regarded my father as if he were the king. In a way, he was. A man sitting on his throne on Lindenvale Hill, running his empire—an empire that would eventually be passed down to me.

Every time I sit in my office—which used to be his—I recall that memory. When I lounge with a glass of scotch, those moments swirl with the aroma whenever I inhale it into my lungs—a scent that used to be sweet but is now vexingly bitter.

Cameron and Brennan had the opportunity to walk away. Cameron did. He got accepted into art school, but he returned to campus to gather his things when we realized Mom was never coming back.

They both sacrificed their futures for me. To help me keep this family afloat because I was so goddamn young when I inherited the Lindenvale Hill estate. But choosing to work together and run the multimillion-dollar empire was our next move.

It was the *only* move.

"Cam and I were talking in the car on the way home, and I think if we are replotting and planting, we should go with the Cosmic Crisp. Long storage life...hardy variety."

WA 38, or the Cosmic Crisp, was an apple variety developed exclusively by Washington State University. It's becoming one of the most sought-after varieties, but we scratched that notion because it has a significantly delayed return on investment and a high probability of market saturation. It's risky, but when the trees are finally able to produce a high-quality product, there's also a possibility the payoff could be substantial.

A privilege that comes with being one of the leading apple producers in the country.

Fuck, this is too much to think about at ten o'clock at night.

Unintentionally, I turn my head, glaring toward the direction of the back door. "If you two are set on the Cosmic Crisp, we can discuss it again tomorrow."

Brennan narrows his eyes at me questionably when I turn to face them again.

"What?" I growl.

My harsh tone pulls Brennan's mouth into a devious smile. "You're just," he waves a hand at me, "on edge." He knits his arms over his chest. "And you have been since you and Taryn walked through that door."

Cameron remains silent.

Jesus Christ. Is it really that obvious?

My little ghost is thoroughly fucking with every part of my body now and not just my head.

Giving them my back, I mutter, "I'm going to take a shower."

Brennan's strangled laugh follows me into the kitchen, the sound grating against my skin. I open our designated junk drawer, reaching to the back to pull out a pair of keys and a phone before marching straight out the back door. I'm barely across the yard when I see Taryn at the bottom, where the grass flattens out in front of my house.

The solar lights along the sidewalk and in the garden reflect off the blades of grass, while the lights on the edge of the house illuminate her silhouette and the ball she throws through the air. Rossco darts after it, his black body temporarily disappearing into the hazy darkness before he reemerges and returns it to her. She crouches down, wrapping her arms around him as she nuzzles her head into his neck.

The gentle touch of the breeze stirs the curtain of hair framing her face, the moonlight painting her high cheekbones silver.

She's beautiful.

It never crossed my mind that someone else might belong here. With us.

But she does, in ways I can't ignore, no matter how hard I try. And that's a big fucking problem.

She stands to her feet, and Rossco drops the ball on one of

her shoes. A giggle rattles her shoulders. I can't hear the addicting sound, but I damn sure feel the way it weaves tightly around my chest, the string pulling tighter the longer I ogle her.

Her mouth shifts into a smile when she throws the ball across the yard, my skin heating in response to the warmth that one expression can exude.

"I thought we were past all the stalking," she says, distractedly watching Rossco.

I don't know why I find it sexy as hell that she can sense my presence like I can sense hers.

She doesn't bother glancing at me, but I catch the amusement laced in her tone. "So, are we going to get this over with now? Or are you going to share your victory with your brothers since they're home early?"

Oh, goddamn.

Does she want that?

I don't share. I divulged that fact the night I chased her through the orchard.

The one line I won't cross. Not with her.

Not because I'm incapable, but because I'm afraid of what seeing her like that would do to me. Being with my brothers behind closed doors is one thing, but seeing her bend and conform to Cameron and Brennan will feed the envious beast concealed in the caverns in my chest. It would drive me to madness, pressing the side of myself that wants to make her mine.

Only mine.

Hypothetically, if we found ourselves in that situation, seeing their hands roam her body would make me want to bury myself deep inside her hot body and choke my brothers to death simultaneously.

I cock my head. "That's a bold thing to say to me."

"Well, Colten Lindenvale, you seem to bring that out of

me." She clucks her tongue. "For some reason, you frustrate the hell out of me, so you can only blame yourself for my insolence."

I stalk toward her, the several yards between us crackling with energy. "And what is it about me that makes you so irritated?"

She breathes out the word as if it's painful to admit. "Everything." She tucks a strand of dark hair behind her ear, nervously peering down at her fingers. Her throat clears. "If I'm honest, I've never really had anyone around to infuriate me. And when you do it—"

She picks up the ball off the ground again and tosses it into the foggy black void in the distance. Rossco bolts after it, leaving us alone momentarily.

My voice lowers an octave. "When I do it…"

"It's going to sound pathetic, so I don't want to say it."

"Say it."

"Colten—"

"Say it, Little Ghost!"

"Fine! Because when you do it, I kind of like it." She pauses. "Nobody has ever been around long enough to piss me off—at least not like you do. Even when you were fucking that girl against the window, you still acknowledged that I was here."

Her lower lip quivers. My fingertips buzz, itching to grab her and trap that bottom lip between my teeth so she doesn't have to wear this sadness transforming her features.

Closing her eyes, she shakes her head. "It's sad, I know. Sometimes, I wish I were that kid who had helicopter parents or an annoying sibling who always grated on my every nerve. I never had that. Sure, my parents were around, but they were always focused on the next adventure, the next house. The next place and yadda, yadda."

Pain prickles behind my ribs, my sternum tightening like a

massive ball python is coiling around my frame. Her words intensify their grip, squeezing the air out of my lungs.

"You call me Little Ghost. And sometimes that's how I feel —at least that's how I felt until you dragged me here against my will. I feel absolutely insane. I should be running. Should've done what any sane person would do and called someone or reported you when you let me go today, but I didn't. Because, for some reason that I'll never understand, I *want* to come back here."

Oddly, I trust her, so I put aside my hesitations and let her take Elena and Tristan today. Watching her with them is simultaneously befuddling and enlightening.

Taryn encourages my little sister's toothy, bright smile to appear more than it ever has. Elena is bold. Becoming fearless. Strutting around with her head held high and a flourishing sense of independence. We haven't been missing Jess that long, but the shift Taryn creates in her little personality is evident.

And Tristan...

Damn, Tristan is entirely different. He's talking to us. Not just because we ask him questions but because he voluntarily chooses to engage. Now, he lowers the Switch to his lap to fully interact instead of mumbling a few words or making sounds of acknowledgment with the screen in front of his eyes. He's initiating conversations, and my heart throbs at the colossal change she's instilling in him.

"But I still feel trapped, Colten," she whispers. The way she articulates my name demolishes the organ in my chest. "And it's not because of you three. It's because I was moving around so much before and never stayed in one spot long enough to form any kind of connection with anyone...Any kind of attachment that made me consider staying. I like it here," she says under her breath. It's a confession I barely catch amongst the voices of crickets and whirr of the breeze through the trees. "I mean, who actually likes being around the people who abducted them?"

I swallow her sincerity, tucking it away with the plethora of unfamiliar feelings she's awakened within me.

Drawn by the magnetic pull, I find myself stepping toward her. Her chest rises and falls, the motion suspended in time as her dark irises bounce between mine.

My hands itch to touch her—to feel her soft, elastic skin molding to my hands.

Instead, I tuck them into my pockets to suppress the urge. "Do you enjoy being around us?"

She nods. "Am I crazy for wanting to stay?" she murmurs.

I don't think she understands the weight those words carry. They've already etched themselves into my brain like the ink branded on my skin.

But as I hold her gaze, the durable part of my soul that has started to melt away since she arrived begins to solidify. Again.

Because saying you'll stay is just as easy as leaving.

THIRTY-THREE | TARYN

The babbling creek below drifts through the trees, complementing the birds chirping in the lush canopy above. The warm breeze whips past me, brushing a lock of hair across my mouth. The strands cling to my lips, and I swipe them out of the way, smiling in contentment. The fresh air is sweet. Revitalizing.

It's hard to believe that Elena and Tristan start school on Monday. Still, I'm grateful the guys decided we needed a fun Saturday activity to say farewell to summer before the kids return to their usual schedules and activities.

The guys have been occupied nonstop, preparing for the early and mid-harvest season. From what they've told me, that means primarily focusing on the plots producing the Gala, Honeycrisp, and Empire apples.

The last two weeks, we only converse in the evenings when they return from work since they are always up and out the door before the kids and I wake up. It's more frustrating than it should be since I was brought here specifically to be a nanny for Elena and Tristan.

But I understand why the guys did it now. The reason why they took such drastic measures to ensure I didn't leave them.

Tristan opened up to me one day while I was helping them write and draw pictures for their dad. Christian Lindenvale, the man behind bars, consistently writes to the two of them without missing a week.

Actually, I've learned their father writes letters to all six of them, though only five are delivered to the house now. Since Jessica's letters are always missing, I assume he's sending them to campus.

Tristan told me they always write back to him, except for Colten. Doesn't surprise me in the slightest.

What does he do with all those letters?

Does he open them and examine the words he wished would've never come in the first place, or does he stash them in the back of a drawer or on a shelf collecting dust?

There's something there. A secret Colten hides in the depths, out of reach. He hasn't said anything, but I feel it when I'm around him.

When I *was* around him.

He's been avoiding me since the night I told him I like being here.

The topic of their mom, however, is brutal. Despite a body never being found, Elena knows she's gone. Colten told her she's never coming back, and she's learned to accept it. That doesn't stop Elena from talking about her, even though she doesn't remember her mother. She imagines the idea of her. Putting pieces together based on the stories her siblings have told her.

But the moment Elena accidentally called me *mom*, my heart broke for her. The worst part? It happened at the dinner table. All eyes from her brothers held her in place while her glassy ones were hooked on me. It was an accident. I know that. But the world stopped momentarily, the slipped word causing the boys' breath to get trapped in their lungs. Their chests were unnaturally still.

Elena apologized shakily, and I soothed the anxiety that flowed out of her afterward. The twins couldn't stop staring at me, and Colten...was Colten.

He ate a few more bites of food, his posture rigid and face brooding, then tossed his plate into the sink and left the room.

That was the last time I saw him that night. Besides a few words here and there, our interactions have been minimal. The sexual tension, on the other hand, is unlike anything I've ever experienced.

Everyone is decked out in their swim gear, ready for a relaxing day at a swimming hole Cameron and Brennan said they discovered one day in high school.

I head to the back of the car and open the trunk, pulling everything we brought with us toward me—towels, the cooler, aired-up pool floaties taking up too much space, beach bags full of snacks, sunscreen, the whole nine yards.

Colten rounds the corner, his eyes instantly glued to mine. He brushes past Brennan and stuffs the keys into the pocket of his shorts. My focus drops to the motion of his hand. I'm no doubt blushing because Colten's lips tip upward, unleashing a flurry of sparks that skitter across my skin.

I didn't realize how much I missed his smirk.

God. I think I want him.

And I wish I didn't.

If there's anything I've learned about Colten Lindenvale, it's that he feels. Everything.

But he doesn't show it, discuss it, or want to acknowledge it in any way, shape, or form. He was a man who instantly had to become the head of a household too young. A young adult who lost his mother and watched as his father was dragged away to prison, only to be left with the responsibility of a multimillion-dollar company and his five siblings.

I don't pity Colten. I admire him.

My parents may not be active in my life, but I still have them. They love me, although it's different from the affection I wished for growing up. But the kind of love between all the Lindenvale children is irreplaceable and inspiring.

Colten's shoulder grazes mine before he comes to a halt. "We're going to go scope out the spot. We'll be right back."

I nod, swallowing. "Okay."

Dear Lord, can he tell I'm frazzled?

His mouth twitches upward. Yep, he can tell.

Colten may not be talking to me much, but I'm thankful he returned my phone and keys. It didn't stop there; he completely surprised me when he said Rossco could sleep in my room.

Peeking around the corner, I see Cameron unbuckle Elena and assist her in getting out of the car seat.

Tristan sprints to meet me at the back, Rossco trotting beside him. "I call the gator floatie!"

"I want the flamingo!" Elena shouts quickly after.

"What if I want the flamingo?" I joke.

Cameron appears beside me with Elena, her purple Little Mermaid one-piece swimsuit making me smile.

"Good luck with that," Cameron scoffs. "She never lets anyone else use that thing. Tells us we aren't allowed to because it's pink."

Elena sweeps her natural brown waves out of her eyes from the breeze blowing through the forest and peers up at me. "We can share!"

"Sounds like a deal." Flattening my lips into a line to conceal my smirk, I side-eye Cameron. "She likes me more, I guess."

His eyes roll. "I've known that for a while now. She isn't shy about voicing her favoritism."

That makes me grin.

Fifteen minutes later, all our stuff is spread across the beach in front of the swimming hole. Elena stands in front of me as I sit crisscross on a towel, her small body vibrating impatiently. My fingers swipe the sunscreen across her skin and blend it into her back.

There will be no sunburns on my watch—not with her delicate skin.

"Can I go *now*?" she whines, eyeing Tristan as he drags the gator floatie into the water while Brennan and Cameron toss a stick so Rossco can fetch it.

Three massive rocks surround the small, deep pool. A rushing creek gushes behind it, but the boulders and other rocks seclude the area, creating a calm swimming spot. A small waterfall flows between two boulders and into the pool, adding to the aesthetic.

This spot is incredible.

The sunlight filters through the trees, warming my skin. Nerves twist in my stomach at the thought of hanging out with Colten, Cameron, and Brennan in my bikini.

I chose one of my more modest options, a maroon halter top that reveals a little cleavage paired with full-coverage bottoms. But I already know I'm going to feel like I'm naked. I already do, and I have a white T-shirt and shorts on.

"Turn around quick," I tell Elena. "You're almost done."

She spins quickly, the rapid movement making her almost tumble into me.

I laugh, squirting a bead of sunscreen on my fingers as I swipe it across her face. "Now you're good to go."

Elena darts away from me, grabbing the pink flamingo floatie on the beach near where Colten is setting up some camp chairs. The size of the flamingo appears massive next to her petite frame as she drags it into the water in her mesh swim shoes.

I watch from afar, mustering the courage to remove my T-shirt.

Ugh. It shouldn't be this hard, yet here I am, nervous as hell about exposing myself. Both Colten and Cameron have already seen the more vulnerable parts of my body.

This is nothing.

Reaching for the hem, I toss my shirt onto the towel next to me. The wind glides across my arms, erupting my skin into millions of tiny goosebumps. After pulling my hair into a high bun, I grab the bottle of sunscreen and apply it to my legs, observing the guys as I rub in the protective layer.

Cameron and Brennan approach Colten, conversing about something I can't quite hear over the rushing water of Cedar Creek. Whatever Brennan said makes Colten laugh, the raspy and warm noise soaking into my skin with the sunscreen.

Rossco sprints up the beach toward me, his fur dripping water onto the sandy shoreline.

"Hey, boy," I croon. "Are you happy to have a water day?"

He pants, his tongue flapping about. Rossco shakes, and I flinch, the little chilly beads of water flying through the air and landing on my skin.

I chuckle, scratching behind his wet ears. "Thanks for that."

My attention lands on Colten while my fingers dig into Rossco's fur. He grips the base of his gray T-shirt in his fists, ripping it off in one fluid motion that leaves my mouth watering. The sunlight kisses the ridges of his sculpted muscles, revealing his flawless abdomen that I've felt pressed against mine, creating the kind of friction that sends my cognizance into a spiral.

Oh, dear God.

Cameron's and Brennan's shirts are the next to go. My hands pause on Rossco, so I can fully ogle their physiques. My eyes hungrily bolt over every inch of tan, exposed skin. They are all incredibly toned. Bodies that should be outlawed because they are so astoundingly distracting.

So distracting that I didn't realize, at some point, I reached for the sunscreen and have a giant blob of white in the palm of my hand. I slap it onto my shins, focusing on rubbing in the silky cream for only a moment before my attention settles back on the guys.

My eyes linger on the mapping of cords in their arms, protruding under their skin.

What would they feel like pressed against my tongue?

They all toss their shirts on a chair, their tendons rippling in a way that propels the heat flooding between my legs. Men swimming without shirts is normal. But at this moment, around the three of them, the look is far from innocent.

They are pussy-dripping masterpieces.

The sunshine licks my arms and legs; the heat is so unbearable that I'm clicking the cap on the sunscreen bottle.

Forget it. I'll cover the rest of my body when I've cooled down because if I don't stop ogling them, I might come right here. Their hands may not be touching me, but I can feel their auras from this far away.

Getting to my feet, I head to the water with Rossco. It's not long before I'm wading past Elena and Tristan, giggling and splashing each other. The ground below my feet melts away into nothingness the farther I swim. The calm waves lick against my neck, the heady combination of hot and cold pulling at my insides.

Inhaling the fresh air into my lungs, my body floats to the surface. Baby blue sky and wispy white clouds through the break in the trees flood my vision. Tipping my head back, I allow my eyes to flutter closed.

I force my breathing into a steady cadence, hoping the tension will seep from my pores and drift away with the current downstream.

A feather of a touch skids across my calf. My eyelids burst open in horror the second something wraps around my ankle, and an arm surges out of the water, crashing into my chest.

A partial screech is extracted from my throat, slicing through the air violently before my body is jerked downward. Entirely submerged, I thrash around, resurfacing for air, only to find two very wet men staring at me with handsome smirks on their faces. As I wipe the water from my eyes, my expression shifts into a glower.

I slam my fist into Cameron's shoulder and shoot Brennan the middle finger behind me. "You both suck. I was trying to relax."

Cameron moves toward me—a shark in water circling his prey. "Is that what you were doing?"

Brennan's tone is amused. "We were just helping you out. Your body flushed red while you were ogling us, so we figured we might help cool you off."

I wade to where I can stand and swipe a hand over my head to slick my hair back. "I wasn't gawking," I grumble.

I definitely was. But they don't need to know that.

Cameron wades toward me with unrushed movements. My heart thrashes. "Are you lying right now?"

"No," I say, forcing the single word off my tongue.

My eyes dart toward Colten on the beach. He's lounging in one of the camp chairs, his eyes penetrating mine as his two brothers draw closer.

My body is humming in response to their unwavering attention, all three of them eyeing me like I'm a bullseye in the center of the target.

"Are you sure?" Brennan taunts playfully. "If Cam and I dip our fingers below your bikini, are you going to be wet for us?"

I turn my head toward him, thinning my eyes. "We're swimming. I'm already wet, assholes."

Is it possible for your heart to increase speed so fast it vibrates behind your ribs? Anxious energy sparkles to every nerve ending.

Cameron presses his chest against my front, his proximity

turning the water around us into flowing hot lava that threatens to incinerate me. "I'm guessing in more ways than one."

I peer up at him, swallowing when another chest presses against my back and a pair of hands grips my waist. Cameron and Brennan sandwich me between them, and as hard as I try to breathe, they are sucking all the oxygen out of the air.

Internally panicking, I locate Tristan and Elena, but they're distracted, playing with something in the water on the shoreline.

"What do you say, brother? Should we find out?" The tip of Brennan's nose skims the slope of my neck, his fingers pulsing into my stomach as he holds me still.

Shit. Shit. Shit!

Colten shifts to the edge of the chair, elbows braced on his knees, his sharp eyes fixed on us intensely. His gaze has my body quivering between his brothers.

I know Colten hates watching—he told me that. But the way he glares at me like I'm the only one here is doing strange things to me. His unmoving demeanor is unreadable.

Does he like it?

Flitting my eyes back to Cameron, I hold his stare as his fingers glide up my inner thigh, skimming the material of my swimsuit bottoms. I purse my lips, striving to keep my composure, distracting myself with the beads of water clinging to his thick, dark lashes.

A corner of his mouth lifts right before a finger slides under the fabric, grazing my clit. From the shore, you wouldn't know he's touching me this erotically, but as he thrusts it inside me, the moan that effortlessly slips from my throat gives me away.

"Goddamn, Bren. She lied to us," Cameron groans. "We already know her pussy better than she does. Maybe we should get to know it a little more."

I'm not even fixated on whether the kids can hear us anymore. They are preoccupied, running across the beach, gathering things for something they are building on the rocky shoreline.

I swear I can visibly see Colten's chest rising and falling. His large hands grip the arms of the chair as though anchoring himself in a desperate attempt to regain control. Colten reaches for his shorts and repositions himself in the chair.

Fuck. Is he hard right now?

He might say he hates watching, but his behavior on the beach tells me something entirely different. Or perhaps he despises every part of this interaction between his brothers and me, but struggles to find the willpower to look away.

The thought turns me into putty between the twins—Brennan's chest against my back and Cameron's pressed against my breasts.

Cameron's finger moves inside me, making me delirious as my walls clench around him. Inattentively, my hands swiftly move to find purchase on his forearms, my fingernails creating crescents in his skin. He nods toward the beach, my brows drawing together when he withdraws his hand from below my bikini.

A few seconds later, the twins swim away from me. I shiver at their absence, my body reacquainting itself with the chilly waters while my core throbs painfully.

My gaze magnetizes to Colten's, both of us in an impenetrable staring contest that neither of us is willing to break.

His eyelids clamp shut. When they open again, my gut swoops violently.

The way he looks at me is downright alarming.

The longer I gape at him, the more my stomach plummets. Since arriving, Colten has terrified and thrilled me to an extent I've never experienced. As he gets up and marches to swipe a bottle of water out of the cooler, the pieces click into place.

It isn't one-sided.

He's frightened of *me*.

Before today, I thought Colten might be the one to destroy me—the one to bend and transform everything I had always wanted in a person.

But I think I was wrong.

Because maybe I'm the one destined to break him.

THIRTY-FOUR | TARYN

I miss the kids. The house is entirely too quiet and boring without them. It's been three days since they started school, and I've cleaned every inch of this house.

Literally.

It was a bit of a struggle, but I managed to pull out the fridge and oven enough to annihilate the dust bunnies and decayed food, some so rotted or hardened that I couldn't tell what it was in its original form.

It was a fun guessing game, though—it kept me distracted enough to avoid dwelling on the unsettling thought that the walls of this silent box might be closing in on me.

Like focusing on the little shriveled fuzzy ball that I gawked at for longer than I needed to, wondering if, at one point, it was a runaway blueberry that rolled under the fridge and disappeared.

Rossco is lying on the sparkling floor with his head on his paw, his ears perking every time the bass drops from the speakers playing my music through the kitchen. There may be no sweet voices echoing through the halls or the patter of bare feet sprinting through the house, but I sure as hell can make my own noise—keep myself company as I've practically done my entire life.

I glance at the clock on the microwave and release a heavy sigh. It's almost noon, and I'm already bored. Each tap of my foot on the wood flooring shuffles through the illusory box of ideas in my head.

Cookies. Now that's an idea. The sugary scent will battle the nose-numbing chemicals hanging heavily in the air.

I could pull up a Pinterest pin since I suck at baking, but instead, my fingers snatch my phone off the counter. I pause the music and tap the contact app to locate Adelaide's phone number.

I've visited her each morning after dropping Elena and Tristan off at school. Sometimes, when it's slow—since not as many tourists visit Cedar Creek Cove now that school has started back up—she will sit and have a cup of coffee with me.

She's quickly becoming a friend, and in my short time visiting her, I've gained a deeper understanding of Adelaide and Cameron's bond. They have been inseparable since they were twelve, when they met on a cliffside. He asked her out several times over the years, but she always politely declined. When I asked why, she told me that her relationship with him was too meaningful to screw up. Which I get entirely when you don't have a lot of them to begin with.

Eventually, he stopped asking, and they continued on like it had never happened. Internally, I called bullshit the moment she said it—I saw her knuckles whiten as she gripped the coffee cup, her throat working as if she were trying to swallow down the truth threatening to surface.

I click on the phone icon and put it on speaker. After a few seconds, the call connects, her bright voice filling the kitchen.

"I didn't think you'd be using my number so fast," she laughs over the sound of some clanking metal drifting over the line. "I just gave it to you this morning."

I lean over the counter and chuckle. "I've already missed your voice. And I'm incredibly bored at home and want to bake."

"*Oooh*. You called the right person, then!"

"I know shit about baking, but I want to make some chocolate chip cookies. Do you have an easy recipe I could follow? Possibly one that's I-suck-at-baking-proof."

"Okay, first, go into the pantry."

"All right," I drawl, picking up my phone and stepping over Rossco to the pantry door. I open it and walk inside, flicking on the light to illuminate the shelves.

Every time I step into the pantry, images of Cameron and me flash across my vision. Our mingling clothes thrown haphazardly across the floor. His head between my legs. Those green eyes observing me firmly as I came apart from his mouth.

I would've settled for the floor if I had known how often Elena and Tristan use the stool. Now, it haunts me. Whenever they climb onto it to collect something off a shelf, my mind wanders back to the memory of my legs spread out, melting for Cameron's talented tongue and his fingers as I found my release.

I blink away the vision, focusing back on the task. "What next?"

"Go to the very back and look at the middle shelf. There will be some—"

"Oh my God, you're a witch!" I squeal, instantly eyeing the large mason jars. I grasp onto one, turning it over in my hands to read the recipe taped onto the jar in beautiful handwriting.

Her vibrant laughter rings in my ears. "Cameron always craves my chocolate chip cookies, so I usually send him home with several jars to last the month. He's also horrible at baking."

"Thank you, that makes this so much easier."

"Just don't burn them," she warns. "The time on the directions will cook them to a gooey texture—" A faint chime interrupts her, and I pause, trying to place the sound. The faint ring registers—it's the bell on the front door of The Honey Hut alerting Adelaide that someone has walked in.

"I have to go. Happy baking!" She ends the call, leaving me smiling at the jar.

Thirty minutes later, I'm standing at the counter licking the dough off the spoon. It might be controversial, but eating raw dough is my favorite part of baking. Not that I do it often, but cookie dough makes me happy, and who am I to deny myself that kind of simple pleasure? Butter and sugar are the ways to my heart.

No wonder Cameron always craves Adelaide's cookies. If the batter is this good, I can only imagine how delicious the cookies are once they're fluffy, baked disks of addictive perfection.

My eyes dart to the oven timer, the neon green light reminding me that I have ten minutes before I need to take them out.

"If I" by Limi blares through the kitchen speakers. I munch on a chocolate chip, my hips absentmindedly swaying as my tongue swipes across the spatula, the sweet flavor dancing on my taste buds.

I can't remember the last time I was in this good of a mood.

I shimmy a few steps to the sink, reaching for the cabinet above to grab a glass for water. My movements pause when I glance out the windows, the car parked outside making my gut drop to my feet.

Uh...

Rapidly flipping around with part of the spatula in my mouth, I lock on to two pairs of eyes gaping at me from the other side of the kitchen island. My stomach flips as Brennan stares at me unblinkingly while Cameron, being the ass that he can be sometimes, smirks.

He finds sneaking up on me amusing.

Seeing them instantly flips the internal switch, turning the shock into searing heat that flushes my chest and overflows, flooding between my legs.

My eyes bounce like little ping-pong balls in my head as I leisurely remove the spatula from my mouth. Their eyes track the movement. "How long have you been standing there?"

Brennan leans over the counter, his fists gripping the edge. "Long enough," he grumbles, not meeting my eyes.

"We came home for lunch and got a show instead. Please keep going," Cameron gestures to me.

He rounds the counter, and I retreat a step, waving the spatula around with some of the cookie dough plastered on it. "Heck no. I didn't expect you to be home, and I'm extremely uncoordinated and terrible at dancing."

"The way you're giving my brother a hard-on suggests otherwise." Cameron's intense tone trickles down the ridges of my spine.

He advances toward me, and I swallow, his focus latching on the expanse of my throat. Each step he takes toward me is thunderous, the vibrations beneath my feet keeping me rooted until he stands tall and menacing before me.

My hand holding up the spatula trembles. He lowers his head, his mouth clamping around some of the sweet dough. The rumble that resonates deep in his chest pulses through the air, igniting a heavier tension between us. He straightens, his tongue fondling his lower lip as he peers deeply into my eyes— a penetrating look that's meant to dissect the thoughts chaotically running berserk in my head.

I'm fighting to keep my composure. This situation should not be as erotic as it is, and yet his steadfast gaze swirls the turmoil in my mind. When his lips lift, I question if he can see the commotion he's creating.

The Lindenvale brothers must have a plethora of broken hearts following in their wake.

Would it be worth it to be one of them?

My voice wobbles as I ask, "Does it taste good?"

"You tell me." Without warning, Cameron's mouth drops and strikes against mine.

He swiftly slips his tongue between my lips, letting me taste the sweet flavor lingering on his taste buds as our tongues fuse together.

Oh, dear Lord, I swear these brothers are going to be the death of me.

The kiss is as soft as his lips, but the arm that snakes around my waist, tugging me closer, draws a whimper from my throat, the faint sound encouraging him to devour me completely. The kiss spirals to desperate need, the tension between us finally snapping like an overstretched rubber band, weathered and strained from resisting for far too long.

As he explores my mouth with his talented tongue, my knees threaten to buckle from the spark that sets my skin ablaze. I let the spatula fall from my hand to place one arm around his neck and thread my fingers through his mussed hair, holding on tightly so I don't fall away from him—he's melting me into a pile of goo, and I'm afraid I'll slip straight through his fingers.

Damn, Cameron knows how to kiss. He has desire flooding between my thighs, my body begging to be touched in the way it shakes for him.

He groans into my mouth, and I hungrily swallow the sound. My world spins, his urgency unleashing sparks into my bloodstream like a drug injected into my veins.

He withdraws from me, exhaling a loud sigh. My eyes flutter open, barely catching the jerking movements of Cameron's head as he gestures to Brennan.

What is he doing?

Cameron moves behind me, his arm staying around my waist the entire time. But it's the other man stalking toward me that has my heart jumping on a trampoline in my chest to lodge itself further into my throat. Cameron tugs my back against his front, sending my heart free-falling back down until it bounces off my ribs and repeats the thrill.

I'm unsure when all my common sense vanished into some ulterior dimension, but I'm blaming it on the roofie they slipped me that night. That's when it all went beautifully downhill.

Brennan's tattooed hand snatches my throat, the pads of his fingers frivolously pulsing into my flesh as he forces my body to press even harder against Cameron's. His mouth lowers to mine as he takes his turn, claiming my mouth. Holy fuck, the all-consuming lust overwhelming me has my hips spontaneously rolling into him to chase the friction. His erection jabs into my stomach, and abruptly, I'm aware of a second one digging into my ass.

A strange noise—somewhere between a moan and a squeal—slips out. Brennan laughs against my lips, the beautiful sound and moisture of his breath eliciting the sheen of sweat coating my skin.

"Look how much you fucking love being between my brother and me," Brennan murmurs against my mouth.

I shouldn't be. *But I want to.*

Cameron's lips glide against the shell of my ear. "Just imagine how much more she would love it if we were both between those pretty legs."

Brennan and I simultaneously shiver at his words.

"Just say the words, Taryn," Brennan urges insistently. "Tell my brother how much you want us."

Most people have a devil and an angel resting on their shoulders, battling for control. I, on the other hand, have two twins taking turns sharing the role of the devil—one behind me and the other in front, their rock-hard cocks rubbing against my clothing. Layers of clothing are baking me from the inside out like the cookies in the oven.

Cameron's fingertips drift over my shoulder and down the length of my arm, summoning goosebumps that pepper my skin. "The next move is yours."

My body moves before I have time to ponder my actions.

If they want to play, then the game is on.

Craning my neck, I grip the back of Cameron's head behind me to slam my lips against his. He nips my bottom lip, groaning into my mouth.

"Fuck, yes," Brennan growls, lowering himself in front of me to grip the backs of my thighs. I break my kiss with Cameron, taking the hint to wrap my legs around Brennan's waist. "Take the cookies out of the oven so they don't burn, Cam."

Brennan carries me through the kitchen to the living room. When I think he is about to drop me onto the couch, he takes us behind it and lowers me to my feet.

Cameron's quick to join us. I'm not quite sure when his shirt came off, but his defined abdomen is glorious as he reaches for the hem of my tank top. He rips it over my head, tossing it onto the back of the couch while Brennan's fingers dip below the band of my leggings, peeling them down my legs. I unclasp my bra, standing before them completely naked.

"God, I've missed these tits," Cameron says huskily, lowering his mouth to one of my perky pink nipples.

He swirls his masterful tongue, egging on the pulse thrumming at my core. Brennan pulls the other one between his teeth, sucking and nipping, both the soothing and painful sensations shooting liquid heat straight to my pussy.

"I want to taste how wet she is," Brennan groans.

He grips my waist, spinning me around so my stomach is in line with the back of the couch. Placing his hand on the ridges of my spine, he pushes down so I'm bent at the hips, lying over the edge on top of the cushions. Weaving an arm under my thigh, he hikes one of my legs up onto the back of the couch, opening me up to them.

Cameron's palm drifts over the apples of my ass, his fingers dragging down and through my arousal that's now dripping down my legs.

"Oh, shit," I tremble, dropping my head to bask in the pleasure.

His fingers vanish, the hot warmth of a tongue replacing his digits between my seam. Cameron walks around the couch and appears in front of me. My body tenses, knowing that Brennan is the one with his head between my legs as his tongue starts to flick my throbbing clit. Cameron lifts his glistening fingers, pushing them into his mouth to lick them clean, and at the same time, Brennan thrusts one into me.

They are both tasting me in two completely different ways, and I've never seen anything so erotic.

I moan, my steadfast gaze locked on Cameron while Brennan continues to wind me tighter with his mouth and his fingers gliding against my walls, strumming that spot that has my balance wavering on the one leg holding my weight up.

Cameron sits on the couch before me, his hand wrapping around my throat as he draws his face closer to mine.

"I want you to taste how addictive you are." Claiming my mouth, his tongue instantly collides with mine while his brother teases my clit in slow, teasing strokes.

Cameron's lips continue to explore mine unhurriedly.

Slowly.

Fucking addictively.

The air shifts, sending chills across every inch of my exposed skin. Something feels wrong. I sense it in how my skin crawls, like the legs of spiders, overwhelming me with an awareness that leaves me flustered.

My gut churns, and the nausea peels my eyes open. They

instantaneously clash with a pair of dark green ones in the foyer—eyes that are usually vivid and alive.

But now, they are the color of grass under a looming sky threatening to unleash brutal rain.

The hue of murky water that veils the monsters lurking just below the surface.

I've never seen them so dark.

Colten's broad shoulders are ridged, his body as unyielding as a stone statue displayed in a museum. His jaw is hardened, his gaze boiling with red-hot anger meant to incinerate anything in its path.

And currently, that's Cameron, Brennan, and me as they devour me in the living room. However, unlike the twins, I'm not oblivious to the brooding man who has sucked all the air out of the room.

The unforeseen sight of him has a magnitude of pleasure flooding between my thighs, where Brennan continues pleasuring me with his mouth and fingers. Cameron nips my bottom lip, one of his hands lifting to fondle my breasts.

Shit.

I reach the apex, my leg trembling and my breath quickening as the surge of pleasure knocks into me like a rampant wave smashing against a pier out at sea.

I whimper against Cameron's lips as he pulls his mouth from mine, examining my expression as I come.

But not once through the crest of my orgasm do my eyes stray from Colten's.

THIRTY-FIVE | TARYN

"**D**amn, she just came all over my fingers and tongue," Brennan grunts.

I inhale an unstable breath. "Colten." I intended for his name to serve as a warning for Cameron and Brennan, but it escapes my lips as a desperate plea.

Cameron turns to brace an arm on the back of the couch, slouching into the cushions beside my head. "*Fuck.* Did Colten watching you make you come?"

I nod apprehensively, my eyes steady on Colten. He crosses one arm over the other, his biceps straining against his gray T-shirt.

Still bent over like a whore with a leg propped up, I mutter, "Yes."

The column of his throat works. "You two are supposed to be on lunch break," Colten grits out with clenched fists now at his sides.

He's mad. Colten's irritation is so hot that the light sheen of sweat glazing his skin glistens from the sun peeking through the windows. I'm afraid he'll start melting and drip onto the floor like acid. I'm sure he wishes it would swallow him whole, considering he nearly walked into a fuckfest between his two brothers and me.

Brennan stands up behind me, his jeans rubbing against my ass. "We are having lunch."

Colten exhales, rolling his eyes to the ceiling. He places his hands on his hips, shaking his head as his jaw flexes.

"You see that, Taryn?" Cameron quips. "That's Colten's I'm-going-to-fucking-kill-someone face." I peer at Colten, his gaze bouncing between the three of us. My focus lands on the growing bulge behind his zipper. "There's no need to look like that, Colt. You've always known Brennan and I are great at sharing."

"Not a fucking chance."

Brennan's wicked laugh seeps through my pores, tensing every muscle in my body. "So, you want to watch then?" he taunts. "We are far from being done with her, so it's either you watch her take our cocks like the good little slut we all know she is, or you leave."

"Come here, Taryn," Cameron orders.

Swallowing hesitantly, I rise off the back of the couch and make my way around it like a newborn calf learning to walk for the first time. My legs feel like jelly after being in that position for so long.

Brennan rips off his shirt, discarding it onto the floor. The grating of Cameron's zipper and Colten's heavy breathing only thickens the nearly suffocating tension hanging in the room.

Standing up, Cameron shoves his pants to his ankles and kicks them off. I come to stand in front of him, his thick erection springing free and jutting straight toward me.

He plops down on the couch, wrapping a fist around his dick as he slowly pumps himself from base to tip. "On your hands and knees. I want you to show Colten how talented you are at sucking cock."

Colten's sharp tone cuts through the air, "I already know how good she is."

I lower myself to my knees as Brennan discards his pants and moves around to sit on the far end of the couch from Cameron and me, so he has a perfect view of my positioning between his brother's legs.

Cameron threads his fingers through my hair, tightening his grip at the nape of my neck. I inhale sharply, the sting pulling a hiss through my teeth. "Do you? Or do you need the reminder?"

Before Colten has time to counter, Cameron guides my mouth to his cock. My lips pop open, letting him guide himself in. My lips stretch to fit his size, his heated focus observing my movements as my cheeks hollow to take him.

I want them. All three of them. And if Colten wants to play voyeur, I will give him something to watch.

My body is so needy, I'm quivering. My hands dart up to grip Cameron's solid thighs for stability. I take him deeper, his length soft against my tongue.

My gaze magnetizes to his, and I watch the way his eyes darken when the tip of his dick punches the back of my throat. The first few tears roll down my feverish cheeks, leaving cold trails against my hot skin, but I don't stop. He rewards me with his firm grip tightening in my hair while he releases a grumble that directly hits my clit.

"Goddamn. Look at how pretty she looks with her lips wrapped around your cock," Brennan says, standing to stalk toward me.

Cameron tugs me off him, his dick withdrawing from my mouth with a *pop*.

Is Colten really going to stand there this entire time? He told me he wouldn't watch, yet here he is, utterly immobile at the edge of the living room with his feet glued to the floor.

I rise onto my knees for Brennan, reaching forward to cup

his balls. My tongue twirls around the head of his cock, swiping up the bead at the top. He cups the back of my skull, holding my head hostage as he snaps his hips forward, fully filling my mouth. I choke around him as he finds a steady pace, moving in and out in a way that has wet sounds piercing the air.

My heart thunders against my ribs, trying to escape and fall between Brennan's feet. Everything about this situation feels sinful, but I've never felt so confident. Self-assurance bubbles under my skin, popping, bursting, and driving me feral for these men.

I may be the one on my knees, but I hold the power to bring them to theirs.

My eyes magnetize to Colten's as Brennan satiates himself in my mouth. His Adam's apple bobs, a silent testament to the internal battle he's facing.

"Are you going to check if she's dripping on our carpet, Colt, or should I?" Cameron's gruff voice comes from behind me.

Colten takes a step toward us, his first movement in the last few minutes beside his chest rising and falling with every shallow breath. His face is still hardened, but his expression sends a jolt of fear down my spine at his entranced state.

Another step.

And another.

Then his feet hit the carpet, and pure fright rolls through me, squashing whatever confidence was budding.

Never mind.

I can't do this; I am way out of my league here.

Colten crouches to my level, his warm scent of cinnamon and leather with a hint of wood enveloping me and driving my senses wild. He drives me wild. Brennan may be stuffing my mouth, but my eyes slice to the side to collide with Colten's.

His raspy voice has my insides coiling. "Are you soaked for my brothers, Little Ghost?"

A shock wave bolts through my body at his question,

leaving me momentarily stunned. Well, it's not a question exactly. A statement. Because he damn well knows that I'm melting for them.

The rough pad of Brennan's thumb caresses my cheekbone. "Open your legs but keep your eyes on me."

I am high on them. All of them. So, I do as he asks and reposition my knees on the floor.

Colten reaches between my thighs, sliding his fingers through my wet center. My eyes clamp shut as I moan around Brennan, feeling and hearing how wet I am when Colten slaps my pussy a few times.

"Fuck. She's soaked," Colten breathes.

"*Shit.* When you touch her like that, her moan vibrates through my cock," Brennan sighs, tossing his head back.

Colten leans into my ear, his warm breath gliding down the slope of my neck. "Should we show them how you prefer to take cock?"

I nod.

Colten's husky voice makes my clit ache and swell. "Sit on the couch, Bren," Colten orders. "I'll show you how Taryn prefers to be fucked."

Brennan removes me from him, and I take a moment to suck a few deep breaths into my burning lungs. Now Cameron is the one watching us with his dick in his hand. Brennan crashes onto the couch, and I move between his legs, grabbing his cock again as he shifts to the edge of the sofa, nudging my lips with his head.

The ruffling of clothes and the grating of a zipper behind me release an army of sharp wings that attack my stomach. They aren't butterflies. It's what I imagine crow wings to feel like. It was as if Colten somehow transferred the crow feathers inked on his arms into my body when he touched me with his fingers.

They are violent.

Frenzied.

Hungry to be quelled by pleasure.

Another noise turns my head—I think it's the legs of the coffee table dragging across the carpet—but Brennan grips my jaw with his thumb and forefinger, lifting my eyes to meet his.

Brennan's head slants. "I want to see the look in your eyes when you take my dick to the back of your throat, while Colten fills your needy cunt."

My teeth sink into my bottom lip, and I nod.

My eyes are steady on his as I lower my mouth onto him. Something thrusts into my pussy at the same time, making my muscles clench. Colten's fingers bend, deliciously hitting that spot that has my toes curling. He withdraws them, replacing them with the hot tip of his cock. He slides it through my arousal a few times before slowly pushing inside me.

Inch by inch, he stretches me, the feeling beautifully hypnotic until he reaches the hilt, pulling out and slamming back into me.

"Oh shit," I cry around Brennan's cock, but it emerges like gibberish. Brennan's mouth tilts in one corner at my inability to speak.

"This is the hottest fucking thing I have ever seen in my life," Cameron groans.

He moves closer to Brennan on the couch as Colten rolls his hips into my ass from behind, his heated and clammy skin slapping against mine. Cameron reaches for my hand, bringing it to grip his rock-hard erection as his brothers use me.

"How does her pussy feel, Colt?" Cameron inquires as my fingers wrap around his length while Bren thrusts between my lips, and Colten's pacing picks up from behind.

Pleasure racks through my body, and the rope coiling in my lower belly starts to tighten.

"Her cunt is gripping me so tightly," Colten exhales.

One hand grips my ass cheek while the other is splayed

across my lower back. He strikes into me from behind, pushing Brennan's cock deeper down my throat every time his hips snap forward.

Colten's fingers travel up my spine, tangling into my hair. "What do you say, Little Ghost? Should we let Cam take your ass?"

I squirm, both of their grips compressing into my damp flesh to keep me in place while their cocks fill me. That would be too much. There's no way I can take all three of them simultaneously. The words loiter on my tongue, but Colten's ruthless thrusting has Brennan's length shoving them back down where they'll never see the light of day.

Colten wraps my hair around his fist, pulling my head up. I wince in pain, sucking in the air I was deprived of the second Brennan's cock falls from my mouth.

Colten withdraws from my center, standing up to settle on the couch. He doesn't release me, my scalp aching when he tugs me along with him. I'm sure in his eyes, some of this is my punishment for what he walked into. Nothing says welcome home for lunch like seeing me sandwiched between his twin brothers as one sucked on my clit while the other devoured my mouth. I'm sure he would've preferred an actual sandwich.

He sinks into the couch, every muscle relaxing against the firm armrest. He pulls his legs up, his muscular limbs sprawling out as he pulls me on top to straddle him. His hands locate the juncture between my hip bones and my soft stomach, his calloused touch igniting a wildfire that coasts across my skin, a bead of sweat trickling down my neck.

My palms flatten against his inked pecs, giving myself purchase to grind my clit along his erection. The electrifying friction sparks the fuse like a firework, anticipating the explosion that will shatter us into pieces.

Shatter our restraint.

Shatter our untouchable little world on the hill because there's no going back after this.

Colten's chest rises and falls under my hands. "Are you ready to take all three of our cocks?" My answering swallow transforms his mouth into a vicious grin. "No turning back now, Taryn."

The way his gravelly voice articulates my name could make me come right here. He said I'm only allowed to come on his cock, so technically, I wouldn't be breaking the rules since his hard length is pressed against my wet center.

His large hand snatches my throat, dragging my chest down to rest against his—my breasts perfectly molding to his pecs as Cameron's hands firmly grip my ass.

Colton's voice lowers to a whisper as his lips skim my ear, a warning laced in his tone. "You're fucking with my entire head, baby. I said I don't share—" He wets his lips. "But here we are, and if you were bent over the couch like a slut for my brothers, I'm going to treat you like one. And good sluts let all their holes be used."

His admonition echoes in my ears, unleashing an impenetrable, suffocating fog that prevents coherent thoughts from forming. Cameron says something, but a strange sense of dissociation washes over me. His voice sounds distant and muffled, as if I'm watching this scene unfold from somewhere far away.

"She's ready," Colten answers.

Shit. Is that what Cameron asked?

Because I'm not sure I am. These Lindenvale brothers are carrying trophies between their legs. I can barely handle one brother when we're fucking around, let alone three.

At the same time.

"Oh, God." I don't mean for my whimper to be audibly heard, but their knowing snickers tell me they liked hearing it.

Brennan stands behind Colten's head, where he's still

relaxed against the armrest. I'm facing Colten and Brennan in this position, and Cameron is...

Fingers slip through my dripping arousal behind me, making me shudder. I brush my chin over my shoulder, observing as Cameron moves a finger to my other tight hole. He inserts a digit and holds my eyes, my muscles clenching and teeth gritting at the intrusion.

A corner of his mouth tips, and he moves his finger in and out as I slowly adjust to it. Taking one is manageable, but when his speed picks up and I release a whimper, hunger flashes across his eyes. He withdraws it, drags two fingers through my center, coating them in my arousal, and repositions them at my back entrance before shoving them inside.

"Ah," I bite out as Cameron works to stretch me so I can fit him.

So I can fit all of them.

The pain intensifies, and I slam my eyes shut, trying to ignore the burning behind my eyes.

A finger dips below my chin, turning my head. "Focus on me and relax your muscles. It's going to hurt, but you can take it." Colten's hands snake toward my back, spreading my ass so Cameron has better access to stretch me slowly.

My lips flatten in a line—the pain slowly morphing into pleasure as the seconds turn into minutes and the discomfort and ache subside. Colten wraps his arms around my back, lowering my lips to his. Words leave Cameron's mouth, but I'm too lost in the feverish kiss with Colten as our tongues strike, heating up the temperature coating my skin. He explores my mouth, our lips moving in sync. Too many emotions and feelings are consuming me when Cameron spits on my ass, dragging his cock through before positioning his tip at my entrance.

I whimper into Colten's mouth nervously, the sound enticing his tongue to sweep and frolic with mine in a way that has my head spinning with dizzying intensity.

Why is it that kissing during sex increases the intimacy level tenfold? He's not even the one slowly thrusting inside me. His brother is. But the flawless man under me is seeping further into my heart with every encounter. Every touch, no matter how minuscule or immense it may be.

My heart rumbles behind my rib cage. A bead of sweat trickles down my back as the living room suddenly feels like a furnace, burning me alive. I push up to draw in a full breath, but Colten grips his dick and wastes no time pressing into my soaked pussy.

"Goddamn. This ass is so fucking tight," Cameron grunts, burying himself to the hilt.

Tears burn behind my eyes at the ache that is as excruciating as it is beautiful. Pleasure can satisfy, but pain stirs the soul, making you feel alive. A muted scream is driven from my lungs, the fullness coiling the taut string in my stomach.

Colten groans, pushing his hips up at a steady, mind-bending pace. Cameron doesn't move, though. He may be inside me, but he's waiting for me to adjust to the feeling of him in my ass while his brother fills my pussy.

"One more, baby," Colten hums.

Why does he keep calling me that? It almost sounds like a declaration.

He couldn't be claiming me in front of his brothers.

Could he?

Do I even want him to?

Yes. Yes, I do.

Instinctively, I lean forward, my lips popping open. Brennan's thick cock drifts along my tongue to the back of my throat, the three of them filling me completely. I should feel dirty. Embarrassed. But I don't. I feel powerful when I make these men unhinged.

Colten thrusts upward under me as Cameron starts slowly

pushing his hips forward. My watery eyes roll upward, clashing with Brennan's green ones.

A tear cascades over my bottom lashes and onto my cheek. His wicked smile spurs my confidence, and I moan around his cock, watching the way his taut abdomen tightens further, showcasing his abs that cut into his tan skin.

"Look at those tears dripping on my cock."

That's what Brennan said that night in the Orchard when I ran. I'm not sure why, but I think Brennan gets off on tears.

"Look at those beautiful brown eyes melting for us," Brennan grunts, swiping his thumb over my jaw to wipe away the saliva dripping down my chin.

Yep. Me crying definitely turns him on. I can feel it in the way the vein under his shaft throbs against my tongue.

"Fuck. Fuck. *Fuck!* I'm not going to last long like this." Cameron's fingers dig into my ass as he starts grinding at a steadier pace from behind now that he's stretched me to fit him.

They say if you pinch yourself, you won't feel other pain because the sharp sensation distracts your brain, momentarily masking any other discomfort. Between Brennan's cock hitting the back of my throat, Colten filling my pussy, and Cameron taking my ass, there are so many emotions and things happening to my body that it numbs the agony. They are dragging me down to the depths, drowning me in euphoria.

Heavy breaths and skin slapping skin overtake the room, their skilled movements fluttering the pulse in my clit, encouraging my oncoming orgasm. My glazed eyes roll to the back of my head.

"None of us are." Brennan's voice hints that he's grinning. "Look at how perfectly she's taking all of us."

"Are you going to show us how grateful you are, Little Ghost," Colten exhales sharply, "and come while we're all buried inside you?"

The slight curve in Colten's dick hits that spot that has my toes digging into the couch. Darkness clouds my vision. I moan in response, letting it consume me. My cheeks are hollow for Brennan as my pussy and ass clench around both Cameron's and Colten's cocks.

"Yes, just like that baby," Colten soothes, his face appearing through my blurry, watery eyes.

Those words haul me into a space where time doesn't exist. Nothing else exists but us. I come around them, my eyes fluttering closed as the surge crashes into me so hard my limbs shake and quiver with the climax.

"Fuck, I'm coming," Cameron bellows, pulling out as hot ribbons fall across my back.

"Shit, me too," Brennan says the second salty streams coat the back of my throat.

Colten doesn't stop. He goes harder. Mercilessly pounding my pussy while I struggle to swallow Brennan's cum as he pulls out of my mouth. I don't know what colossal storm is raging in Colten's head, but his fingers wrap around my throat like a vise.

He covers my mouth with his, his tongue immediately demanding entrance. I cry out at the overwhelming emotions consuming me, our teeth clashing and lips fueling the flames.

Holy hell.

I shriek against his lips as Colten draws a second orgasm from me, but only for him. His dick jolts, pulsing his cum inside of me as he finds his release with me. My chest cracks open, letting this man sink deeper into my soul.

The realization dawns on me that he doesn't have a condom on. Neither did Cameron. But I can't bring myself to care as I feel his hot release dripping down the inside of my thighs as he draws out both of our orgasms.

His lips brush gently against mine, and he slows his pace, riding out both of our orgasms. He lifts his face from mine, gaping at me with heated eyes. The look almost makes me forget that Cameron and Brennan, completely satiated, are staring at us. But it's not long before the intensity gleaming in Colten's eyes alters into confusion, then something else entirely that seizes my breath.

We all exist in complete silence, and I can see the war raging behind Colten's green irises. He looks like he's about to break, and my heart thrashes.

He lifts me off him, shaking his head at himself.

He's spiraling, and all I want to do is save him—to wrap my arms around him and tell him I'm sorry for dragging him into this mess when it bends his morals.

Hauling himself off the couch, he irritably reaches for his pants and shirt on the floor and does what he always does.

He leaves the room without another word to any of us.

Brennan and Cameron peer at me, their scrutinizing gazes feeling like ants crawling up my limbs.

"Colten, wait," I holler.

Grabbing the blanket off the couch, I wrap it around my naked body, chasing after him. But he's already gone. I hustle through the foyer, down the hallway, and out the back door, which he didn't even bother to shut. I sprint across the yard, extremely aware of their cum leaking down my thighs, but I'm too focused on the brooding man marching up his porch steps.

"Colten, please stop," I yell. "Just talk to me!"

It's as if his body hits a wall. His shirt is clenched in his fist, but his pants are on. The muscles in his back are rigid, his shoulders so broad and strained that I could slam my fist against him and break bones.

My heart sinks like a boulder tossed into the deepest trench in the sea when he keeps walking and slams the door behind him.

I stand there with the blanket wrapped tightly around me. It's fine. If he doesn't want to face me now, I know there's one thing I can do that he won't be able to ignore.

Because Colten Lindenvale hates it when I run.

THIRTY-SIX | TARYN

"My pencil keeps breaking," Elena whines, tossing the yellow pencil onto the table with as much irritability as a five-year-old can muster. Her pouty lips stick out as she watches the pencil roll across the table and tumble to the floor.

Tristan glances up from his math problems, rolling his eyes. "You keep pressing down too hard."

"No, it's the pencil," she counters, knitting her arms over her chest.

I toss the cucumbers and tomatoes I picked from the garden this afternoon into the salad bowl, watching them argue. "And I think you two need to clean up and get ready for dinner," I interrupt.

They both sigh, push their chairs away from the table, and exit the room, muttering to each other under their breaths.

I stood out in the trickling rain, picking at various plants for over an hour earlier, thinking Colten would either get fed up with my pathetic lurking or return to work where I could snag him for a chat before he left.

He's done neither.

This whole afternoon, since our...fuckfest at lunch, he's been locked away in his house. And I know that because I tried the front door. There's a back door, too, but that one was also locked. Then I wandered around to his bedroom windows with a dripping wet Rossco trailing behind me, but the shades were drawn. I couldn't see in, and he couldn't see out.

That solidified my scheme, so I'm planning to make a "break for it" after dinner, since I'm doubtful he'll attend. That notion is proved true when Cameron and Brennan wander into the kitchen and shake their heads with apologetic expressions, hinting that their chat with him didn't go as planned.

"I figured." I sigh, leaning over my hands on the countertop.

They both stare at me. The only reason there is awkward silence right now has nothing to do with what happened earlier between all of us. We are more concerned about Colten and the internal battle he's facing. One that we initiated.

We acted thoughtlessly.

The kids might not have been home today, but we should've known Colten could catch us.

Brennan flattens his lips. "It's our fault. We pushed him too far."

I reach for the plate of cookies on the counter, unable to resist. At least taking them out early before we lost ourselves in each other resulted in some perfectly chewy cookies. I always prefer them undercooked anyway. I take a bite while they watch me.

"It's my fault," I shake my head, choking on the words. "He said that first night in the forest that he would never share."

He told me he has been losing control since he brought me here, and I can't help but feel like this is my doing. The lust disoriented me. I wasn't thinking clearly, and as much as I loved feeling all three of them, my skin crawls with distress.

I don't regret it per se. But I don't feel good about it either.

Colten won't talk to any of us. He's doing what he always

does: surrendering himself to the chaotic thoughts in his head and allowing them to run amuck.

Sad laughter shakes Cameron's chest. "Yeah, he's always been the brother who...struggles to share his possessions."

I taper a brow. "So, he's possessive over me." It's not a question; I'm saying it out loud so my brain can process it.

"Well, something clearly happened between you two when we took Jessica to school. It's not hard to guess what it was," Brennan's tone alludes. He reaches for the plate of cookies, and I impulsively swat at his hand, smacking the back of the wrist. "Ow!" He points to my fingers digging into the soft dough. "You're eating one. I guess the lack of sharing skills is something you and Colten have in common."

Smirking at him, I tear off half of my cookie and hand it to him right as Elena and Tristan amble into the kitchen. Perfect timing. They both eye the cookie with bright eyes and huge shit-eating grins.

Elena opens her mouth, but Cameron reads her mind, instantly cutting her off. "After dinner." He hands Tristan a dinner plate and wanders to the oven, starting to dish some spaghetti on Elena's. "And you have to eat at least half your plate if you want a cookie."

"*Sooo*, what did he say when you talked to him?" I ask, shifting my attention to Brennan as Elena grills Cameron about why she can't have a cookie before dinner.

Got to give her credit for trying.

Brennan shrugs, wiping his fingers on his jeans as he finishes chewing. "Barely anything. He was pretty piss—mad." I chuckle at his save since Elena and Tristan are in the room. "He said he would be eating dinner at home and proceeded to get rid of us by saying he'd see us at five tomorrow morning in section fifteen."

"Dang. He must be really mad if he told you to meet him at

five." Colten may go to work early, but the twins are usually out of the house by seven.

Cameron focuses on the pot of spaghetti he's dishing onto plates but joins in on the conversation. "He said something about a heat wave tomorrow, so he wants to get fertilizing done early, which is crap if you ask me. Knowing him, he'll probably get started around four to release some pent-up frustration before we join him."

On that note, "I'm going on a run after dinner." I grab a plate from the stack on the marble island.

Cameron hands Elena her plate by the oven, glaring at me suspiciously. They still look at me like that whenever I say I'm going on a run. I go on a run most mornings now, and clearly, I always come back.

"You went on one this morning, and it's dark outside," Cameron mentions distrustfully.

"Yes, but Colten won't talk to either of you and there's only one way he'll talk to me." Their eyes burn through my skull as my gaze bounces between them. "Which is also why I need to ask a favor from you two."

I WRIGGLE my hands into my sweatshirt pocket, soaking in the warmth. My eyes flutter shut, fully appreciating the scent of the river mingling seamlessly with the breeze. I inhale a deep breath, letting the cool air calm my anxiety and heated lungs. When I close my eyes, the water lapping against the cliffside below sounds like a calm ocean on a sunny day.

It's peaceful and quiet. But when I open my eyes, panic courses through my veins like my blood is one with the rushing river below.

I'm fearful of heights, yet here I am—staring down at the dark moonlit waters shimmering with silver light that's too mesmerizing to walk away from. I step closer to the edge, my eyes rolling with each wave smashing against the rocks thirty feet below—the water drifting across the little ledge at the bottom, barely rising above the water's surface.

I'm not sure what persuaded me to step up to the brink. There's just something stunningly haunting about the pitch-black water. It's so petrifying that I would forever sink into a cold void of murky water if I jumped.

A flash of light glimmers off the blades of grass swaying in the breeze, making my heart beat a little harder—faster with the growing sound of tires crunching gravel.

I don't have to turn around to know the car speeding down the driveway is Colten's truck. The hum of the diesel engine is enough of a sign, the sound vibrating my bones the closer it gets.

Turning my chin over my shoulder, my eyes thin into slits at the oncoming headlights. He gets to the spot right before the significant bend in the road, slamming on his brakes.

I can't decide what's more unsettling—that he doesn't exit immediately or that his face is hidden behind tinted windows. But I don't have to witness his expression to know that he's pissed at me. The fact that he's here means Cameron and Brennan played their part. He won't talk to me willingly, so here I am, attempting to get him to speak to me with the only way I know will work.

He throws open the door, hopping out. The second his shoes hit the ground, a spark of adrenaline smashes into my heart head-on.

"Are you fucking kidding me, Little Ghost?" he seethes, stalking toward me with shoulders so tense and strained that he rivals the Hulk. "What the hell are you thinking? I thought we were over this shit."

"I think," I drawl, "I'm trying to do whatever I can to get you to have an honest conversation with me. You're sulking around and ignoring us after..." I release a heavy sigh.

His broad arms cross over his chest, the front of his muscular frame shadowed by the headlights behind him. His silhouette is flawless. "After I fucked you with my two younger brothers."

I swallow. "Yeah—that."

A grumble comes from the depths of his throat. Colten's light, disdainful laughter tightens my sternum. "You're one to talk. You have no right to tell me you want to have an honest discussion when you're running. Is that why you're leaving?"

"I wasn't leaving, Colten."

His intense eyes pierce mine. "Bull. Shit. I want the truth, Taryn."

Pursing my lips, I shift my weight anxiously. "It's the truth." Taking a few steps toward him, I see his shoulders visibly stiffen. "Because when I run, I know you'll come find me. I've never had anyone in my life who cared enough to chase after me when I leave, but I also don't think you've ever had anyone go to such drastic lengths to show you they care either." I tap my sternum with my finger. "I care, Colten. This was the only way to get you to talk to me."

He pulls his fingers through his mussed hair. "I don't want to talk about it, Taryn. Leave it alone. It's over. Done. In the past."

"Doesn't sound like it's in the past."

"Well, it is! Because every time I think about it, I hate—" He clears his throat, and my features falter.

"You hate what? Me?"

Throwing his hands frustratedly around, he growls, "Fuck. No!"

"Then what? What do you hate?" I push.

"Those were my brothers, Taryn." He gestures up the road toward the house. "The ones I'm supposed to be looking out for. Setting an *example* for! And here I am, having a foursome with my twin brothers because, for some reason, I want you so badly. So badly that I'm going fucking insane! I'm barely able to control myself when I'm around you."

The breath in my lungs hitches, my pulse jumping so violently that I wonder if it's trying to magnetize to his. They're probably in sync.

I blink, dropping my gaze to the grass below my shoes. "So, you hate that it happened."

When I peek back up, his tongue swipes over his bottom lip. The silence pulls at the tension between us as we stand in the grassy expanse, near the orchard that flanks both sides of the road and spills toward the cliffside. The only sounds are the waves kissing the rock below and the breeze ruffling through the trees.

The breath he blows out traps mine in my lungs. "I loved it too much and loathed it a fucking lot." His eyes dart between mine as he advances toward me. "I want you, okay? Is that what you want to hear?"

Words evade me.

"Or maybe I should get on my knees, bury my head between your legs, and stroke your clit with my tongue while I whisper against your pussy that all I fucking want is for you to be mine, and only mine. I. Want. You," he reiterates.

I shake my head, feeling my heart tighten in my throat. "And why is that a problem?"

"Because I can never give you all of me, Taryn...I know that's a lot to ask of someone. You'll have to accept the parts I allow you to have."

"Why?" I breathe, focusing on the moonlight flickering in his gaze.

"Because I know how much of yourself you can lose when you give over everything you are to someone."

My head tilts, my heart breaking at the emotion slipping through his tone.

It is a lot to ask someone, but I know his baggage. Well, not all his baggage; it is more like a carry-on with the things I've collected here and there over the last couple months: facts about his childhood, his parents, and what happened five years ago.

He's tormented by all of it.

For some reason, all I want to do is be a sliver of his relief. I see how hard he works. I see how he loves his family unconditionally. He'd do almost anything to ensure they're happy and protected. Jessica said Cameron is the brother who loves hard, but I've come to realize Colten Lindenvale loves effortlessly despite the shit he's been through. He just doesn't recognize it.

I step into him so my breasts brush against his chest, his focus landing on the movement in the expanse of my throat. "Okay," I whisper.

Lines form between his brows while he peers down at me so profoundly that something catches fire deep in my soul. "Okay, what?"

"I accept whatever you'll allow me to have, Colten."

The emotions crossing his features are unlike anything I've ever seen. It's a seamless blend of awe and reprieve, and my heart swells in response.

He lifts his hand, letting his fingers drift over the skin on the underside of my jaw. "Are you sure? It's a lot to ask of you, and I don't want you to resent me."

A smile tugs at my lips. "I resented you once, and here we are."

His palm flattens on the back of my neck. Colten's head dips, his lips brushing mine so softly that an eruption of sparklers fizzles through my nerves. His tongue flicks against my bottom lip in an unhurried, playful stroke, and my mouth parts, searching for more. Our tongues intertwine, pulling a groan from his chest that vibrates against mine.

"Come home with me," he whispers against my lips, the silent request striking my pulsing clit.

Pulling away, I stare up at him. "I have a feeling you might drag me there anyway."

"Damn straight, Little Ghost."

Lowering his body, he grips the backs of my thighs, lifting me effortlessly into his strong arms and carrying me toward his truck. Cradling the back of my head, his lips find mine again, his sweet taste driving me wild.

But a twinge of doubt pierces through the bliss because he didn't say, 'I can't give you all of me.'

He said, 'I can *never* give you all of me.'

THIRTY-SEVEN | COLTEN

Have I said I'm screwed yet? Like majorly fucked because I can't stop thinking about her.

I can't stop lusting after her.

And my hands won't stop drifting over Taryn's delicate, naked body sprawled under my sheets as if she belongs on my bed with them. And I'm starting to think she does.

I said I could never give her all of me. It's what I've told every woman who's stepped into this house before. Yet I didn't quite convince myself when I said it to her. Because I'm starting to wonder if she's the one person I could let go for.

And that thought is terrifying. The clang of those internal alarm bells echoes in my skull. She's everything I told myself I could never have if I wanted to protect my family.

What you could have with Taryn was everything you vowed you'd never let yourself desire.

But as I rest my arm on the pillow behind my head, my eyes scan her soft features beside me. Taryn's button nose points toward the ceiling, and her eyelashes fan over her rosy cheeks, dusted with freckles. The moonlight shines on the orchard outside my bedroom, casting long shadows that creep across the grass and through my windows.

My chest aches, as if whatever I'm feeling for her has sunk its sharp claws into my heart and refuses to let go. Taryn is so beautiful and perfect that it hurts.

Perfect for this family.

Perfect for me—though admitting it means risking everything.

Are some things worth annihilating yourself for?

Yes.

But there's so much at stake. I wouldn't be the only one facing the consequences if this relationship—well, whatever the fuck we are—turns into a catastrophic event. Two sweet, innocent faces in that house think the world of the girl next to me.

I wish I weren't wandering aimlessly in my head all the time. Making decisions would be a lot goddamn easier if I didn't have to contemplate how my actions affect my family.

"You're staring." Taryn's gentle, post-sex, sleep-ridden voice catches me off guard. Her eyes flutter open, whatever force between us pulling them to mine.

"Hmm?"

She shifts to face me, her hair draping over the pillow. "You've been staring at me for the last five minutes."

"Oh— Yeah. I can't seem to stop." When did I suddenly decide to respond with full-blown honesty?

Her eyes flit between mine. "If this is making you uncomfortable, I can leave. If you want?"

She begins to sit up, but impulsively, I reach for her. I pull her into my frame, sitting up against the bed frame. "Please stay."

She pulls up the duvet to cover her stunning breasts, fiddling with the red polish on her nails as her skin slowly melts into mine. I admire the special relationship she shares with Elena, one that is unlike any of ours. They always wear the same color when it's time to repaint their nails, and whenever I see a new color flash before my eyes—or when Taryn's fingers wrap around my cock—it's a reminder that my little sister is falling for her just as hard as I am.

God. We're all fucking attached.

Taryn drags me back to the present. "You're not used to this. Are you?"

"What?"

"Women staying." She says it so innocently—so confidently because she knows exactly how my interactions before her have ended. "Every night I saw you bring a woman in, she would leave a few hours later. But you're asking *me* to stay. Why?"

Her probing question tightens my tendons. *It feels different*, I want to say, but I don't. "Because my cock likes your cunt more."

She glares at my response, the expression releasing something that had been tightly wound inside me for a very long time.

I sigh, not wanting to talk about it but unable to stop myself —which is nothing new since she seems to have that effect on me. "My parents' marriage wasn't always a mess. It was the kind of relationship I looked up to. One I knew I wanted someday— until one random month, it shifted into something I didn't."

She listens intently, her eyes locked on my face while her fingertips tenderly drift through the hair on my chest.

"My mom's temperament was the first to change. Sometimes, it was subtle, but when it worsened, she and my dad became increasingly detached, which led him to an alcohol addiction. They fought constantly," enough that I would shield my siblings from their wrath in my room until two in the morning when it finally stopped, when they were too tired to continue. "They were in love, and then they weren't. When nothing changed, and they were caught in this repetitive cycle of arguing and resenting each other for years, my father chased her down and ultimately brought it to an end."

Her fingers still on my pec. "What do you mean 'chased her down'?"

"My mother, Jane, tried to leave the night before she disappeared when one fight escalated," I sigh. "He followed. He returned. She didn't. It's painfully fucking simple to put the pieces together, especially after—" The words disintegrate on my tongue.

I'm not looking at her, but I know her chest rises and falls weightily by how her skin lightly rubs against mine. "And that's what you believe? That she ran, and he—murdered her."

My tone raises an octave, becoming defensive. "It's what I know, Taryn. There's nothing to believe if I saw it happen." I'm not screaming at her, but I can't stop the hurt from blending with my voice.

Her muscles harden to stone beside me, and I side-eye her. She's not breathing now. But I expected that. It's the same way I felt when I walked in on them that night.

"What do you mean you saw it happen, Colten?" She chokes out my name.

Fuck.

Somehow, she pulls the truth out of me despite my internal quarrel to keep it in the depths of my soul where it's festered and rotted. "It's exactly what it sounds like. The sight of my mother's blood is burned into my brain like a fucking cattle brand, Taryn!"

She sits up hastily, clutching the blanket to her chest. "You saw your father murder your mother?" she utters disbelievingly.

"Yes," I answer firmly.

"That's a big accusat—"

"It's not a fucking accusation!" Emotion clogs my throat. "I was there. I saw the shattered dresser mirror and her blood dripping on the floor. I saw—"

My eyes burn, the tip of my nose tingling.

She reaches up, cupping my face as her thumb moves in gentle, circular motions on my cheek. "It's okay," she murmurs.

I swallow, rolling my shoulders back to alleviate some of the strain. "When I walked into the room, he was holding a bloody shard of glass in one hand and a bottle of scotch in the other. When she saw me, she ran and told me she would be back. It's been five years, Taryn— Five years!"

We sit silently, her fingernails gliding over the ink on my bicep. "Jessica said you disappeared for three days after that."

The air I draw into my lungs hangs heavy, swirling and expanding until I can barely breathe.

My brothers and I rode our bikes for miles in the summers. We always passed this dirt road, and we decided to explore it one day. The two-mile, unkempt path passed through a thick forest of Douglas firs and other vegetation, but what was at the end of the road was something we never expected.

High on the cliffs overlooking a small canyon where a creek flowed into the Columbia stood a cabin. The abandoned, weathered wooden structure, with broken windows and a stone chimney, had succumbed to years of exposure, yet it remained magnificent. It was our refuge, a place we retreated to when our parents began to argue more frequently. There were times we nearly threw parties out there, where we could drink underage and hook up, but something about it felt sacred. It seemed like it would lose all its meaning if we brought anyone else there.

No one else knew about it. That was until a year later, after we discovered it.

We were stunned to see a young girl standing dangerously close to the edge. At first, we thought she was a ghost. With bright blonde hair and milky skin, she appeared almost silver against her black dress and the dusky sky, staring down at the creek below. It was eerie. But we soon realized she wasn't a figment of our imagination or a soul trapped in a second dimension haunting the cabin. She was seeking a safe place to escape the thoughts tormenting her mind, and like us, the cabin became her sanctuary.

Taryn sits up, analyzing my expression with warm eyes.

"There's this abandoned cabin on the Altair Bluff Cliffs," I begin. "My brothers and I discovered it long ago, and it became one of our favorite places that nobody else knew about. That next morning, when my father returned home with dried blood on his hands and shirt, and my mom didn't, that's where I went. I packed a backpack, took my bike, and camped there for three days while I tried to process everything—"

To this day, I still haven't processed that night. As I've gotten older, the memories from that night are cloudy, but all the significant elements remain vivid and unchanged.

The blood.

The sickly-sweet scent of scotch on my father's breath.

The shards of reflective glass littering the carpet.

"Then I went home because I had five siblings who needed me more than I needed to be alone. From that point on, I swore I would never leave them again, and I would do whatever I could to protect them since I was more focused on myself during those three days than on the people I should have been concerned about around my father."

Her brows pull together. "Is that why you don't drink?" I hold her eyes. "I've never seen you with a beer, only with glasses of scotch. And I've never actually seen you drink them. I drank your glass that one night…"

My cock twitches at the thought. Yes, I painfully remember that. "The scotch on your tongue when I kissed you was the first time I had tasted liquor in five years."

"You've been sober for five years?"

"Alcohol controlled my father, and I promised I would never give it dominance to control me."

"So, you always make yourself a glass but never drink it?"

It sounds ridiculous when she says it like that.

My head moves back and forth. "The scent of it in my hand, but my willpower not to let it course through my veins, reminds me that I'm in control."

"That is very—"

"Eccentric?"

Her lingering eyes attract mine. *Who's the one staring now?*

"I was going to say admirable," she mumbles softly.

"Not sure I would call it that since it's the easiest decision I ever made. My father once told me that a man only fails when he gives up entirely."

She twists her lips thoughtfully. "Then, despite whatever happened that night, I think the one thing you can take away is that your father showed you exactly what that looks like. And even though he gave up on your mom—your family," she chokes on the emotion clogging her throat, "you never have. That's why it's admirable. Because even after all the shit he's put you through, you're still here, and you've become exactly what your family has needed."

I've never thought of it that way. It's easier to resent him. To picture his face on the target my brothers and I set up in the orchard for archery practice when we need to blow off steam.

For the first time in a long while, I'm thinking about the pile of unopened letters in my desk drawer—a stack that grows taller every week—wondering if they are filled with apologies and "I'm sorry." Or if they loiter there with excuses I don't fucking want to hear.

I've never had the urge to open them. It would be like dragging the blade of a letter opener through a freshly stitched wound that has never healed.

Yet the glint of curiosity in my mind ponders if they would bring a new wave of clarity. But as I stare at the picture frame across the room on my dresser of my siblings and me that I had taken of us last summer, I don't think I'm ready to open that can of worms yet—or if I'll ever be ready.

THIRTY-EIGHT | TARYN

Unblinkingly, I stare at the screen, the contact on my phone stirring the anxiety swirling in my stomach. It's been months since I talked to my parents.

I haven't updated them, and they've sent nothing to me.

Well, I guess that's not true. They have. But it's just a collection of pictures of them in Costa Rica, unaware that their daughter was abducted and is now living in a completely different state from the last time they spoke to her.

It's been a week, but the conversation Colten and I had in his bed plays on a loop in my mind. He watched his father murder his mother. And yet, here I am, anxious to talk to two people who still love me.

Who I still have.

Even if our love looks slightly different in how we don't talk or see each other very often, it's still there. And my heavy heart sinks in my gut, knowing I haven't been as grateful as I should be.

Why do we only appreciate what we have when we witness others' misfortunes?

I exhale slowly, digging my fingers into Rossco's fur as he

lies on my bed, mustering up the courage to tap the call button before I change my mind. I press the button, and the phone rings; each chime in my ear feels like an invisible cord is wrapping around my chest, tightening like those old phones with the cord plugged into the wall.

Perhaps they won't answer. If they call back, at least I'll feel a bit better knowing that, to some degree, they are looking out for me.

"Taryn," my mom's bright, cheerful voice drifts over the line. Sometimes, it's crazy how similar we sound, especially now that I'm older.

The words come out destructed as emotion worms up my throat. "Hi, Mom."

"Peter, get in here! Taryn's on the phone," she yells away from the speaker. "How's Arizona honey? Is it hot there?"

My tongue feels like sandpaper when I lick my dry lips. "I'm not in Arizona anymore. I— Uh...followed a job to Washington."

The line remains silent for a few seconds, and I pick some dried grass out of Rossco's coat, setting the blades on my bedside table. He rolls over onto his back, begging for a belly rub. I can never say no when he asks.

"Well, that's exciting. Why didn't you tell us?"

Tears swell behind my eyes, and I shrug, knowing she can't see me.

I could tell them the truth: I came here for a teaching position but was deceived by three brothers and abducted to be a nanny. Yet, that doesn't even feel like the truth anymore because the reality is that I enjoy it here. It's the first place in a long time that has started to feel like home, but with that comes the apprehension.

Maybe it's my imagination, but my room in the tower feels smaller than it used to. The vast expanse of the orchard makes it seem like the property line is closing in day by day. Perhaps it's because I spend so much time on the hill, or maybe the carefree girl who loved to bounce around now wonders if she could truly be happy settling down somewhere.

Maybe I'm more like my parents than I care to admit.

But settling down here? Could I learn to push past the anxiety of staying in one place and learn to love the steadiness?

Colten and I aren't exclusive; at least, we haven't had that conversation despite how much we've fucked. I've spent several nights in his bed, and every morning, I wake up to his handsome face next to me. Yet, there are two other men in this house with whom I have had physical relations with. They could very much be affected by a decision like that if I only choose one of them.

Shit. I am in over my head.

I sniffle, and she fills the void with her motherly tone when I don't say anything because I don't have a good excuse. "Well, if you're happy, we're happy. So, you said you followed a job? Oh —your dad is here now!"

"Hey, sweetheart! We miss you," my father says, nearly breaking me completely.

God, why did I ever think that they didn't care?

I hear it in their joyful voices, more so now than I ever did, and I can't help but wonder if it's because of Lindenvale Hill.

Or they're just having a blast in Costa Rica.

I shake my head at myself, willing away the thought.

What this fragile family has gone through is incomparable to my relationship with my parents. I may be a world away from mine, but at this moment, I feel closer to them somehow.

"I miss you too. And yeah, Mom, I'm a nanny for a family in Cedar Creek Cove."

"A nanny?" my dad says, surprised. "I thought you were teaching?"

"She moved to Washington," my mom informs him, her voice farther away from the phone as she catches him up.

"Do you like the family?" he asks.

The smile that transforms my lips is instant. "Yeah. I really do. They own Lindenvale Hill Orchard."

With my mom's response, I can practically sense her eyes bugging out of her head. "Really?"

"Wait, isn't that the family where the father was charged with the murder of the mother?" my dad cuts in.

"I'm surprised you know about it," I say.

"We might travel a lot, but we don't live under a rock, sweetheart." My mom chuckles.

My dad's warning is clear. "Just be careful."

For the next half hour, they tell me about their recent travels, and I tell them about Cedar Creek and the Lindenvale kids. When I tell them how much I'm making nannying for them, the line goes silent, and I think they've stopped breathing.

My mom takes a deep breath. "No wonder you aren't teaching! Well, we are very happy for you."

"We need to leave to make our dinner reservation, but please don't take as long to call us next time, okay?" My heart sinks into my stomach like a boulder at my dad's comment.

That's what they always say.

Because I'm always the one to reach out.

The one to initiate a phone call or a text.

Never them.

I nod, letting the first tear fall free from the corner of my eye. "Okay."

"We love you, Taryn," my mom declares. She already sounds distant from the phone.

"Love you guys, too."

Then the line goes dead, and I swallow down the reaction I've felt too many times after phone calls like this. Placing my phone on the nightstand, I pad across my floor to go back down and join the twins, Elena, and Tristan since it's a Friday night and the kids don't have school tomorrow.

Rossco follows me down to the first floor, but the chatter from the kitchen is accompanied by music from the opposite end of the house. The soft sound of a piano drifts through the foyer. Curiously, I turn left, heading toward the living room and hallway leading to the master bedroom.

Cameron's room.

As I amble down the hallway, I notice the music isn't coming from his room but through a cracked door at the end of the dark hallway that is always locked. Delicate yellow light creates a line across the wood floor, drawing me closer. When I reach the door, I stand and listen to the ballad playing over speakers momentarily before nudging it open.

My head tilts as I absorb the office-like space. It's not an office, though. I stand still, my eyes scanning the wooden table filled with tubes of paint and jars of brushes in various sizes. The light from the sconces on the wall casts a warm glow against the black walls and dark wood finishes. On the other side of the room, an easel stands with a dark canvas covered in shades of red, dark green, and black.

I know I shouldn't be in here, but I can't stop myself from entering the room. The scent of oil paint hangs heavy in the air, pulling me in. The three walls that aren't windows facing the yard are covered in framed paintings against the dark walls, and suddenly, the recognition hits.

The artwork in this room is in the same style as the masterpieces hung throughout the house and the paintings displayed above Colten's bed and in his living room. As I walk toward a wall, my eyes drop to the cursive handwriting—a signature I never bothered to seek out whenever I passed the canvases.

But now, the barely legible cursive is recognizable.

Cameron Lindenvale.

I analyze the room, my body moving from painting to painting. His style is abstract realism, all of them landscapes or plant life.

It's breathtaking.

It is the kind of talent that has your jaw dropping and eyes watering because it evokes emotion.

"Of course, the one time I leave the door open to go to the bathroom, you find your way in here."

Cameron's raspy voice from the doorway startles me, but I can't stop staring at the painting of a forest before me, featuring what looks like a young girl standing in the middle of a dirt road. She has light blonde hair and is wearing a black dress that contrasts beautifully with her pale skin and the deep greens of the trees. It's dark. Eerie. Hauntingly striking since it's the only painting that depicts a person.

There's something about this one. But I can't quite put my finger on it.

"Sorry. It's just— These are incredible, Cameron. Why have you never mentioned that you paint?"

He walks up beside me, stuffing his hands in his pockets. "Because it's personal to me."

My gaze finds his. "But they hang throughout the house."

"But you would've had no idea I created them unless you found this room," he contradicts.

True. My lips twist to the side, my eyes magnetizing to the painting again. "This one is my favorite. There's something about it."

He shifts his weight, both of us gaping intently at his artwork. "It's my favorite too." And I believe him. His voice is lighter. Brighter. Proud.

I study the brushstrokes across the canvas, some messy and some not, to create that abstract realism look. But each stroke is perfectly placed.

"Who is she?" I can't help but ask.

His lips lift. "My muse."

The silence stretches, and classical music fills the void.

Although I never considered him a classical guy, I can see why it accompanies him while he creates these masterpieces.

He steps away from me, wandering to the unfinished canvas he's working on. When I turn to look at him, I realize he isn't wearing a shirt. Random splatters of paint cling to his muscular chest and arms.

"Why are you in here, Taryn?"

"I was curious, I suppose. But also—" I swallow, considering whether this is the right time for this conversation. However, it must happen eventually, so I see no reason to prolong it and complicate the situation more.

He tapers a brow.

"I like Colten," I breathe. An immediate weight lifts off my shoulders, hearing the confession out loud.

Eyes narrowing, he surveys my expression and smirks. "I've known that for a while."

"I still need you, though. I don't want this to change our friendship." *Wow, that sounded desperate.*

He grabs a dirty, paint-smeared rag from the table and places his hands on his hips. "I've seen you two together, and I know how you are around Brennan and me. You're different with him." He shakes his head. "I've noticed it since that first week, even though I wish I didn't—" He tightens his lips. "It's okay. Really. This won't change anything."

"But will that make things awkward if I tell you I want him? We all did things—together."

"Yes, we did," he agrees. "But I wouldn't change what happened. Family comes first, Taryn, and he's better with you. Colten's put everything on the line for this family, and I have no intention of taking away the one good thing that has happened to him since Mom disappeared."

I swallow, nodding as tears swell in my eyes, hearing him care for his brother like this.

God, Cameron is going to make some woman so lucky one day.

"But there's one thing you should know about Colten," he says, and I straighten my spine. "He makes decisions with his head and ignores his heart. He's been through a lot over the years and despises it when people break their promises. So, if you're choosing him, I need you to think carefully about your decision before it goes too far. Because if he gets hurt again, I don't think there'll be anything to save him this time."

THIRTY-NINE | COLTEN

Reaching up to one of the branches, I wrap the string lights around it, pulling to tighten them. I climb down the ladder and head to the bed of my truck, where the generator hums through the otherwise quiet orchard. I plug in the cord, watching as this part of section nine brightens from the dainty lights I wove in a zigzag pattern through the apple trees.

They drape over the picnic blanket I set up with a few candles and a vase of flowers I picked from the garden because I have no idea what the fuck to get a woman for her birthday.

Taryn seems like the type of person who values thoughts over things. I respect that about her.

After work, I ran into town to The Honey Hut and picked up a chocolate cake I had Adelaide make just for her. It's currently waiting in the cooler in the truck, but the twins—along with Elena and Tristan—are making her dinner first, and later tonight, I'll be bringing her out here.

I settled with a grand gesture because she never talks about needing things, and I still want to make up for everything I've put her through. And for some goddamn reason, I love the bright smile on her face when she's surprised and caught off guard. A smile that makes my lungs and heart feel full, like they could explode at any moment.

That's what she does to me.

Crouching down to the flowers, I nervously rearrange them in the large vase on the blanket.

Standing up, I take one last look around at my pathetic attempt at a birthday gift. Section nine isn't far from the house, so I figured we could walk to it. Tucking my hands into my sweatshirt pockets, I begin the walk back to the house between the rows of trees on either side of me, my head swimming with doubts.

This is so stupid. Why did I think this was a good idea?

When I return to the house, I slip off my hood as I walk through the doorway. The scent of butter and garlic wafts through the room, making my mouth water. Smells like they've got a good handle on dinner.

My body jolts as something crashes and shatters on the floor.

Maybe not.

"I'm sorry! I didn't mean to!" Elena's sweet, anxiety-ridden squeak comes from the kitchen.

They told Taryn she couldn't leave her room for an hour while they got everything ready, so I assume she is still upstairs.

Multicolored balloons are scattered haphazardly around the foyer, leading into the dining room and kitchen. On the table, lit candles, a bowl of salad, and happy birthday napkins from Tristan's party earlier this year are displayed. Streamers are chaotically taped to the walls, twisting and attaching to opposite sides of the room.

I hustle into the kitchen, seeing Brennan and Tristan blowing and tying more balloons while Elena sits on the counter beside the stove with a wooden spoon. Cameron appears from the pantry with a broom, reaching for the broken glass and beer puddle on the floor that Rossco is helping clean up.

"Watch where you step. She knocked my beer off the counter," Cameron mutters, amused.

"Come here, Rossco," I call. He turns toward me, and I crouch down to pet him as Cameron cleans up the mess.

"Don't forget to stir, Elena," Cameron reminds, snatching a towel off the counter.

She sticks the spoon back in the homemade Alfredo sauce, stirring it around as steam billows into the air. Her teeth sink into her bottom lip, entirely focused on her task.

After Cameron gets everything cleaned up, he removes the noodles from the stove and strains them, tossing them into the sauce.

"All right, I think that's enough balloons. I feel like I'm going to pass out," Brennan sighs, smacking the balloon he had just finished blowing up away from him.

"Do you think she'll like it?" Tristan wonders, looking around.

I grin. "Oh, I definitely think she will like it."

That response earns me a smile from him, and I cling to the expression.

"Can I go get her now?" Elena asks. How she drawls out the word *now* suggests she's already asked multiple times.

Brennan rolls his eyes. "All right, go get her."

She hops off the counter rapidly, sprinting out of the room as fast as her little feet will carry her.

Cameron turns off the burner and reaches into the fridge to grab another beer. After popping off the top, he carries his beer and the pan of Alfredo into the dining room, placing the pasta on the pot holder.

Brennan, Tristan, and I follow him, pulling out the chairs as we settle into our usual spots.

"How was school today?" I ask Tristan while we wait for the girls to return downstairs.

He shrugs. "I played with a snake I found at recess."

Brennan and I frown simultaneously. I'm unsure why we are both staring at him like this; his fascination with reptiles is not surprising in the slightest. We've caught him playing with lizards in the rock beds outside multiple times when he wanted to avoid us, at least before Taryn arrived.

Brennan peers at him. "What did you do with it?"

I reach for my water, bringing it to my lips.

Tristan's eyes widen as if he is reluctant to share. He fiddles with his napkin. "I put it on a girl in my class who was sitting and reading on the bench. Then she got me in trouble."

That. That I was not expecting.

Brennan's eyes widen, and I choke mid-swallow, the water caught in my throat.

"And why would you do that?" Brennan questions.

Another shrug. "I was bored, and she's annoying."

I smirk. "You probably just put gasoline on the fire."

Tristan looks up at me from across the table, one of his blue-green eyes twitching. "What does that mean?"

Brennan laughs. "It means you just started a war. She might be more annoying now."

Tristan crosses his arms, rolling his eyes.

"Come on. Come On!"

"Okay, okay." Taryn chuckles at Elena, the approaching sound causing the hair on my arms to stand on end.

We all turn our heads, watching as they descend the stairs. When Taryn sees everything, a lovely blush colors her cheeks, creeping up the slope of her neck and across the curve of her breasts. Her genuine smile quickens my breath.

"Oh, you guys. This is too much!" she says, tilting her head.

When they enter the dining room, Elena grabs the chair and pulls it out for her.

Taryn didn't even mention that today is her birthday. I remembered it from the application she submitted for the teaching position. I seem to recall everything I read about her. When I informed my brothers, they came up with this plan. Judging by how she is brightly beaming, I can tell she is stunned.

"How did you guys even know it was my birthday? I didn't say anything."

"We know everything about you, remember?" Cameron smirks.

She purses her lips, attempting to hide her grin. "Right."

"And we made your cards," Elena shouts, jumping to snatch them off the table. She stands beside Taryn's chair and hands them to her.

She opens them one by one, smiling at Tristan and Elena's card and then laughing at the one Brennan and Cameron gave her. It makes my skin itch, wondering what the twins wrote.

She opens mine next.

I have a surprise for you.
Meet me on the porch after dinner.
- C

After she reads it, her eyes instantly collide with mine. She nods, suppressing a smile.

My pulse batters, and I take a sip of water, my focus not leaving her.

I'll see you on the porch after dinner, Little Ghost.

"Where are we going?" Taryn wraps her arms tightly around her body.

The chilly night air is a little colder than I had anticipated, but luckily, she's in a sweatshirt, and I have a few blankets and pillows set up in the truck bed.

When I remain silent, she glares at me. "You guys already surprised me with dinner," she whines, walking beside me as we reach the edge of the mowed lawn where the orchard meets the yard.

"What's your point?"

She rolls her eyes and huffs out a breath, glancing around at the dark trees engulfing us. Her eyelids turn into little slits as her focus finds me again. "Should I be running?"

"Do you want to run?" I challenge.

"You're making me feel like I should, since you're being all shady."

A thrill shoots through my veins. Snatching her arm, I tug her into me, her breath quickly exiting her lungs.

Lowering my head to hers, I brush my warm lips against the skin below her ear. "If you want to run, then run," I gesture ahead of us toward the direction of the quaint party for just the two of us that I set up. After a minute of walking—or running—she'll start to see the string lights flickering through the trees.

"I'll make you a deal. I'll give you a minute head start, but if I catch you, I want your clit on my tongue while my cock is buried in your throat."

She visibly shudders, my dick twitching at how responsive she is to my words. "God, your mouth sometimes."

Without another word, she wiggles out of my grasp and starts running, each beat of her feet against the ground encouraging the drumming in my chest.

I start walking in the same direction, because she is bound to lose anyway.

She just doesn't know it yet.

A minute later, I see her ahead, standing motionless under the starry sky with the moonlight filtering above. The glow of the string lights in front of her highlights her flawless silhouette. I usually don't drive my truck through the empty rows between the trees, but I made an exception tonight.

Ambling up behind her, I keep my hands tucked in my pockets. Lowering my lips to the curve of her neck, I press a soft kiss there, fighting the urge to groan at her taste. "Happy birthday, Little Ghost."

The movement in her throat moves against my mouth. She spins rapidly, her arms wrapping around my head as she buries her face in my neck. Something wet drips down my chest, the wake of her tears searing through my flesh and cutting open my heart.

Fuck. She hates it.

"I'm sorry. I should've gotten you a better gift," I growl, pulling my fingers through my hair.

Her head shakes against me. "No. Uh—" She inhales a deep breath, pulling back. Bunching up her sweatshirt sleeves, she rubs the cloth under her eyes. "This is the nicest thing anyone has ever done for me."

Her confession brings some comfort. "I didn't know what to get you."

Taryn's lips tilt upward as I reach for her hand, interlacing our fingers. Her touch shoots liquid fire up my arms and straight to my cock, and I start to think about all the ways I could make her look at me like that again, with big eyes sparking with contentment—like I just handed her the entire world under a canopy of hanging lights.

I walk her over, and she sits on the blanket as I go to the truck, pull out the boxed cake in the cooler, and set it in front of her. Then I grab the lighter and light the candles around the perimeter of the blanket before dishing out a few pieces of cake onto our plates. We sit on the blanket, diving into the fluffy pillow of perfection.

She hums, and I feel the sound deep in my bones. "Holy shit," she chews. "Adelaide has magic hands. This is the best cake I've ever had."

As I place the fork in my mouth, I lick off the frosting, noticing her eyes follow the movement of my tongue. Even before Adelaide took over The Honey Hut, we always bought our cakes from her grandmother. Adelaide definitely has a talent of her own. It might even rival her grandmother's.

"Did Tristan tell you what he did today?" I ask her.

She pauses mid-chew. "No."

Her face scrunches in worry, and I laugh. "He got in trouble because he put a snake he found on a girl in his class."

Her eyes widen. "No, he didn't," she says through chuckles.

I nod, but the expression that crosses her features next is concerning. "What?"

"It's times like this when I miss teaching. Sometimes, the things kids do can be so—unexpected." A sad smile lifts the corners of her mouth. "They always kept me on my toes." The flames from the candles flicker, the yellow glow licking her skin. "One time, before I secured the first-grade position in Arizona, I was subbing for this seventh-grade English class. When I pulled the chair out from my desk, luckily, I looked down." She stifles a laugh. "A student glued tacks to the cushion."

My eyes narrow. What the hell? Why is that funny?

"That's fucking horrible." However, I feel like I can't say much since my friends and I regularly played pranks and some-times took things a little too far. But not to that extent.

That's just psychotic.

And if Taryn was my teacher when I was in school.

Fuck. I would've been so distracted.

Maybe I would've tried to get her attention, too, now that I'm thinking about it.

She shrugs, the grin on her lips adding a wave of heat that licks up my arms. "Yeah. But I've found that in situations like that, all they're looking for is a reaction. So, I didn't give them one—whoever it was. While they read the book they were reading as a class, I just stood."

"Did you tell someone?" I lean back against my hands, placing my empty plate on the blanket.

"Afterward, I did. As painful as it would've been if I had sat down, I don't know—" She weighs her words. "It felt powerful to maintain my composure. I was twenty-one then, so the fact that I could hold it together in a situation like that made me realize I might be cut out for teaching. It's hard work, but it's gratifying to recognize the kind of example you can set and how many young minds you can influence."

And there it is.

That is the exact reason she is so perfect for us.

Perfect for Elena and Tristan.

But my gut is filled with guilt because, at this moment, I don't think I can be selfish with her. As much as we need her here, maybe we can make something work. On Monday, I will call Alaric Sinclair, my former principal at Cedar Creek High, and see what I can do to get her a teaching position.

Holding out my hand to her, she hesitantly places her fingers on my palm, and I pull her on top of me, drawing a gasp from her. Her body is draped over mine, and the inferno in my chest rages.

I want to fuck her all the time, but now? I want to kiss the shit out of her. Intertwining her fingers in my hair, she stares down at me amiably.

Why is it that I have a strong urge to give her everything?

I wanted to keep her here because it was what my family needed after Mom disappeared and Dad was taken away.

I needed to give *them* everything.

And yet, as I stare into the flames dancing in her irises, my chest swells. Although I'm determined to keep her here, I'm starting to learn that Taryn Meyers is the one person I can't be selfish with.

FORTY | COLTEN

Dropping the barbell, I swipe the sweat off my brow with my forearm, the cords in my arms pulled tight. My tendons are ablaze, the fire spreading up my biceps, shoulders, and neck. Reaching for the towel on the bench, I wander over to the fan propped in the corner of the room. The movement of air washes over my skin, cooling the moisture seeping through my pores.

I heave a breath of exhaustion, dragging the towel down my face.

I'm overworking myself.

I'm painfully aware of how my body craves to sink into my soft mattress at the end of each day. But not before having my little ghost under me with my cock buried inside of her, where she can fully haul me to the depths where sleep is the next to consume me.

It's dangerous.

I'm getting used to falling asleep beside her and waking up to kiss her forehead before I pet Rossco at the foot of the bed and sneak out of the room to begin my early days. Even though the demons in my mind shake my sanity and scream at me that getting comfortable will inevitably destroy me in the long run, it feels natural.

She seems to be the most normal thing in the world.

I made the call—contacted my old principal and asked if he had any positions open at the elementary school. He did.

I was relieved and pissed off simultaneously when he informed me that their fifth-grade teacher is pregnant and due in a month. They are looking to hire someone for the position temporarily. When I told him Taryn might be interested in full-time teaching, he said there's a possibility—if she fits with the students and staff—that they could hire her permanently, depending on what happens at the end of the school year. So, I sent him everything she had sent me when she applied for our faux job listing.

I'm still on edge about the idea. But after hearing her talk about how much she loved teaching the night of her birthday, I didn't want to be the one to stand in the way of something she's so passionate about. I would be taking her away from kids who could use her radiance. Her warmth. And after seeing her with Elena and Tristan, I can't keep her contained on the hill. I'm just not sure when I'll tell her.

I peer out the gym windows. The sun sits on top of the trees on the horizon outside the shop, and the dark blue sky is painted with wisps of white clouds. I turn, and something gray in the corner of the windowsill catches my eye.

Tossing the towel over my shoulder, I walk over, grinning at the painted rock. A smile that quickly turns into a smirk. Taryn painted rocks with Elena and Tristan weeks ago, and yet every time I find one in a random spot, it brightens my day in the simplest way.

Picking it up, I rotate the smooth oval rock in my hand. But this specific one is unlike the others I've found because this is a masterpiece with a painting of perky breasts and rosy nipples.

Yeah. That was Taryn.

I laugh to myself, pulling my fingers through my damp hair matted from the sweat on my forehead, trying to ignore the ache in my cock.

Damn, I want to get home.

I place the rock back, deciding that whenever I'm working out, it will bring a smile to my face, knowing she put it in here. But I also pray to God, for her sake, that Elena and Tristan didn't observe her paint that one.

Jesus. I don't need Elena's artwork turning into little erotic pictures at the age of five.

Snatching my water bottle off the bench, I turn off the fan and hit the lights before shutting the double barn doors and hopping in my truck. I round the major bend in the road that scales the cliffside, picking up speed when I hit the straight part leading to the hill.

When I get into the house, the sound of joyful laughter vibrates my bones.

"Can we make it bigger?" Tristan shouts from somewhere in the living room.

I freeze, my brain trying to process the mess in front of me that will be hell to clean up. Random dining room table chairs are propping up blankets, and the entire living room and part of the foyer are now a sea of covers, pillows, and sheets.

Even though I can't see her, I hear Taryn shout, "I don't think we can make this any bigger!" They must be in separate parts of this giant fortification.

"Bigger," Elena seconds, taking Tristan's side.

"I don't think your brothers will be thrilled if we take the sheets off their beds," Taryn replies.

A corner of my lips curls up, and I twirl my keys around my finger, the metal clanking and silencing their voices. "The brothers probably won't be too happy anyway if we're the ones that have to help clean up this mess."

"Colten!" Elena shrieks. "Come find us!"

I raise a brow at the fort." I don't think I'll ever be able to find you."

"Well, good. Because it's our fort anyway, and you're not allowed inside," Taryn answers straightforwardly.

"My house, my rules, Little Ghost," I remind, unable to help the arrogance in my tone. I bite back a laugh. "And last I checked, this fort is in *my* living room."

I practically feel the breath in her lungs cease, my body soaking in the effect I have on her across the room like it's ecstasy. The heavy air sits on my shoulders, the weight pushing my feet forward as if the only relief is to see her.

Placing the keys in my pocket, I walk to the part of the floor designed to be the opening—two dining room chairs making a tunnel—that leads into one part of the fort that begins in the foyer.

My tired and sore muscles protest when I crouch down and start crawling on the sheets, but the giggling from somewhere in the fortress shoots determination through my bloodstream. Tristan hurries toward me on his hands and knees, startling me with the brightest smile on his face. The sight is enough to smash into me with the power of a freight train, nearly knocking me out and leaving me breathless. He should've had this kind of smile on his face for the past five years, and I hate that I couldn't be the one to put it there, but I am grateful that Taryn did.

He just needed more—more than his siblings doing every-thing they could to bring him out of the thick shell that was almost impossible to pierce through.

But he didn't need us.

He needed someone else who'd willingly decide to be a constant in his life. He needed to know that there was another person out there who cared about his happiness.

On all fours, he closes the distance and sits before me, crossing his legs. "I can't let you through, brother."

I snicker. He recently picked up "brother" from Cameron and Brennan. My panic meter buried behind my sternum wobbles. I wonder what else he's picked up from them. If the twins are more cautious around Elena, I assume Tristan knows a lot more than he leads on.

I raise a brow. "Where are the girls?"

He shakes his head.

"Do I need to bribe you to take my side instead?"

His eyes narrow into slits, challenging me. "What does bribe mean?"

"It means I give you something you want so you can give me what I want."

His face twists in thought as he taps his finger on his chin in a steady rhythm. "Can you teach me to use the bow?"

That is not what I was expecting. I anticipated him asking for a later bedtime or something he usually whines about, like wanting more dessert.

But this? The unexpected demand warms my face, catching me off guard. Years ago, I told him he would have to wait until he was eight, and the twins and I would take him.

When he was around five or so, Jess would walk him and Elena down to the shop, and they would watch us set up a target. His intrigued eyes always followed, his quaint voice whispering to Jessica if he could try. I wanted to let him. I did. Because it was one of the few times he showed interest in something. But he was still too small to use the first bow my dad bought me when I was eight.

But there are no hesitations. I don't see why he couldn't learn now.

"Deal," I say, reaching out my hand instantly.

He shakes it, that optimistic smile returning. "I'll go get Elena. Taryn is by the windows in the back corner of the living room."

Spinning away from me and crawling through the tunnel,

he darts farther into the fortress as if it's swallowing him whole. Tiny bursts of laughter drift through from the left side near the sectional, and the cackle of laughter, followed by a scream, tells me that Tristan has found Elena.

Turning right, I head deeper into the back corner of the living room. The room lights filter through the shades of white and gray fabric as I worm my way through, trying to ignore the painful ache seizing my muscles from my workout not even thirty minutes ago.

I get to a small, tented room and take another right. Damn, this fort is massive. It must have taken them all afternoon to set this up.

"Little Ghost," I singsong.

The hairs on my arms stand on end, keeping me alert.

She's close.

I don't have to look at her to know she took that swift intake of air that she does when she's startled. But on this side of the fortress, there's silence. On the other side, I hear lots of giggling and hands and knees thumping on the floor.

My blood is pumping in my ears, the pounding as loud as the first night when I chased Taryn through the orchard and she figured out who I was. Rounding the coffee table, my eyes land on a flap of sheet that subtly peeks into the corner of the living room. A sliver of movement through the opening shoots adrenaline through my heated veins.

Wasting no time, I flip open the flap of sheets and crawl through, my eye trained on hers as she stares at me with wide eyes.

She crosses her arms furiously, shifting on the pillow she's sitting on. "Tristan is a traitor! He told me he was on my side and wouldn't let you in."

I tilt my head, an impish smile playing on my lips. "Blood comes before beauty, Little Ghost."

She purses her lips together to hide her grin, her eyes

shifting into little slits to evaluate me. Fuck, I love it when she looks at me like that.

Moving the last few feet toward her, I crowd her space, pushing her down onto the pillows so her body is underneath mine. Her legs willingly open for me, and I settle between them.

Lifting my hand to her face, I trace her jawbone with my fingertips. "I found the gift you left me on the window ledge in the gym." I *tsk* at her. "I hope you aren't teaching my little siblings to paint erotica. You remember the rules; their minds are fragile. At this point, I think you like being punished."

She pushes herself up a little on her elbows, her face drawing closer to mine. "It's not a punishment if I enjoy it," she whispers, her breath fanning across my mouth.

My fingers dig under her long-sleeved T-shirt, running up her soft abdomen. They paint her rib cage and drift across the undersides of her breasts. "Were those breasts painted on that rock supposed to be these?" Wriggling under her sports bra, I roll a nipple between my thumb and index finger, pinching it lightly.

She squirms under me. "*Mhmm.*"

How the hell did I give this woman all the control to drive me absolutely insane?

I roll my hips, my hardening cock creating friction against her core. Dropping my mouth to hers, I brush a light kiss against her lips as I thrust into her with way too many layers between us.

A reserved whimper escapes her, the sound driving me to deepen the kiss. My tongue brushes against Taryn's, and I devour every part of her as if that shrill moan could feed my starving soul.

I'm infatuated with her.

Placing an arm above her head to keep myself propped on top of her, my other hand gives each of her breasts the attention they deserve. She raises her hips to chase the friction while her fingers pull through my hair.

I want to fuck her right now. I should carry her back to my place so she can writhe below me and come on my cock all night, but I'm not sure where my brothers are, and someone needs to watch Elena and Tristan.

Pulling back, I mumble against her lips, "Where are Cameron and Brennan?"

"They went to pick up pizzas at Crocks," she says against my mouth, her lips clashing with mine again.

My hand exploring her body glides below the waistband of her leggings, drifting over soft skin until I feel the wet heat pooling between her legs. She's so fucking wet it makes my dick pulse inside my gym shorts.

I lower my head, releasing an exasperated groan. "Shower with me after dinner?" I plead quietly so that Elena and Tristan don't hear wherever they're lurking.

She nods. The words come out breathlessly as my fingertip swipes over her clit, her back arching. "You *really* need one."

Pulling my hand out from the inside of her leggings, I bunch up the T-shirt near my armpit, lowering my nose to it. "It's not that bad," I lie.

I flinch when her fingertips drag over the painful bulge in my shorts. "Yes, I'll shower with you. As long as I can clean this cock off with my tongue."

Jesus. That mouth.

Growling, I capture her mouth again, biting her bottom lip as I picture my wet dick sliding between her beautiful lips while water droplets grace her smooth skin.

"Hello? Anyone home?"

Both of our bodies freeze instantly at the voice. The living room is now completely quiet because I can't hear Tristan or Elena either.

A few moments later, Elena squeals, "Jessica!"

A ruckus coming from the other side gives me enough time to quickly peel my large frame off Taryn's. I adjust my dick in my shorts while she fixes her shirt, breathing heavily. It's like we're fucking teenagers almost getting caught doing something we're not supposed to be doing.

We both crawl out of the fort, and Jess has her arms wrapped around Tristan and Elena.

"Do you see how big the fort is?" Tristan asks her.

"It's huge! Definitely bigger than the one I made with you guys earlier this summer," Jess chuckles.

I push myself up off the floor when we reach the fort's entrance, and I swipe back my hair, smiling as Jessica's kind eyes find mine.

"I didn't know you were coming home." Why is my voice all high-pitched and shit?

A knowing smirk tilts Jess's lips.

Shit. She knows.

Jessica shrugs, pushing her pin-straight brown hair behind her shoulder. "It was a last-minute decision. I wanted to come home for the weekend!" She rubs circular motions on Elena's back since she's attached like a barnacle to her leg.

Taryn appears out of the fortress behind me with rosy cheeks.

Jess has a shit-eating grin on her face, her green eyes flickering with delight. "I see you two are more acquainted now. Are you finally friends?"

Friends.

The word churns like hot acid in my stomach, like my body is rejecting the notion.

Everything about Taryn thrills me: her sugary citrus scent, the way I can read her emotions effortlessly when I peer into those big brown eyes, holding them captive as she does with mine.

Her tongue.

Her lips.

I'm obsessed with the words that emerge from someone so feisty and kind simultaneously. She is selfless. Despite how hard I tried, she makes my family happy in ways I never could.

Since I first found her, Taryn Meyers has consumed my thoughts. And that vital artery in my chest aches whenever she slips into my mind or I'm near her.

I have her. But not in the way my heart craves her.

FORTY-ONE | TARYN

"You've only been in college for a month. How are you seeing someone already?"

Jessica shrugs at Cameron's interrogation about the guy she's been seeing, her cheeks turning that shade of pink that reminds me of the pink hollyhocks growing in the garden outside. Her three older brothers examine her like a specimen under a microscope.

I doubt she wanted to tell them, but she couldn't stop smiling when they asked how her classes were going earlier. They instantly knew something was up, and since then, they haven't stopped grilling her. She's probably contemplating why she came home for the weekend.

Her eyes bounce between the boys as we all lounge around the clean living room, which was hell to clean up because now I have a ton of laundry to fold tomorrow. Elena and Tristan are too busy to participate in this conversation. Not that they'd want to. They are more entertained by seeing how long they can hold their Oreos in their milk before half of it sinks to the bottom.

Her eyes clash with mine, and I give her an apologetic smile from my position on the floor as I scratch Rossco's stomach. "Oh, give her a break."

"No, I want to know who the guy is," Brennan snaps, leaning over his knees.

Colten smirks, reaching for the nearly empty pizza box and grabbing a slice. I think it's like his sixth one. But he said he didn't have lunch today, so I can't say I'm surprised.

"You guys brought Taryn home and literally couldn't keep your dicks—"

"Jessica," Colten warns.

Jess huffs out a breath, and I laugh, all stares from the boys now directed at me.

"What?" I look between them. "She's not wrong, and you know it."

Cameron leans back into the couch cushions and knits his arms, releasing an annoyed sigh. "I still don't like the idea."

My eyes roll. "You would say that even if she had been dating the guy for months."

"I'm her brother," he counters, "I'm not supposed to like anyone she's seeing."

Jessica glances down at her light blue fingernails, picking at some of the paint near her cuticles. "And we're not actually dating, so..."

It's probably the wrong thing to say on her part because the boys' eyes thin, their dangerous gazes not giving an inch. It's not hard to assume what thoughts are rummaging through their thick heads.

"I want a name," Brennan demands, pointing his finger at her.

Colten shoves the rest of his crust in his mouth, wiping his hands on his shorts. "I need a shower." Standing, my eyes clash with his, his head giving an elusive nod toward the back of the house.

I scratch behind Rossco's ears. Sometimes, he is the perfect escape plan for situations. "And I'm going to take Rossco out before we head upstairs," I say.

"Real subtle, guys," Brennan mutters.

Cameron's features scrunch together. "It's like nine p.m.— Do you guys want to come back after and watch a movie or something?"

Colten's already walking to the back of the house when his voice bounces off the walls. "Sure."

Elena's selective hearing chooses this moment to focus on the conversation. "I want to watch a movie!"

"You need to go to bed soon, Little Miss," Jess tells her.

Elena's lips pout, and her tiny arms cross over her chest. "Fine."

"Wanna go outside?" I ask Rossco. His black ears perk upward, and he hastily flips over and darts to the foyer. Standing, I tuck a strand of hair behind my ear. "I'll be back."

On my way out of the living room, their eyes follow every step I make. I swear I can sense their gazes still lingering even after I disappear and walk down the hallway to the back door. They aren't exactly oblivious to what's about to happen, but I'd rather not make this situation any more awkward than it already is.

Walking down the hill, Rossco follows me to Colten's front door. My knuckles barely rasp against the door before it opens, a hand whizzing out and tugging me inside hurriedly. He shuts the door behind Rossco and me, hauling me into his arms.

His lips crash down onto mine before I can take a proper breath. His tongue pushes past my lips, freeing a fluttery mess of wings that chaotically attack my stomach and relocate to my chest.

Our hands roam, and our bodies seem to gravitate toward the shower in his room as if it's the only place we are meant to be at this moment in time. My fingertips trail over his firm pecs beneath his shirt, my touch working its way to his defined V-line that leads straight to his dick that my mouth and pussy are already salivating for.

When I reach under the band of his athletic shorts, dragging my nails against his skin, the tremble coursing through his body fuels the fire burning between us. It's consuming all of me, and it's hot. Scorching. Everything about Colten is beginning to burn me alive, so slow and addicting.

Dragging me along, he bursts through his bedroom door and into the darkened space. The room that was just still and silent is now alive with our erratic breaths and thundering hearts.

"Shower. Now," he demands against my lips.

"Yes, sir." Turning away from him, he pats me on the ass before I quicken my pace.

Stepping through the threshold into the bathroom, my eyes roam to the wall of windows, the orchard directly outside welcoming the rain that the dark, gloomy sky is releasing. The patter of water tapping against the roof grows louder.

I've always loved the rain. The fresh scent, the ground vibrating with life and color after it quenches its thirst. The musty dirt scent that fills the air.

At first, I found the row of windows in the bathroom odd. Extremely odd. But the greens outside contrast nicely with the deep gray tile and black accents with forest green towels to complement the space.

Also, when I was roaming around the outside like a stalker and trying to get him to talk to me, I noticed that the windows looking into the bathroom were tinted with a mirror-like quality. Being the weirdo I am, I stepped up to the glass to peer inside. I could see into the bathroom, but not unless my nose pressed against the glass. I bet there is still a smudge there.

"And you better be naked and wet when I get in there." Colten's raspy voice slips through to my ears smoothly from the bedroom.

The strings under my already sensitive skin tighten. "I'm already wet," I taunt, reaching into the shower to turn on the water.

"Jesus," he mumbles, making me smile. I love that I have that effect on him. Seeing him come completely undone by using a few words is my kryptonite.

Reaching for the hem of my shirt, I discard it on the ground next to the large walk-in shower. I hear a *thunk*, my ears perking at the sound of a drawer closing in the bedroom.

I step into the shower with only a thin sheet of glass as a barrier to catch water droplets so they don't collect on the floor. Moving under the spray, I close my eyes, allowing the hot water to glide down my face and body, the temperature adding to the heat already blazing my skin.

Before I know it, he accompanies me in the shower, his strong and calloused hands reaching for my naked form. His fingertips pulse into my hip bones, but the hard length under his palm, pressing against the outside of my thigh, has my breath expelling from my lungs.

It's not his cock.

Oh, shit.

The hammering of my heart pounds in my ears. The drumming reminds me of the moment in *Jurassic Park* when the massive predator's heavy footsteps are advancing. The noise is slow. Steady. But fucking terrifying. It's probably a strange comparison, but it's fitting.

I know exactly what it is with just the chill, soft touch of the silicone. Braving a glance down, my eyes drop to my pink rabbit vibrator. His lips roam over the curvature of my neck, his tongue lapping at the droplets cascading down. The sight of my vibrator electrifies my nerves, firing a dose of excitement that fogs my brain.

"Do you know how long I've thought about using this on you?" Colten's gravelly murmur vibrates my shoulder. I shake my head. "Since I went to the house and picked up all your things, Taryn. Fucking months ago. The moment I saw this, I knew I wouldn't be stuffing you with only my cock."

Oh. My. God. The things he says and does with his mouth should be illegal.

"Tell me, Little Ghost. Which hole do you want my cock in?"

My mouth opens, the hot spray from the shower hitting my tongue. I don't have the chance to answer because he pushes my body forward, hauling one of my legs up onto the bench.

His arm snakes up my back and around my neck, one of his hands cupping the front of my throat. He positions me so I'm bent over with my head up and back arched.

"It doesn't matter what you want." Damn, I love how controlling he can be with me. "I have yet to stretch your ass, and I won't be satisfied until I've claimed you everywhere. Did you like it when my brother fucked your ass while I was taking your cunt?"

I whimper, remembering the way my body reacted to the pleasure and pain of being so full of Colten, Brennan, and Cameron. "Yes."

His merciless laugh ignites a wildfire in my chest. His hand with my pink rabbit moves to the front of my body, and he drags the tip of it through my wet slit. "My dick is going to wipe away any trace of my brothers. After I'm done with you, the only name and cock you'll be able to remember is mine."

He drags it over my sensitive clit, and I whimper. Shoving it inside me, my pussy clenches at the beautiful feeling of my vibrator, but thankfully, he leaves it turned off. I know once his dick is inside me, I'll only last about one second if the vibrator is turned on. I would combust as quickly as the snap of his fingers.

He thrusts it in and out leisurely, the magnificent burn in my belly heightening. Colten releases his hand from clutching my throat and withdraws the toy from my pussy, moving the tip of it to my back hole.

My body trembles, and he flattens his palm over one of my shoulder blades. "Relax your muscles, Taryn. I need to prepare you to take me. We're in the shower, so this is going to be a little harder, but I'm not waiting any longer to claim every part of you."

I nod frantically, nipping my bottom lip. He slowly nudges it inside me, the intrusion and burn building the tears behind my eyes. God, it hurts, but it did the first time. The only thing keeping me sane is recalling how euphoric it felt the first time after I had finally adjusted to Cameron's cock after he stretched me to fit him while Colten was buried in my pussy.

Once the vibrator feels like it's fully inside me, he starts thrusting it in and out at a slow pace that has my delirious mind spinning and my legs trembling beneath me. Water droplets from the spray glide down my face, and I lick my lips, realizing the salty taste on my tongue must be a mixture of the water blending with my tears.

"Oh, shit, Colten." The pain starts morphing into pleasure, as my body heats to a temperature hotter than the shower and thick steam that lingers in the air.

He groans, reaching in front to cup one of my breasts as he starts to move the toy faster. I moan, dropping my head between my shoulders. I arch my back up, involuntarily pushing my ass up to chase more of the friction.

"Look at you," he coos. "Such a good girl letting me get you ready to take my cock in your ass."

"I need you inside me," I breathe, craning my neck to peer at his handsome features. I don't care how much it's going to hurt—I want to feel everything.

My eyes track the movement of the water dripping over his pecs and the ridges of his abdomen. How he looks with tatted skin pulled tight over firm muscles and those piercing green eyes is enough to make me explode. But I can't. Not yet.

"Fuck, I love it when you beg for me, baby. I'll give you anything you want."

His sincere and calm tone tells me he means that.

He removes the toy, and my body tenses at the loss. But I know what's coming next, and once his length is inside me, it's going to hurt again before it's euphoric. He cleans the toy with soap quickly before he spits into his hand, grips his dick, and pumps it from base to tip a few times. Then he's nudging at my back entrance. I observe the way the veins in his arms protrude against his skin. I wet my lips.

The way his fingers flex on his length is mesmerizing. The way he runs his tongue along his top teeth before clenching his jaw, because he is trying to maintain control, is enough to heighten my pleasure.

He's breathtaking.

"Take a deep breath, baby. I need you to let me all the way in."

I think I let Colten all the way in a long time ago. Despite how badly I didn't want to at the time.

Inhaling deeply, I relax into his arms as his hips push forward into my ass. I grit my teeth and slam my eyes shut. It still burns, but not as badly now that he's prepared me to take him. He adjusts my hips and the way my leg is propped up on the bench, opening me up to him further. Reaching in front of me, he swipes the toy across my clit, and I moan at the erotic feeling of my sensitive center being played with while he's taking my ass. He pushes the vibrator inside me, and I clench around him, releasing a sound that can't be described as a moan or a whimper—it's somewhere exquisitely in between.

I glance over my shoulder, watching the stunning man claim my body—my soul—in more ways than he already has.

"Just like that, baby. You're doing so good for me," he grunts in praise.

Between Colten thrusting the toy in and out of my pussy and his thick cock, he is filling me completely.

I feel him everywhere.

In my core.

He's in my head.

He's consuming my heart.

"Fuck," he mutters. Using his free hand, he grips my ass with his fingers to open me wider. "Do you love how I can still give your pussy exactly what it needs while I fuck this tight ass?"

The pain dulls more, shifting into a kind of pleasure I've never experienced—one that's heavy and intoxicating, tainting my bloodstream. "God, Colten. I'm going to come if you don't stop saying things like that to me."

Of course, he doesn't stop. "Then come. Show me how much you love my cock, baby."

His words fade, my cresting orgasm overtaking any thoughts swarming in my head.

"Fucking say it," he demands. "Tell me you love my cock."

My release hits me with a power that has my foot losing traction on the wet tile floor. My pussy throbs around the pink rabbit and his dick as my orgasm explodes, hauling me over the precipice.

Through the black fog overshadowing my vision and brain, my heart overtakes my mouth. "I love you," I mutter breathlessly, struggling to come down from the high.

"Shit, Taryn," he drawls.

Instantly, those words register to both of us, but his cock is already pulsing inside me—filling me with his hot release. I'm not sure if his orgasm started happening before or because I said that.

His motions still momentarily before his abdomen

collapses on top of my back. Removing the vibrator and dropping it to the shower floor, both of his hands grip my waist. My heart crawls into my throat.

I didn't mean to admit that out loud.

No. No. No!

Goddammit, Taryn.

Now, I wish my mouth was full of something other than my swift tongue. If he'd had my mouth occupied, too, those words would've had a better chance of emerging unintelligible.

He slips out of me as quickly as he retreats from the shower. Colten snatches a towel from the metal bar on the wall, and I grab my own. My quick steps hurry after him out of the bathroom and into his room. He wraps the towel around himself, tucking in a corner to secure it around his hips. We have barely been out of the shower for thirty seconds, so both of us are dripping on the wood flooring and area rug under his bed frame.

"Colten!" His shoulders stiffen. "Please talk to me," I plead. Tears burn behind my eyes, the tip of my nose tingling with overwhelming emotion. "You don't have to say it back, I just—I just..." I don't know. It's not untrue. I do. I love him, and I've felt it for weeks, but I didn't think I'd admit it without thinking. And definitely not this soon.

"Taryn..." He pulls his fingers through his wet hair, still facing away from me. But the moment his hand drops, so does the topic I know without a doubt he wants to avoid.

Just turn around, please.

I don't know why I care so much, but I want him to face me —to fight it out with me instead of battling whatever is in his head like he always does.

Fight with me.

Yell at me.

Tell me you don't love me.

Just don't go through it alone because I know you *always* do it alone.

"Please," I beg in a near whisper, the sound barely audible even to my own ears.

He lowers his head, his chest rising and falling in such a depressed manner that my heart smashes against my ribs, attempting to shatter them so it can impale itself.

Tears stream down my face, and I slam my eyes shut, my heart breaking. Doubts churn inside my head, demolishing anything positive and hopeful in their path.

"It wasn't something I just said in the moment," I admit. "I love all of you." The hot streaks from my tears cool against my flushed cheeks.

He doesn't answer me—the silence deafening.

Gasping in a shaky breath, I stare at the man who's terrified of love. I can't blame him. I know his past. "But I can't hold on to the hope that you might someday say it back when there's a chance you never will."

I didn't think his shoulders could slump any more than they are, but they do. I just poured my heart out into a puddle of vulnerability on his floor along with the water below my bare feet.

I stand timidly, waiting. Longing for him to say something. Anything. But he doesn't.

It's the hardest thing I've ever done, but I turn away from him, retreating to the bathroom, rapidly covering my exposed skin and fragile heart with the clothes I left on the floor. When I walk out, he's perched on the edge of his bed with his head resting in his hands while Rossco sits on the floor, peering up at him, concerned.

Colten doesn't look at him either. He barely breathes.

But his complete silence speaks louder than any word could.

Message received.

Leaving him alone, I exit the house, leaving Rossco behind too. He's an emotional support presence Colten might need more than me, so I open the door and step out into the chilly night.

Alone.

Despite the fresh air, it feels suffocating. And through the tears and blurry vision, everything around me creeps in full force. The walls are closing in, the pressure sitting on my chest like one of those bloated dead whales that wash up on the beach.

I can't be here right now, so running back up the hill through the angry downpour, I run through the house, feeling heated gazes on me from the living room.

I just need a night to myself.

And it's not going to be here.

FORTY-TWO | COLTEN

Words I was so fearful to hear sink their talons into my hardened soul, grasping the part of myself I've kept suppressed—the part that has always needed to hear them but has been petrified of the consequences. They're clinging to the weak man, trying to get me to say the words I've felt for weeks but haven't wanted to acknowledge.

Taryn said she loves me.

And I didn't fucking say it back.

I'm not entirely ignorant. I know I love her, and honestly, I think it's been festering from the moment her defiant spirit marched out of the office when we first officially met. I knew everything about her before then because of all the research I had done before we chose her. But having her physically in front of me was unlike anything I had conjured up in my head. The seed was planted the moment I saw her—rooted itself, and has woven its way through my veins, around my bones, and covered my heart with the invasive feeling I'll never shake.

I glance up from my hands and meet a pair of brown eyes.

But they aren't hers.

And I wish with everything in my broken soul that they were Taryn's.

She left. Walked out the door after she laid everything out on the line while I've been wallowing like an idiot because my heart and brain are clashing for governance. They still are. My heart wants her. It's fighting to make her mine in all the ways she isn't already. Yet my brain understands that she's gone.

That she walked out on me like my mother did all those years ago.

Exactly how my grandparents left and never spoke to my family again after their daughter vanished.

How my damn father was arrested and is incarcerated because the love in his marriage failed at some point in time, and he wasn't man enough to try and fix it.

Her words echo in my head.

"But I can't hold on to the hope that you might someday say it back when there's a chance you never will."

I want to.

Fuck. I want to shout it at her to get my head out of my ass since I promised myself I'd never say those words to anyone unless it were my siblings.

People always seem to leave and never come back. But the thought of losing Taryn...

She is virtuous. She is gentle. She loves and accepts the darkest parts of me.

If surrendering my control so I can love her in all the ways she deserves can annihilate me, then I will forever consider her my ultimate risk. And if all fails, her loving me exactly how I am right now will be my greatest reward.

"I fucked up. Hard," I say, reaching out to feel Rossco's thick coat below my sweaty palms. "But I think you already know that."

He blinks at me, his tongue lolling to the side when I scratch behind his ears. "Let's go get our girl," I murmur.

Our girl.

My girl.

Mine.

I don't know how long I've been sitting alone, but I pick up my stressed and weighted frame off the bed, go to my dresser, and tug on a pair of sweatpants and a white T-shirt. My brisk, beating heart increases my pace as I march into the closet, grabbing a sweatshirt before I make my way to the front of the house and slip on my boots.

The rain pelts down on my hood relentlessly, soaking through the cloth. The back door light of the main house guides me through the yard with Rossco on my tail. With too much intensity, I fling the back door open, letting it slam against the exterior of the house. I'm through the hallway and in the foyer before it has time to shut.

I lower my hood, and Rossco shakes his damp coat over the wood floor at my feet. I should clean it up so nobody slips, but Taryn is my priority. And I vow right here that she will always be one of my priorities.

Three pairs of eyes in the living room snap to me. Elena and Tristan must be in bed.

I clear my throat, the weight of their gazes making my skin itch. "Is she upstairs?"

Brennan's arm is draped over the back of the couch, and his eyes fall to his lap. Jessica says nothing from the recliner.

Cameron's disheartened regard, though...that one slices through every muscle and embeds in my bones. Swiping a thumb across his bottom lip, he leans over his knees, pinning me with his glare. "You want to clue us in on what's going on?"

My chest caves, my lungs squeezing out the words. "She told me she—"

"She what?" Brennan pushes, slanting his head.

My pulse batters. "Loves me."

Lines form between Cameron's brows. "So, what's the fucking problem then?"

I don't want to admit it—that I am a complete asshole for letting her walk away like that, but honesty wins. "I couldn't say it back."

Jess lifts a hand to her mouth in shock. "That explains it," she mutters through her fingers, but the words are precise and clear, striking with a force that weakens my knees.

"Colten..." Cameron's pained sigh has my hands balling into fists at my sides. "You can't punish yourself or Taryn for what happened between Mom and Dad. You aren't them." He shakes his head. "And if you take things further with her...I know you'd go into it knowing you'd want your relationship to look nothing like what theirs did those last few years before Mom disappeared."

Emotion slithers up my throat, clogging my airway and making it difficult to draw even half a breath.

He's right.

Yet the infection of fear still lingers in the depths of my mind.

But how I feel about her? Yeah, that sensation has spread and numbed all the hurt and agony that has coexisted over the past five years.

When I don't speak, Brennan lifts his eyes to meet mine. "But do you? Do you feel the same way?"

My fingers pull through my damp hair. "Fuck. I should've said it back." The sound of a car door slamming jolts my body. "Where is she?"

Cameron reaches for the coffee table, grabbing his beer. "She said she needed a night alone. So, she's headed back to the house. Gram and Bumpa's old place."

Fuck. Fuck. FUCK!

I stride to the window, watching her truck speed around the

circular driveway. Her red taillights, glowing through the down-pour and light misting of fog, taunt me as they disappear.

"Shit!" Turning rapidly without a second thought, I tear through the kitchen, seizing the Aston Martin keys from the counter, and march back through the foyer to the front door.

My body is reacting on its own. She's pulling me toward her as if we're bound by an invisible force. The growing distance between us is lengthening the void, and I'm determined to close the distance.

I crave her closeness.

Her soft, malleable body plastered against mine.

I'm addicted to how my heart pulses wildly whenever she's nearby. I'm captivated by the brightness and vibrancy that flickers across those brown irises. They make me feel lighter whenever they're imprisoned by mine.

God, I love the way she makes me feel.

But right now, I'm combatting the same soul-wrenching feeling that attacked me all those years ago when I left my siblings for those few days after Mom disappeared.

I didn't look at her after she said those words to me. I couldn't. But her pleading eyes were so powerful that I felt the dejection pooling in my gut like poison.

Hurling my body into the front seat, water drips off my hair and cascades down the side of my temple. Turning on the igni-tion, I slam my foot on the gas pedal, cursing myself for letting her walk away.

Cursing myself because *I'm* the reason she left.

I round the circular driveway, flicking on the wipers to clear the droplets of rain pelting the windshield from the low cloud cover. Accelerating down the driveway with the solar lights on both sides, I enter the orchard, slamming the pedal harder as if I could smash it into the floor. Luckily this car is a hell of a lot faster than my truck. A red glow appears through the rain and fog in the distance, the sight of her truck dangerously escalating the cadence of my heart hammering violently.

Please slow down when you see me.

I've always loved chasing her. But right now?

Fuck that.

I want her in my bed. I want to say the words I know she wants to hear. I want my hands tangled in her silky, dark hair and her body trapped below mine because that's where she belongs. With me. *With us.*

Nearing her vehicle, I flash the brights, but she doesn't slow.

I slam the steering wheel with my fist. "Please slow down!"

But nothing happens.

We race through the orchard. A storm may be raging around us, but my focus is on calming the chaos I have unleashed.

Gaining on her, I flash them again, holding my breath.

Red brake lights illuminate the wet gravel, but the moment I realize where she is—where we are in the orchard—time slows.

The water droplets gliding down the slope of the windshield.

The boom of my pulse echoing in my ears.

The searing current of panic that poisons my bloodstream the moment her taillights vanish off the cliffside, leaving an endless abyss of darkness that swallows everything in its wake.

FORTY-THREE | TARYN

I never understood what people meant when they said something played behind their eyes in slow motion. I tried to envision it sometimes. The ability to have that power seemed intriguing.

No matter how hard I tried, it wasn't something I could comprehend.

But now? I feel it.

I see it in how my headlights reflect off the murky waves of the Columbia River while the lingering glint of Colten's lights dances in my vision.

The understanding hits me as hard as the impact of my truck smashing through the water's surface.

There's so much adrenaline and horror coursing through my body that I don't feel anything when my forehead smashes into the steering wheel. I also don't feel the pain when my chest hits the front with such force that I wonder if my ribs might shatter and puncture my heart.

Also, the out-of-body experience.

Yeah. I comprehend that now, too.

Nevertheless, this is my fault.

"You'll have to accept the parts I allow you to have."

Colten said that to me weeks ago, and I accepted it. Accepted him. That's what you do when you care for someone so profoundly because you fell for all the good parts somewhere along the way.

The bad parts of Colten, though? They've morphed into something I respect. He is overly protective of his family, which is why he has layers upon layers of barriers encasing his heart. *They* come first, and they will always come first.

Loving me means allowing himself the opportunity to be hurt. And when Colten is broken, he thinks his vulnerability not only infects him but weakens his family.

His rejection stings.

So badly. But I understand why he did it and it would be easier if I didn't. Easier if I could hate us for dragging each other along when we knew breaking each other was inevitable.

I was feeling trapped when he didn't say the words back. Observed as the imaginary walls closed with each moment of silence when he didn't utter a word. The walls squeezed me tighter than any place I had been before.

But the reality is, despite Colten not saying he loved me, I hope a part of me healed him, even if it was the slightest bit. I know he feels something for me, even if he isn't sure what it is. He feels everything.

I saw what he is like when he lets go. The tension that tugs at his jawline when he's trying so hard not to give in, but he would take one look at me and let his walls collapse for a little while.

He collapsed some of mine. The parts of me that told myself I would never find a place I wanted to settle.

With him, I would have.

The timer slowly *ticks, ticks, ticks* away the deeper my truck sinks, and the regret I didn't sense before fills my veins as water floods the floor of my truck.

I shouldn't have run. People leaving is the one thing that kills him, and that's precisely what I did. That was my last thought the moment his headlights appeared behind me. I knew the bend in the road was there, but I was going too fast. Distraction overcame me because the man who said he couldn't give me everything realized he shouldn't have let me go.

Now it's too late.

My head pulses wildly, feeling like someone is taking a sledgehammer to my skull, repetitively beating down to haul me into an unconscious state. Everything in my vision is blurred, and my body is focusing heavily on the pain I can now feel everywhere and not only in my heart.

Lifting a hand to my face, I massage my fingers into my temple, releasing a groan.

Think, Taryn.

Get out.

Get out.

Get out.

My eyes begin to focus, the horror registering so fast as the truck dives nose-first into the blackened river. Icy water laps at my legs, my whole body already shivering from the ache blending with a substantial dose of panic. Without wasting another precious second, my hand flies to my seat belt. My body is flung forward over the steering wheel, my hand struggling to reach it, but I manage to unclasp myself.

Waves crash against my driver's side window, and the water's surface splatters with the downpour of rain. The water in the cab is up to my waist now, and from what I know, the only way to get out of this is to crawl out the windows.

Reaching for the old crank on my door—because of course, my truck is a dinosaur—I wind it, the window coming down only slightly. Each crank gets more challenging as my strength dwindles and my head spins. I swallow the acid creeping up my throat when it no longer budges, and I'm left with an open window with two inches of space.

In a sinking car.

Tears cascade down my cheeks, my hands violently shaking and cold to the point where the numbness gradually overtakes all my limbs. Managing to glance into my back seat shadowed by the inky darkness of the stormy night, the tiny flicker of hope I have that I can find something to break the window disappears.

I'm cold.

My head is throbbing.

My limbs are aching.

My heart fucking hurts, and as I watch the last wave crash against the window and turn into nothing but a pitch-black void dragging me under, my brain tells me I'm going to die.

Some people say regrets are all you think about when death comes calling. I always hoped that wouldn't be the case, but for me, it's true.

Images of my parents with their warm smiles cross my vision. I know they love me. I shouldn't have cared that I was the one who always initiated the conversation. I should have called them. Reached out more. Because even if they don't reach out first, I still want to hear their voices.

God. Cameron, Brennan, Tristan, and Elena. People always leave them, and now I'm just another name on that list.

I needed a breather—some space to be alone after pouring my heart out to Colten and receiving deafening silence in return. And now my gut churns with guilt, wishing I would've sat in my room in the tower before making any rash decisions.

To fight harder instead of walking away.

Nobody has fought for him before.

He fights for his family, but nobody fights for him.

Colten's handsome face flashes before me in a medley of beautiful images until he is the only person consuming my thoughts. Like the first time my eyes magnetized to his translucent green ones when he opened the school door for my "interview." When he caught me in the orchard and called me his *Little Ghost* for the first time. The effortless smiles that tug at his lips when he's around his family. The butterflies he gave me that night when he surprised me with my birthday picnic under the lights in the orchard. All the moments I've felt him move inside me like he was the one piece I've been missing all along. The piece that made life feel less hollow and kept me grounded.

He keeps me grounded.

"I'm sorry I left," I whisper, the words coming out shaky from the shivers impacting my weak body. Colten can't hear me, but I wish there were some way I could make him feel them.

But I'm down here, and he's up there.

The water is higher, pouring through the slit in the window. It's drifting up to my neck.

The water level rises.

Up.

Up.

Up.

Water trickles down my cheeks, and I can't tell if the wetness is from my eyes or the river. But when I lick my lips, and the salty flavor coats my tongue, I know it's my tears.

I hope you'll forgive me one day.

Then I inhale my last, deep breath, letting the river overtake me. My head completely submerges, but my eyes are still open.

One second feels like one minute. Thirty seconds feels like a lifetime of drowning. Then, the front of the truck makes contact with something underwater, and the back tailgate slowly drifts down to even out. But my taillights, still shining through the darkness, reflect off what appears to be rock.

I must be on a ledge that's part of the cliff.

I glance out my driver's side window one last time, my lungs burning and screaming for oxygen. But the pain starts to numb when my eyes snag on something silver glinting in the distance outside my driver's side window.

My heart plummets as fast as my truck did when the realization hits.

The last thought that crosses my mind before my eyes close and my body surrenders is that my vehicle isn't the only one the river has claimed.

FORTY-FOUR | COLTEN

My body is hurled into a free fall.

Not the good kind where your stomach dives, tossing you into an addicting adrenaline rush. It's the type that slams your heart into your gut when you realize the nightmare is a living, breathing thing.

"Fuck! Taryn," I bellow in the cab of the Aston Martin as I slam my foot on the gas pedal, trying to keep my eyes focused on the approaching curve through the heavy rain obstructing my view.

Yet all I can concentrate on is her.

The terror flashing through her eyes.

The fearful thoughts swarming her head.

The thought of her beautiful body being hurt in any way floods the sides of my vision with red.

But she is. She must be with a fall like that.

It's a thirty-foot drop to the water, and as I start to slow the car, so I don't follow her off the cliff, my dread devours me.

"Siri, call Cameron," I yell, the valuable seconds ticking by before my car answers with, "Calling Cameron."

Each ring rattles my bones, but then he answers the call. "Did you find he—"

"I need you to call 911 and get them here as fast as possible. Taryn—she..."

Cameron's tone is laced with alarm. "She what?"

Oh, fuck.

How the hell am I going to get her out of this?

It could be thirty minutes before first responders arrive, and we don't have that long—a few minutes at most.

"Her truck went off the cliff." My eyes burn, my hand clutching the wheel as if I can shatter it into a million pieces, exactly like my heart is.

"Oh, shit! Brennan," he shouts, not bothering to remove the phone from his ear. "Call 911 and get them here now."

"What?" Brennan's muted, confused reply drifts through the phone from wherever he is in the house.

"Do it now," Cameron snaps. "Taryn's truck went off the cliff!"

I attempt to swallow the anxiety, but it stays glued to the inside of my esophagus. "We're going to need a helicopter, Cam," I manage to say with an obstructed windpipe as I fling the door open.

"Wait," Cameron says frantically. I pause. "What are you going to do?"

He already knows the answer to that question, and I don't have to think about it. "I'm jumping in."

"Are you fucking kidding? That drop—"

"We've cliff-dived plenty before," I rush out, "And there's no other fucking option, Cam! Unless you want her to drown—"

"Just— *Shit*. Just be careful." A few words are exchanged in the background before he talks again. "First responders are on their way, and Bren and I will be there as quickly as we can."

Acid burns my throat, tears pooling in my eyes.

"And, Colten?"

"Yeah," I breathe heavily, jumping out of the car.

"I love you."

"I love you too, brother."

The call is disconnected, and the rain pelts my head, dripping off my hair and down my temple as I open the trunk to find something. Anything that can help me get her out.

My brain pounds against my skull, making it hard to form cohesive thoughts since she is the only thing I see.

Reaching into the trunk, I haul a black bag forward, digging through the contents and tossing them aside until I find what I need. Thank fuck we all keep a set of tools in our cars. Grabbing the screwdriver, I leave the car running and track through the mud to the edge of the cliffside.

Her truck is nosediving into the river, her headlights and red rear lights taunting me under the waves as she sinks further. Glancing around briefly, I notice a rock shelf above the water, big enough to fit us both, just ten feet from her submerged vehicle.

If I can get her out—

When I fucking get her out, we will have to wait there for the helicopter. With the thirty-foot cliffside, there's no other way.

Swimming isn't an option.

Gripping the screwdriver handle in my hand, I blow out a breath and notice that her truck hasn't sunk any further.

"Hold on, Little Ghost."

Inhaling a deep breath, I jump off the side, my veins flooding with adrenaline. The sound of rain hammering the surface grows louder until the water engulfs me and bubbles ring in my ears. Jumping from that height pushes me farther down into the river, so I open my eyes and locate her truck when the water settles around me.

Quickly kicking myself up to the surface against the current, I prepare myself to take the last breath I'll need if I'm going to save her. Filling my lungs, I hold my breath, pushing my body downward. The closer I get, the lack of movement in the cab cracks all the bones in my sternum, urging me to gasp for air.

But I can't.

I won't.

Come on, baby, fight for me.

Reaching for the door handle to keep myself steady, fight-or-flight for her tears through my soul. I'd rather it be me succumbing to the Columbia than her.

Through the driver's side window—open slightly—her brown hair floats around her face like the tentacles of a jellyfish, beautifully gliding through the ocean. But nothing about her pale face, floating limbs, and open eyes is angelic.

It's fucking horrifying, and not even half a second passes before my fist clenching the screwdriver drives into the glass. The metal tip smashes into the side where the glass is weaker. The inferno in my lungs rages, my brain screaming at me to focus on the breath in my lungs instead of hers.

She is my oxygen.

Taryn was my first breath of fresh air since that horrific night. The night that stabbed and scraped into my skin with a serrated blade. She has filled my torn flesh and implanted herself in all the holes.

She is my lifeline, and I refuse to let her go this way. Taryn will hear the words I should've said.

Spiderwebs form in the glass. One more blow causes the window to shatter, and the shards flutter into the truck and around me, settling onto the rock platform below it.

My hand releases the screwdriver, and I instantly reach for her. The headlights flicker a few times before the river devours us completely.

Breaking the surface should be relieving. My lungs should be able to draw in the air they need to satisfy them. To keep them inflating and deflating the way they are meant to function so I stay alive.

They don't.

Because Taryn is slack in my arms.

Her dead weight hangs over my shoulder, my body fighting against the waves and current to the ledge in the distance I saw from above before I jumped.

Her head is lolled, wet hair clinging to her lifeless face. My ears concentrate on catching any breaths, listening for anything expelled from her.

Wading through the river, my body tensely holding on to her, I wipe the water from my eyes to see more clearly through the dark. It does little against the rain.

"Come on, Taryn, I need you to wake up!"

No response, but I didn't think I would get one.

She's not dead.

She won't die like this.

Even if it meant begging the Grim Reaper to take my soul in place of hers, I would do it without hesitation. I would crash down onto my knees and give myself over because the world needs her more than me.

I thought the clouds were raging above before. Flashes of lightning brighten the wet rock walls and surface around me, the sky's screams and angry voices crackling through the air as I slap a hand onto the ledge, pushing her weak body up before me.

Our clothes cling to us like a second layer of skin. I should be shivering, convulsing from the chilled waters of the Columbia and the relentless rain. My body should be reacting to the cold encasing my skin instead of heating to temperatures that rival hell because of how angry I am at myself for letting this happen.

Pulling my frame up on the ledge, the jagged rocks dig into my knees as I crawl toward her head. Her lifeless eyes stare into the unforgiving heavens. Water droplets cascade down her creamy and colorless skin.

"Taryn, baby," I whisper shakily, lifting my hand to the skin below her jaw, my fingers jittering against where the pulse in her neck should be responding.

Fluttering.

Dancing.

Giving any sign of life.

But there is nothing.

Rain in my gaze is replaced with the lick of flames, awakening my insides with a drive I've never known. Raising my body above hers, I bring my hands to her chest, starting chest compressions. I reach far back into the storage box in my memory, frantically pulling out the contents until I locate the CPR class I took as a lifeguard for a summer.

My knuckles turn white as I force some of my weight into a rhythmic motion against her fragile chest, attempting to fight the hold of death. My hands tremble uncontrollably, but I try to push through.

Fuck!

My arms burn, and my mouth mutters numbers out loud, counting the compressions.

"Breathe," I shout the command into nothingness, the world around us insignificant and blurred. "Breathe, Taryn!"

My desperation overtakes my hands, and my movements come faster as fear grips me. Removing my hands, my thumb fondles her cold lower lip with a hue of blue only icy waters can create.

Lowering my mouth to hers, I draw oxygen into my lungs, then force my life, my breath, into the girl who has completely destroyed my world in the best way possible.

Taryn Meyers was destined to upend my life and devastate my control. And as my lips press into hers, I realize I never want to go a day without that aching burn deep in my chest that stirs with the craving to be closer to her, even when it's impossible.

"You make me better, baby," I mumble against her lips.

I rise above her, starting chest compressions again, digging my hands deeper this time, feeling the splintering of bone beneath my palms.

A faint ripple in her throat catches my eye.

"Come back to me," I grunt breathlessly. "Lash out at me. Show me that fight I've seen in you since the beginning. Breathe so I can get on my knees and lay my heart at your feet and beg for your forgiveness before I tell you how much I love you—how badly and profoundly I've loved you since you sat across from me in that office."

Her blue lips part, her eyes blinking away the rain collecting in them. I hold on to the last sliver of hope wherever it's hiding in my soul.

Yes, Little Ghost! Breathe for me.

Convulsing, her body twists to the side, expelling and coughing water out of her lungs onto the rock ledge below her. Sucking air back into her lungs, she frantically flails, her eyes widen in horror, locking me in place.

"It's okay, I've got you—"

"Colten." My name emerges, tattered and raw from her throat. "The car!" My eyes hold her frightened ones. "Your mother's car—"

She grips me for stability, my heart lurching into my throat at the mention of my mother, but Taryn's eyes flutter, her head lolling backward as oblivion consumes her.

FORTY-FIVE | TARYN

The scent of chemicals hanging heavy in the air drifts into my nose.

Why does it burn?

The sterile aroma of antiseptics penetrates the heavy fog in my head with its potency. My chest rises and falls while darkness blankets my vision. The clinical smell unsettles me.

Peeling my weighted eyelids open gradually, piercing light spurs the overwhelming headache near my temples, stirring the nausea in my stomach. I scrunch my face in response to the bright light.

My breathing quickens at the sharp pain digging into my sternum as if someone were using one of those mechanical screwdrivers to drill into my bones.

My body hunches over slightly, and a groan parts from my lips. The inexorable aching turns my breathing shallow.

Shit. Why is it hard to breathe?

Breathe.

I couldn't breathe.

Images of dark waters smash into my cognizance, flashes of my memory resurfacing.

My truck went off the cliff. I couldn't escape. I sucked in too much water. I was drowning.

My eyes fly open to dispose of the horrific memory, and my pained lungs draw in quick breaths since I can't seem to get enough oxygen.

The ceiling, blurry at first, comes into focus. The fluorescent fixtures overhead drill into my eyes, the bright white room grinding the panic into granules of sand that scrape under my skin.

A faint, feminine voice spills into my ears. "Taryn?"

Ugh. My head feels like an anchor threatening to drag me back down to that dark place. Managing to turn my focus, my head falls to the side, my eyes taking in the woman before me.

A woman who should be countries away and not where... well, wherever I am.

"Mom?" I croak, my sandpaper tongue barely speaking the words.

She rushes to my side next to a monitor and an IV machine, the corners of my eyes briefly registering the room. The stark white walls burn my vision. A wooden door is open, leading to a hallway where someone in navy scrubs rushes past. Glancing down, I see the transparent cords draped on the bed attached to the catheter taped on the inside of my elbow, feeding my veins.

My stomach rolls. I hate the hospital. But I'm guessing I didn't have a choice by the looks of it.

"Oh, sweetheart," my mother sighs in relief, lifting a hand to my cheek and stroking the skin.

I lean into her touch, soaking up her warmth. I didn't realize I could miss a hand's temperature so much—it's unique to her. There was always something so comforting about her— her hugs, her warm palms.

Her cropped, brown, layered hair is tickling her shoulders. When I peer into her eyes, it's like gazing into a mirror. I've always thought they reminded me of chocolate whiskey.

Pain rolls through my body, a tear slipping from the corner of my eye, drifting down my feverish cheek as I stare at her, trying to convince myself she's not a mirage. "How are you here right now?"

Her thumb wipes away the moisture. "Your boyfriend called us," she says softly. "Told us what happened. We hopped on a flight immediately." She swallows, her gentle fingers tucking a strand of hair behind my ear.

Wait...what?

I adjust my body to try and sit up, but she urges me not to by placing her hands on my chest. She doesn't touch me hard, but I feel everything. At this point, even the stroke of a feather could have me hunching over in pain. Well, if I could manage to hunch over, which I think is impossible right now.

"Where is he?" I murmur, the frantic pace of my heart stabilizing the consistent pain in my ribs.

She steps to the side, revealing a body in one of the visitor chairs against the wall in the room. Even asleep and exhausted, Colten's handsome features have my heart rate spiking, but then an aching follows behind my rib cage. His head is perched uncomfortably on his shoulder, his chest rising and falling steadily.

My eyes remain trained on him when I respond to something my mom mentioned earlier. "He's not my boyfriend," I clarify.

My mother glances at him, and we both stare. I'm sure the same thought is running through her head because how can he sleep like that with his legs straight out and crossed at the ankles and his head using his shoulder as a pillow? It looks incredibly uncomfortable.

Her attention finds me, and she grins. "That's not what he said."

The slow spread of a smile overtakes my lips.

Boyfriend, huh?

"Breathe so I can get on my knees and lay my heart at your feet and beg for your forgiveness before I tell you how much I love you— how badly and profoundly I've loved you since you sat across from me in that office."

His voice—those words—circulate in my head on a loop as if I'm never supposed to forget them. It's like a song carved into a record, but the tune and lyrics were engraved into my heart instead.

I'm unsure how I heard him say that or how I registered his words, but I think that admission grasped onto my soul and wrenched me out of death's cold fingers, ready to claim me.

"You were—dead," my mother chokes. "He saved you..."

Raking my eyes over his exhausted form, I suppress a smile at his slightly parted lips. Lips that have always made me feel alive, but now they're the reason I'm breathing.

"I think in a lot of ways we've saved each other," I tell her honestly.

A tear falls off her bottom lashes, and she wipes it away. "Your father." She swallows the emotion. "I'm going to go get your father."

Pressing her lips to my forehead, she hurries out of the room, the silence settling around me. Turning my head toward the ceiling, my eyes flutter closed, and I attempt to draw in calming breaths.

I wince in pain. Damn. Why is a tiny person in my chest scraping my bones against a cheese grater?

Try again.

In through my nose, out through my—

"I know you need to breathe to live, Little Ghost, but don't hurt yourself." Colten's smooth, sleep-ridden voice numbs the pain.

Turning my head on the pillow toward him, his vibrant light green eyes clash with mine. They take my breath away, which probably isn't healthy right now, considering my state.

The corner of his mouth tilts up as he pushes himself off the chair and strides to my bedside. Lowering his head to mine, his lips brush against my temple so lovingly that my heart splinters as if I could transfer the pieces to where we're connected and embed myself into him.

Lifting my left arm, I place my hand on his jaw, the weight of his head falling into my hand. "At least the pain is a reminder that I'm living. Thank you for jumping in and saving me." I stroke the stubble on his cheek with my thumb.

Straightening, he sits in the chair beside my bed, the one I assume my mom was in before I woke. He reaches for my hand, grasping it tightly enough as if he'd lose me if he let go.

His thumb moves in soothing, circular motions on my wrist. "You wouldn't be in here if it wasn't for me." Shaking his head, he twists his lips to the side, emotion swirling in his glassy eyes. "I shouldn't have let you go—"

I squeeze his hand tighter. "And I shouldn't have run," I whisper, all the emotions hitting me because this is equally our fault.

Yes, he should have answered me back and said something instead of nothing when I said I loved him. But I'm used to running or at least leaving when I feel any kind of discomfort or angst.

"We share the blame for this, Colten. I won't allow you to carry the weight of this on your own."

His eyes lift to mine, flashing with something I've never seen in his gaze. It's empathy. But then his eyelids shut, the thoughts swarming in his head, working against him.

"But you're *here* because of me," he says again. His tone is laced with grief. "Your ribs are fractured, Taryn."

Ah. That explains the immense pain I'm in.

"I literally broke you when I..." The words die on his tongue. He flattens his lips, his eyes shifting to the other side of the room where the single sink sits with some cabinets.

I drag my bottom lip between my teeth and shake my head. "I don't understand," I say, not following.

The words get lodged in his throat. "I broke you when I gave you CPR."

"The CPR you gave me when you saved my life?" A tear falls over his bottom lash, and it breaks my heart watching it trail down his flushed cheek and the dusting of hair on his jaw that looks like it grew overnight from his stress and worry alone. "Colten, my truck went off a cliff, and my body smashed into the wheel." He winces, his eyes darting to a corner of the room to avoid my eyes. "Please look at me," I plead, a near whisper. His eyelids slam shut and he exhales a shaky breath before pulling his gaze back to mine. "I drowned. You saved me. Even if it wasn't the fall and impact that caused it, rib fractures can happen even when you're doing CPR correctly—"

"But I was so hard on you," he murmurs.

"'Breathe so I can get on my knees and lay my heart at your feet and beg for your forgiveness,'" I repeat his words. He glances up, eyes scanning mine as his brow furrows in disbelief. I wasn't sure if he said it, but now I'm sure. "I don't need you to lay your heart at my feet, Colten, because yours is the reason mine is beating again."

The column of his throat works as he swallows. "You heard me?"

"I'm not sure how...it was almost like a distant voice in a sea of nothingness. I didn't feel pain at that moment. Everything was dark and lifeless, but the one thing I heard clearly was your voice."

His head falls between his shoulders, his body physically shaking. He picks up his head, his cheeks flushed as he peers at me. "So, I'm assuming you heard the rest then?"

My lips tug upward, and I nod, the tears stinging behind my eyes.

"Goddammit." He rakes his other hand that isn't holding

mine through his hair. I don't think there is any circulation in my fingers, but I am perfectly okay with it. "I didn't think you'd hear me. I didn't want to tell you that way..."

"Then tell me when you're ready," I say genuinely.

"Taryn—"

I squeeze his hand. "I'm serious, Colten. I don't need to hear it today. I don't need to hear it tomorrow. Hearing you say it at all—even if it was your distant voice in that unforeseen moment—is all I need right now. You are all I need right now."

Standing, he leans over my bed, his head dipping to mine. Colten's lips brush over mine so softly. He's not close enough, so my left hand drifts behind his head to tug the hair at the nape of his neck, bringing him closer. He groans into my mouth, and I swallow the sound. Tilting his lips, he deepens the kiss, his tongue entering my mouth and flicking against mine, injecting sparks back into my bloodstream, making me feel even more alive. If he keeps kissing me like this, I'll be healed by the end of the day.

Colten makes me feel high. A pain relief method I would happily overdose on. Again. And again.

"Fuck," he feathers across my lips. He kisses the corner of my mouth. "Thank you—" His lips press into my nose. "—for coming—" He peppers his mouth against my cheek, and I whimper. "—back to me. My beautiful little ghost."

"Always," I exhale as his forehead rests against mine. Moving my spine, I hiss at the agony. He quickly stands up, looking at me with concern. "I'm okay," I reassure him. He nods. "And thank you for calling my parents. I haven't seen my mom and dad in over eight months; I didn't realize how much I needed to see them after all this time."

He leans into the bed, rubbing a lock of my hair between his pointer finger and thumb. "Your parents love you, Taryn. It's evident. They may have their own way of showing it, but the moment I called, they instantly bought tickets to fly out here to make sure you were okay." I peer at my red-painted nails, pulling my lower lip between my teeth. "Cameron and Brennan are back at the house, but I told them you're awake, so they are bringing everyone here to see you. They were the ones who got the helicopter and first responders to us."

My frantic eyes meet his. "Are they okay? What about Elena and Tristan—"

"They sat them down and told them what happened. They were shaken up, but they want to come see you."

I smile.

He rakes his fingers through his hair. "Oh, and your parents are going to stay with us for a week. Your mother insisted on getting a hotel since she said she wasn't sure of their plans after this, but I insisted they stay with us. I hope that's okay."

A vibration of movement deep in my memory begins to bounce gradually off the inside of my skull. Tapering my brows, I focus on the recollection, the images playing behind my eyes, dragging me back down to drowning in my truck. I couldn't breathe. It was dark. But I looked out the window one last time before my eyes closed and saw something in the distance. It was metal.

My hand flies to my mouth, tears pooling in my eyes.

It was her. He said they never found the car. That her vehicle disappeared when she did.

"Colten, your mom," I stutter through the tears, the burning image of the silver SUV coexisting with my truck underwater.

His eyes fall to the impeccable white tile flooring below his shoes, the fluorescent light catching his Adam's apple bobbing.

His eyes glass over, the look terrifying me more than I thought possible. "You said something about her before you passed out," he swallows. "I felt it in my gut. I knew you wouldn't mention her out of nowhere like that."

He pauses, running his hands over his face, keeping me from seeing the emotion tearing through him.

My chest rises and falls heavily despite the ache. "Colten," I mutter worriedly.

When his eyes find mine, my stomach sinks. "Your truck wasn't the only car they pulled out of the river this morning. You found my mom, Taryn."

FORTY-SIX | TARYN

"Are you sure you want to do this?" Staring out the windshield, my eyes scan the multiple chain-link fences with razor wires twisted at the top.

Colten doesn't say anything.

The only sound between us is the air conditioning blowing in the cab; once in a while, his loud exhale penetrates the silence. Goosebumps break out over my unshaven legs from the chilly air drifting through the vents. Bending over in any capacity right now shoots pain throughout my sternum and fragile fractured ribs, so shaving my legs has been on the back burner until it's no longer excruciating to reach my legs.

Tugging the fuzzy blanket farther up on my lap, we gaze at the prison looming before us.

He didn't want me to come. But when I caught him sneaking out of bed early this morning, I knew something was wreaking havoc in that brain of his.

It's a Saturday. He rarely works on Saturdays.

He assumed I was using the bathroom, but when he emerged from the closet, fully dressed, I asked him what he was doing, and he frustratedly pushed his fingers through his hair.

A few days after my accident, Jane's body was discovered in her car, and Colten submitted a visitor's application to the prison where his father is held. His application was approved yesterday, and he made an appointment to visit today, planning to drive the three hours there and back by himself.

Now that we're here, I think he's having second thoughts.

It's been a week. A rough week.

Mourning has overtaken the house as if they had lost Jane just yesterday. Which I guess, in a way, they did. Besides Colten, they've always held on to some minuscule sliver of hope, thinking she was out there somewhere.

She was...just not where they expected.

Jane had never left the property.

Elena doesn't understand and keeps asking why she can't see Mommy. They've tried to sit down and explain it to her in a million ways that a five-year-old might apprehend, but she can't grasp that even though they found her, it's only the shell of who used to be her mother. Tristan remains quiet again, diving into his Switch to distract himself from a house plagued by the loss of Jane Lindenvale.

Cameron and Brennan have found various ways to keep themselves busy and keep the brutal truth from infesting their minds. Jessica hasn't gone back to school yet; she reached out to her professors to let them know the circumstances, so she's working online for another week until things are more settled than they are now.

On the other hand, my parents have been staying in their grandparents' old place—my old rental—until they figure out where they are going next. It's been nice to have them around. The heart-to-heart I had with my mom one night over a glass of wine on the porch while we watched Elena and Tristan throw the ball to Rossco will be one of my favorite moments with her.

Colten and the twins were showing my dad around the property at the time, but the moments alone that we'd desperately needed started turning into a plan for me to join them on a new adventure once a year. Maybe it was almost losing my life or knowing that the Lindenvale siblings lost Jane, but my mom and I mended something that was torn between us.

Time is fleeting.

Temporary.

And after all that's happened, we both want to try harder.

I like to believe my parents have been a comforting presence when they come to the house. They don't want to intrude, but Colten has invited them to dinner at the house multiple times. Elena loves my mom. One night, when I was tucking her into bed, she whispered that she thinks of my mom like her grandma. It warmed my heart, especially after all this fragile family has been through. But day by day, little by little, the air becomes a little less heavy.

I don't think things will ever go back to normal. Jane Lindenvale will finally be laid to rest in a cemetery the boys picked out later this week.

But each movement is a step toward healing.

The sound of Colten swallowing draws my attention. "I don't know what to say to him— It's been five years."

"I think you know exactly what to say to him; you just need to find the right way to bring it up." He nods, reaching for the door handle. "I'll be right here when you get back."

Rounding the front of the car, he strides up to my door and tugs it open. I peer into his green eyes as he softly reaches for my hand.

His hand shakes, so he clutches mine tighter. "Will you come with me?"

The simple request has my chest clenching and my heart so tight it could rupture. The impact alone could refracture whatever healing my ribs have accomplished in the last few days.

The Colten who stands in front of me now is far different than the man who lured me to Cedar Creek Cove. He was the kind of man to dig a bottomless hole and entomb all his emotions in the unfathomable depths. A man who could easily slip on a mask, deceiving the world by leaving a layer between him and whatever feelings were eating away at his flesh.

But the barrier has fallen, crumpled into a pile of ash at his feet. I want to collect the dust and hold it in the palms of my hands to prove to him how effortlessly I love his imperfections. The things he finds too weak to share but the things I find beauty in.

Because he is a remarkable brother. A protective parental figure who has shoved everything else aside to ensure his siblings feel valued. Cared for. So they know they are a priority—that they are set up to strive in life despite the memories that linger in that house like an old scent that permanently intertwines with the threads in a carpet or the paint on the walls.

He's carried the weight of it all.

The company.

Their bills.

The vast property that could have swallowed them all.

Colten had to grow up exceptionally fast because he witnessed what failed love looks and feels like. It left his family vulnerable, but he picked up the pieces and held them together without blinking an eye.

Now he's here, searching for answers because Jane's car at the bottom of the river only stirred up more questions about what happened that night.

After we make our way to the designated visitors' entrance, Colten and I show our driver's licenses before they screen us and give us temporary visitor badges. Escorting us to the visitation room, Colten grabs my clammy hand, refusing to let go. I grip his bicep as we brush past guards, their eyes locking onto us as we pass.

I've never set foot in a prison. It's unsettling.

Concrete walls and floors synchronize with the harsh light,

highlighting the beige accents here and there. Black cameras dot the ceilings and corners of the hallways, reminding me that people are watching every move we make.

My body trembles when we come to a halt.

"Right this way," the female correctional officer says, opening the door and leading us into the visitation room, separating guests from the inmates.

We step inside. It looks exactly like the movies, a wall of glass through the center of the room with telephones for communication and metal chairs that look like they could freeze my ass in under a minute. Other correctional officers stand in the room, observing and scanning the few people visiting other convicts.

She motions to two chairs. "Take a seat, and they'll bring him in."

The nervous tremble in Colton's tone breaks my heart. "Thank you."

He pulls out a chair for me, and I take a seat, holding my breath at the shot of pain that smashes into my ribs.

He takes a seat, eyeing me suspiciously. "Are you okay?"

"Yeah," I partially lie. He's what matters. I'm here for him. I am attempting to ignore the pain as much as I'm trying to forget I might be coming face-to-face with a murderer who was plastered on the news for months, years ago. I throw his question back at him. "Are you okay?"

He rolls his lips, leaning back against the metal backing of the chair with his arms crossed. "I'm not sure."

A door on the other side of the room, behind the glass, opens, revealing a man in a khaki-colored jumpsuit. His downcast expression is fixated on the concrete floor below his shoes, giving us a clear view of his short, cropped brown hair. Colten's father's wrists are shackled together as the guard leads him farther into the room.

Colten stills unnaturally beside me, his hand tightly gripping mine. Christian finally looks up, his shoulders rigid at seeing his son. He blinks a few times, their eyes holding each other's while they process what's in front of them. Then, Christian's focus locks on me.

Heavy eyes take me in, his face void of any expression. He lifts a hand to his peppered facial hair, scratching at his jawline with his fingernails. The dark circles under his eyes make him appear twenty years older than he is, but the handsomeness that was once there still lingers. I hold his gaze for a second longer, noting that he and his son probably had identical color irises at one point. Not anymore. There is an overlay of gray. They are lifeless.

At the same time, Colten and Christian reach for the phones, unsaid words passing between them. Pulling the phone between us, we both lean into it to hear.

Christian clears his throat. "When they said one of my sons was here to see me, I didn't expect—" He pauses, swallowing.

"Me?" Colten finishes, his tone laced with a huskiness I usually find charming. But at this moment, he's holding back; it's as if his vibrating hands are trying to transfer some of his resentment to me so he doesn't lash out.

His father nods slowly, the silence sitting heavily.

Christian's eyes locate mine, and Colten stiffens beside me. "You must be Taryn," he says. I shift uncomfortably, not particularly enjoying the way my pulse is battering in response to him knowing who I am. "Tristan has talked about you in his letters."

He has? Tristan never allowed me to read them, even though I helped Elena with hers. He needed help addressing the letters but would seal the envelope before giving them to me.

Christian's gaze lands back on his son. "How are they?"

Colten exhales a breath. "Confused. Distraught. Missing a father who doesn't deserve to be missed."

I wince while his father's weak frame tenses at his son's unsympathetic words.

"I—" His father sighs, clutching the phone so hard his knuckles turn white.

"*Hmm?* Are you going to try to defend yourself? Because it's too late for that. We found her, and there's nothing you can—"

"You found her?" He chokes, his eyes glassing over with a look that completely flips my stomach. *Why does he look like that?* "Is—is she okay?"

Colten's brow furrows irritably, and my heart lurches into my throat.

"What are you talking about?" Colten snips. "Of course she's not fucking okay." His voice rises, and I peer around at the guards staring at us apprehensively.

His eyes don't stray from Colten's. "Where is Jane?"

My head tilts at his question. Either he is insane and pulling up a mask to hide the truth, or he is genuinely as confused as I am.

Colten releases my hand, pointing an index finger up to the glass. "In a morgue! She's in a damn morgue, Dad!"

"Colten," I warn through gritted teeth, pulsing my fingers into his thigh gently.

His chest rises and falls, his cheeks flushing with fury. Compared to this cement box, it is a vibrant hue contrasting everything else around us. "No, Taryn! He needs to know that we found her, despite his best efforts to make sure she would never be found!"

"I don't know what you are talking about," Christian whispers into the phone. It's not the kind of hushed tone used to conceal truths, but one that genuinely shows me this man is perplexed.

"No?" Colten taunts. "You didn't run her car off the cliffside into the Columbia when she was still inside? Because we have her body," he points to his chest, "my mother's body! Taryn's truck went off the cliff, and she found her car..." The inhale Colten takes is loud and booming.

Christian closes his eyes, his face flushing as a tear falls onto his cheek. He scrunches his features as if he's in pain. "I lost her," he mumbles into the phone.

"We all lost her!" Colten clarifies. "Because of—"

"No," Christian shakes his head, Colten's movements freezing. "There's so much you don't know about what led to that night," he murmurs. "After you came into our room and found us, and she drove off, I went after her."

Colten peers at him disbelievingly. "I know."

"No, you don't." His dad exhales. His eyes flit to mine briefly before settling back on his son. "I looked for Jane all night, but I never found her."

FORTY-SEVEN | COLTEN

Whatever oxygen is filling the rooms on both sides of the glass seems to be sucked out rapidly. Taryn stills beside me, her eyes wide. The air in my lungs dispels, my eyes shifting into slits to glare at my father, who doesn't appear to be breathing.

"What do you mean you never found her?" I question the man who I look like in more ways than I care to admit.

My jawline and dark hair are identical to his. Before he was arrested, his muscular frame rivaled what mine is now. Working out was as effective as alcohol when it came to stress.

It's the eyes, though. That's the major transformation. They're haunting. Buzzing with lies behind the layer of confusion, attempting to muddle my focus and distract me.

He's playing me.

"Do you remember that morning? The morning I came back to the house. You never left the porch—"

"Yes, I remember it quite well." The memory is branded into my brain permanently, seared into the bone of my skull, where even my corpse someday will never be rid of the horrific recollections.

Taryn's thumb rubs in circular, rotating motions on my leg. Her attempt to soothe me tenses my muscles, but the reminder that she is here is all I need.

Christian's fingers adjust their grip on the phone, and he sighs, closing his eyes. When they open, they hold Taryn and me in place. "After she ran out, I chased after her. I thought she was headed to her parents', but when I pulled in front of their house, her car wasn't there, and they said they hadn't seen her. When I returned that next morning, it was because I searched for Jane all night, but I never found her."

"I don't believe you," I mutter through gritted teeth.

Lies. Lies piled on top of fucking lies.

"What do you remember?" he asks, my heart plummeting into my stomach, creating a commotion that leaves me struggling to breathe. "When you first walked into our room... What do you remember?"

My jaw pops. The wrath circulates through my veins. I don't want to do this. But it's why I'm here, isn't it? To get answers. To relive the past because it has already haunted me every single fucking day since it happened.

"It's okay," Taryn croons from beside me. "I'm here."

The warmth of her fingertips caressing my thigh works to dissolve some of the boiling rage. If I erupt in this visitor's room, they'll toss me out and leave me feeling as empty as when I came in. I want to move on. I owe it to *her* to try to settle the past.

The images flash behind my eyes.

The bloody glass in one of my father's hands.

The bottle of liquor in the other.

The broken shards of mirror scattered on the floor.

The blood soaked into the carpet.

My mother clenching her hands to her bloody stomach.

"When I walked in, I saw—she was holding her stomach where you stabbed her. I saw you try to murder her!"

Another tear falls from his dead eyes, and it makes me want to send my fist flying through this glass partition to smack it off his face. He doesn't deserve to cry for her.

"It was her wrists..."

My heart just fucking stopped beating. Taryn holds her other hand up to cover her mouth, inhaling an audible breath beside me.

I stare at him expectantly. "What do you mean by 'her wrists'?"

He shakes his head. "It wasn't her stomach, Colten. It was her wrists."

Sweat seeps through my pores, chilling instantly. "So you slit her—" His head moves from side to side again, and my mouth falls shut.

No. No. No. She wouldn't willingly leave us that way. She wouldn't.

He clears his throat, his eyes holding mine. "After Tristan was born, something changed. It was gradual, something festering day by day. It also started happening around the same time the company picked up, increasing my hours away from home...away from her."

I listen intently, the room blurring around me as his story becomes my focus.

"God, I used to love touching her," he whispers, closing his eyes. "The way she would melt into me. She was the love of my life, and back then, when I met her, I knew it instantly." Taryn stirs beside me, leaning closer to the phone gripped in my hand. "She started looking more exhausted than usual. There was this physical distance that started growing, and whenever I would touch her—hug her—she would push me away." He shakes his head. "I didn't understand it, but I never bothered to ask her what was wrong. I ignored it... Ignored her. Life was so good until it suddenly wasn't."

My heart thumps aggressively in my chest.

I remember it—the beautiful days when Mom and Dad would take Cam, Bren, Jess, baby Tristan, and me to our grandparents or on the boat. The family dinners at the table were full of laughter and vibrancy. Those days, I always felt warm, thinking nothing would ever change. But I was naive then.

"When Tristan was around one," he continues, "your mother would disappear randomly for hours at a time. Some nights, she wouldn't even come home." That timeline slides through my mind. Around that time, Dad started to find refuge at the bottom of a bottle. That's when his addiction began.

"I thought she was having an affair," he mutters. He rubs a palm over his cropped hair. "After a few months, I confronted her about it. She screamed at me—she was defensive. Jane turned the blame on me, claiming she would leave for hours because she was burnt out from caring for our five children alone and needed time to herself. I didn't understand it at the time. For years, there were good days and really low days. She would be fine one moment and breaking down the next. But when she got pregnant with Elena, things got worse. She started disappearing again. Around you kids, her mask was flawless, but alone...her and I." Another tear cascades down his cheek. "She was withdrawn and resented me for focusing more on the company than our family."

The correctional officer steps behind him. "You have ten more minutes." Their voice trickles through the phone enough for me to hear.

My dad nods, glancing back at me.

I tilt my head, acid rolling in my stomach. "Was she having an affair?"

He inhales, his chest rising heavily before dropping. "No." Chills run up my arms, my hair standing on end. "One night, when you boys were alone with the kids, and Elena was a newborn, I followed her. She pulled into a parking lot—" His voice catches in his throat. "All those years, she was seeing a therapist, and I didn't even know."

A lump lodges in my throat. "Did she ever find out you followed her?"

He nods. "I was drunk when I drove there. She saw my truck out the window and confronted me about it later that night. I begged to do counseling with her. We were so off the rails, Colten. If she was trying to better herself, I wanted to do it alongside her. I wanted our old selves back...I wanted the woman I fell in love with, and I wanted to be the man she married again."

Taryn's hand vanishes from my lap. "What did she do when she found out you followed her?" she stutters from nerves.

His tired and red eyes flit to hers. "She said I didn't trust her. That week, I tried harder. I would get home early and make dinner; I would take you, boys, out with the bow. I would clean and do little things around the house that I thought she would appreciate. She told me she would be home late one night, so when she came home and saw we were eating dinner together without her, something inside her broke."

Another memory resurfaces from earlier that evening, seizing my body until it's all I can fixate on.

Reaching for my beer, I take a sip, scanning everyone at the table as we all lounge around with full stomachs from the steaks Dad made. I smile at Jess, holding my new sister, Elena, across from me with my dad. Cameron sits on one end of the table while Tristan sits beside me in his high chair, and Brennan sits on my other side. It's the first time in months we've had Cameron here since he's visiting from school. Mom walks through the front door, her sad eyes settling on us as my dad sips his scotch.

"Honey, you're back." Dad smiles at her, but she stares at him blankly.

"Mom, I got an A on my math test today!" Jessica beams, rocking Elena in her arms.

"That's awesome," she tells her, but her tone is void of emotion.

Why is she so sad? Shouldn't she be happy to see us? She's been gone all afternoon.

"I left you some dinner in the fridge," Dad says. "And I got most of the chores done on your list in the kitchen."

She raises a brow, pushing a section of hair behind her shoulder. "You touched my list?"

My dad stills in the chair beside me. "Yeah, I came home early and wanted to—"

A fake smile barely touches her lips. "Well, it looks like you all are doing just fine without me."

"Jane," Dad exhales, pushing his chair away from the table.

She raises a hand, stopping him, disappearing out of the room without another word.

WHEN SHE LEFT the room while we were all sitting there, my dad didn't run after her. He just snatched his glass off the dining table, draining all his scotch. He walked into the kitchen, returned with the bottle, and poured himself more.

I can still feel the uncomfortable silence clinging to my skin and the bitter taste of the beer I was drinking plastered on my tongue. I pushed the beer away, acid swirling in my gut because whenever he grabbed a bottle, chaos was sure to follow.

The air crackles with energy, electrifying my skin. It's funny how traumatic experiences can erase everything, all the other essential details, until the only thing displayed in your vision is the horrific parts playing before your eyes.

That night shifts. My memory warps and twists until the

puzzle pieces settle into place. My throat burns, and the center of my heart tears directly down the middle. Is it possible to throw up your vital organs?

My father lifts a hand to his face, his soft and broken voice drifting through the phone. "I ignored the signs...I should've seen the goddamn signs and gotten her help."

Looking up from his lap, his face is red and puffy. He sniffles, wiping his nose on his sleeve.

"She wouldn't just—" The words die on my tongue. I can't say them. I swallow. "Why then? Why right after Elena was born?"

His eyes fall from mine. "After Tristan was born, we wanted to be done."

"What do you mean?" I say through gritted teeth. "Your marriage?"

He shakes his head, the simple gesture confusing me more than anything he has said thus far. "Kids. We didn't want any more kids."

"But Elena—"

"Was an accident."

Motherfucker. My baby sister will never fucking hear those words. I will never allow the truth to be embedded in her little brain like a parasite.

He continues. "Around the time Tristan turned one, Jane told me she didn't feel right. Her hormone levels were all over the place. We were completely in love one moment, and it was as if we had completely lost everything the next. She told me she couldn't handle another pregnancy, but..." His mouth shuts briefly, his chest rising and falling. "Being pregnant again while we already had you five exhausted her. And by that time..." He swallows. "I was already an alcoholic and was around less and less. Then Elena was born, and whatever was holding her together snapped."

Taryn moves her hand back to my lap, her warmth battling the cold air blanketing my skin.

"When I heard glass shatter that night, I ran to her. But I was too late. There was so much blood. She..." he stutters through tears. Inhaling a deep breath, he peers up at the ceiling. "She had the piece of glass in her hand. I tried to stop her, but I had drunk too much, and instead, I grabbed it out of her hand out of anger. I wanted to ask her why. Why hurting herself was the only answer, but you opened the door before I could get the words out..."

My raspy voice barely emerges. "You tried to stop her."

"After you caught us, I chased after her. She must have lost control or died before—" My dad slams his eyes shut. "I looked all night, Colten, but I never found her."

Taryn stirs beside me, her brain probably going haywire since her truck went off that same cliff.

My blood simmers, bubbling below my skin. "Why didn't you defend yourself in court? You both left us completely, and I had to pick up all the fucking pieces and keep this family—my family—together!"

I thought he killed her. But she did it to herself because we were all too negligent to see the signs. And I can't help but feel like part of her death was my fault, too. I was old enough to know that something was wrong. But I thought it was their marriage. I thought it was my alcoholic father driving her away. I thought my dad fell so far off the deep end that he wanted to dispose of her, but when she went off that cliff, he, in a way, was with her.

He flattens his lips, the movement pulling at something deep inside my chest. "I didn't kill her, but I'm responsible for her death in every way. She may have cut her wrists, but I was the blade of the glass."

FORTY-EIGHT | TARYN

My palms flatten over the fabric draping over my body. The halter top hugs my neck tightly, and I wrap my arms around myself. I drop my head, my eyes gliding over the silk, which resembles black water cascading down my body. The bottom rests on the blades of grass as if it could soak into the ground.

I've never stood in a cemetery.

I've never attended a funeral.

I fiddle with my hands, exhaling a weighted breath, my ears tuning into the buzz of a lawnmower off in the distance as the silent hum of birds drifts through the air. A gentle breeze whips through the tree above us, rattling the red-tinted leaves and coating my bare arms in a layer of goosebumps.

I want to do more. Find a way to help Colten and his siblings process the loss of their mother.

In reality, they lost Jane five years ago. They have lived every day not knowing what happened until Colten visited their father. Cameron, Brennan, and Jessica know the harsh details of her death—that they lost their mother to the depression that quietly took hold of her. But Tristan and Elena... God, those poor kids, their young minds can't process the truth.

I'm twenty-four, and I'm still struggling to process it.

They know their mom was in an accident five years ago, when Jane's car went off the cliff and ended up at the bottom of the river. Everything beyond that, though, will be revealed with time.

In a way, I know Colten, Cameron, Brennan, and Jessica feel responsible for not noticing the signs of Jane's depression sooner. Their guilt is palpable, and it's easy to imagine them wondering if they could've done something.

I'm sure the what-ifs haunt them, and I feel so protective of this family that I wish I could take away their pain.

Now, whatever condition they found Jane's body in is prepared to be buried six feet underground, with only the Lindenvale kids and me to pay respects to the woman who raised them. A mother who felt completely alone at the end of her life. A woman who should still be here.

Blank faces in black formal wear stare down into the hole as Elena throws a handful of dirt at the mother she never knew. It sprinkles down onto the shiny oak casket, littered with other handfuls each Lindenvale child has taken turns tossing below. She turns away, nuzzling her face into the curve of Colten's neck. His arms are wrapped tightly around her, holding her to him.

For the last several days, Colten has barely left Elena's side unless he's at work or we're sleeping. She has become his everything. I mean, she already was, but it's different now. I've seen it in his eyes. His admiration for her was beautiful before, but now it's a cosmic kind of love. She may have been an accident, but she will never be that to him.

"Do you think she's in heaven?" Tristan asks, staring at the damp dirt caked on his hand.

Cameron places his arm around his shoulders, tugging him closer. "She's somewhere beautiful."

"And I'm sure wherever she is, she misses you," Brennan adds.

My heart splinters, sending a dull ache through my still-tender ribs. Colten glances at me. Even though this day is about them and their movement toward healing, he has still made me feel seen, stealing looks here and there throughout the small ceremony. I'm unsure if his glimpses are to make him feel more comfortable or to make me feel like I belong here, even though I feel like I should be anywhere other than intruding on this last intimate moment they have with their mother.

He gives me a single nod to move closer, and I move toward him. One hand drifts around my waist and pulls my body against him while his other arm holds Elena. His soft black suit melts into my skin, and my head leans against his muscular shoulder, accepting his comfort the same way I'm trying to comfort him.

He holds me. I grasp onto him.

Nodding, Tristan whispers, "I miss you too, Mom."

We stay there for a few more minutes, letting the natural buzzing and chirping sounds in the cemetery fill the void.

Tears cascade down Jessica's flushed cheeks. Using the long sleeves of her dress, she lets them soak into the material, blowing out a breath. "Well, I think we need something to lighten the day." Her siblings look at her with melancholy faces. "You guys want to go to The Honey Hut?"

Elena turns, the side of her head finding comfort against Colten's chest. He peers down at her while she gazes at the plot, and a faint grin pulls at his mouth. He tucks a strand of brown hair behind her ear. "Nothing sounds better."

"I miss you," "I love you, Mom," and "We'll visit you soon" are murmured as goodbyes. And together—a storm of black on a cloudless day coasting through the quiet cemetery—we all walk toward the car. A young family, leaving their mother to rest peacefully below the maple tree her children chose for her.

A short drive from the cemetery later, the bell on the door of The Honey Hut rings, notifying everyone of our presence. Only a few patrons lounge around the café, some sipping on late afternoon coffees and others chewing on pastries. Eyes settle on us, their questioning gazes heating the room.

Sometimes, I wonder how long it's been since all the Lindenvale children were seen together, as they mostly keep to themselves on the hill. We all match in black attire, so it's expected that people will stare, form theories, and contemplate why we look the way we do. But if they soak in the expressions on the Lindenvale kids' faces, the answer is simple.

"Can I go look and see what I want?" Tristan asks, eyeing the case of pastries picked over since it's late afternoon and the weekend.

Brennan ruffles his hair. "Pick something good, so I can steal a bite."

"I'm going with him!" Elena drops Jess's hand and runs to the counter with him, her short black dress with a bow rippling behind her like water and her matching flats clapping on the floor.

My eyes scan the room as the guests return to their computers or conversations. Behind the counter is vacant. Adelaide must be in the back. We all move forward, Cameron parting from us. He walks around to the side and opens the door to slip behind the counter as if it's where he belongs. Grabbing a white paper coffee cup, he wanders over to the three carafes of coffee next to the espresso machine and pours himself one. He jumps up onto the back countertop and sways his legs, sipping at the hot drink, steam billowing in front of his face. I watch in amusement.

Chuckling, I glance at Jess. "Does he usually act like he owns the place?"

She rolls her eyes. "Considering he spends most of his time here, if he's not on the hill, yes."

"If he's late to work or missing, he makes it pretty easy to find him." Colten grins.

"Yep," Brennan pops the P, "wherever *she* is, he is usually somewhere near."

She. Meaning Adelaide.

As if on cue, she strolls out of the back kitchen in her usual black apron. Her hair is curled with a gold claw clip, keeping half of it out of her face. The long pieces drape over her purple knit fall sweater. The cozy look is topped off with dark skinny jeans and knee-high brown boots that I would kill to pull off the way her toned legs can.

Her eyes zero in on Cameron, and she snaps her fingers, her index finger pointing downward as a command. "Get off my counter, Cameron Scott."

He hides his smirk behind the rim of the paper cup. "I love it when you boss me around."

I observe her snatching a white towel off the countertop and rolling the material. She whips it at his legs, and he sets down his cup, seizing her wrist when she goes for another blow. He tugs her toward him, and she giggles, pushing away from him.

For some reason, I can't pull my attention away from them. Their fondness for each other is evident in their movements and flushed faces. Evident in the way their eyes cling to each other like there's nobody else in the room. It's a look I've only seen Cameron wear once before. I sift through the files in my head, trying to locate the exact moment I first saw this expression on his face. Then, the memory whips out of the box and straight into my hands. It's when we were in Cameron's studio, staring at a painting of a young girl alone on a dirt road winding through the woods.

Colten's palm presses into the small of my back. "Let's go grab a seat, Little Ghost."

I smile up at him, nodding, letting him direct me away from the front of the café and toward the back, where Brennan is lounging on the antique couches, watching Elena and Tristan indecisively figure out what they want. Jess points to something in the case, and Elena eagerly bobs her head up and down in approval.

Brennan places an arm over the back of the couch. "So, what happens now?"

Colten raises a brow, taking a seat on a couch opposite him. I lower myself beside him.

He rubs a hand over his jawline. "Like, is Dad going to try and get out of prison now that we know—you know...that mom had been struggling when she died?"

Colten exhales a breath, leaning back with his arms crossed. "He said he was going to leave it alone. He feels responsible. But it wouldn't surprise me if, one day, he decides to challenge the charges. But he would need to hire a defense attorney. There would be more trials; they would pull up her mental health history with the therapist, look for inconsistencies with the case and forensics, and probably drag Gram and Gramps back in it. So much shit would have to happen again." A heavy sigh parts from his lips. "We'll deal with it when or if that time ever comes. He made his choice. It won't be easy, but we all deserve time to heal."

Flipping his head toward me, he places his hand on my thigh, his fingers pulsing into my flesh. "You still haven't told me what my father said to you before we left the prison."

A faint smile tugs at my mouth.

"You have two minutes left," the correctional officer tells Christian, and he nods.

"Colten, can you hand the phone to Taryn?" he asks from the other side of the glass barrier.

Colten's eyes shift into little slits, scrutinizing his father. Placing my hand on his bicep, I run my thumb up and down on his skin. His attention shifts to me.

"It's okay," I assure him. "I'll talk to him."

He lifts his frame from the chair, handing me the phone. Tugging his fingers anxiously through his hair, he paces toward the door to wait for me, leaving me alone with a man I've never spoken to—a man I've only seen in articles and on the news. But here he is in the flesh, asking to speak with me.

My pulse beats wildly. What could he possibly want to say to me?

Clearing my throat, I shift in my seat. My skin prickles in response to Colten's eyes boring into me from behind.

"I don't have much time, but I want to thank you." Opening my mouth to speak and ask why he's thanking me, he quickly cuts me off. "You don't need to say anything. The rest of my children have sent me letters for years, but I'd be lying if I said I wasn't waiting for a particular letter every week since I've been in here."

My heart drops, and Christian's intense gaze hooks on to mine. He rubs his red eyes with his fingers before looking back up. But his focus isn't on me. His attention is on his son. "I can't tell you how happy I was when six letters arrived a few weeks ago instead of five. I knew whatever was in Colten's letter would hurt like hell, but I needed to hear it."

Colten sent him a letter? Why, after all this time?

"He told me my failures have made him a better man—that my failures have made him the man his family needed when I couldn't step up as a father." I focus on a part of the glass where I can see Colten's reflection toward the back of the room. "I have failed a lot in *my lifetime, Taryn. But the one thing I'll never forgive myself for is that my son said he hasn't believed in love for the last five years."*

He rolls out his shoulders, swallowing. "But then he said he met someone who changed his mind...I think you and I both know who that is."

The breath in my lungs evaporates. My heart batters against my ribs, and I have the overwhelming urge to reach up and clench my chest.

The officer steps up behind him. "Time is up."

Christian holds my gaze for a moment, silence passing between us.

He flattens his lips, taking one last look at Colten. "Take care of them."

My reply to his plea is effortless. "I will."

FORTY-NINE | TARYN

Purples and pinks blend into an ombre of colors with wispy clouds streaking across the sky like someone took a paintbrush to the atmosphere and made it their own personal masterpiece. The vibrant hues reflect off the water of the Columbia, the view easing the vibration of panic in my bones.

My feet hang off the truck bed, dangling and swaying. The chilly air soaks into the black silk fabric of my dress, the wind catching the loose cloth, making it ripple like the waves below.

I'm forced to take this corner on the cliffside almost daily while driving or riding with one of the guys. Shortly after my accident, Colten paid a construction company to build a barrier. And though the guardrail eases some of the panic that vibrates in my bones whenever I get close to the cliffside, each day is more manageable.

Like today.

Colten pulled his truck off the road to a spot where we could watch the sunset over the water. At first, I refused to come anywhere near the cliff that nearly killed me. But once I saw the view, my heart craved to watch it. To soak in the chilly fall air while a picturesque landscape is sprawled out before me.

The edge of the orchard is behind us. Leaves rustle in the wind, some falling from branches and fluttering to the earth below. Occasionally, I can hear the pounding of apples crashing to the ground. Inhaling a deep breath, the scent of algae and wood lingers in the air, sweeping off the river.

Colten rounds the corner of the truck, gripping his black suit jacket and tugging it off. The white shirt stretches against his forearms, his strong shoulders rippling when he removes his tie. Placing the garments on the side, he lifts himself up to sit beside me, the truck bouncing with his weight.

Blankets and pillows are in the bed, and he reaches for a blanket. Whipping it out, he lays it on my legs and wraps his arm around me, tugging me closer. His leather and cinnamon scent envelops me.

Today was a heavy day.

The funeral.

All the beautiful words he said about his mother and the woman she was still echo in my mind.

I wish I could've known Jane and met the woman who raised the resilient man sitting beside me.

The last five years have been hell for Colten. The weight he's had to endure. The armor he had to carry around to be the man his family needed. But I've fallen in love with him because when the dark and evil parts of the world consumed his parents, he refused to let go and let it destroy him, too.

He rests a hand on my thigh, peering at the world expanding before us. I, on the other hand, keep my eyes locked on him.

"Today, I remembered why I promised myself I would never fall in love," Colten says, keeping his eyes on the river.

My heart throbs in my chest, unsure where this is going. "Okay..."

His tongue darts out, wetting his bottom lip. "They were my example of love. I saw the moments they couldn't keep their hands off each other—the way they smiled at each other...God, the way he wrapped my mom in his arms."

I place my hand on his, intertwining our fingers.

"My parents were the perfect example of what love should look like. Just as quickly, they became an impeccable standard of everything it shouldn't." His face turns to mine, his bright green eyes holding me captive in his gaze. "I focused on the nothingness in their relationship, Taryn. The parts that were too dark and bitter even to contemplate wanting to give myself over to something that could eventually tear me apart. But every single day, I have put my family first. All my decisions revolve around them because they are my everything. And despite what happened with my parents, loving my siblings is effortless. Easy."

My eyes flit between his.

"I dragged you here for them, but waking up each morning, knowing you were in my house, in my head, knowing that you could be mine if I just told you how badly I wanted to love you in every way possible, drove me to the brink of madness. I should've said those words to you in that shower, and I'm sorry I didn't."

I reach for his face with my other hand, stroking his jawline with my fingers. "Colten, you don't have to apologize—"

"No, I do." He latches onto my hand lovingly, tightening his grip around it. "When your truck went off the cliffside, I briefly thought about what a future without you would be like." His hand releases mine, but before my body chills at the loss of him, his index finger presses below my chin, keeping it steady so he can peer into my eyes. "And now I understand that whether it's failed love or a loveless life, they are both equally empty and hollow."

His thumb drifts over my bottom lip. "I wasn't lying when I

said I've loved you every day since we found ourselves sitting across from each other in that office. Because since that moment, you have stirred the dormant parts of my soul, Little Ghost."

My heart thunders. The artery bounces around the inside of my chest as if it can burst out of my sternum and magnetize to his.

We may be in our black attire from earlier, but as the sun dips below the horizon, the world engulfing us is bright and vibrant.

His green eyes reflect the sunset, and suddenly, I'm gazing into a living kaleidoscope of colors. "I'm in love with you, Taryn Meyers."

Not wasting a second, I swing my leg over his lap, straddling him in my dress on the edge of his truck bed. My lips collide with his, my body showing him exactly how I feel. His head tilts, his hands reaching around to cup my ass and pull my core flush with his. I deepen the kiss, letting my tongue dance with his in a way that has my soul catching fire in my chest. My ribs protest my movement as I grind on his growing cock, but I ignore the pain because there's only room for one feeling right now.

"I love you, Colten," I breathe against his lips, my fingers fondling the first button on his white dress shirt. I pop them open one by one, revealing the expansive tattoo on his chest. "I have been yours since you first called me Little Ghost." He looks up at me, his lips swollen and glistening. "But despite the nickname, you always see me."

"Always."

I turn my head, eyes scanning the landscape before the colors disintegrate and pave the way for the night.

"It was brave to bring me here to the cliff," I say honestly. "I only got out of the hospital a week ago. Remember? You should, because you've never left my side."

My head quickly turns back toward him when he shifts his body under mine. He leans backward, his arms around my waist, dragging me down with him. He lies against the pillows and blankets, and I fall onto his chest.

"I remember. You're never allowed to go back there."

I smile at him. His hands grip my waist, his strength and muscle flipping me over effortlessly and gently so he doesn't egg on the pain in my ribs. I'm trapped beneath his frame, the open flaps of his shirt taunting me with his flexed abdomen. God, those hard lines are perfection.

He must sense my neediness. Rolling my dress up to expose my black thong, he presses the solid ridge of his cock confined in his dress pants against my pussy, grinding on top of me. The moan I release has his fingertips pulsing into my skin.

His lips brush against the shell of my ear. "On second thought, I'll make you a deal." Moving to the slope of my neck, I feel the tilt of his lips against my heated skin. It makes my clit throb, muddling my head so I can't think straight. "The next time we find ourselves in that hospital will be when you're having my baby."

Gripping onto the collar of his shirt, I pull his face to mine. "Colten Lindenvale, you have yourself a deal."

A groan of pleasure rattles his chest, the sound transferring a vibration that impales my bones the second his lips crash against mine again.

Sometimes, I wonder if I would've found my way to him without the teaching position. I contemplate what would've happened if he hadn't lured me to Cedar Creek. But, to be honest, I don't think I believe in fate.

I believe in decisions.

That our decisions, minuscule or vast, hold power to control us and the future we allow ourselves. Our personal choices can create a shock wave that ripples and affects others around us, even when we don't believe they do. But how we handle things determines the outcome and how we move forward.

Me?

I've always moved forward too quickly—hopping from one place to the next with no sense of direction. Here with them, Lindenvale Hill feels like home. In the bed of this truck, with the orchard on both sides and the river stretching before us, peace overwhelms me.

Because the moment I was forced to slow down, I finally found my center.

EPILOGUE | COLTEN

11 MONTHS LATER

The cool fall air brushes against my overheated skin from days of exhausting myself. A honeyed, fried scent with a hint of crisp apple catches the breeze and swirls around the field.

Music blares through the speakers on the stage while the band sets up for their set, providing entertainment for the crowd. People swarm the stands lined in all directions, collecting produce from local vendors and looking at products from small businesses and artists around Washington. My favorite booths are the ones serving apples—Lindenvale Hill apples—in unique ways, which is always a favorite for guests visiting the hill.

Kids run around with caramel apples in hand, bouncing from fair rides to cornhole games, scarecrow-making tables, and bobbing for apple buckets. Bales of hay, pumpkins, and corn stalks decorate the venue.

Looking around at it all, I can't help but grin. The festival looks like it used to years ago. Like it never stopped.

There's a warmth in the air now. A sweetness I can taste on my tongue instead of a bitter flavor that lingered before I decided to cancel the Lindenvale Harvest Festival after Mom disappeared.

I never thought I would be here. Hosting another festival with a clear mind, admiring how families roam the property. It feels like it used to—back when I was a teenager, soaking in the moments with my family. Sure, it's different now, knowing what Mom went through and that our father still sits in prison, but the future grows brighter each day.

And when I turn, my future is walking toward me. My little ghost. Taryn's body sways to the music, her beautiful eyes taking in every detail of the festival she worked so hard to help me with. Elena smiles, my eyes instantly noting the hole in her mouth where one of her teeth should be. She runs toward me, the love of my life following behind her.

Elena crashes into my leg, her power making me take a step back to keep myself from falling over. "Whoa there!" I try to regain my balance. "Looks like someone finally got that tooth out."

She shows me her pearly white teeth, pointing at the hole. "Isn't it cool? It's under my pillow now!"

"She literally just ripped the thing out during breakfast this morning." Taryn laughs. "Tristan couldn't even finish his breakfast because it grossed him out too much."

I haven't seen her all day except this morning when she woke up with my cock inside her at five a.m. Her heavy eyes took a second to open, but when I pulled a nipple into my mouth to suck on it, her cunt started to weep for me, her back arching off the bed, craving me deeper. She's my favorite way to wake up. And after drawing out two orgasms from her and filling her pussy with my cum, I kissed her goodbye and slipped out the door, so she could fall back asleep.

I had too much to do today.

Opening an arm out so she can come closer, she tucks herself into my side. Her warmth radiates through me, causing my pulse to hammer faster than it has all week. She always does that to me, but it's different now—a tapping under my skin that I want to make permanent.

Pressing my lips into her forehead, I ask, "Where are Jess and the twins?"

Jessica came home from college this weekend for the harvest festival. When I told her my plan a few days ago, I said I wanted to make this festival memorable for us again, since we'd been absent for over five years. She nearly skipped all her classes because she was so excited.

"Cameron and Brennan were waiting for Jess to finish up with a paper. They should be meeting up with us in a little while," she says.

"Hi, Miss Taryn!" a small voice yells from afar.

We turn our heads and find a girl with her mom at one of the stands near us.

Taryn smiles, her features bright as she waves to her student. "Hi, Claire."

Last winter, Taryn stepped into a temporary teaching position at Cedar Creek Elementary. Once the school year ended, Alaric Sinclair, my former principal, offered her a full-time fourth-grade teaching position. She takes Elena and Tristan to school, brings them home in the afternoon, and we take turns taking them to sports practices and games.

"I really want to go on the hay bale ride!" Elena points at the tractor sitting near the entrance with the trailer attached and bales of hay piled on top to look like seats.

My heart jumps. Here we go.

"Don't you think we should wait for everyone and all go together?" Taryn suggests, running the palm of her hand over Elena's brown hair.

Elena shrugs. "We could go twice!"

Taryn looks at me, waiting for an answer.

"You guys go. I let Phillip know you want a private ride, and then when Jessica, Cam, and Bren get here, we can all go."

When Taryn turns to look at the tractor, Elena winks at me. The movement is flawless and smooth. I have no idea where she learned that. She's been doing it a lot recently.

I wink back, stuffing my hands in my pockets as Taryn rotates back toward us and smiles. My hands tremble in my pockets, and when she stares at me for a second, I wonder if she can sense my nerves controlling my body.

Chill out. Calm down. She doesn't know anything.

She holds her hand out, and Elena grasps it. "All right. We'll see you back here in a little while?" Taryn asks me.

"I'll see you in a little while," I reassure her.

Walking hand in hand to the festival entrance, I turn and hustle back to the shop at the side of the venue, where my truck is parked. I let Phillip know the girls are ready for the ride, and I triple-check that he knows where they're going, which is different from the festival map showing the hayride route.

This is a particular route I had explicitly picked for *her,* and I have about fifteen minutes before Phillip arrives with them. Luckily, everything is set up and ready to go, and the twins should be there now with Jessica.

Everything is falling into place.

Hopping into my truck, I open the glovebox, taking out what I need. Admiring the box, my thumb swipes over the velvet as my future flashes before my eyes. And she is everything I want.

EPILOGUE | TARYN

The tractor engine roars in front of us as the trailer takes us down the dirt road. Cars pass us on their way to the venue, kids' hands waving out the windows as we pass them.

This is a big hayride for only two people, but I shouldn't be complaining. It's with one of my favorite people.

Elena picks up a piece of straw, pulling the strand between her index finger and thumb. She seems a little off today, but I can't put my finger on it. I wanted to take coffee to Colten this morning since I know he has been working like crazy to get this festival set up, but three seconds after I mentioned it, she ripped her damn tooth out. The thing was bleeding like crazy, and Tristan nearly fainted at the sight of her blood soaking into the white napkin.

This girl always surprises me, I swear.

I peer around us, noticing the direction we are going. Reaching into the back pocket of my jeans, I remove the folded festival pamphlet. Unfolding the paper and flipping to the section with the hayride, I study the route.

"We aren't going the right way."

Elena sits across from me, her head flying up from the straw she's fiddling with across from me. "Yeah, we are."

"No, we are supposed to be headed toward section ten in the orchard," I inform her, twisting my lips to the side.

She flattens her lips. "Well, we own it. We get special treatment."

I guess. "And technically, you own it. I don't," I joke.

She mumbles something to herself, grinning as she tosses the strand of hay into the wind, watching as it flutters away and lands on the road.

The sun has disappeared, and the world around us is blanketed in reds and oranges, matching the festival and autumn mood. Chills break out across my arms, so I tug my black sweater sleeves over my hands to keep them warm.

"Hold on," Phillip calls over the engine.

His demand catches me off guard. The tractor turns, and Phillip slows the speed, taking us down the ditch and between two rows of apple trees on either side. We drive down the rows for a few minutes, and the peaceful ride calms my thumping heart. I lean back against the bale behind me, ignoring the fact that hay is going to get caught in my woven sweater.

I'm too happy and content to care.

The trees pass, the world gets darker, but the smile that spreads across Elena's face is too cheerful to ignore. She's practically vibrating in her seat, but when I start to eye her suspiciously, something glowing above catches my eye.

And the thought that this is just a normal hayride that every other guest has gone on today instantly diminishes.

Tilting my head upward, string lights zigzag above us in the trees as the tractor and trailer pass under them. It's like a tunnel of lights carrying us deeper into the Lindenvale Hill Orchard. My pulse quickens, the lights sitting amongst the sunset sky like one of those aesthetic photos you stare at because you wonder if it's real. And my pounding pulse attempting to burst out of my skin tells me it's real.

The tractor pulls to a stop, and I turn my head toward Phillip, wondering what's going on.

"Why are we stopping?" I call out, but there's no answer. He sits in the confined space with his head forward, not paying attention to anything I say.

That's strange.

Rotating back to Elena, my breath is expelled from my lungs. I blink, and sure enough, she's gone.

Poof.

Just disappeared into thin air like she was never there in the first place.

Adrenaline transfers through my bloodstream, shooting straight to my head and racing heart. I hurriedly stand up, cautiously strolling to the end of the trailer to hop off and walk on solid ground. As I make my way around the side of the trailer, something comes into view in front of the tractor in the distance. The ceiling of lights continues, glowing amongst the apple trees and guiding my way.

When I get next to the tire, nearly as big as I am, I freeze.

Holy shit.

When a gut feeling tells you something is going on, you're probably right. But in this case, I'm glad I didn't think too hard about why everyone was acting so strangely today.

Blinking a few times doesn't rid me of the breathtaking view in front of me.

Colten is in a navy suit that stretches across his muscles with a burgundy tie, the ink from his tattoo peeking above the collar. Standing on a circular carpet, his hands are clasped in front of him, with large jars of sunflowers decorating the perimeter around him.

It's almost been a year since we found ourselves sitting in that truck, making promises that we never wanted to let go of.

But this smile—the one on his face right now—makes me breathless. Because with this one look, I know what's ahead is a sweet, sweet, sweeter life.

But it's not just him. Behind him, making a half circle around the carpet, are Cameron, Brennan, Jessica, Tristan, Elena, and Rossco. The family who took me in, who I now consider my own. They stare at me with grins on their faces as I stare blankly from nerves.

I wanted this. Knew I wanted *him* from nearly the beginning when he sucked me up in this whirlwind life. And though every nerve ending in my body crackles and bursts like vibrant fireworks exploding against the night sky, I already know my answer.

"Yes."

The grins on the twins' faces show me that I didn't say my response in my head like I thought I did. Crap.

Colten smirks. "I didn't ask you anything yet." His teasing tone sends sparks flickering between my thighs.

Stepping onto the carpet, he holds his hand out, palm up, waiting for me. I place my hand in his as he tugs me forward, my chest crashing into his with the impact of two waves in the sea colliding with each other. I expel a sharp breath.

"Well," I stutter. Come on, Taryn, get yourself together. "Whatever you ask me, my answer will be yes. I always seem to say yes to you."

He lifts a hand, his thumb caressing my cheek. "I can be very persuasive that way, can't I?"

I hum in agreement, nodding.

I purse my lips, trying to hide my smile, glancing at the Lindenvale kids. Elena can barely contain herself. Cameron has his arm around Tristan, and Jessica and Brennan are staring at me like they never thought Colten would be here, experiencing a moment like this.

"So, if I ask you to stay here forever, with us." He pauses, waiting for my answer.

My eyes flit to his. "I would say yes."

"If I told you that someday, I want to see you have my children..."

"I would say yes, because I dream of that too."

He groans. "If I ask you if you'll let me love you until we both cease to exist—"

"I would say living a long life with you is all I want," I say honestly.

His fingers move to the skin below my jaw, tilting my face higher. "If I asked you to marry me, right here, right now, what would you say?"

The heart encased inside my chest flutters, the butterflies in my stomach with wings of fire burning me from the inside out. My anxious body shakes at his question, and I wonder if the vibrations are transferring through the ground because his frame is damn near trembling as much as mine.

I smirk at him, my lips buzzing. "I would ask you where the officiant is."

Without another word, Cameron steps forward, taking a piece of paper out of his jacket pocket as Jess steps forward with what looks like a marriage license and a few pens.

"Oh, you are completely serious," I breathe, glancing at his siblings in shock before looking back into Colten's eyes.

His hand lowers from my face, and at the same time, his body gravitates toward the carpet. Getting on one knee, he reaches into his pocket, removing a black velvet box.

God, yes. A million times yes, and he hasn't even asked me yet.

He opens the lid, revealing a large band with emerald-cut diamonds all the way around. The stones reflect the glow of the string lights above us, making my eyes widen. The ring is gorgeous in every way an object can be. A promise that will tie me to him for eternity.

He blows out a breath, the box shaking in his hands. "I've practiced the words I wanted to say to you a million times, but I'm so nervous I can't fuc—remember," he catches himself, and I chuckle. Colten's soft smile is so handsome that I take a mental image of this moment."I love you, Taryn Meyers, and I want to love you every day of my life. I want to celebrate all the good and love each other through all the bad. Because when I was at my lowest, you showed up, a ghost in my darkness, and showed me how beautiful a future could be if I don't let other people's pasts define mine."

A tear cascades down my cheek, and Colten rises to wipe it away with the pad of his thumb before taking the ring out of the box. "Even when we're both torn from this world, my ghost will dance with yours."

My eyes hold his as he places the ring on my finger. "Is that a promise?"

"Yeah, Little Ghost. It's a promise."

THE END

ACKNOWLEDGMENTS

First off, I have to thank my crazy, wonderful brain, because *The House on Lindenvale Hill* was entirely inspired by a dream, right down to the character names. This story has had a chokehold on me since I woke up that morning a few years ago, and it's surreal to think it's now a physical book. I worried for so long that the idea of a woman trapped in the center of a massive apple orchard with a broken family wouldn't feel believable, that it might be too far out there, but I ran with it anyway. I've never been so glad I trusted my gut. Taryn and the Lindenvale kids hold such a special place in my heart. It's wild to think they aren't real, because to me, they are beautiful figments of my imagination that I'll always carry with me.

To my readers, and to those of you who stuck with me through a year of relentless teasing and marketing, thank you for your patience and for sharing the hell out of this book. This was originally meant to be my debut, but it spent some time out in the world and in publishers' hands, trying to find its place, before I decided to self-publish it. I have such high hopes for this story, and I truly believe it will travel to places I never expected and resonate with many of you in the same way it resonates with me.

To my family, this book was supposed to be a secret, and I didn't tell you about *The House on Lindenvale Hill* until I landed an agent. Although you aren't allowed to read it, I know you are still supporting me in every way and never fail to ask me for updates.

Shout-out to my incredible husband. You've been by my side through all the milestones, wins, and hard moments. I love you.

To my editor and proofreader, Rumi, and my beta readers, Melissa and Clair, you helped me polish this story in every possible way. I was so nervous stepping into my first book, and your excitement and eagerness to help me refine this world mean more than I can find the words for. I will always be grateful.

We're not done with the Lindenvale brothers just yet. Because if you're anything like me, I'm willing to bet Cameron has already claimed a corner of your heart.

I hope you're ready to give him all of it.

XOXO,
Cassidy

ABOUT THE AUTHOR

Cassidy Cole is known for her dark and fiery romance novels. From a young age, she was fascinated by the vivid dreams and unconventional thoughts that played out in her mind. Now, she brings them to life, weaving these ideas into her books.

Cassidy embraces the seclusion of her writing space, where coffee keeps her grounded by day, and wine or beer fuels the night. She lives with her husband and two dogs, finding peace in the shadows where her stories take shape.

Connect with her on her social media or her newsletter (The CassCult) for the latest updates on books, teasers, events, and more.

Instagram & TikTok: @cassidycoleauthor
Website: www.cassidycoleauthor.com